STAR WARS®

DARK NEST III
THE
SWARM WAR

By Troy Denning

STAR WARS

DARK NEST III
THE
SWARM WAR

TROY DENNING

BALLANTINE BOOKS • NEW YORK

Star Wars: Dark Nest III: The Swarm War is a work of fiction. Names, characters, places, and incidents are the products of the author's imagination or are used fictitiously. Any resemblance to actual events, locales, or persons, living or dead, is entirely coincidental.

A Del Rey Mass Market Original

Published in the United States by Del Rey Books, an imprint of The Random House Publishing Group, a division of Random House, Inc., New York.

DEL REY is a registered trademark and the Del Rey colophon is a trademark of Random House, Inc.

ISBN 978-0-345-46305-0

Printed in the United States of America

www.starwars.com
www.delreybooks.com

OPM 9

For David "DJ" Richardson
Good friend

ACKNOWLEDGMENTS

Many people contributed to this book in ways large and small. I would like to give special thanks to the following: Andria Hayday for her support, critiques, and many suggestions; James Luceno for brainstorming and ideas; Enrique Guerrero for his thoughts on the Chiss; Shelly Shapiro and Sue Rostoni for their encouragement, skillful editing, and especially for their patience; all the people at Del Rey who make writing so much fun, particularly Keith Clayton, Colleen Lindsay, and Colette Russen; all of the people at Lucasfilm, particularly Howard Roffman, Amy Gary, Leland Chee, and Pablo Hidalgo. And, of course, to George Lucas for sharing his galaxy with us all.

THE STAR WARS NOVELS TIMELINE

1020 YEARS BEFORE STAR WARS: A New Hope

Darth Bane: Path of Destruction

33 YEARS BEFORE STAR WARS: A New Hope

Darth Maul: Saboteur*

32.5 YEARS BEFORE STAR WARS: A New Hope

Cloak of Deception
Darth Maul: Shadow Hunter

32 YEARS BEFORE STAR WARS: A New Hope

STAR WARS: EPISODE I THE PHANTOM MENACE

29 YEARS BEFORE STAR WARS: A New Hope

Rogue Planet

27 YEARS BEFORE STAR WARS: A New Hope

Outbound Flight

22.5 YEARS BEFORE STAR WARS: A New Hope

The Approaching Storm

22 YEARS BEFORE STAR WARS: A New Hope

STAR WARS: EPISODE II ATTACK OF THE CLONES

Republic Commando: Hard Contact

21.5 YEARS BEFORE STAR WARS: A New Hope

Shatterpoint

21 YEARS BEFORE STAR WARS: A New Hope

The Cestus Deception
The Hive*

Republic Commando: Triple Zero

20 YEARS BEFORE STAR WARS: A New Hope

MedStar I: Battle Surgeons
MedStar II: Jedi Healer

19.5 YEARS BEFORE STAR WARS: A New Hope

Jedi Trial
Yoda: Dark Rendezvous

19 YEARS BEFORE STAR WARS: A New Hope

Labyrinth of Evil

STAR WARS: EPISODE III REVENGE OF THE SITH

Dark Lord: The Rise of Darth Vader

10-0 YEARS BEFORE STAR WARS: A New Hope

The Han Solo Trilogy:
The Paradise Snare
The Hutt Gambit
Rebel Dawn

5-2 YEARS BEFORE STAR WARS: A New Hope

The Adventures of Lando Calrissian

The Han Solo Adventures

STAR WARS: A New Hope YEAR 0

STAR WARS: EPISODE IV A NEW HOPE

0-3 YEARS AFTER STAR WARS: A New Hope

Tales from the Mos Eisley Cantina
Galaxies: The Ruins of Dantooine
Splinter of the Mind's Eye

3 YEARS AFTER STAR WARS: A New Hope

STAR WARS: EPISODE V THE EMPIRE STRIKES BACK

Tales of the Bounty Hunters

3.5 YEARS AFTER STAR WARS: A New Hope

Shadows of the Empire

4 YEARS AFTER STAR WARS: A New Hope

STAR WARS: EPISODE VI RETURN OF THE JEDI

Tales from Jabba's Palace
Tales from the Empire
Tales from the New Republic

The Bounty Hunter Wars:
The Mandalorian Armor
Slave Ship
Hard Merchandise

The Truce at Bakura

6.5-7.5 YEARS AFTER *STAR WARS: A New Hope*

X-Wing:
Rogue Squadron
Wedge's Gamble
The Krytos Trap
The Bacta War
Wraith Squadron
Iron Fist
Solo Command

8 YEARS AFTER STAR WARS: A New Hope
The Courtship of Princess Leia
A Forest Apart*
Tatooine Ghost

9 YEARS AFTER STAR WARS: A New Hope
The Thrawn Trilogy:
Heir to the Empire
Dark Force Rising
The Last Command

X-Wing: Isard's Revenge

11 YEARS AFTER STAR WARS: A New Hope
The Jedi Academy Trilogy:
Jedi Search
Dark Apprentice
Champions of the Force

I, Jedi

12-13 YEARS AFTER STAR WARS: A New Hope
Children of the Jedi
Darksaber
Planet of Twilight
X-Wing: Starfighters of Adumar

14 YEARS AFTER STAR WARS: A New Hope
The Crystal Star

16-17 YEARS AFTER STAR WARS: A New Hope
The Black Fleet Crisis Trilogy:
Before the Storm
Shield of Lies
Tyrant's Test

17 YEARS AFTER STAR WARS: A New Hope
The New Rebellion

18 YEARS AFTER STAR WARS: A New Hope
The Corellian Trilogy:
Ambush at Corellia
Assault at Selonia
Showdown at Centerpoint

19 YEARS AFTER STAR WARS: A New Hope
The Hand of Thrawn Duology:
Specter of the Past
Vision of the Future

22 YEARS AFTER STAR WARS: A New Hope
Fool's Bargin*
Survivor's Quest

25 YEARS AFTER *STAR WARS: A New Hope*

Boba Fett: A Practical Man*

The New Jedi Order:
Vector Prime
Dark Tide I: Onslaught
Dark Tide II: Ruin
Agents of Chaos I: Hero's Trial
Agents of Chaos II: Jedi Eclipse
Balance Point
Recovery*
Edge of Victory I: Conquest
Edge of Victory II: Rebirth
Star by Star
Dark Journey
Enemy Lines I: Rebel Dream
Enemy Lines II: Rebel Stand
Traitor
Destiny's Way
Ylesia*
Force Heretic I: Remnant
Force Heretic II: Refugee
Force Heretic III: Reunion
The Final Prophecy
The Unifying Force

35 YEARS AFTER STAR WARS: A New Hope
The Dark Nest Trilogy:
The Joiner King
The Unseen Queen
The Swarm War

40 YEARS AFTER *STAR WARS: A New Hope*

Legacy of the Force:
Betrayal
Bloodlines
Tempest
Exile
Sacrifice
Inferno
Fury
Revelation
Invincible

*An ebook novella

DRAMATIS PERSONAE

Alema Rar: Gorog Night Herald (female Twi'lek)

Ben Skywalker: child (male human)

C-3PO: protocol droid

Cal Omas: Galactic Alliance Chief-of-State (male human)

Corran Horn: Jedi Master (male human)

Emala: War Profiteer (female Squib)

Gilad Pellaeon: acting Galactic Alliance Supreme Commander (male human)

Gorog: mastermind (Killik)

Grees: War Profiteer (male Squib)

Han Solo: captain, *Millennium Falcon* (male human)

Jacen Solo: Jedi Knight (male human)

Jae Juun: Galactic Alliance Intelligence agent (male Sullustan)

Jaina Solo: Jedi Knight (female human)

Kyp Durron: Jedi Master (male human)

Leia Organa Solo: Jedi Knight, copilot, *Millennium Falcon* (female human)

Lomi Plo: Gorog Queen (female human . . . mostly)

Lowbacca: Jedi Knight (male Wookiee)

Luke Skywalker: Jedi Grand Master (male human)

Mara Jade Skywalker: Jedi Master (female human)

R2-D2: astromech droid

Raynar Thul: UnuThul (male human)

Saba Sebatyne: Jedi Master (female Barabel)

Sligh: War Profiteer (male Squib)
Tahiri Veila: Jedi Knight (female human)
Tarfang: Galactic Alliance Intelligence Agent (male Ewok)
Tenel Ka: Jedi Knight, Queen Mother (female human)
Tesar Sebatyne: Jedi Knight (male Barabel)
Unu: the Will (Killik)
Wuluw: Communications Aide (Killik)
Zekk: Jedi Knight (male human)

PROLOGUE

The bomb lay half buried in the red sand, a durasteel manifestation of the brutality and unreasoning fear of its makers. It had fallen from orbit in a long fiery tumble, then planted itself tail-first atop the dune opposite the nest. Its heat shield was still glowing with entry friction, and the casing was so carbon-scored that the marks emblazoned on its side could not be read. But Jaina and Zekk needed no identifiers to know they were staring at a Chiss megaweapon. The thing was the size of a beldon, with a bulge on its nose that could house anything from a baradium penetrating charge to the triggering laser of a planet-buster warhead.

When it grew clear that the bomb was not going to detonate—at least not *yet*—Jaina finally let out her breath.

"We need a better look at that thing," she said.

Along with Jacen, Zekk, and the other three Jedi on their team, she was standing in the mouth of the Iesei dartship hangar, gazing up three hundred meters of steep, sandy slope toward the bomb. Every couple of seconds, a turbolaser strike would crack down from orbit, melting a rontosized crater of pink glass into the dune and raising a ten-story plume of dust that often obscured their view.

"We need to know what the Chiss have up their sleeves," Zekk agreed.

"We *need* to get out of here," Jacen countered. "Or am I the only one who still feels the Force-call?"

"No—" Zekk said.

"—we feel it, too," Jaina finished.

The call had arisen a few hours earlier, in the middle of a StealthX assault that had failed to turn back the Chiss task force. The summons was coming from the direction of the known galaxy, a sense of beckoning and urgency that was growing more powerful by the hour, calling the Jedi Knights back toward Ossus, demanding they return to the Academy at once.

"We *all* feel it," Tahiri said. She furrowed her scarred brow, then turned to Tesar and Lowbacca. "At least I think we do."

The Barabel and the Wookiee nodded in agreement.

"It iz hard to ignore," Tesar said.

"And we shouldn't try," Jacen replied. "Something bad must be happening for my uncle to summon us all like this. Even Luke Skywalker can't pull on the Force that hard without suffering for it."

"Maybe not," Jaina said. "But it will only take a few minutes to look at that bomb. I think we have time."

"It must be some kind of secret weapon," Zekk added. "We'll need an R-nine unit—"

"And some testing equipment," Tesar finished. He and Lowbacca started toward the interior of the near-empty hangar, where a few dozen Killiks with rosy thoraxes and green-mottled abdomens were bustling over the team's battered StealthXs—repairing and refueling, but not rearming. The StealthXs had run out of shadow bombs the previous day, and they had depleted the nest's store of actuating gas that morning. "We will collect it and catch up."

Jacen quickly moved to block their way. "No."

Tesar's neck scales rose and Lowbacca's fur bristled, and they glared down at Jacen without speaking.

"Think about it—they're *Chiss*," Jacen said. "It could be a trap. Maybe that bomb isn't meant to detonate until we're out there trying to examine it."

Tesar and Lowbacca clucked their throats and looked over their shoulders toward the bomb. They were not yet Joiners, but Jaina and Zekk could sense their thoughts well enough to know the pair were being influenced by Jacen's argument. And so was Tahiri, of course. She did not need to be a mindmate for Jaina and Zekk to know she had fallen under Jacen's sway. She was always rubbing her forearms over him, and whenever he looked her way, she suddenly had to blink.

Zekk let out a grudging chest rumble, then Jaina said, "We wish your thinking had been this clear at Supply Depot Thrago."

"We don't know that my thinking *was* unclear," Jacen said. "Not yet, anyway."

Zekk frowned. "Our raid was supposed to delay the war—"

"—not start it," Jaina finished.

Jacen shrugged. "The future is always in motion." He looked away, then added, "It's too late to undo what happened after the raid. We should respect Uncle Luke's summons and return to Ossus at once."

"And abandon Iesei?" Zekk asked. Jaina and Zekk had not been with Iesei long enough to join its collective mind—in fact, living with a nest other than Taat seemed to be weakening their own mental link—but Iesei felt like a sibling to them, and they were bound to it through the Will of the Colony. "With the Chiss preparing to land?"

"We won't save the nest by staying," Jacen said. "It's better to leave while we still can."

"Why are you in such a hurry?" Jaina asked.

When Jacen's only reply was a flash of anger, she tried to sense the answer through the Force-bond they shared as twins, but she felt nothing. And neither did Zekk, who still shared most of what she thought and felt. Since the raid on Thrago, Jacen had been shutting them both out—perhaps because Jaina and Zekk had grown so angry with him when he took a reckless shot and nearly turned the raid into a massacre. Or maybe Jacen was hiding something. Jaina and Zekk could not tell. They only knew that his withdrawal from the twin bond was one of the biggest reasons they no longer trusted him.

After a moment, Jacen finally replied, "I'm in a hurry because it's prudent. If we stay, all we can do is kill a few dozen Chiss—and what good would *that* accomplish?"

Jaina and Zekk had no answer. They knew as well as Jacen did that Iesei would be wiped out to the last larva. The Chiss assault force was just too large and well equipped to be stopped.

But there was still the bomb. If they could find out what it was, there was no counting the number of other nests they might save.

"Jacen, no one is keeping you here," Jaina said. "Leave whenever you want."

"We're going to look at that bomb," Zekk added.

Jaina turned to Tesar. "Give us a one-minute head start. If Jacen is right about this being a trick—"

"—we will know soon enough," Tesar finished. "Go."

Lowbacca added a groan assuring them that he and Tesar would be close behind.

Jacen finally opened their twin bond, flooding the Force with his alarm and concern. "Jaina! Don't—"

Jaina and Zekk ignored him. Jacen only opened the twin bond when he wanted something, and right now what he wanted was for them to leave the bomb and start home. They turned away, springing out of the hangar mouth and dropping five meters down the slope of the nest-dune. Almost immediately it grew apparent that the bomb was no trick. A ripple of danger sense prickled their necks, then a barrage of turbolaser bolts crashed down from orbit and pelted their faces with hot sand. They dived away in opposite directions and somersaulted down the slope half a dozen times, then rose to their feet and Force-leapt across a five-meter trough onto the opposite dune.

The turbolasers followed, filling the air with the fresh smell of ozone. The slope of the dune turned into a churning mass of sand, half spraying through the air while the rest growled down the slope in a series of eerie-sounding avalanches. Now working against gravity, Jaina and Zekk began to ascend toward the bomb in sporadic Force leaps. Sand scratched their eyes and filled their noses and throats, but they remained within the roiling cloud, trying to hide from the Chiss sensors and make themselves more difficult to target.

They were barely halfway to the bomb when they felt Jacen, Tahiri, and what remained of the Iesei nest racing up the slope behind them. The intensity of the barrage abruptly decreased as the Chiss gunners began to spread their fire, and the silhouettes of hundreds of Iesei appeared in the surrounding haze. The insects were scurrying up the hill on all sixes, their antennae waving as they overtook Jaina and Zekk.

A moment later the silhouettes of Jacen and Tahiri emerged from the sand cloud and came to Jaina's side.

"So the bomb *isn't* a trick," Jacen said. "This is still a bad idea."

"Then what are *you* doing here?" Zekk asked from behind Jaina.

"Looking after you two," Jacon said. "Uncle Luke won't be very happy if I go back without you."

Jaina frowned and started to protest; then a deafening bang echoed across the desert. The dune gave way beneath their feet, and the Jedi found themselves being swept down the slope in a giant sandslide.

For a moment Jaina and Zekk thought the Chiss gunners had finally hit the half-buried bomb. Then they heard the distant roar of engines and realized the bang had been a sonic boom. Jaina waved her hand, using the Force to clear a hole in the dust cloud. A black plume of entry smoke was blossoming against the yellow sky, descending from the dark sliver of the Chiss assault cruiser that was raining fire down on them.

"Drop ship!" Jaina shouted. "Be ready!"

"Iesei, take cover!" Zekk added.

An instant later, an endless string of silver flashes erupted from the head of the smoke plume. The Killiks pushed their heads into the sand and began to dig, while the Jedi used the Force to pull themselves free of the sandslide and yanked their lightsabers off their utility belts.

A blue cascade of cannon bolts began to sweep across the dune, its deep *thump-thump*ing an almost gentle counterpoint to the crashing roar of the turbolasers. Jaina and Zekk stood expectant for what seemed an eternity. There was no use trying to run or take cover. Drop ship weapons systems were designed to spread a carpet of death around their landing zones. Often, they laid fire as thick as twenty bolts a square meter.

An eerie chorus of squeals arose as the cannon strikes found the buried swarm of Iesei, and the haze grew heavy with the bitter smell of scorched chitin. More bolts began to sizzle down all around Jaina and Zekk, raising chesthigh sand geysers and charging the air with static. They raised their lightsabers and yielded control to the Force, then started to whirl and dance across the dune, dodging incoming fire and deflecting it into the ground beside their feet.

Zekk took a cannon blast full on his blade and was

driven to his knees. Jaina spun to his side and tapped two more bolts away, only to find herself badly out of position as a third dropped toward her head.

Zekk's lightsaber swept up just centimeters from her face, catching the bolt on the blade tip and sending it zipping across the dune. Jaina spun away from another attack and glimpsed Jacen and Tahiri standing back-to-back, Jacen holding his hand above their heads, cannon fire ricocheting away as though he held a deflector shield in his palm. *That* was something Jaina and Zekk had never seen before.

Then the fusillade was past, leaving in its place a slope of churned sand strewn with pieces of smoking chitin and flailing, half-buried Killiks. Jaina and Zekk started toward the crest again, but it was clear they would never reach it ahead of the Chiss drop ship. The sandslide had carried them to the bottom of the dune, and with most of the Iesei dead or dying, the turbolaser gunners were once again beginning to concentrate their fire on the Jedi.

Tesar and Lowbacca arrived from the hangar, Tesar floating an R9 unit behind him, Lowbacca carrying a rucksack full of equipment over his shoulder.

"This one does not like this," Tesar rasped. "Why do the Chisz send a drop ship instead of a fighter? Would it not be easier to hit the bomb with a missile than to recover it?"

"A concussion missile would leave pieces," Jaina said.

"And we can still learn a lot from pieces," Zekk added.

"If they want to protect their secret, they need to keep the bomb out of our hands completely," Jaina finished.

Lowbacca rowled another thought, suggesting that maybe the assault cruiser had run out of missiles. It had used thousands just fighting its way to the planet.

The drop ship completed its attack pattern, then stopped firing as it descended below the effective altitude for its fire-control apparatus. The vessel itself was a fiery wedge of ceram-metal composite at the tip of the smoke plume, no more than forty meters long and perhaps half that at the base. Jaina and Zekk and the others continued to ascend the slope in Force leaps, but there was no sign of any healthy Killiks—either the laser cannons had gotten them all, or the survivors were staying hidden.

The turbolaser strikes continued to come, obscuring the Jedi Knights' vision and slowing their progress, but failing to stop them entirely. It was difficult enough to hit moving targets from orbit, without those targets having the Jedi danger sense to warn them when a strike was headed their way.

The team was halfway up the slope when the turbo-laser barrage suddenly ended. Jaina and Zekk would have thought the drop ship was landing, except that the roar of its engines continued to build. They used the Force to clear another hole in the dust cloud. The drop ship was much closer than it sounded, but that was not the reason the barrage had stopped.

High overhead, above the dispersing column of entry smoke, the tiny white wedge of a Star Destroyer was sliding across the sky toward the assault cruiser. Small disks of turbolaser fire were blossoming around both vessels, and a pair of flame trails were already angling down toward the horizon where two damaged starfighters had plunged into the atmosphere.

"Is that an *Alliance* Star Destroyer?" Tahiri asked, coming to Jaina's side.

"It must be," Tesar said, joining them. "Why would the Chisz fire on each other?"

"They wouldn't," Jaina said.

She and Zekk reached out to the Star Destroyer in the Force. Instead of the Alliance crew they had expected, they were astonished to feel the diffuse presence of a Killik nest.

A familiar murk began to gather inside their chests. Then Zekk gasped, "Unu!"

Lowbacca groaned in bewilderment, wondering how a nest of Killiks had come by a Galactic Alliance Star Destroyer.

"Who knows? But it can't be good." Jacen stopped at Jaina's side. "Maybe *this* is why Uncle Luke is trying to call us home."

"Maybe," Jaina allowed. The murk inside began to grow heavy, and the mystery of the Star Destroyer's arrival began to seem a lot less important than the bomb. "But we still have to find out what that bomb is."

"*We* do?" Jacen demanded. "Or UnuThul does?"

"We *all* do," Zekk said.

Jaina and Zekk continued toward the top of the dune. Without the barrage churning up sand and dust, the air was beginning to clear, and they could see the crimson wedge of the drop ship descending the last few meters to the sand. Its nose shield was still glowing with entry heat, and the multibarreled laser cannons that hung beneath the wings were hissing and popping with electromagnetic discharge.

Then the drop ship's belly turret spun toward the Jedi and began to stitch the slope with fire from its twin charric guns. Jaina, Zekk, and the others raised their lightsabers and started to knock the beams back toward the vessel. Unlike blaster bolts—which carried very little kinetic charge—the charric beams struck with an enormous impact. Several times Jaina, Zekk, and even Lowbacca felt their lightsabers fly from their grasps and had to use the Force to recall the weapons.

The Jedi Knights continued up the dune in sporadic leaps, taking turns covering each other, seeking the protection of craters or mounds of sand when they could, but always advancing toward the crest of the dune and the bomb. When it grew apparent that the turret guns would not be enough to hold them at bay, the drop ship dipped its nose to give the laser cannons a good firing angle. The blue-skinned pilot came into view through the cockpit canopy. Sitting in the commander's seat next to him was a steely-eyed human with a long scar over his right eye.

Jagged Fel.

Jaina stopped in her tracks, so astonished and touched by old feelings that a charric beam came close to sneaking past her guard. She had been the one to end their romance, but she had never quite stopped loving him, and the sight of him now—commanding the enemy drop ship—filled her with so many conflicting emotions that she felt as though someone had tripped her primary circuit breaker.

Fel's gaze locked on Jaina, and a hint of sorrow—or maybe disappointment—flashed across his face. He spoke into his throat mike; then Zekk's large frame slammed into Jaina from the side and hurled them both into the glassy bottom of a turbolaser crater.

Before Jaina could complain, Zekk's fear and anger were boiling into her. Suddenly she was rebuking herself for trusting Fel, then she and Zekk were wondering how she could have been so foolish . . . and how their minds could have come unjoined at such a critical moment.

Sand began to rain down from above. They felt the crater reverberating beneath them and realized the dropship's laser cannons had opened fire.

"You're—*we're*—supposed to be over him!" Zekk said aloud.

"We *are* over him," Jaina said. She could feel how hurt Zekk was by the tumultuous emotions that seeing Fel had raised in her, and that made her angry—at Fel, at herself, at Zekk. Did Zekk think she could *make* herself love him? "We were just shocked."

Zekk glared at her out of one eye. "We have to stop lying to ourselves. It'll get us killed."

"*I'm* not lying," Jaina retorted.

She rolled away from Zekk, then scrambled up the crater's glassy wall and peered over its lip toward the drop ship. As she had expected, a squad of Chiss commandos had dropped out of the vessel's belly. Dressed in formfitted plates of color-shifting camouflage armor, they were racing along the crest of the dune toward the unexploded bomb. Instead of the recovery cables or magnetic pads that Jaina had expected, they were carrying several demolition satchels.

Zekk arrived at Jaina's side and peered up the slope. They wondered for a moment why the Chiss would go to the trouble of landing a party to blow up the bomb. A few hits from the drop ship's laser cannons would have done the job more than adequately.

Then they understood. "Vape charges!" Zekk shouted.

The Chiss equivalent of thermal detonators, vape charges left nothing behind to analyze. They *disintegrated*. But they could not be delivered by missile. Like thermal detonators, they were infantry weapons. They had to be thrown or placed.

Jaina snaked a finger over the edge of the crater and pointed at one of the drop ship's laser cannons, then used the Force to scoop up a pile of sand and hurl it up the barrel. The weapon exploded, vaporizing one wing and ripping a jagged gash in the fuselage.

Fel's eyes widened in shock, and Jaina and Zekk lost sight of him as the drop ship rocked up on its side and flipped. It landed hard in the sand, and a chain of blasts shook the dune as the remaining laser cannons exploded. The vessel rolled back onto its belly and began to belch smoke.

A pang of sorrow shot through Jaina's breast, and Zekk said, "We can't worry about him, Jaina—"

"He wasn't worried about us," Jaina agreed. Her sorrow was quickly turning to rage—at Zekk and at herself, but most of all at Fel—and her hands began to tremble so hard she found it difficult to hold on to her lightsaber. "We know."

Now that the laser cannons had fallen silent, Jaina leapt out of the crater and led the charge toward the top of the dune. Half the Chiss commando squad stopped and started to lay fire down the slope, while the rest raced the last few meters to the bomb and began to string a linked line of vape charges around it.

Jaina and the other Jedi Knights continued their ascent, deflecting the charric beams back toward the Chiss who were working to set the charges. Four of these commandos fell before their fellows realized what the Jedi were doing, but the survivors were too well trained to lose focus.

By the time Jaina and the others neared the crest of the dune, the charges had been placed and the survivors were scrambling to rejoin their companions. The squad leader fell back behind the rest of the squad and began to punch an activation code into a signaling unit built into the armor on his forearm.

Jaina pointed in the leader's direction and used the Force to tear his hand away from the buttons, and the rest of the Chiss turned their charric guns on her.

Zekk stepped in front of Jaina, deflecting beam after beam into the leader's chest armor. The impact drove him back toward the wreckage of the drop ship, finally splitting his armor when he came to a stop against the hull.

Then Tesar and Lowbacca and Tahiri were among the surviving commandos, batting their charric beams aside, kicking their guns from their hands and ordering them to surrender.

The Chiss did not, of course. Apparently more frightened of becoming Killik Joiners than of dying, they fought on with their knives, their hands, leaving the Jedi no choice but to kill, amputate, and Force-shove. Intent on securing the triggering device, Jaina and Zekk circled past the brawl and started toward the squad leader, who lay crumpled and immobile beside the drop ship.

And that was when a loud groan sounded from the hull. Jaina and Zekk paused, thinking the craft was about to explode. Instead, it rolled away from them, revealing a dark jagged hole where the near wing had once connected to the fuselage.

Realizing someone had to be using the Force, Jaina and Zekk glanced over their shoulders and found Jacen looking in the drop ship's direction. He smiled, then nodded past them toward the vessel.

When Jaina and Zekk turned around again, it was to find a coughing, brown-haired human staggering out of the fuselage. He was covered in soot, and he looked so stunned and scorched that it seemed a miracle he was moving at all.

"Jag?" Jaina gasped.

She and Zekk started forward to help, but Fel merely stooped down and depressed a button on the dead squad leader's forearm.

The signaling unit emitted a single loud beep.

Fel did not even glance in Jaina and Zekk's direction. He simply turned away and hurled himself over the far side of the dune.

Jaina and Zekk spun back toward their companions. "Run!"

Jaina's warning was hardly necessary. The rest of the Jedi were already turning away from the confused commandos, Force-leaping toward the bottom of the dune.

Jaina and Zekk found Jacen and adjusted their own leap so they came down on the slope next to him.

"You planned that!" Jaina accused her brother.

"Planned *what*?" Jacen asked.

He leapt the rest of the way to the bottom of the dune, where he was joined by Tahiri, Tesar, and Lowbacca. Jaina and Zekk landed next to the group an instant later.

"The vape charges!" Zekk accused.

"You helped Jag!" Jaina added. As Jaina made her accusation, she and Zekk were turning back toward the bomb—now about three hundred meters above, still at the top of the dune. "You don't *want* us to recover this weapon!"

"That's ridiculous. I was only trying to save Jag's life." Jacen's voice was calm and smooth. "I thought you would thank me for that."

"Ask *Jag* to thank you," Jaina snapped.

She and Zekk raised their hands, reaching out to grasp the vape charges in the Force, but they were too late. A white flash swallowed the crest of the dune. They threw up their arms to shield their eyes, then heard a deep growl reverberating across the desert and felt the sand shuddering beneath their feet.

When they looked up, the top of the dune was gone—and so was the bomb.

ONE

Star Pond had calmed into a dark mirror, and the kaddyr bugs had fallen mysteriously silent. The entire Jedi academy had descended into uneasy stillness, and Luke knew it was time. He ended the meditation with a breath, then unfolded his legs—he had been floating cross-legged in the air—and lowered his feet to the pavilion floor.

Mara was instantly at his side, taking his arm in case he was too weak to stand. "How do you feel?"

Luke's entire body felt stiff and sore, his head was aching, and his hands were trembling. He tested his legs and found them a little wobbly.

"I'm fine," he said. His stomach felt as empty as space. "A little hungry, maybe."

"I'll bet." Continuing to hold his arm, Mara turned to leave the meditation pavilion. "Let's get you something to eat . . . and some rest."

Luke did not follow her. "I can last another hour." Through the Force, he could feel nearly the entire Jedi order gathered in the lecture hall, waiting to learn why he had summoned them. "We need to do this now."

"Luke, you look like you've been hanging out in wampa caves again," Mara said. "You need to rest."

"Mara, it's *time*," Luke insisted. "Is Ben there?"

"I don't know," Mara said.

Although their son was finally beginning to show some

interest in the Force, he continued to shut himself off from his parents. Luke and Mara were saddened and a little disturbed by Ben's detachment, but they were determined not to push. The turmoil in the Force during the war with the Yuuzhan Vong had left him somewhat mistrustful of the Jedi way of life, and they both knew that if he was ever going to follow in their footsteps, he would have to find his own way onto the path.

"Does Ben really need to be part of this?" Mara's tone suggested the answer she wanted to hear.

"Sorry, but I think he does," Luke said. "Now that Jacen has convinced him that it's safe to open himself to the Force, Ben will have to make the same decision as everyone else. All the students will."

Mara frowned. "Shouldn't the children wait until they're older?"

"We'll ask them again when they become apprentices," Luke said. "I don't know whether I'm about to save the Jedi order or destroy it—"

"*I* do," Mara interrupted. "The Masters are pulling the order in ten different directions. You have to do this, or they'll tear it apart."

"It certainly looks that way," Luke said. With Corran Horn and Kyp Durron at odds over the anti-Killik policies of the Galactic Alliance, it seemed as though every Master in the order was trying to impose his or her own compromise on the Jedi. "But whether this is successful or not, it's going to change the Jedi order. If some students don't want to be a part of that, it's better for everyone to find out now."

Mara considered this, then sighed. "I'll have Nanna bring Ben over." She pulled out her comlink and stepped to one side of the pavilion. "And I'll let Kam and Tionne know you want the students there."

"Good. Thank you."

Luke continued to look out over the dark water. He had spent the last week deep in meditation, sending a Force-call to the entire Jedi order. It would have been easier to use the HoloNet, but many Jedi—such as Jaina and her team— were in places the HoloNet did not cover. Besides, Luke was trying to make a point, to subtly remind the rest of the order that all Jedi answered to the same authority.

And the strategy had worked. In every arm of the galaxy, Masters had suspended negotiations, Jedi Knights had dropped investigations, apprentices had withdrawn from combat. There were a few Jedi stranded on off-lane worlds without transport and a couple unable to suspend their activities without fatal consequences, but for the most part, his summons had been honored. Only two Jedi Knights had willfully ignored his call, and their decision had surprised Luke less than it had hurt him.

A familiar presence drew near on the path behind the meditation pavilion, and Luke spoke without turning around. "Hello, Jacen."

Jacen stopped at the entrance to the pavilion. "I'm sorry to disturb you."

Luke continued to look out on the pond. "Come to explain why Jaina and Zekk aren't here?"

"It's not their fault," Jacen said, still behind Luke. "We've had some, uh, disagreements."

"Don't make excuses for them, Jacen," Mara said, closing her comlink. "If you felt Luke's summons, so did they."

"It's not that simple," Jacen said. "They may have thought I was trying to trick them."

Luke finally turned around. "Tesar and Lowbacca didn't seem to think so." He had felt three other Jedi Knights return to Ossus along with Jacen. "Neither did Tahiri."

"What can I say?" Jacen spread his hands. "I'm not *their* brother."

Mara frowned. "Jacen, your sister used you as a pretext

and we all know it. Let's leave it at that." She turned to Luke. "Nanna's on the way with Ben, and Kam says the students have all been waiting in the lecture hall since this morning."

"Thanks." Luke joined her and Jacen at the rear of the pavilion, then gestured at the path leading toward the lecture hall. "Walk with us, Jacen. We need to talk."

"I know." Jacen fell in at Luke's side, between him and Mara. "You must be furious about the raid on the Chiss supply depot."

"I was," Luke admitted. "But your aunt convinced me that if you were involved, there had to be a good reason."

"I was more than involved," Jacen said. "It was my idea."

"*Your* idea?" Mara echoed.

Jacen was silent a moment, and Luke could feel him struggling with himself, trying to decide how much we could tell them. He was trying to protect something—something as important to him as the Force itself.

Finally, Jacen said, "I had a vision." He stopped and looked into the crown of a red-fronded dbergo tree. "I saw the Chiss launch a surprise attack against the Killiks."

"And so you decided to *provoke* the Chiss just to be certain?" Luke asked. "Surely, it would have been better to warn the Killiks."

Jacen's fear chilled the Force. "There was more," he said. "I saw the Killiks mount a counterattack. The war spread to the Galactic Alliance."

"And *that's* why you attacked the Chiss supply depot," Mara surmised. "To protect the Galactic Alliance."

"Among other things," Jacen said. "I had to change the dynamics of the situation. If the war had started that way, it wouldn't have stopped. Ever." He turned to Luke. "Uncle Luke, I saw the galaxy die."

"Die?" An icy ball formed in Luke's stomach. Considering the turmoil the order had been in at the time, he was beginning to understand why Jacen had felt it necessary to take such dire action. "Because the Chiss launched a surprise attack?"

Jacen nodded. "That's why I convinced Jaina and the others to help me. To prevent the surprise attack from happening."

"I see." Luke fell quiet, wondering what *he* would have done, had he been in Jacen's place and experienced such a terrifying vision. "I understand why you felt you had to act, Jacen. But trying to change what you see in a vision is dangerous—even for a Jedi of your talent and power. What you witnessed was only *one* of many possible futures."

"One that I can't permit," Jacen replied quickly.

Again, Luke felt a wave of protectiveness from Jacen—protectiveness and secrecy.

"You were protecting something," Luke said. "What?"

"Nothing . . . and everything." Jacen spread his hands, and Luke felt him draw in on himself in the Force. "This."

They came to the Crooked Way, a serpentine path of rectangular stepping-stones, set askew to each other so that walkers would be forced to slow down and concentrate on their journey through the garden. Luke allowed Mara to lead the way, then fell in behind Jacen, watching with interest as his nephew instinctively took the smoothest, most fluid possible route up the walkway.

"Jacen, do you know that you *have* prevented what you saw in your vision?" Luke asked. He was meandering back and forth behind his nephew, absentmindedly allowing his feet to choose their route from one stone to the next. "Can you be certain that your own actions won't bring the vision to pass?"

Jacen missed the next stone and would have stepped onto the soft carpet of moss had he not sensed his error and caught his balance. He stopped, then pivoted around to face Luke.

"Is that a rhetorical question, Master?" he asked.

"Not entirely," Luke replied. He was concerned that Jacen had fixed the future again, as he had when he had reached across time and spoken to Leia during a vision at the Crash site on Yoggoy. "I need to be sure I know everything."

"Even Yoda didn't know everything," Jacen said, smiling. "But the future is still in motion, if that's what you're asking."

"Thank you," Luke said. Fearing dangerous ripples in the Force, Luke had asked Jacen not to reach into the future again. "But I still wish you hadn't acted so . . . forcefully."

"I had to do something," Jacen said. "And when it comes to the future, Uncle Luke, don't we *always* plot the next jump blind?"

"We do," Luke said. "That's why it is usually wise to be cautious."

"I see." Jacen glanced up the Crooked Way, where the steeply pitched roof of the lecture hall loomed behind a hedge of bambwood. "So you summoned the entire Jedi order to Ossus to do something cautious?"

Luke put on an exaggerated frown. "I said *usually*, Jacen." He let out a melodramatic sigh to show that he was not truly angry, then said, "Go on ahead. I can see that you're a disrespectful young nephew who delights in embarrassing his elders."

"Of course, Master."

Jacen smiled and bowed, then started up the Crooked Way, now taking the straightest possible line toward the lecture hall. Luke watched him go, wondering whether the jump he was about to make with the future of the order was any less bold—or blind—than the one his nephew had made in attacking the supply depot.

"You have to do *something*," Mara said, sensing the drift of his thoughts. "And this is the best choice."

"I know," he said. "That's what worries me."

Luke followed, taking his time, concentrating on the musky smell of the garden soil, deliberately focusing his thoughts on something other than the address he was about to give. He already knew what he needed to say—*that* had grown very clear to him as he learned more about the growing rift in the order—and overthinking it now would only interfere with the message. Better to let the words come naturally, to speak from his heart and hope the Jedi would listen with theirs.

By the time they reached the eastern gable of the lecture hall, a familiar calm had come over Luke. He could sense the Jedi waiting inside the building, tense with anticipation, all hoping that he could resolve the impasse that was threatening to tear the order apart. That much was clear, but he sensed more: frustration, animosity, even bitterness and rage. The disagreements had grown intense and personal, to the point that several Jedi Masters could barely stand to be in the same room.

Luke slid open the instructor's door and led the way down a short, wood-floored hallway. As they approached the sliding panel at the end, the Jedi on the other side sensed their presence, and the low murmur in the auditorium died away.

Mara kissed Luke on the cheek, then whispered, "You can do this, Luke."

"I know," Luke said. "But keep a stun grenade handy just in case."

Mara smiled. "You won't need a grenade—they're *going* to be stunned."

She pulled the panel aside, revealing a simple but soaring auditorium with pillars of pale wood. The Jedi were gathered in the front of the room. Kyp Durron and his supporters were clustered near the left wall, and Corran Horn and his group were bunched along the right. Jacen and Ben sat in the middle with the Solos and Saba Sebatyne, while the students were interspersed in small groups along both sides of the center aisle.

Luke was shocked by how small the gathering looked. Including the students and Han, there were just under three hundred people in a hall that had been designed to hold two thousand—the academy's entire complement of Jedi and support staff. The vacant benches were a stark reminder of how small a bulwark the Jedi truly were against the dark forces that always seemed to be gathering in the unwatched corners of the galaxy.

Luke stopped in the middle of the dais and took a deep breath. He had rehearsed his speech a dozen times, but he still had more butterflies in his stomach than when he had faced Darth Vader on Cloud City. So much depended on what he was about to say . . . and on how the Jedi responded to it.

"Thirty-five standard years ago, I became the last guardian of an ancient order that had thrived for a thousand generations. During all that time, no evil dared challenge its power, no honest being ever questioned its integrity. Yet fall it did, brought low by the treachery of a Sith Lord who disguised himself as a friend and an ally. Only a handful of Masters survived, hiding in deserts and swamps so that the bright light that was the Jedi order would not be extinguished."

Luke paused here and exchanged gazes with Leia. Her face had been lined by four decades of sacrifice and service to the galaxy, yet her brown eyes still shined with the intensity of her youth. At the moment, they were also shining with curiosity. Luke had not discussed what he intended to say even with her.

He looked back to the other Jedi. "Under the guidance of two of those Masters, I became the instrument of the Jedi's return, and I have dedicated myself to rekindling the light of their order. Ours may be a smaller, paler beacon than the one that once lit the way for the Old Republic, but it *has* been growing, both in size and in brilliance."

Luke felt the anticipation in the Force beginning to shift toward optimism, but he also sensed concern rising in his sister. As a Force-gifted politician and a former Chief of State, she realized what he was doing—and she could see where it would lead. Luke pushed her worries out of his mind; he was doing this to save the order, not to aggrandize himself.

"We have been growing," he continued, "until now."

Luke looked first toward Corran and his supporters, then toward Kyp and his.

"*Now* we are threatened by a different enemy, one that I brought into our midst through my misunderstanding of the old practices. In my arrogance, I believed we had found a better way, one more in tune with the challenges we face in our time. I was wrong."

A murmur of soft protest rustled through the hall, and the Force near both Kyp and Corran grew unsettled with guilt. Luke raised his hand for silence.

"In the order I envisioned, we served the Force by following our own consciences. We taught our apprentices well, and we trusted them to follow their own hearts." Luke looked directly into Leia's troubled eyes. "It was a splendid dream, but it has been growing more impractical for some time now."

Luke returned his gaze to the other Jedi. "My mistake was in forgetting that good beings can disagree. They can evaluate all of the evidence and study it from every angle and *still* reach opposite conclusions. And each side can believe with pure hearts that only *their* view is right.

"When that happens, it's easy to lose sight of something far more important than who's right and who's wrong."

Luke fixed his eyes on Kyp, who managed to avoid looking away despite the color that came to his face. "When the Jedi are at odds with each other, they are at odds with the Force."

Luke shifted his gaze to Corran, who responded with a contrite lowering of the eyes. "And when the Jedi are at odds with the Force, they can't perform their duty to themselves, to the order, *or* to the Alliance."

The hall fell utterly silent. Luke remained quiet—not to build the suspense, but to give every Jedi time to reflect on his or her own part in the crisis.

Ben and the students were sitting very still, with their chins pressed to their chests. But their eyes were darting from side to side, looking for clues as to how they should respond. Tesar Sebatyne flattened his scales—betraying the shame he felt for helping precipitate the crisis, and Lowbacca slumped his enormous shoulders. Tahiri sat up straight and stared stonily ahead, her stiff bearing an unsuccessful attempt to disguise her guilty feelings. Only Leia seemed unaffected by the subtle chastisement. She sat with her fingers steepled in front of her, studying Luke with a furrowed brow and a Force presence so guarded he could not read her emotions.

When the mood in the hall began to shift toward regret, Luke spoke again. "I've meditated at length, and I've concluded that *how* we respond to a crisis—the one facing us now or any other—is far less important than responding to it together. Even with the Force to guide us, we're only mortal. We *are* going to make mistakes.

"But mistakes by themselves will never destroy us. As long as we work together, we'll always have the strength to recover. What we *can't* recover from is fighting among ourselves. It will leave us too exhausted to face our enemies. And *that* is what Lomi Plo and the Dark Nest want. It's the only way they can defeat us."

Luke took a deep breath. "So I'm asking each of you to

rethink your commitment to the Jedi. If you can't place the good of the order above all else and follow the direction chosen by your superiors, I'm asking you to leave. If you have other duties or loyalties that come before the order, I'm asking you to leave. If you cannot be a Jedi Knight first, I'm asking you not to be a Jedi Knight at all."

Luke took his time, looking from one shocked face to another. Only Leia seemed dismayed—but he had expected that.

"Think about your choice carefully," he said. "When you are ready, come to me and let me know what you have decided."

TWO

A stunned silence still lay over the lecture hall as Leia stepped onto the dais and started after her brother. As a Jedi Knight, it was hardly her place to challenge a decree from the order's most senior Master, but she knew what Luke was doing . . . even if *he* did not. She entered the small corridor behind the dais, and that was when Han caught up and took her arm.

He slid the panel shut behind them, then whispered, "Hold on! Don't you want to talk this over before you quit?"

"Relax, Han. I'm not leaving the order." Leia glanced down the corridor, toward the golden light spilling out the entrance to the lecture hall's small library. Inside, calmly awaiting the storm, she could sense her brother's presence. "I just need to talk some sense into Luke before this gets out of hand."

"Are you sure?" Han asked. "I mean, you're not even a Master."

"I'm his sister," Leia retorted. "That gives me special privileges."

She strode down the corridor and entered the library without announcing herself. Luke was seated on a mat at the far end of the room, with a low writing table before him and the HoloNet access terminal at his back. Mara stood beside him at one end of the table, her green eyes as hard and unfathomable as an eumlar crystal.

When she saw Leia, Mara cocked her brow. "I doubt you're here to pledge your obedience to the order."

"I'm not." Leia stopped in front of the table and glared down at Luke. "Do you *know* what you've just done?"

"Of course," Luke said. "It's called the Rubogean Gambit."

Leia's aggravation gave way to shock. "You're taking control of the order as a ploy?"

"He has to do *something*," Mara said. "The order is falling apart."

"But the Rubogean Gambit?" Leia protested. "You can't be serious!"

"I'm afraid so," Luke said. "I wish I wasn't."

Leia reached out to her brother in the Force and realized he was telling the truth. He was filled with disappointment— in Kyp, Corran, and the other Masters, in himself, in her. The *last* thing he wanted was to take personal control of the order, but Mara was right. Something had to be done, and—as usual—it fell to Luke to do it.

Leia considered her brother's plan for a moment, growing calmer as she reflected on his other options—or rather, his lack of them.

Finally, she said, "Your provocation isn't strong enough. Most of the Jedi in that hall *want* you to take over. They won't resist you."

"I hope they'll change their minds once they reflect on it," Luke answered. "If not, then I'll *have* to take control of the order."

"For its own good." Leia's rusty political instincts began to trip alarms inside her head. "Do you know how many despots have said the same thing to me?"

"Luke is *not* a despot." Mara's voice grew a little heated. "He doesn't even *want* control."

"I know." Leia kept her gaze on her brother. "But that doesn't make this any less dangerous. If the gambit fails, you'll be reducing the order to a personality cult."

"Then let's hope my ultimatum helps the Masters find a way to work together again." Luke's eyes grew hard. "I will not let them tear the Jedi apart."

"Even if it means anointing yourself king of the Jedi?" Leia pressed.

"Yes, Leia—even if it means *that*."

Surprised by the sudden sharpness in her brother's voice, Leia fell into an uneasy silence. It was clear Luke had already made up his mind. That alone made her worry. He had reached his decision without seeking the benefit of her political experience—and the fact that she could think of no better plan made her worry even more.

When the silence became unbearable, Han stepped to the end of the table opposite Mara. "Okay, I'm lost. Will somebody please slow down and tell me what the blazes a Rubogean Gambit is?"

"It's a diplomatic ploy," Leia explained, relieved to have an excuse to break eye contact with Luke. "You distract your counterpart with a provocative assertion, hoping he's so upset that he doesn't notice what you're really doing."

"In other words, you pull a bait and switch." Han scowled at Luke. "So you *don't* want the Jedi to put the order first?"

"Actually, that's what I *do* want," Luke said. "Our problem now is that everybody puts the order last. Corran thinks we exist to serve the Alliance, and Kyp is convinced we should follow nothing but our own consciences. Meanwhile, Jaina and *her* team believe our first duty is to protect the weak from aggression."

"I'm with you so far," Han said. "Where I make a bad jump is the part where you take full control. If you don't want to be king of the Jedi, why are you using this swindle to slip it past everyone in the order?"

"Luke is trying to unite the Masters against him, Han," Leia explained.

"Yeah, I get that part." Han furrowed his brow, clearly even more skeptical of what was happening than Leia was. "But like I said, if Luke doesn't want to be king, why try slipping it past everyone?"

"Because being sneaky is the only way to convince the Masters I really want this," Luke said. "The threat has to be big—and it has to be *real*. If I'm too obvious, they'll know I'm trying to manipulate them, and it won't work."

Han thought this over for a moment, then said, "That makes sense. But it's still risky. How do you know they'll catch on to this Rubber Gambit or whatever it is?"

"Han, they're Jedi *Masters*," Mara said. "They caught on before Luke finished his speech."

Luke suddenly lifted his chin and looked past them toward the entrance to the library. "This will have to be the end of our discussion. The first Jedi is coming to tell me her decision."

A sad heaviness began to fill Leia's chest. "Of course."

She took Han's hand and turned to go. Danni Quee was already coming through the entrance, her blue eyes shining with unshed tears. When she saw Leia and Han already in the room, she stopped abruptly and looked a little flustered.

"I'm sorry." She started to withdraw. "I'll come back later."

"That's okay, Danni," Leia said. "We were finished here, anyway."

Leia started to lead Han past, but Danni put up her hand to stop them.

"Please don't leave on my account. This won't take long, and what I have to say isn't private." Without waiting for a reply, Danni turned to Luke. "Master Skywalker, I hope you won't think I don't value what I have learned with the Jedi because I came to this decision quickly, but I was never a true member of the order, and my future lies with Zonama Sekot. There is still so much to learn from her that I'd be lying to myself if I said that the Jedi came first. I wish you and the Jedi the best, but I'm going to return to Zonama Sekot."

"I understand, Danni." Luke rose and stepped around the table, then took her hands in his. "You were a tremendous help to the Jedi in our most desperate hour, but we've all known for some time that your destiny lies elsewhere. Thank you, and may the Force be with you always."

Danni smiled and wiped her eyes, then embraced Luke. "Thank *you*, Master Skywalker. And please come see us when you can. Sekot would enjoy visiting with you again."

"I will," Luke promised. "I'd enjoy visiting with her, too."

Danni released Luke and embraced Mara and Leia and Han, then left the room.

She was barely gone before Tenel Ka, the Queen Mother of Hapes, strode in. She held her dimpled chin high and her shoulders square, but the resolve in her eyes was more heartbreaking than reassuring.

Tenel Ka flashed Leia a sad smile, then turned to Luke. "Master Skywalker, I would like nothing more than to place myself entirely at the Jedi order's disposal." She bit her lip, then reached under the Jedi robe she had donned for her visit and removed her lightsaber from its clip. "And if there were only myself and my daughter to consider, perhaps I would.

"But that would be irresponsible. I am the sole ablebodied sovereign of an interstellar empire, and if I were to relinquish my throne, my nobles would spill lakes of blood fighting to take my place." She held out her lightsaber to

Luke. "It is with great regret that I must surrender this. I simply cannot fulfill the duties of a Knight in the Jedi order."

"I understand." Luke accepted Tenel Ka's lightsaber, then pushed it back into her hand. "But please keep your lightsaber. You earned the right to carry it, and that can never be taken away."

Tenel Ka managed a sad smile. "Thank you, Master Skywalker. Your gesture means a great deal to me."

"Thank *you*, Queen Mother," Luke said. "You may have assumed other duties for now, but you carry within you everything that a Jedi Knight is. Perhaps one day you will be free to return to the order. There will always be a place for you."

Tenel Ka's smile turned more hopeful. "Yes, perhaps that is so."

She embraced Luke with her one arm, then surprised Leia by embracing her and Han. "You mean more to me than I will ever be able to tell, my friends. I am going to miss you both."

"Miss us?" Han replied. "This isn't forever, kid. We're going to visit, you know."

"That's right," Leia added, returning the Queen Mother's embrace. "Your security chief may not allow baby holos, but I still want to see your daughter—and if we have to come all the way to Hapes to do it, we will."

Tenel Ka stiffened in Leia's arms. "That would be . . . nice." She stepped back, her anxiety permeating the Force. "Be sure to let us know when you are coming, so we can arrange the proper security."

"Of course." Leia had to force herself not to frown. "Thank you."

Tenel Ka gave Leia and Han an uneasy smile, then turned her attention to Luke and Mara as well. "Goodbye. May the Force be with you all."

The Queen Mother spun and left the room so quickly that neither Leia nor anyone else had time to wish her the same.

Han frowned after her. "That was weird."

"Something about the baby," Leia said. "There's a reason she won't let anybody get a good look at it."

"Maybe she's embarrassed," Han said.

"Han!" Leia and Mara exclaimed together.

"Look, she still won't say anything about the father," he said. "I'm just saying that maybe there's a reason. Maybe she's not proud of the guy."

"You know, Han might be right," Luke said. "Not that she's embarrassed, but maybe there's something she doesn't want the galaxy to see. How would her nobles react if the heir to the Hapes throne was less than a perfect beauty?"

Leia's heart sank. "Oh, no. That poor woman."

"I'm glad you let Tenel Ka keep her lightsaber, Luke," Mara agreed. "She may need it."

They all stared out into the corridor after the Queen Mother, pondering the lonely circumstances of her life, wondering how they might be able to help, until another set of footsteps echoed down the passage. A moment later, Corran Horn appeared at the entrance to the library and bowed respectfully.

"Master Skywalker, would now be a good time to speak with you?" he asked.

"Of course." Luke glanced meaningfully in Leia and Han's direction, then returned to his mat behind the writing table and sat. "Come in."

Leia took Han's hand again and started past Corran. "Excuse us, Corran. We were just leaving."

"Please don't, at least not yet," Corran said. "I've already said this to the rest of the order, and I'd like you to hear it, too."

Leia glanced at Luke for permission, then nodded. "If you wish."

Corran went to the center of the room and clasped his hands behind his back.

"Master Skywalker, first I would like to apologize for the part I've played in this crisis. I can see now that in complying with Chief Omas's request that I become the order's temporary leader, I was playing directly into his hands."

"Yes, you were," Luke said.

Corran swallowed, then fixed his gaze on the wall behind Luke's head. "I assure you, it was never my intention to usurp anyone's authority, but when it grew clear how bad Jedi relations had grown with Chief Omas and the Alliance, I felt something had to be done. I can see now how badly mistaken I was."

"Mistakes are always easy to see in retrospect," Luke said mildly.

Corran glanced down at Luke, clearly uncertain how he was taking the apology. "But I *do* carry the good of the order utmost in my heart."

"Good," Luke said.

"That's why I think it might be best if I left." Corran's voice was choked with emotion. "My presence can only be a divisive element."

"I see." Luke braced his elbows on the writing table, then rested his chin on his steepled fingers. "Corran, isn't this the second time you have offered to leave the order for its own good?"

Corran nodded. "It is. After the destruction of Ithor—"

"Don't let there be a third," Luke interrupted. "I won't stop you next time."

Corran frowned, clearly confused. "Stop me?"

"Corran, you may have been naïve for believing the Yuuzhan Vong would honor their word, but *they* destroyed Ithor, not you," Luke said. "And the mistakes that led the

Jedi into our current crisis are more mine than anyone else's. So please stop trying to shoulder the entire galaxy's guilt by yourself. To be honest, it makes you look a bit pompous."

Corran looked as though someone had detonated a stun grenade in his face. "Pompous?"

Luke nodded. "I hope you don't mind me telling you that in front of others, but you're the one who invited them to stay."

Corran glanced over at Leia and Han. "Of course not."

"Good," Luke said. "Then we're all settled? You're going to continue as a Jedi, and your loyalty to the order comes first?"

"Yes." Corran nodded. "Of course."

Luke smiled broadly. "I'm glad. We couldn't afford to lose you, Corran. I don't think you realize just how valuable you are to the order. The Jedi *do* have a duty to support the Galactic Alliance—far more than we have been—and nobody represents that viewpoint better than you do."

"Uh, thank you." Corran remained in the center of the room looking confused.

After a moment, Luke said, "That's all, Corran. Unless there's something else—"

"Actually, there is," Corran said. "I think the other Masters have all chosen to stay, as well. After I spoke with them, they asked me to tell you they would be waiting in the auditorium."

"They did?" Luke raised his brow and tried to avoid showing the satisfaction that Leia sensed through their twin bond. "I guess I should go hear what they have to say."

Leia stepped aside, then she and the others followed Luke into the auditorium. The room was even emptier than before, with Kyp, Saba, and the rest of the Masters gathered in a tight cluster near the front of the speaking dais, holding an animated conversation in barely civil tones. Tesar, Lowbacca, Tahiri, and Tekli were seated together a few rows back, trying not to be too obvious in their eavesdropping. Jacen sat on the opposite side of the aisle, appearing more interested in his conversation with Ben than in whatever the Masters were whispering about.

The rest of the order was gone—presumably sent away by the Masters so they could have a private conversation with Master Skywalker. The fact that Jacen, Tesar, and the others had been asked to stay suggested that the conversation was going to be about the Killiks. Apparently, Luke's plan had at least made the Masters willing to talk again. Leia doubted they would agree on anything, but talking was a start.

When Han saw the gathering of Masters, he hopped off the dais and held his hand out toward Ben. "It looks like we're going to be a little out of place at this meeting, partner. Why don't we go back over to the *Falcon* and work on that warp vortex problem I was telling you about?"

Ben's eyes lit up. He started to say good-bye to Jacen—until Kenth Hamner rose and spoke from among the Masters.

"Actually, Captain Solo, we'd like you to stay."

Han cast a worried look in Leia's direction, and she knew they were thinking the same thing: that Jaina and Zekk were going to be a big part of this conversation.

"Yeah, sure," he said. "Whatever you want."

Ben twisted his freckled face into a sour expression. "What about the *Falcon*'s vortex problem?"

"Don't worry about that, kid," Han said to him. "Vortex stabilizers don't fix themselves. It'll be there waiting when we're ready."

"Perhaps Ben's Defender Droid could take him home."

Kenth glanced toward the speaking dais. "If that's acceptable to the Masters Skywalker?"

"Of course," Mara said. She looked toward the back of the hall. "Nanna?"

The big Defender Droid stepped out of the shadows, then extended her metallic hand and waited as Ben reluctantly shuffled up the aisle to join her.

Once the pair had left the hall, Kenth turned to Han. "Thank you for staying, Captain Solo. We know your affiliation is informal, but you're an important part of the order, and your opinion has always carried a great deal of weight with the Masters."

"Always glad to help," Han said cautiously. "So what's this about?"

"In a minute." Kenth waved Han toward a seat. Clearly, the Masters had come to an agreement about one thing—they were going to meet Luke's gambit with a united front. "First, we would like to ask how Master Skywalker sees family fitting into his new view of a Jedi's commitment to the order."

"I'm not saying we have to abandon our loved ones," Luke said, stepping between Leia and the Masters. "But obviously, any Jedi is required to be away from his or her family for extended periods."

When Luke remained between Leia and the Masters, she took the hint and stepped off the dais, then went to Han's side. They both sat on the bench with Jacen.

As Luke and the Masters continued to clarify just what Luke meant by "placing the order first," Han leaned close to Jacen's ear.

"Tenel Ka left the order," he whispered. "Thought you'd want to know."

"I already did," Jacen answered. "Uncle Luke didn't leave her much choice, did he?"

"It only formalizes what we've all known for some time,"

Leia said. Jacen and Tenel Ka had been close throughout their teenage years, and Leia did not want Jacen to allow Tenel Ka's departure to influence his own decision. "Tenel Ka's duties as the Queen Mother already prevent her from participating in the order in any meaningful way."

Jacen smiled and placed his hand on Leia's knee. "Mom, I'm not going to disappear again. I've already decided to stay."

Leia was so relieved that she suspected even Han could feel it, but she kept a straight face and said, "If that's what you think is best for you, dear."

Jacen laughed and rolled his eyes. "Mother, your feelings betray you."

"I suppose so." Leia grew more serious, then asked, "What has Tenel Ka told you about her daughter?"

"Allana?" Jacen's presence suddenly seemed to disappear from the Force, and his tone grew guarded. "What about her?"

"We mean, what is Tenel Ka hiding?" Han demanded. "Mention the kid, and she closes up like a rabclab in ice water."

"What makes you think Tenel Ka would tell *me* anything?" Jacen asked.

"She obviously *has*," Leia said. "Or you wouldn't be trying to dodge our questions."

Jacen stared at the floor. Leia had the sense that he wanted to tell them, but was struggling with whether he had the right. Finally, he met Leia's gaze.

"If Tenel Ka finds it necessary to keep her daughter out of the hololight, I think we should trust that she has good reason."

Han looked past Jacen to Leia and nodded. "Luke was right."

Jacen's eyes widened. "About *what*?"

"About Allana," Leia said. "If she were, uh, *afflicted* in some way, Tenel Ka would need to keep the child hidden. The Hapans' obsession with beauty goes beyond the neurotic. I can't imagine what they might do if the heir to their throne was blemished."

The alarm in Jacen's expression began to fade. "Don't bother asking for details. I don't know them."

Leia could tell by the way Jacen avoided her eyes that he was lying, but she decided to let it go. He clearly felt that they were already asking him to betray a confidence, and pressing him any harder would only make him less forthcoming.

"We know all that we need to," Leia said. "I only hope Tenel Ka realizes we're here to help."

"Mom, Tenel Ka has more money than Lando, and dozens of Jedi friends," Jacen said. "I'm pretty sure she knows she can get all the help she needs."

"Hey, we're just worried about her," Han said. "Poor kid—whatever's wrong, I'll bet the problem came from the father."

Jacen frowned and was silent for a moment, then said, "I'm sure you're right, Dad. And if this is your way of asking if I know who the father is, it's not going to work."

Han pretended to be hurt. "You think *I'd* snoop?"

"I *know* you would," Jacen said. "That's the Zeltron Lead you just tried. You taught it to me when I was ten."

Han shrugged. "And I didn't think you were listening."

Leia's attention was drawn to the gathering of Masters by a sudden lull in their conversation. She looked up to find Luke seated on the edge of the dais, motioning everyone forward. As they all approached, she sensed a certain hopefulness in her brother's presence.

"The Masters have agreed that the order's first responsibility during any crisis is to respond in a coherent and united fashion," he said. "Now the question is, what are we going to do about the Killiks?"

"That's why we asked all of you to stay," Tresina Lobi said, turning to Leia and the others. "You know more about the Killiks than any of us, so your insights will guide our decision."

Luke nodded his agreement. "I'd like to ask Jacen to share his vision with the rest of us."

"Vision?" Corran asked.

"It's why I organized the attack on Supply Depot Thrago," Jacen explained, going to stand between the Masters and the dais. "I saw the Chiss launch a massive surprise attack against the Killiks."

Kenth frowned. "Surely, you didn't think that you could prevent—"

"Let him finish," Luke said, raising his hand to silence the Master. "Jacen's plan was desperate, but not unreasonable given the circumstances at the time—especially our own disarray."

Jacen continued, "What really frightened me about the vision was that the Chiss failed to destroy the Colony. Instead, I saw the Killiks mount a counterattack, and the war spread to the Galactic Alliance."

"Let me see if I understand this," Corran said, frowning in confusion. "You saw the war spreading to the Galactic Alliance, so you attacked the Chiss to keep that from happening? That sounds crazy, Jacen."

Jacen nodded. "It's convoluted, I know. But I felt we had to change the dynamic. Obviously, the Chiss are *still* attacking—"

"And the Galactic Alliance is *still* being dragged into the war." Kenth's tone was sharp. "Not only are we fighting in the Utegetu Nebula now we have the Chiss mobilizing against us because they think we gave the *Ackbar* to the Killiks. I don't see that your attack accomplished anything except to hasten the war—and make everything vastly more complicated."

"It convinced the Chiss they couldn't win with a quick strike," Han said, coming to Jacen's defense. "At least now there's *some* chance you can bring this mess under control before it erupts into a galaxywide bug stomp."

"Han is right," Corran said. "Besides, debating our past mistakes—whether or not they *were* mistakes—won't solve this problem. We need to talk about how we're going to stop this war before it gets out of control."

The Masters nodded their agreement, but fell silent and stared at the floor, clearly reluctant to launch into the same argument that had been threatening to tear the order apart for several months. After a few seconds, Corran, Kyp, and even Saba began to cast expectant glances toward Luke, clearly hoping he would take the lead. He remained silent, determined to force the Masters to work through the problem themselves and develop their own consensus.

Finally, Jacen spoke up. "I know how to stop the war."

Everybody's brow—including Leia's—went up.

"Why am I not surprised?" Kyp asked. He ran a hand through his unruly hair, pausing to scratch his scalp. "Okay, let's hear it. You seem to be the only one with any ideas."

Jacen stepped over next to Luke, placing himself squarely in front of the Masters. His determination hung heavy and hard in the Force. He was going to stop the war. Too much would be lost if he did not.

"We kill Raynar Thul."

"*What?*"

This was cried by several Jedi at once, among them Tesar Sebatyne and the other young Jedi Knights who had accompanied Jacen on the raid against Supply Depot Thrago. Even Leia found herself wondering if she had heard Jacen correctly.

"Did you see *that* in your vision, too?" Corran asked.

He turned to the other Masters, shaking his head in disapproval. "We talked about this before."

Luke frowned. "We did?"

"When you and Han were captured on Woteba," Mara informed him. "It was our backup plan."

"And now it should be our primary plan," Jacen said calmly. "It's the only way to prevent the war."

"Go on," Luke said.

"Most insect species have an immense mortality rate," Jacen explained. "One egg out of a thousand might produce a larva that survives to become an imago and produce young of its own. When Raynar became a Joiner—"

"But killing Raynar would destroy the Colony!" Tesar rasped.

"I believe that's the point," Kenth said. "They *have* declared war on two other galactic civilizations."

Lowbacca roared an objection, protesting that the Dark Nest was causing all the trouble.

"Jacen has obviously given this a lot of thought," Luke said, raising his hands for quiet. "Why don't we hear him out?"

"Because hearing Jacen out is dangerous," Tahiri said, glaring at Jacen. "He says one thing and means another."

Coming from Tahiri, whom the Solos had considered practically their own daughter since Anakin's death, the comment was especially stinging. Leia would have admonished her for her rudeness, had Luke not done so first.

"That's enough!" Luke scowled first at Tahiri, then at Tesar and Lowbacca. "This debate is among the Masters, and when we *ask* for your opinion, you're going to give it in a civilized fashion. Is that clear?"

Tesar's scales stood on end and Lowbacca's fur ruffled, but they joined Tahiri in nodding. "Yes, Master."

"Thank you." Luke looked back to Jacen. "You were saying?"

"When Raynar became a Joiner, the Killiks began to value the lives of individual nest-members," Jacen continued. "Their population exploded, they began to strip their own worlds bare, and that's when the Colony was born and began to infringe on Chiss space."

"But will killing Raynar change that *now*?" Saba asked from the front bench. "The Killikz have already changed. This one does not see how removing Raynar will change them back."

"Because the change is a *learned* behavior." Jacen was obviously ready with his answer. "Raynar is the only element of their personality that *innately* values individual life."

"So we remove Raynar, and they unlearn the behavior?" Kenth asked.

"Exactly," Jacen said. "Raynar's ability to project his will through the Force is what binds the individual nests into the Colony. If we remove that, the nests will need to survive on their own."

"The nests will either return to their normal state or starve," Kenth said. "Either way, the problem takes care of itself."

"Not exactly," Corran said. "You're forgetting the Dark Nest. By all accounts, they're already running the Colony from behind the scenes. If we take out Raynar, what's to prevent Lomi Plo from taking over?"

"We have to take her and Alema Rar out, too," Jacen said. "I'm sorry, I thought that was a given."

When no one objected, Luke asked, "So everyone agrees on that much, then? The Dark Nest must be destroyed."

"Assuming we can," Han muttered. "We've tried that before, remember?"

"We've learned a lot since then," Jacen insisted. "This time, we'll succeed."

"I'm glad you're so confident, Jacen," Kyp said. "How about letting the rest of us in on the secret?"

"I already have," Jacen said. "We're going to eliminate Raynar and his nest, too."

This drew a pair of snorts from Tesar and Lowbacca, but a warning glance from Luke was enough to silence the two Jedi Knights.

"Now I'm really lost," Corran said. "If we have to destroy the Dark Nest anyway, why don't we just stop there and *reason* with Raynar?"

"I wish we could," Leia said. "But Raynar's mind was shattered by the *Flier*'s crash, and the Killiks have a very fluid concept of truth. When you put those two things together, you can't count on him to behave rationally. We only persuaded him to abandon Qoribu by convincing him that if he didn't, *all* of the nests there would turn into Dark Nests."

"That's true, Mother," Jacen said. "But the real problem is you *can't* destroy the Dark Nest without killing Raynar. As long as there is an Unu, there will be a Gorog."

"That'z zilly," Tesar scoffed.

"Not at all." Cilghal spoke in a soft voice that had a quieting effect on the whole argument. "I began to suspect the same thing myself when the Dark Nest reappeared in the Utegetu Nebula."

Corran, Kenth, and even Luke looked stunned.

"Why?" Luke asked.

"Do you remember our discussion about the conscious and unconscious mind?" Cilghal replied.

Luke nodded. "I believe you put it this way: 'Like the Force itself, every mind in the galaxy has two aspects.' "

"Very good, Master Skywalker," Cilghal said. "The conscious mind embraces what we know of ourselves, and the unconscious contains the part that remains hidden."

"I thought that was the subconscious mind," Corran said.

"So did I, until Cilghal explained it," Luke said. "The

subconscious is a level of the mind between full awareness and unawareness. The *unconscious* remains fully hidden from the part of our minds that we know. Right, Cilghal?"

"You have an excellent memory, Master Skywalker," she said.

"Wait a minute, Cilghal," Kyp said. "You're saying that Jacen is actually right? That even if the Dark Nest didn't exist, the Colony would create one?"

"I am saying that Jacen's theory fits what we have observed," Cilghal replied. "To the extent that the Colony is a collective mind, it makes sense for it to create an unconscious. And you cannot destroy an unconscious mind without also destroying the conscious mind."

Cilghal paused and swiveled one bulbous eye toward Tesar, Lowbacca, and Tahiri. "I am sorry, but if this theory is correct, it is simply impossible to destroy the Dark Nest without destroying the Colony. One accompanies the other."

"Then Jacen's theory is wrong!" Tesar rasped.

"That is always possible," Cilghal admitted. "But it explains everything we have observed, and that makes it the best working theory we have."

"So we kill one of our own?" Corran shook his head harshly. "I can't believe that's our best option. It goes against everything I feel as a Jedi. We're not assassins, we don't betray our own, and we don't destroy entire civilizations."

"Corran, we talked about *that*, too," Leia reminded him. "It's because Raynar *is* a Jedi that we must act. He's become a threat to the galaxy, and it's our responsibility to stop him."

"I understand that he's a threat," Corran responded. "But if he's as shattered as you say, we shouldn't be trying to kill him—we should be trying to help him."

"May the Force be with you on *that*!" Han scoffed.

"You'll need it. Raynar's more powerful than Luke, and he doesn't *want* your help."

Luke cocked his brow at Han's assessment of his relative strength, but looked more surprised than insulted and did not protest.

"Corran, think about what you're asking," Leia said. "Exactly *how* do you suggest we help Raynar? You know how difficult it is to hold a regular Jedi against his will, and Raynar's resources are immensely more vast. I'm afraid we have to face the reality of the situation."

"So you're agreeing with Jacen?" Corran asked. "You think our only choice is to kill Raynar?"

The question struck Leia like a kick in the stomach. She had known Raynar since he had come to the Jedi academy on Yavin 4 as the haughty child-heir to the Bornaryn Shipping Empire, then watched him mature into the sincere young man who had volunteered to accompany Anakin on the ill-fated strike mission to Myrkr. The thought of actually sending Jedi against him made her lips tremble with sorrow. But she had seen for herself, when the Killik fleet attacked in the Murgo Choke, that he had no such qualms about assaulting his former friends.

Leia nodded sadly. "Yes, Corran," she said. "I think Jacen is right. Our best option is to take out Raynar. In fact, it is our duty."

Corran's face reddened, and Leia knew the exchange was about to get rough.

"Our *duty*?" he demanded. "What about Jaina and Zekk?"

"What about them?" Han shot back.

"They're Joiners, too," Corran pointed out, still looking at Leia. "Will you be so eager to kill *them* when they take Raynar's place?"

Luke raised a hand in an effort to restore calm, but the

damage had already been done. The question had heated even Leia's blood, and Han immediately went into full boil

"They're not *going* to take Raynar's place!" Han shouted.

"You can't know that," Corran replied. "Jaina has always done as she pleases, and now she's with the Colony." He turned back to Leia. "So I want to know: will you say the same thing when we have to go after Jaina and Zekk?"

"That's a baseless question, and you know it!" Leia said.

"Not really," Kyle Katarn said. "I, for one, would find your answer relevant to Raynar's case."

"Huttwash!" Kyp protested. "Jaina and Zekk have already demonstrated that they're Jedi first. It's not relevant at all."

"Then why aren't they here?" Kyle pressed.

"Probably because they're trying to stop a *war*," Han retorted.

And they were off, voices rising, tempers flaring, gestures growing increasingly sharp. Corran continued to press the Solos about what they would do if Jaina and Zekk were running the Colony instead of Raynar. Han and Leia continued to insist it was a moot question, and Kyle, Kyp, and the rest of the Masters continued to line up on both sides of the issue, taking increasingly rigid positions.

Within minutes, it grew apparent that they had reached an impasse, and Leia sensed her brother's frustration building. His attempt to unite the Masters had failed miserably. They were no closer to reaching a consensus now than they had been while he and Han were trapped in the Utegetu, and even Leia could see the situation was only going to grow worse.

"Thank you."

Though Luke spoke softly, he used the Force to project his words into the minds of everyone present. The effect was immediate; the argument came to a sudden halt, and the entire group turned to face him.

"Thank you for your opinions." Luke stepped back onto the dais. "I'll consider them all carefully and let you know what I decide."

Kyp frowned. "What *you* decide?"

"Yes, Kyp," Mara said. She stepped toward him and locked eyes with him. "What *Luke* decides. Don't you think that's best?"

Kyp's brow rose, then he looked around him at the faces of the other Masters—many still flushed with the emotions of their argument—and slowly seemed to realize what Leia already had: Luke was taking control of the order.

Before Kyp found the breath to answer, Han turned and started up the aisle toward the exit, his boot heels clunking on the wood floor. Leia started after him, almost running to catch up. Luke seemed content to watch them go in silence, but not Saba.

"Jedi Solo, where are you going?" the Barabel demanded.

"With Han," Leia replied. "To get our daughter back."

"What about the order?" Saba asked.

Leia did not even turn around. "*What* order?"

THREE

The Yuuzhan Vong's attempt to reshape Coruscant into the image of their lost homeworld had brought many good things to the planet, and fresh y'luubi was one of the best. Taken from Liberation Lake no more than three hours before smoldering, it had a rich, smoky flavor that filled Mara's entire head with pleasure. She held the spongy meat on her tongue, allowing it to dissolve as she had heard was proper, and marveled at the succession of spectacular tastes. The flavor went from smoky to sweet to tangy, then ended with a sharp, spicy bite that made her mouth water for more.

"The y'luubi are unbelievably wonderful, Madame Thul," Mara said, addressing their host. She and Luke had barely been back on Coruscant for a week before Madame Thul arrived aboard the *Tradewyn* and sent a message to the Jedi Temple inviting them to dine with her.

"The whole meal is," Luke added. "Thank you again for insisting that we meet here."

Aryn Thul—Raynar Thul's mother and the chairwoman of the board of Bornaryn Trading—smiled politely. "I'm so pleased you're enjoying it." A gaunt, almost frail woman with gray hair and durasteel eyes, she carried herself with a dignity and grace appropriate to the shimmersilk gown and Corusca gem necklace she had chosen for their "casual" dinner. "I was told Yuza Bre is the finest restaurant on Coruscant."

"By all accounts," Mara said. "I understand reservations are usually required months in advance. I can't imagine why it's deserted tonight."

"You can't?" Tyko Thul asked. A large, round-faced man with short graying hair and hazel eyes, he was the brother of Madame Thul's late husband—and the chief operating officer of Bornaryn Trading. He turned to Madame Thul and shared an arrogant smile. "It appears the Jedi are not quite as all-knowing as we are led to believe."

"We shouldn't judge that on the basis of a restaurant, Tyko. I doubt corporate acquisitions are very high on their list of concerns." Madame Thul turned to Mara. "As of this morning, the Yuza Bre is a Bornaryn property. Buying it was the only way to guarantee our visit would remain private."

"Buying a restaurant was hardly necessary, Madame Thul," Luke said in a guarded tone. "If there's something you need to discuss in private, I would have been happy to meet you aboard the *Tradewyn*."

Given the argument among the Masters over whether to eliminate Raynar, both Mara and Luke had found the timing of Madame Thul's dinner invitation suspicious. But Luke had been a friend of the Thuls since Raynar attended the Jedi academy on Yavin 4, and Mara had convinced him that *if* Madame Thul knew about the argument, declining the invitation would be viewed as evidence that he agreed with those who felt the only way to resolve the Killik crisis was to kill her son.

Madame Thul frowned. "Luke, we have been friends since before Bornan died." Her tone remained nonchalant, but Mara could sense her anger—and her fear—in the Force. "Surely, you know me well enough to realize that if I wish to discuss something with you, I will."

"Does that mean you don't wish to discuss *anything*?" Luke asked.

"It means that you aren't the primary reason I bought Yuza Bre." Madame Thul allowed herself a guilty smile. "This happens to be Chief Omas's favorite restaurant. As you can imagine, from now on, he is going to find it difficult to make reservations."

"That seems rather petty," Mara said. Madame Thul struck her as a woman who appreciated frankness, so she spoke bluntly. "And it's hardly likely to sway his attitude regarding the Colony."

Madame Thul shrugged, her blue eyes twinkling with mischief. "I have been trying to be heard on this for months, but that Jenet assistant of his refuses to schedule an appointment. This seems as good a way as any to make my displeasure known."

"I'm sure it will accomplish *that*," Mara said. "But if feeding y'luubi to the Skywalker family is how you show displeasure with the Jedi, I'm sorry to inform you it isn't working."

She smiled, expecting Madame Thul to do likewise and utter at least a polite little laugh. Instead, the chairwoman fixed her with a steely-eyed glare.

"I really don't understand, Mara." She turned to Luke. "Is there some reason I *should* be displeased with the Jedi?"

"That isn't for us to say," Luke answered. "You're certainly aware of the Jedi's role in the recent trouble between the Colony and the Alliance."

"Of course," Madame Thul said. "You were crucial in keeping the nest ships trapped inside the Utegetu Nebula."

"So the answer to your question depends on you, Chairwoman Thul," Mara said. "Where do your loyalties lie?"

It was Tyko Thul who answered. "Our loyalties lie where they always have—with Bornaryn Trading. We have outlasted three galactic governments . . . and we'll outlast this one."

"What about family?" Luke asked, addressing the question to Madame Thul. "I'm sure your loyalties also extend to Raynar."

"Our interests in the Colony are very important to us, yes." Madame Thul's voice grew icy. "Obviously, Bornaryn will do *whatever* we must to protect them—and at the moment, we are well positioned to be extremely effective."

"For example, Bornaryn has diversified into exotic starship fuels," Tyko added. "Just yesterday, we acquired Xtib."

A tense silence fell over the table. Xtib was the processing company that produced TibannaX, the special Tibanna isotope used in StealthX engines to conceal their ion tails.

After a moment, Mara raised her eyes and locked gazes with Tyko. "I hope you don't intend that as a threat, Chief Thul. We're a little short on patience these days."

"Is there a reason Bornaryn would *need* to threaten the Jedi?" Tyko asked, refusing to be intimidated.

"You're obviously aware of our discussions regarding Raynar," Luke said, rising. "Rest assured that the Jedi would never take such an action lightly, but we *will* do what we must to bring this war to a swift end."

"Thank you for your frankness, Master Skywalker." Some of the stateliness seemed to drain from Madame Thul's bearing, and she motioned for him to return to his chair. "I don't know why, but I do take some small comfort from the reluctance in your voice. Please stay and finish your dinner."

"I'm afraid that isn't possible," Luke said.

"But we *would* like to know how you came by your information," Mara added, also rising. Her stomach was knotting in anger, though not because of any threat Bornaryn Trading might pose to the Jedi's TibannaX supplies. Someone—almost certainly a Jedi—had betrayed the confidence of Luke and the order. "Who told you?"

Madame Thul lifted her brow. "You truly expect me to reveal that?"

"You really don't have a choice," Mara said.

"This is outrageous!" Tyko snapped.

He started to rise, but Mara flicked a finger in his direction, and he dropped back into his chair, paralyzed by her Force grasp. Gundar, the thick-necked bodyguard who had been doubling as their waiter, reached for his blaster and started to leave his station near the kitchen.

Luke wagged a finger at the hulking human, then used the Force to pin him against a wall and looked to Madame Thul.

"I take security breaches very seriously," he said. "Don't make me use the Force on you."

Madame Thul sighed, then looked away. "You mustn't be too hard on them," she said. "They were convinced they were doing the right thing."

"They always are," Mara said. "Who was it?"

"The Barabel and his Wookiee," Madame Thul said. "Tesar and . . . Lowbacca it was, I believe."

Mara could sense Madame Thul's truthfulness in the Force, but she still found it difficult to believe—if only because it proved just how deeply divided the order remained even *after* Luke's gambit.

"It makes sense." Luke sounded as defeated as Mara was shocked. "I had just hoped for better."

"If you are disappointed, perhaps you should look to yourself for the reason," Madame Thul suggested. "Tesar and the Wookiee have good hearts, Master Skywalker. They would not betray your confidence unless they believed they had no other choice."

"Or unless they were under the Colony's control," Mara said. She turned toward the restaurant's transparisteel wall and looked across the green glow of Victory Square, toward the golden sheen of the Jedi Temple's giant pyramid. "They *were* back among the Killiks for more than a month."

Luke's concern—or perhaps it was sorrow—permeated the Force-bond Mara shared with him, but he retained a neutral expression as he spoke to Madame Thul.

"Thank you for your hospitality," he said. "The y'luubi was beyond description. I'm sure the Yuza Bre will continue to prosper under Bornaryn's ownership."

"You really must leave?" Madame Thul asked.

"I'm afraid so," Luke said. "Until the troubles with the Colony are resolved, it's probably better for Bornaryn Trading and the Jedi to keep their distance."

Madame Thul nodded. "I understand. But before you go, I hope you'll allow me to make one gift to you—friend to friend."

Tyko's eyes widened. "Aryn, I don't think that's a good idea. We might still have a use—"

"I doubt it." Madame Thul scowled at her brother-in-law. "It's obvious that we're not going to sway Master Skywalker with a *droid*, so we may as well give it to him."

Mara frowned. "A droid?"

Madame Thul smiled. "You'll see." She turned to her bodyguard. "Gundar, you can bring in ArOh now."

Gundar activated a remote, and a terrible squealing arose in the kitchen. A moment later, an ancient R series astromech droid lurched into view, its locomotion system so corrupted and corroded that it resembled an ancient sailing ship zigzagging into a headwind. Someone had recently made an effort to polish its brass casing, but the tarnish along the crevices and seams was so thick, it looked like paint.

"An antique droid?" Mara asked.

"A very special antique." Madame Thul waited until the droid had wandered within arm's length of the table, then reached out and gently guided it to her side. "Master Skywalker, allow me to present Artoo-Oh, the original proto-type for the R-two astromech line."

Luke's jaw fell. "The *prototype*?"

"So my systems supervisor assures me," Madame Thul said. "I'm told it contains the original Intellex Four droid brain. I hope it will prove helpful in working through Artoo-Detoo's memory problems."

"I'm sure it will!" Mara gasped. "Where did it come from?"

"An abandoned warehouse, apparently," Madame Thul said. "It was owned by Industrial Automaton, which Bornaryn recently purchased. Of course, their records were *almost* completely useless in locating the prototype."

"Industrial Automaton?" Mara asked. "Ghent said the Artoo was an Imperial design."

"Misinformation," Tyko said. "Imperial Intelligence waged a deliberate campaign to obscure the origin of all the Empire's vital military technology."

"Then the designer of the Intellex IV droid brain *wasn't* an Imperial?" Luke asked.

"Not when he worked on the R-series." Tyko shrugged. "Who can say what happened later? He might have become one, or he might have been forced into their service. All our historians could determine was that his identity has been deleted from all known databases regarding the R-series."

"But you have the prototype," Madame Thul said. "I hope you can find what you need there."

"I don't know what to say," Luke said. "Thank you!"

" 'Thank you' will be quite sufficient," Madame Thul said. "Every man should know his mother."

"I'm sure it will be very helpful," Mara said. "But what made you think of it? Artoo's memory problems aren't exactly common knowledge outside of the Jedi order."

Madame Thul smiled. "Tesar and the Wookiee," she said. "I told you—they have good hearts."

FOUR

With dozens of battered transports hanging on the wax-coated walls at every possible angle and swarms of orange worker-Killiks floating war cargo through the microgravity, the Lizil hangar looked even busier than the last time Han and Leia had visited. The largest available berth was a wedge near the top of the sphere, and even that looked barely big enough for the bulky *Dray*-class transport the Solos had borrowed from Lando to complete their disguise. Han rolled the *Swiff* onto its back and began to ease toward the empty spot.

Leia inhaled sharply, then activated the landing cams and studied the copilot's display. "Wait. Our clearance is only half a meter."

"That much?"

"Han, this isn't the *Falcon*."

"You don't have to tell *me*," Han said. "This big tub handles like an asteroid."

"I believe Princess Leia is suggesting you might not be adept enough with this vessel to berth in such a confined space," C-3PO offered from the back of the flight deck. "Your reaction speed and hand-to-eye coordination have degraded twelve percent in the last decade."

"Only when you're around," Han growled. "And quit telling me that. My memory is fine—and so's my driving, metal mouth."

"What I'm *suggesting*," Leia said, "is that it's a tight fit, and you promised Lando you wouldn't scratch his ship."

"And you think he believed me?"

"I *think* we should wait for a larger berth to open up," Leia said. "We're not going to win the Colony's confidence by causing an accident."

"We don't need their confidence." Han jerked a thumb toward the *Swiff*'s huge cargo bay. "When they see that big magcannon we've got back there, they're going to *beg* us to take it out to the front lines."

"That's quite unlikely, Captain Solo," C-3PO said. "Insect species rarely have a sense of charity, so it simply would not occur to them to appeal to your compassion."

"Han means they'll be eager to contract with us," Leia said. "Which is all the more reason to wait. We don't want to overplay our hand. Jaina and Zekk will still be in the front lines when we get there."

"*Wait?*" Han shook his head and continued to ease the *Swiff* toward the landing spot. One of the adjacent transports, an ancient Republic Sienar Systems *Courier*-class, had extended its boarding ramp into the space he intended to occupy, but he wasn't worried. The *Swiff*'s landing struts were far enough apart to straddle the ramp, and the Lizil workers streaming up and down the incline were used to dodging ships. "It could take days for another berth to open."

"It won't take more than an hour." Leia pointed out the top of the cockpit canopy. "That Freight Queen is making ready to leave."

Han looked, but instead of the Freight Queen, his gaze fell on a sharp-looking Mon Calamari Sailfish berthed directly "below" them in the middle of the hangar floor. The ramp was down, and there were two Flakax standing guard outside, keeping watch over a ragged mob of Verpine, Vratix, and Fefze who seemed to be waiting for an audience with the captain of the Sailfish. The sight sent a cold shudder down Han's spine. He did not like seeing that many different insect species gathered in one place—it made him think they were planning something.

Instead of admitting that—he knew Leia already thought he was paranoid when it came to bugs—he asked, "Is that a LongEye booster on the back of that Sailfish's rectenna dish?"

"How should I know?" Leia asked, frowning at the vessel. "And why would I care?"

"Because that's what Lando adds to the sensor package on all his ships," Han said. "Including that Sailfish he sold to Juun and Tarfang."

"The one they traded to the Squibs?"

"That one," Han confirmed.

Leia eyed the Sailfish for a moment, now clearly as interested in the vessel as Han was. Over the years, the Solos had crossed paths many times with the Squibs, an enterprising trio who liked to operate on the edge of any legal system to which they were subject. The last time, however, the trio had gone too far, helping the Killiks slip a swarm of commando bugs aboard the *Admiral Ackbar*.

Finally, Leia said, "I'm sure Defense Force Intelligence will be very interested in the answer—and what its connection might be to all those different insects loitering outside."

"So I'm not the only one who thinks that's weird," Han said.

"It really isn't that far out of the ordinary," C-3PO said. "When one considers that sixty-seven percent of the ship crews in this hangar are insects, it's barely a statistical deviation."

"Sixty-seven percent?" Han repeated. He looked around the hangar more carefully, paying more attention to the crews and their ships. As C-3PO had pointed out, there *were* an awful lot of bugs, and fully half of the vessels had been manufactured by Slayn & Korpil—a Verpine company. "This is beginning to give me the creeps."

"It could be just the war," Leia said. "Maybe the Killiks feel more secure dealing with insects."

"And that doesn't worry you?" Han asked.

"I said *maybe*," Leia replied. "We'll need to take a closer look."

"May I suggest you do that *after* we finish berthing?" C-3PO asked. "We seem to be in danger of setting down on top of another ship!"

Han glanced at his display and saw that one of the strut-cams showed a landing skid poised to set down atop the Courier's dorsal observation bubble.

"Relax, chipbrain." Han fired an attitude thruster to spin the *Swiff* back into proper position. "It's a tight fit, so I'm using the Sluissi twist."

"The Sluissi twist?" C-3PO asked. "I have no record of that maneuver in my memory banks."

"You will in a second," Han said.

He fired another thruster to stop their rotation, then felt a faint shudder as the edge of the landing skid grazed the Courier's hull. The worker-bugs scattered, and an instant later the *Swiff* touched down and settled onto its struts. Han sank the anchoring bolts and instructed the ship's droid brain to initiate the automatic shutdown sequence, then looked over to find Leia staring out her side of the cockpit canopy.

"I didn't know Wasbo mandibles could open that wide!" Leia said.

"That *was* a great berthing." Han unbuckled his crash webbing, then went to the back of the flight deck. He turned in a slow circle, displaying the elaborate robes, long-haired wig, and white contact lenses he wore as part of his disguise. "Everything in place?"

"Very Arkanian," Leia said. "Just don't draw attention to your hands. That little finger still looks too thick."

"Yes, the disguise would be far better if you had *removed* your ring finger," C-3PO agreed. "Amputation always results in a more convincing four-fingered hand, and I calculate Lizil's current chance of recognizing us at fifty-seven point eight percent, plus or minus four point three percent."

"That so?" Han asked. "How about we disguise *you* as a one-armed cleaning droid?"

C-3PO drew his head back. "That hardly seems necessary," he said, inspecting the green patina that had been applied to his outer casing. "Droids seldom attract much attention anyway. I'm certain my costume will prove perfectly adequate."

"And so will Han's," Leia said, joining them. She was disguised as a Falleen female, with a face covered in fine green scales, beads and combs adorning her long hair, and a spiny dorsal ridge showing through her shape-hugging jumpsuit. "How do I look?"

"Good—great, even." Han flashed a lustful smile, openly admiring the athletic figure Leia was developing under Saba's rigorous training regimen. "Maybe we have time to—"

"What happened to getting our clearance to enter the war zone?" Leia interrupted. She pushed past him, shaking her head. "At least I know the artificial pheromones are working."

Han followed her aft, fairly certain that it wasn't the pheromones he was reacting to. He and Leia had been married for nearly thirty years, and not a day passed when he still did not ache for her. It was as though his attraction to her had been growing a little stronger every day, until one morning he had awakened to find that it was the force that held his galaxy together. It was not a feeling he really understood—perhaps the cause lay in his admiration of her spirit of adventure, or in his love for her as the mother of his children—but it was something for which he was deeply, immensely grateful.

"You're welcome," Leia said.

"What?" Han frowned. Now, whenever anyone read his thoughts, it made him worry he was on his way to becoming a Joiner. "I didn't say anything."

"Not aloud." Leia turned around and gave him a sly reptilian grin that he found rather . . . stirring. "But I'm a Jedi, remember? I sensed your gratitude through the Force."

"Oh . . . yeah." Han found it embarrassing to get caught being so sentimental, even by Leia—*especially* by Leia. "I was just thinking how grateful I was you wanted to come along."

"And I can tell when you're lying, too." The outer corners of Leia's reptilian brows rose. "And why *shouldn't* I have come? Jaina is my daughter, too."

"Take it easy—I didn't mean anything," Han said. "I was talking about that whole 'Jedi come first' thing Luke is pulling. It couldn't have been easy for you to leave with me."

"Luke has to do what he thinks is best for the order," Leia said, avoiding a direct answer to the question. "We have to do what we think is best for Jaina and Zekk. The two aren't mutually exclusive."

"Right," Han said. "But I get the feeling Luke and Saba would've felt a whole lot better about it if they had actually *sent* us to get Jaina and Zekk back."

"I'm sure they would have." Leia started toward the hatch again. "But I don't know if I can support Luke's decision to make himself Grand Master of the Jedi."

"Come on," Han said. "It's not like he had any other choice—and you know he'll do a good job."

"Of course," Leia said. "But what happens to the order when Luke is gone? That's a lot of power for one being to wield, and power corrupts. The next Grand Master might be more susceptible to its dark influence than Luke."

"Then you're worried about nothing," Han said. "You

saw how the Masters were. Without Luke, the order won't last a year."

"I know," Leia said. "And that worries me, too."

They reached the main hatch, where Cakhmaim and Meewalh were waiting in their disguises. The Noghri were doing their best to waddle about and cock their heads in the characteristic expressions of curious Ewoks, but somehow they still looked far too graceful. Han slipped the voice synthesizer into his mouth, then turned and spoke to the Noghri in a deep, booming tone.

"Try to be a little clumsy," he said. "Maybe drop some stuff and trip once or twice."

The pair looked at Han as though he had asked Ewoks to fly.

"Well, do what you can," Han said.

He lowered the boarding ramp and nearly gagged on the clammy, too-sweet air that rolled through the hatchway. The cacophony of ticking and thrumming was even louder than the last time he was here. A dozen waist-high Killiks with deep orange thoraxes and blue abdomens appeared at the bottom of the ramp and started to ascend without requesting permission.

Han stepped aside and—gritting his teeth at their lack of ship etiquette—waved the bugs aboard. They brushed past him and immediately began to spread out through the *Swiff*, running their feathery antennae over every available surface and clacking their mandibles in interest.

Han waved them toward the stern. "This way, my friends," he said, trying to give his best impression of a down-on-his-luck Arkanian technolord. "We have something truly special for you."

Three of the Killiks thrummed their chests and came over, but the rest continued to explore the ship. Han motioned Cakhmaim and Meewalh to keep an eye on the others, then smiled and led the way back to the main cargo hold. Knowing the insects would investigate every meter of the ship, he and Leia and the Noghri had taken pains to shoot any hint of their true identity out the disposal tube, but he still had beads of nervous sweat trickling down his ribs. Given how things had gone in the Utegetu Nebula, it seemed unlikely that Lizil would react well to discovering who he and Leia really were.

When they reached the cargo hold, Han made a show of depressing the slap-pad that opened the hatch. "I present the Magcannon Max, the finest piece of magnetic coil artillery in the galaxy."

The three Killiks stepped through the hatch, then stopped inside and craned their necks back to stare up at the weapon's armored housing—all three stories of it. Han nodded to Leia, who went over to the base of the weapon and began a carefully rehearsed sales pitch in the sultry—if completely artificial—voice of a Falleen.

"The economical Magcannon Max delivers a planetary-defense-grade firepower in a self-contained package. With a fully shielded housing and an internal sensor suite, this naughty girl can find a bombarding Star Destroyer as easily as she can spill its guts."

Leia flashed a winsome Falleen smile, then turned to lead the way toward the weapon's giant, telescoping barrels. Instead of following, the Killiks turned to Han and began to thrum their thoraxes.

"They would like to know how they move a weapon of this size," C-3PO translated. "Does it have its own propulsion system?"

Han addressed the bugs directly. "*You* don't move it. We transport and install wherever you need it—even in the war zone." Han gave them a regal Arkanian smile. "Our service package is superior."

All three bugs turned and left the hold.

Han frowned and started after them. "So you'll take it?"

The last Killik in line turned and fixed Han with its bulbous green eyes. *"Rrrub uur."* It shook its head emphatically. *"Buubb rruuur uubbu, rbu ubb rur."*

"Oh dear," C-3PO said. "She says the Colony has no use for weapons emplacements. The Chiss are overrunning their worlds too fast."

The Killik started up the corridor again, chest rumbling.

"But the repeating blasters and thermal detonators in the secret weapons locker inside the wall behind the main engineering terminal will prove very useful," C-3PO translated. "Lizil has left a dozen shine-balls and fifty waxes of golden membrosia at the foot of the boarding ramp in exchange."

"That's all?" Han followed them to the ramp, where Cakhmaim and Meewalh were already bringing the shine-balls and membrosia aboard—still looking far too graceful for Ewoks. "We didn't come all the way—"

Han's objection came to an abrupt end when he found himself unable to continue down the ramp after the bugs, held immobile by the Force.

Leia came and took him by the arm. "Lord Rysto, there's no use forcing the situation," she cooed in her Falleen voice. "If Lizil doesn't want the gun, we'll just have to find another way to sell it."

Leia's words began to calm Han immediately. He was allowing his frustration to affect his judgment—and that could be very dangerous indeed, given how deep they were inside enemy territory.

Han placed his hand over Leia's. "Thank you, Syrule—you're right." He looked down toward the Mon Calamari Sailfish sitting below them in the middle of the hangar floor. "And I think I know just where to start looking."

FIVE

With most of the Jedi order off chasing pirates or reconnoitering for Admiral Bwua'tu in the Utegetu Nebula, the Knights' Billet on the tenth floor of the Jedi Temple was next to deserted. The only Jedi Knights present were the trio Luke had ordered to meet him here—Tesar, Lowbacca, and Tahiri—and the air had a stale, uncirculated smell. Tesar and Lowbacca were waiting in the conversation salon near the snack galley. Tahiri was in the exercise pen at the far end of the suite, working on a lightsaber form with thirteen fist-sized remotes whirling around her. Judging by the smoke haze visible through the transparisteel walls, the remotes' sting-bolts were set high enough to inflict burns.

Luke leaned close to Cilghal, who stood next to him with an armload of sensor equipment. "Can we do this in the salon?"

"We can detect aural fluctuations anywhere," she said, nodding. "But you know that won't answer your real question."

"It'll help," Luke said. "If their minds are still joined, then it's more likely they have fallen under Raynar's control."

"And if we find their minds *aren't* joined?"

"Then I'll know that telling Madame Thul about the debate over Raynar was their own choice," Luke said. "And I'll take action."

Luke led the way toward the salon. He could feel how concerned Cilghal was by his angry reaction to the Jedi Knights' betrayal, but he felt amazingly certain of himself. The other Masters had left him no choice but to play the Grand Master fully—to run the order as he thought best and demand full obedience from everyone in it.

As Luke and Cilghal drew near, Tesar and Lowbacca rose from the snack table where they were sitting and watched the two Masters approach with an unblinking, insect-like stare. They were both wearing their formal robes, but not their equipment belts or lightsabers. Tahiri remained in the exercise pen, concentrating on her light-saber form and paying no attention to the arrival of the two Masters.

Luke motioned Cilghal and her equipment to the adjacent table, then took a seat opposite the pair and motioned them to sit. He did not summon Tahiri from the exercise pen. Madame Thul had not actually named Tahiri as one of the Jedi who had warned her about the plans to target Raynar, so Luke was content to let the young woman continue exercising—for now.

He remained quiet, studying the two Jedi Knights across the table while Cilghal completed her preparations. Nothing in the Force suggested they were under the Colony's control, but that meant little. Unless Raynar happened to be exerting the Colony's Will at that very moment, Luke suspected there would be nothing for him to sense.

Lowbacca watched Cilghal prepare her equipment, his scientific mind seemingly more interested in her calibrations than in the reason he had been recalled to the Jedi Temple. Tesar, on the other hand, was so nervous that he began to hiss and smack his lips in an effort to keep from drooling.

Finally, Cilghal nodded that she was ready. Luke did not

bother to explain the equipment. Like all Jedi who spent more than a few days among the Killiks, Lowbacca and Tesar had submitted to dozens of aural activity scans as part of Cilghal's research.

"I'm sure you know why I ordered you to meet me here," Luke said.

Lowbacca nodded and groaned, saying that it probably had something to do with what they had told Aryn Thul.

"We can explain," Tesar added.

"I doubt it." Luke's tone was sharp. "But please try."

"We had no choice," Tesar said.

Lowbacca growled his agreement, reasserting the argument that destroying the Colony would be immoral.

"And so would assazzinating a friend," Tesar added. "Raynar was our hunt-mate. Killing him would be wrong."

"Maybe," Luke said. "But that decision isn't yours to make."

Lowbacca countered with a long, stubborn rumble.

"Jedi Knights *do* serve the Force," Luke answered. "But now they serve it through the Jedi order. We've seen what happens when everyone goes in their own direction. We paralyze ourselves, and our enemies flourish."

Lowbacca rowled the opinion that being paralyzed was better than following a yuugrr out on its limb.

Luke frowned. Yuugrrs were dim-witted predators famous for stealing Wookiee children out of their beds, then trying to shake their pursuit by going out on a thin limb. More often than not, the limb broke, plunging the yuugrr, the child, and sometimes the pursuers into the depths of the Kashyyyk forest.

"If you're calling me a yuugrr, I'm not sure I follow your analogy." It was a struggle for Luke to keep an even tone; he felt so betrayed by the pair that it required an act of will to remain interested in their reasons. "What's it supposed to mean?"

"Not that *you* are a yuugrr," Tahiri said, joining them. Sweat was still pouring down her face, and there were several holes where the remotes had burned through her jumpsuit and raised burn blisters. "You're *following* one— and you're taking the whole order with you. We had to do something."

"*We?*" Luke asked. He resisted the urge to send Tesar to fetch some bacta salve from the first-aid kit. This was no time to appear nurturing, and besides, Tahiri's mind still had enough Yuuzhan Vong in it that she probably enjoyed the pain. "Madame Thul didn't mention your name."

"Only because these two didn't tell me what they were doing." Tahiri shot Lowbacca and Tesar a dirty look. "Otherwise, I would have been right there with them."

Luke did not bother to hide his disappointment. "I appreciate your honesty, but I *still* don't understand."

"It's not complicated." Tahiri took a seat between Lowbacca and Tesar, rubbing her forearms against theirs in the Killik manner. "You listen to Jacen as though he were a senior Master, and his advice can't be trusted. He has his own agenda."

"*Jacen* isn't the one who broke confidentiality," Luke retorted. "And he doesn't know what I've decided about Raynar, either."

"But you do lizten to Jacen," Tesar rasped. "You cannot deny *that*."

Lowbacca grunted his agreement, adding that both Luke and Mara gave more weight to Jacen's opinion than to anyone else's. They seemed to think, Lowbacca continued, that taking a five-year furlough made him a better Jedi Knight than the Jedi who had been serving the order and the Alliance all along.

"Jacen's experience is unique," Luke said. "We all know that."

Even to him this sounded more like an excuse than a reason. The truth was that he valued his nephew's opinion because of what Jacen had learned about other Force-using traditions—but also because Jacen was the only person whom Ben would trust to be his guide to the Force. And that certainly *did* make Jacen a favorite in the Skywalker family—they were parents, after all.

Luke glanced over at Cilghal, reaching out to her in the Force with a single question in mind. She raised a webbed hand and gave it an ambiguous flutter that Luke interpreted to suggest a moderate correlation in the aural activity of the three Jedi Knights—enough to suggest there was still a link, but certainly not the complete fusion typical of Joiners.

Luke returned his gaze to Tahiri and the others. "But I value your opinions just as highly. If Jacen has a different agenda, what is it?"

All three Jedi Knights let out nervous throat-clicks. Then Tahiri said, "We haven't been able to figure that out."

"But it had zomething to do with the attack on Supply Depot Thrago," Tesar said.

Lowbacca added a long growl noting that Jaina had refused to fly with her brother since the attack. She was convinced Jacen had deliberately been trying to provoke the Chiss.

"I'm sure he was," Luke said. "The way he explained it to me, that was the only way to prevent the Chiss from launching the surprise attack he saw in his vision."

Lowbacca and Tesar shot uncomfortable glances at each other, but Tahiri kept her unblinking eyes fixed on Luke.

"We think Jacen may be lying about his vision."

Luke's brow shot up. "I didn't sense any lies when he told *me* about it."

"Were you trying to?"

"Jacen is very good at hiding his emotionz," Tesar added.

Lowbacca nodded and grunted that half the time, even Jaina could not feel him in the Force anymore.

"Then *you've* caught him lying?" Luke demanded. "These are very serious charges."

"We haven't actually *caught* him," Tahiri said.

Lowbacca oorrwwalled a clarification, explaining that the facts just did not add up.

"The Chisz were still stocking the depot with fuel when we attacked," Tesar added.

"And there were half a dozen frigates mothballed there," Tahiri finished. "They hadn't even fired the main reactors."

"Your point being?" Luke was growing impatient with their innuendo. It was the favorite weapon of the character assassin, and he expected better of Jedi. "Had Jacen told you the Chiss surprise attack was imminent?"

Tesar and Lowbacca glanced at each other, then Tahiri shook her head. "No, Jacen never said *that*."

"But when the Chisz *did* attack, their assault was improvised," Tesar said. "They did not have enough forward support."

Lowbacca nodded emphatically, adding that the secret weapon they had deployed against the Iesei had obviously been rushed through development. Otherwise, the bomb would not have failed to detonate on its initial use.

"The failed bomb—and everything else you've told me—tends to *support* Jacen's vision, not cast doubt on it," Luke said. He had found the trio's report about the failed bomb as worrying as it was incomplete. Given the Chiss willingness to deploy Alpha Red during the last war—and to run the risk of wiping out the entire galaxy along with the Yuuzhan Vong—he viewed the mysterious bomb in a very ominous light. "Clearly, the Chiss *have* been making war preparations. Forcing their hand may have been the only way to salvage the situation."

"You're saying Jacen did the right thing?" Tahiri gasped. "Even if the Chisz were *not* ready to attack?"

Luke nodded. "Sometimes it's better to hit first— especially if you see the other guy reaching for a thermal detonator."

He stared into the unblinking eyes of each Jedi Knight for several moments, wondering where he could have gone so wrong in their instruction. Perhaps he had been too hesitant to impose his own values on such a diverse group of students, or perhaps he had failed to present them with enough moot dilemmas to develop a proper moral center. All he knew for certain was that he had failed them *somewhere*, that he had not prepared them to face the soul-corrupting ruthlessness of the war against the Yuuzhan Vong, or instilled in them the strength to withstand the power of Raynar Thul's Will.

After a few moments of silence, Luke stood and stared down at the three Jedi. "You are not going to blame Jacen for your actions. Even if he *had* lied about his vision—and I don't believe he did—what you did was inexcusable. In going to Madame Thul with this, you betrayed me, you betrayed the other Masters, and you betrayed the Jedi order."

The three Jedi Knights were not disconcerted in the slightest. Tahiri and Tesar met Luke's gaze with an unblinking glare that was somewhere between anger and disbelief, and Lowbacca let out a very Killik-like chest rumble that suggested he was more angry than remorseful.

"You are a fool to place your faith in Jacen!" Tesar rasped. "He is nothing but a shenbit in a snake'z skin. You trust him with your hatchling—"

Lowbacca snarled a warning to the Barabel, telling him that he was only going to make Luke angrier by mentioning *that*.

"Mentioning what?" Luke demanded.

"Nothing," Tahiri said. "We didn't see it for ourselves, so we don't even know if it's true."

"If *what's* true?" Luke demanded.

Lowbacca gave Tesar a sideways glare, then grooowled a long reply explaining that Jaina and Zekk had caught Jacen blocking some of Ben's memories.

"*Blocking* memories?" Luke asked.

"Ben saw something upsetting," Tahiri explained. "Jaina and Zekk caught Jacen using the Force to prevent him from remembering it."

Luke scowled, the anger he already felt rising to rage. "If you're making this up—"

"We are not," Tesar insisted. "Jaina and Zekk saw it. They saw Jacen rubbing Ben's brow and felt something in the Force."

Lowbacca weighed in with a low rumble, explaining that Jacen had told them it was a technique he learned from the Adepts of the White Current.

"I never heard of anything like that from them," Luke said. "What memory was Jacen trying to block?"

Tahiri shrugged. "You'll have to ask him—he's not much into sharing these days."

Luke could sense that Tahiri was telling the truth, but even without the Force he would have believed her. While Jacen had returned from his five-year sojourn with remarkable skills, he had also returned a far more mysterious person, often deflecting or flatly refusing to answer questions about his experiences. It was as though he believed that no one who had not taken such a retreat for himself was entitled to share in the wisdom it yielded.

"I'll certainly ask Jacen about the memory blocking," Luke said. "But I fail to see what that has to do with *your* betrayal."

Although he was still fuming inside—especially at the

trio's efforts to deflect his anger onto Jacen—Luke paused to give them an opportunity to make the connection for him.

When they did not, he asked, "Then I am to assume that you're not suggesting Jacen has blocked *my* memory of something?"

Even Tahiri's eyes widened with shock, and Tesar said, "Yesz—I mean no—we have no reason to believe he has blocked *your* memoriez."

Luke looked to the other Jedi Knights for confirmation, then nodded when they remained silent.

"Very well," he said. "Before coming here today, I gave this matter a great deal of thought, and nothing you've said has convinced me I was wrong."

Lowbacca began to moan, asserting that everything they did was for the good of the order—

"I know that's what you think," Luke said, raising a hand to silence him. "But what *I* think is that you would rather believe Jacen has betrayed his family, friends, and the order than admit that the Colony is on the brink of plunging the galaxy into the eternal war he saw in his vision."

Tesar ruffled his scales. "That is zilly! We are not under the Colony'z influence!"

"I'm sorry, Jedi Sebatyne," Cilghal said, speaking for the first time since the discussion had begun. "But we can't know that for certain. Your minds *are* still connected, at least rudimentarily, and Raynar was able to exert a considerable influence over you even *before* you were exposed to the collective mind."

"So you're going to base your decision on the *possibility* that we're Joiners?" Tahiri stared at Luke as she asked this, her green eyes as hard and emotionless as olivon. "That's not like you, Master Skywalker."

"If you're asking me to give you the benefit of the doubt,

you're right," Luke said. "There are many questions about *why* you betrayed the order, but there are none as to *whether* you did. You tried to influence my decision by bringing pressure to bear from Madame Thul."

The three Jedi Knights continued to stare at him, their emotionless eyes neither blinking nor flicking away as they awaited the rest.

"Your actions cast serious doubt on your desire to remain Jedi Knights," Luke said. "I suggest you go to Dagobah to reflect on the subject."

"Dagobah?" Tesar rasped. "You are sending us on *vacation?"*

"On retreat," Luke corrected. "To meditate on what it means to be a Jedi Knight."

Tahiri and Lowbacca exchanged glances, then Tahiri asked, "For how long?"

"Until I send for you," Luke replied. "And if you have any desire at all to remain members of the Jedi order, you *will* obey me in this. I'll take any failure—for any reason whatsoever—as your resignation."

SIX

Leia watched in confusion as Han started down the wall, picking his way through the crowded transaction hangar of the Lizil nest toward the suspicious Sailfish. With Defense Force Intelligence actively searching for the Squibs, the Lizil nest seemed a likely place for the trio to take refuge—and Han clearly intended to use that fact to find Jaina. What Leia did not understand was *how*—and, if she knew her husband, neither did Han.

Leia instructed C-3PO and the Noghri to stay with the *Swiff*, then descended the ramp and started after Han, her feet *squeck-squeck*ing in the soft wax that lined the interior of the nest. It took only a few steps before the microgravity, the lack of perspective, and the cloying smell began to unsettle her stomach. She clamped her jaws shut and focused her thoughts on Han, trying to guess what outrageous plan he was developing—and whether it had any chance of working.

A few steps later, Leia caught up to Han and leaned close. "Han, what are you doing?"

"Maybe *they're* interested in a Magcannon Max." Han pointed at the Sailfish, now close enough for a visual inspection. The black box behind the rectenna dish was, indeed, one of Lando's distinctive LongEye boosters. "It looks like they're dealers."

"Have you lost your *mind*?" Leia hissed. "We can't let the Squibs know we're here!"

"Sure we can," Han said. "They're not going to tell anybody."

"They're not?"

"No way." Han glanced around, then whispered, "Juun and Tarfang used to work for those furry little backstabbers. And the last thing they want is for me to tell Lizil that it was *their* employees who helped me and Luke escape Saras on Woteba."

"You don't think they've already told Raynar?" Leia asked.

"Are you kidding?" Han asked. "These are *Squibs*. They'd never admit they played a part in anything that went wrong—especially something that fouled up the Dark Nest's plans."

Leia raised her brow—and felt the scales of her artificial Falleen face ripple in response. "And since they didn't admit it right away—"

"It'll look really bad if *we* tell the Killiks now," Han finished.

"That's what I like about you."

"Handsome as well as rich?" Han asked.

Leia shook her head. "Resourceful . . . and just a little bent."

She gave him a coy smile—then felt a small vibration between her shoulder blades as her disguise reacted to her expression and dispensed a shot of attraction pheromones. A sparkle of lust immediately came to Han's eyes, and he cast a longing glance back toward the *Swiff*.

"Easy, boy!" Leia hissed. *"Later."*

"Okay." Even in his Arkanian disguise, Han looked crestfallen. "Will you wear the costume?"

Leia had to resist the temptation to hit him, for they had reached the hangar "floor" and were in full view of dozens of bustling Lizil. They circled around an old Gallofree light transport, then pushed through the small crowd of insects waiting outside the Sailfish.

Leia followed Han to the foot of the boarding ramp, where they stopped in front of two huge Flakax guards. Standing a little taller than a Wookiee, with sharp beak-like proboscises, black chitinous shells, and long ovoid abdomens hanging beneath their thoraxes, the pair made truly intimidating sentries—especially since Flakax who left their homeworlds tended to become psychopaths.

"We're here to see the Squibs," Han said, hiding the fear that Leia could sense behind the bluster of an Arkanian technolord. "Tell them they still owe us for Pavo Prime."

The sentries' huge, compound eyes studied Leia and Han indifferently.

"It wouldn't be wise to keep us waiting," Leia pressed. "We happen to be old friends."

This drew a chorus of amused clacks and hisses from the insect crews waiting outside the Sailfish, and one of the Flakax held out a three-pincered hand.

"Appointment vouchers cost fifty credits each."

"*Appointment vouchers?*" Han repeated.

"You expect us to stand here for nothing?" the second Flakax demanded.

Leia stepped forward, craning her neck back to stare up at the Flakax's wedge-shaped head. "We don't need an appointment voucher," she said, using the Force to influence the insect's mind. "We're expected."

"They don't need a voucher," the first Flakax said. He stepped aside and motioned the Solos aboard. "The Directors are expecting them."

The second remained where he was, gnashing his mandibles and blocking the base of the ramp. "They are? *Now?*"

"Yeah." Han pulled a credit chit from his pocket. "What's the going price for being expected? Ten?"

The Flakax flattened his antennae. "Twenty-five."

"*Twenty-five!*" Han objected. "That's—"

"A paltry amount, not worth the effort to negotiate," Leia interrupted. "Why don't we just add it to the Directors' account, Lord Rysto? That way everyone will be happy."

"Very well." Han continued to glare at the Flakax, but passed the credits over and slipped back into the character of a haughty Arkanian. "If the Squibs object, I'll instruct them to bring the matter up with you."

The Flakax gave a little abdomen shudder, but stepped aside and waved Leia and Han through the Sailfish's air lock. The air aboard the vessel was stale and musky, and the broad oval corridors typical of Mon Calamari designs were so packed with weapons, power packs, and armor that it was only possible to walk single file. Leia followed Han into the forward salon, where a pair of Verpine pilots stood facing the interior of a large, curved table piled high with trinkets and gadgets. On the other side of the table, a single Lizil Killik stood behind three seated Squibs.

". . . grateful for the cargo," one of the Verpine was saying. "But we need more delivery time. If anything goes wrong, we won't make the date."

"What could go wrong?" the Squib on the left asked. With graying fur, a wrinkled snout, and red bags under his big brown eyes, Grees looked as though he had aged sixty years in the thirty that had passed since Leia had first met him. "Just follow the route we give you. Everything will be fine."

"It's the Chiss that concern us, Director," the second Verpine explained. "Tenupe is on the front lines, you know."

"That's why we saved this run for *you*," the Squib on the

right said. One of his ears no longer stood up straight, instead lying at an angle like a broken antenna. And his voice was so harsh and raspy that Han barely recognized it as Sligh's. "We wouldn't trust just *anyone* with this, you know. We have placed our complete faith in you. Consider it a gift."

The two Verpine glanced at each other nervously; then the first said, "We've heard the Chiss are moving fast. What happens if they overrun the base before we deliver? There's no one else out there who would want your TibannaX—especially not so much."

Han's heart began to pound in excitement. As far as he knew, there was only one use for TibannaX: it was fuel for Jedi StealthXs.

"Ark'ik, you came to us begging for a cargo, but all you have done since we granted it to you is ask *What if this? What if that?*" Emala said. Seated between Grees and Sligh, her eyes were covered in a milky film, and the tip of her nose was cracked and bleeding. She shook her head sadly and looked away from the two Verpine. "Honestly, we are beginning to think you aren't grateful."

The antennae of both Verpine went flat against their heads. "No, we're very grateful, Director," Ark'ik said. "We just don't want to fail you."

"And we don't want that either," Sligh said. "We thought you two were ready to be major players in the war business. But if you're not interested . . ."

"*We'll* take the cargo," Han said, stepping into the cabin.

The first Verpine—Ark'ik—turned with fury in his dark eyes, but his anger swiftly changed to confusion as Leia slinked toward him in her Falleen costume.

"I hope you don't mind." She touched him through the Force, implanting the suggestion that she was only repeating what he already believed. "But you don't need this run. Too many things can go wrong."

"Mind? Why should we mind?" Ark'ik asked. "Too many things can go wrong—"

"Ark'ik!" The second Verpine slapped the first in the back of the head. "Fool! She's using her pheromones on you."

Leia did not bother to correct him. One of the reasons she had chosen a Falleen costume was that it would camouflage many of her Force manipulations as the result of pheromones.

"So?" Ark'ik asked his companion. "This run doesn't have anything to do with *our* fight anyway."

"So be quiet!" The second Verpine turned to the Squibs. "We'll take the run, Director—but we may need another wax. It's a long trip."

"Another wax?" Grees was immediately up and standing in his chair. "Who do you think you *are*? You'll take the three waxes we're giving you and be grateful."

"There's a war on!" Sligh added. "We're lucky we can get *any* black 'brosia out of the Utegetu."

The second Verpine let out a long throat rasp, then dropped his gaze. "Forgive us, Director. I didn't mean to be greedy."

Emala shook her head sadly. "You disappoint us, Ra'tre. We give you a chance to be a part of history, and you try to take advantage." She motioned toward a corridor, and a much younger Squib with red-brown fur and black ear tufts entered the salon. "Krafte will tend to the details. Be sure to tip generously. It makes his charts more accurate."

"Of course." Ra'tre bowed nervously. "Thank you!"

He took Ark'ik's arm and dragged him after the young Squib.

Once they were gone, Han joined Leia in front of the table. "Quite an operation you have here," he said. "Brokering war cargo *and* pushing black membrosia? The Hutts could learn a few things from you."

Emala sat up with pride. "You're not the first to say so."

"Not that it's any business of yours," Grees said. He leaned forward, his nose twitching and his eyes narrow. "Do we *know* you?"

Before Han could launch into his indignant act, the Killik standing behind the Squibs began to rumble its thorax—no doubt explaining that Lizil had already "transacted" with them.

Leia stepped closer to the Squibs' table. "Actually, you might remember us from Pavo Prime," she said. "And before that, we worked together on Tatooine."

"Tatooine?" Sligh reached across the table, then took Leia's hand and rubbed it across his cheek. His ears went flat against his head. "You!"

"Brub?" Lizil demanded.

"We're old friends." Leia kept her gaze fixed on the Squibs, who were all trying to slowly lower their hands out of sight below the table—no doubt reaching for their holdout blasters. Though the possibility had not occurred to her before, the trio would have good reason to assume that she and Han had come to retaliate for the part the Squibs had played in the capture of the *Admiral Ackbar*. "There's nothing to be upset about—isn't that right, Sligh?"

"We'll s-s-see," Sligh stammered.

"Just don't try anything," Grees warned. "You're not as quick as you used to be."

Lizil cocked its head and stared at Leia out of one bulbous green eye. *"Uuu rru buur?"*

"Sligh is nervous because we haven't seen each other in a long time," Leia said, taking a guess at what the insect had asked.

"And Sylune and I looked a lot different back then," Han added.

"I'm sure our appearance must be shocking," Leia said to the Squibs. "But there's no need to be alarmed. We're not here to start trouble—as long as no one else starts it, either."

She cast a meaningful glare at the Squibs' hands, and all three returned their palms to the edge of the table.

"Then why *are* you here?" Grees demanded. "Lizil already told you the Colony doesn't need a magcannon."

"Can't an old friend pay a social call?" Han smiled and fixed Grees with a threatening glare. "I just wanted to tell you that I ran into a couple of your contract employees not so long ago. They were a great help to me and a good friend of mine." He glanced at the Killik behind them. "I thought maybe I should tell you about it."

"No!" all three Squibs said together.

"We mean there's no need," Sligh added quickly. "We already know everything."

"You're sure?" Leia asked. "Even about how they—"

"We *heard*!" Grees said. He turned toward the same corridor from which Emala's son Krafte had emerged. On cue, a small female with silky black fur appeared. "Now we really are very busy. Seneki will see you out."

"That's all the time you have for your friends?" Han turned toward the black female and shooed her back toward the corridor. "I'm hurt!"

Seneki froze halfway into the salon and looked to Emala for instruction.

"Time is money," Emala said, waving Seneki forward. "You understand."

"Not really," Leia said. She held her hand out to Seneki—presumably Emala's daughter—and used the Force to hold her back, drawing a gasp of surprise from the young Squib. "But I'm beginning to think we really should talk about your employees. You could take a lesson from them in politeness."

The three Squibs sighed and looked at each other, then Emala shook her head and said, "You *know* how valuable our time is, and our schedule is very tight today. You'll just have to buy another—"

"Maybe we can make it worth your while," Leia interrupted.

"I doubt that," Sligh said. "If you'll just leave—"

"We're not leaving," Han growled. He turned back to Leia. "You were saying, Syrule?"

Leia smiled and propped her hand on her hip. "Well, I'm sure the Colony wouldn't want our magcannon to end up in the hands of the Chiss or the Galactic Alliance."

Lizil clacked its mandibles in a very definite "No!"

"Then maybe we should sell it to our old friends," Leia said. "I'm sure *they* could find a safe buyer for it—and that way, we would be free to run a load of cargo to Tenupe."

"Tenupe is in a war zone," Sligh said. "The Colony only allows insect crews to run supplies into war zones."

"So talk to them for us," Han said. "It looks like you've got plenty of pull around here."

"*Ruruuruur bub?*" the Killik asked.

"Lizil wants to know why you're so interested in Tenupe," Emala translated.

"We're not," Han answered. "It's the StealthXs we want to see."

The Squibs, who had almost certainly figured out that Han and Leia wanted to see Jaina and Zekk, rolled their eyes.

But Lizil asked, "*Bub?*"

"We have a client who could benefit from the technology," Leia answered. She smiled conspiratorially. "And I'm sure it would only *help* the Colony's war effort if the Galactic Alliance suddenly had to divert even more resources to chasing pirates in stealth ships."

Lizil's antennae tipped forward in interest; then the insect turned to Grees. *"Uubbuu ruub buur?"*

Grees sighed, then said, "Sure, we'll vouch for 'em." His sagging red eyes glared blaster bolts at Leia. "And if they disappoint you, we'll make sure they take their secrets to the grave with them."

SEVEN

Luke usually sensed when the outer door to his office suite in the Jedi Temple was about to open. Today, however, he was so engrossed in Ghent's work that he did not realize he had a visitor until someone stopped at the entrance to the inner office and politely cleared his throat. The micrograbber in Ghent's hand jerked ever so slightly, and a tiny *tick* sounded somewhere deep inside R2-D2's casing. The slicer uttered a colorful smuggler's oath—something about Twi'lek Hutt-slime wrestlers, which he had no doubt learned during his stint in Talon Karrde's smuggling syndicate. Then he slowly, steadily backed the micrograbber out of R2-D2's deep-reserve data compartment.

"That didn't sound good," Luke said. Without turning around, he motioned whoever was at the door to wait there. "How bad is it?"

Ghent turned his tattooed face toward Luke, his pale eyes appearing huge and bug-like through his magnispecs. With his unkempt blue hair and tattered jumpsuit, the scrawny man looked more like a jolt-head from the underbelly of Talos City than the Alliance's best slicer.

"How bad is what?"

"Whatever it is you're swearing about," Mara said. She was kneeling beside Ghent, holding a handful of ancient circuits they had taken from the R2 prototype Aryn Thul had given them. "It sounded like you dropped the omni-gate."

"I heard it hit inside Artoo," Luke said helpfully.

Ghent nodded. "Me, too," he said, as though it were an everyday occurrence.

He retrieved a penglow from his tool kit and shined it down into R2-D2's casing, slowly playing the beam over the internal circuitry without answering the original question. Luke accepted the neglect as the price of genius and reluctantly turned toward the entrance to his office, where his nephew Jacen was waiting in his customary garb of boots, jumpsuit, and sleeveless cloak. Now that he had shaved off the beard he had grown during his five-year absence, he looked more than ever like his parents, with Leia's big brown eyes and Han's lopsided smirk.

"Twool said you wanted to see me." Jacen glanced toward Ghent and Mara. "But if I've come at a bad time—"

"No, we need to talk." Luke motioned him toward the outer office. "Let's go out here. I don't want to disturb Ghent."

"That's okay," Ghent said, surprising Luke by reacting to a remark that *wasn't* directed at him. "You're not disturbing me."

"I think Luke needs to talk with Jacen privately," Mara explained.

"Oh." Ghent continued to work, peering through his magnispecs into R2-D2's data compartment. "Doesn't he want to see if the omnigate works?"

"Of course," Luke said. The omnigate was a sliver of circuitry Ghent had found inside the prototype droid. Supposedly, it was a sort of hardware passkey that would unlock all of R2-D2's sequestered files. "You mean you're ready?"

"Almost," Ghent said. "And you'd better not leave. The omnigate is pretty deteriorated—it might not last long."

"You've figured out a way to unlock Artoo?" Jacen started across the room without seeking permission from Luke. "You can bring up a holo of my grandmother?"

"Sure." Ghent pulled his micrograbbers out of R2-D2's data compartment, then flipped up his magnispecs. "Either that or lose Artoo's entire memory to a security wipe."

"At least the risks are clear," Luke said, following Jacen back over to the slicer's side. This was hardly the reason he had sent for his nephew, but Jacen had almost as much right to see the lost holos as Luke himself. "Which is more likely?"

Ghent shrugged. "Depends on how much you trust the Thul woman. Her story makes sense."

Luke waited while Ghent's gaze grew increasingly distant . . . as it often did when the slicer actually had to discuss something.

After a moment, Luke prompted, *"But?"*

Ghent's eyes snapped back into focus, and he restarted the conversation where he had left off. "But if that isn't the real Intellex Four prototype in there, the omnigate will trigger every security system your droid has. We'll be lucky if *our* memories aren't erased, overwritten, and reformatted."

"So it depends entirely on whether Aryn Thul is being honest with us?" Mara asked.

"And on whoever sold *her* the prototype," Ghent said. "Droid antiquers are always getting crisped by counterfeit prototypes."

"That's one thing we don't have to worry about," Mara said. "Nobody is going to swindle Aryn Thul. That woman is a business rancor."

Luke turned to Jacen. "What do you think?"

Jacen finally looked surprised. *"Me?"*

"You have an interest in this, too," Luke said. The conversation he wanted to have with his nephew would be difficult enough, so it seemed wise to reassure Jacen that he was still held in high regard. "You should be part of the decision."

"Thanks . . . I think." Jacen furrowed his brow, then said, "Madame Thul certainly has reason to be suspicious of you—even angry. But I don't see any advantage to her in erasing Artoo's memory."

"So you think we should try?" Luke asked. The answer had been exactly what he *wasn't* looking for, relying as it did on calculation and logic instead of the insight and empathy that had been Jacen's special gifts before the war with the Yuuzhan Vong had changed him. "You want to take the chance?"

Jacen nodded. "I don't see that Madame Thul could gain anything by slipping you a counterfeit omnigate."

"That's not what Luke asked," Mara said, apparently sensing Luke's disappointment. "He wants to know how you *feel* about it."

"How I *feel*?" Jacen's eyes lit with comprehension. "That's a silly question. How do you *think* I feel?"

Luke smiled. "I'll take that as a go-ahead." He turned to Ghent and nodded. "Do it."

"Okay, nobody even breathe for a second." Ghent flipped his magnispecs down. "I need to seat the omnigate."

As Ghent lowered his micrograbbers into R2-D2's data compartment, Luke's heart began to beat so hard that he half feared the pounding would break the slicer's concentration. As much as he wanted to learn his mother's fate, more depended on the omnigate than filling the gaps in his family history.

During his stay on Woteba, the Dark Nest had insinuated that Mara might be trying to hide her involvement—during her days as the Emperor's Hand—in the death of Luke's mother. Of course, Luke had realized even then that the insinuation was unfounded. But the known facts left just enough room to keep doubt alive, and doubt could be a very stubborn enemy . . . especially when it was bolstered by the Dark Nest.

Lomi Plo thrived on doubt. If she sensed any doubt in a person's mind at all, she could hide behind it in the Force and make herself effectively invisible. That was how she had nearly killed Luke the last time they met . . . and if he hoped to defeat *her* the next time, he had to cast aside all doubt—in Mara, in himself, in his fellow Jedi. To a greater extent than he had admitted to anyone except Mara, that was one of the driving forces behind his reorganization of the Jedi order. He simply could not allow any doubt in his mind about where it was going.

A few moments later, Ghent let out a sigh of relief and pulled the micrograbbers from the data compartment.

"Okay, you can breathe now," he said. "The gate is attached to the sequestered circuit."

He flipped Artoo's primary circuit breaker, and the little droid came to life with a sharp squeal.

"It's okay, Artoo," Luke said. "Ghent has just been working on those memory problems you've been having."

R2-D2 swiveled his dome around, studying the stacks of prototype parts surrounding him, then trained his photoreceptor on Ghent and beeped suspiciously.

"He didn't add anything you need to worry about," Luke said. "Now, show us what happened between my mother and father after he finished in the Jedi Temple."

Artoo started to squeak a refusal—then let out an alarmed whistle. He spun his photoreceptor toward Luke and reluctantly chirped a question.

"Your parameters are too vague," Ghent chastised. "He probably has a thousand files that fit that description."

"I mean after the file he showed to Han and me in the Saras rehabilitation center." Luke tried to remain patient; he suspected R2-D2 was just stalling to buy time to defeat the omnigate, but it was possible that the droid really did need a more specific reference. "It's the record you stole from the Temple's security system, where my father supervised the slaughter of the students."

Though Luke had already told Jacen and everyone else in his family about the record, he still felt a jolt in the Force as Jacen and the others were reminded that the deaths and screams of the innocents had actually been caught on holo.

When R2-D2 still failed to activate his holoprojector, Luke said, "I think my request is clear enough, Artoo. Stop stalling, or I *will* have Ghent wipe your personality. You know how important this is."

R2-D2 gave a plaintive chirp, then piped a worried-sounding trill.

"I'm *sure*," Luke said.

The droid emitted an angry raspberry, then tipped forward and activated his holoprojector.

The veranda of what looked like an elegant, old-Coruscant apartment appeared in the holo. Padmé Amidala rushed into view, followed closely by a golden protocol droid that looked very much like C-3PO. A moment later, Anakin Skywalker appeared from the opposite direction and embraced her.

"*Are you all right?*" Padmé asked, pulling back a moment later. "*I heard there was an attack on the Jedi Temple . . . you can see the smoke from here!*"

Anakin's gaze slipped away from hers. "*I'm fine,*" he said. "*I came to see if you and the baby are safe.*"

"*Captain Typho is here. We're safe.*" Padmé looked out of the holo, presumably toward the Jedi Temple. "*What's happening?*"

Anakin's response was muffled as the protocol droid blocked their view of Padmé and Anakin, then the droid asked, "*What is going on?*"

"Is that See-Threepio?" Jacen gasped.

Luke shrugged and motioned for quiet. He would solve

the mystery of the golden protocol droid later, after he discovered what had become of his mother.

"You can't be any more confused than I am!" the golden droid said, replying to a string of squeaks and beeps from R2-D2.

He moved out of the way, and Anakin and Padmé came back into view.

". . . Jedi Council has tried to overthrow the Republic—"

"I can't believe that!" Padmé exclaimed.

A furrow appeared in Anakin's brow. "I couldn't either at first, but it's true. I saw Master Windu attempt to assassinate the Chancellor myself."

The golden droid's head filled the holo again. "Something important is going on. I heard a rumor they are going to banish all droids."

R2-D2 beeped loudly in the hologram, and Mara hissed, "That *has* to be Threepio. No other droid is that annoying."

"Shhhh . . . not so loud!" C-3PO said in the holo. R2-D2 beeped more softly, then C-3PO's head disappeared from the holo again. *"Whatever it is, we'll be the last to know."*

Padmé was seated on a bench near the edge of the veranda now. "What are you going to do?"

Anakin sat next to her, his face growing resolute. "I will not betray the Republic. My loyalties lie with the Chancellor and the Senate."

"What about Obi-Wan?" Padmé asked.

"I don't know," Anakin replied. "Many of the Jedi have been killed."

"Is he part of the rebellion?" Padmé pressed.

Anakin shrugged. "We may never know."

They both stared at the floor for a moment, then Padmé shook her head in despair.

"How could this have happened?"

"The Republic is unstable, Padmé. The Jedi aren't the

only ones trying to take advantage of the situation."
Anakin waited until Padmé met his gaze, and his voice assumed a more ominous tone. *"There are also traitors in the Senate."*

Padmé stood, and her expression grew uneasy. *"What are you saying?"*

Anakin rose and turned her to face him. *"You need to distance yourself from your friends in the Senate. The Chancellor said they will be dealt with when this conflict is over."*

"What if they start an inquisition?" Padmé's tone was more angry than frightened. *"I've opposed this war. What will you do if I become suspect?"*

"That won't happen," Anakin said. *"I won't let it."*

Padmé turned away from him and was silent for a time, then she said, *"I want to leave, go someplace far from here."*

"Why?" Anakin seemed hurt by her suggestion. *"Things are different now! There's a new order."*

Padmé refused to yield. *"I want to bring up our child someplace safe."*

"I want that, too!" Anakin said. *"But that place is* here. *I'm gaining new knowledge of the Force. Soon I'll be able to protect you from anything."*

Padmé studied him for several moments, her expression changing from disbelieving to disheartened as she contemplated his battle-sullied clothes. Finally, she let her chin drop.

"Oh, Anakin . . . I'm afraid."

"Have faith, my love." Seeming to miss that it was *him* she feared, Anakin took her in his arms. *"Have faith, my love. Everything will soon be set right. The Separatists have gathered in the Mustafar system. I'm going there to end this war. Wait until I return . . . things will be different, I promise."*

Anakin kissed her, but he must have sensed the misgivings that Luke could see even in the tiny holo—the fear of what he was becoming—because he stopped and waited until she looked into his eyes.

"Please . . ." His voice assumed just a hint of command. *"Wait for me."*

Padmé nodded, lowering her eyes in surrender. "I will."

Anakin studied her for a moment; then, as he turned and approached R2-D2's position, the file ended.

Luke and the others remained silent for a moment, he and Mara and Jacen pondering Padmé's final words, trying to match her expressions to her tone. When she told Anakin that she was afraid, had she been thinking of the anti-war inquisition she had mentioned? Or of what the future held for *them*?

Mara was the first to break the silence. "No offense, Luke, but your father gives me the shudders."

"Why is that?" Jacen asked, sounding genuinely puzzled.

Mara raised her brow in surprise. "You didn't catch the subtext? That little threat when he told her to distance herself from her friends in the Senate?" She frowned. "I *know* you're more sensitive than that."

"What I saw was a man worried about his wife's safety," Jacen replied. "That's *all* I saw."

"You didn't find him a little controlling?" Luke asked. He was really beginning to worry about his nephew's emotional awareness; it was as though all of the tenderness had evaporated from his soul during his sojourn to explore the Force. "Even when he had completely dismissed her wish to go someplace safe?"

"He promised to keep her safe *there*." Jacen gave them a lopsided smile. "From what I've heard about Anakin Skywalker and his abilities, he was probably telling the truth."

"I guess that's one way of looking at it." Mara's tone implied that she chose to look at the exchange another way.

"But maybe Luke and I are reading too much into it, as you suggest. There's not much detail in a holo that size."

"And maybe you have more context to place it in than I do," Jacen allowed. "I'm not saying it was the right thing—just that I understand what he was thinking."

"Good point—sometimes we forget that Anakin Skywalker was only human." Luke turned to R2-D2. "Artoo, show us the next—"

"Uh, you might not want to do that," Ghent interrupted.

Luke frowned. "Why not?"

Ghent frowned back. "Didn't I tell you that the omnigate is pretty . . ." He glanced at R2-D2, then apparently decided it would not be wise to mention how deteriorated the gate was in front of the droid. ". . . that it was *used*?"

"Yes," Mara said. "That doesn't explain why we shouldn't view the next file, though."

"In fact, it tends to suggest we *should*," Jacen said, "while everything is still working."

Ghent just stared at them blankly.

"Well?" Luke asked impatiently.

Ghent shrugged. "It's your omnigate, I guess."

Luke furrowed his brow, waiting for an explanation, but Mara—who knew the slicer far better from their days working for Talon Karrde—said immediately, "You'll have to tell us the problem, Ghent. Why is a *used* omnigate so risky?"

"Oh." He knelt beside R2-D2 and deactivated the droid again, then said, "You don't want to overheat a deteriorated gate. It's too easy to melt it."

"So we just have to wait for it to cool off?" Jacen asked.

"That would help," Ghent said.

"Only *help*?" Mara asked.

"Well, we're probably overheating the gate every time we use it," Ghent said. "It was in pretty bad shape."

"You're saying it's just a matter of time before it goes?" Mara clarified.

"Yeah—it could go the next time you use it, or the time after that," Ghent said. "I don't think it will last three times."

Luke exhaled in frustration. "Is there anything we can do about that?"

Ghent thought for a moment, then nodded. "I could try to copy its architecture."

"How risky is that?" Mara asked.

"It's not," Ghent said. "Unless, of course, I make a mistake."

"But then we'd have a backup in case the first gate melted?" Luke asked.

Ghent looked at him as though he had just asked a very foolish question. "Well, that *is* the idea of making a backup."

"Then why didn't you just say so in the first place?" Jacen demanded, growing uncharacteristically impatient with the communicationally challenged slicer. "What's the drawback?"

"Time," Ghent said. "It takes a lot of time—especially since I don't want to make a mistake."

"Time could be a problem," Luke said.

So far, he had been content to let the Jedi continue on the sidelines of the war, trying to rebuild Chief Omas's confidence in the order by hunting down pirates and adjudicating quarrels among the Alliance's member-states. But he was not willing to continue that approach forever. Sooner or later, the Jedi would need to take action . . . and a deepening tickle in the base of his head was beginning to suggest it would be sooner.

Luke hated to let his personal history interfere, but before the Jedi went into action, he needed to be free of his doubts. Mara had assured him that she had never been involved in anything concerning Padmé Amidala, and Luke believed her. But the possibility remained that the Dark Nest's insinuations were true: that Padmé might have lived under an alias for fifteen or twenty years, and that Mara—then Palpatine's assassin—might have been sent to track her down without knowing her true identity. If Luke were to have any chance at all of defeating Lomi Plo, he needed to know what had happened to his mother—to banish utterly from his heart the last ghost of doubt about Mara's involvement.

When Ghent merely continued to look at him without speaking, Luke sighed and asked, "How long would it take to build the backup?"

Ghent shrugged. "It'll be faster than trying to figure the algorithm and original variables for the universal key you used last—"

"Okay, I understand." Luke closed his eyes and nodded. "Copy it—but don't do anything that would prevent me from taking the original back and using it in an emergency."

"Emergency?" Ghent seemed confused. "How could looking at a bunch of old holos be an emergency?"

"It *could*," Mara told him. "You don't need to know why."

Ghent shrugged. "Okay." He flipped his magnispecs down and reached for his micrograbbers. "No problem with the emergency thing."

Luke waited until the slicer had started work, then turned to Jacen. "Let's move to the outer office and leave Ghent to his work."

"Oh yeah—the *conversation*." Jacen started toward the door, then stopped and glanced over his shoulder. "Aren't you coming, Aunt Mara? After all, you're the *really* angry one."

"I wouldn't say angry, Jacen."

"No?" Jacen gave her a crooked Solo smile. "*I* would."

EIGHT

The private hangar, hidden deep under several metallic asteroids on the rear side of the nest, appeared much more orderly than Lizil's main hangar. Two dozen Slayn & Korpil transports hung on the walls in neat rows, taking on everything from blaster rifles to concussion missiles to artillery pieces. There was no "transacting"; nothing was being removed from the vessels, and there was not a membrosia ball in sight.

Han swung the *Swiff* into an open berth near the exit membrane, using the attitude thrusters to stick the landing pads to the wax-lined floor extra firmly. The hangar was crawling with big bugs—Killik and otherwise—and he had no intention of firing the anchoring bolts until he was sure a quick departure would not be needed.

"We sure picked the wrong disguises for this job," Han said, eyeing the bustling swarm. "I don't see anything that isn't a bug anywhere."

"That's odd, Captain Solo," C-3PO said. "I don't see any bugs at all. The Verpine are a species of mantid, the Fefze are more closely related to beetles, and the Huk are much closer to vespids than—"

"I don't think Han actually meant *bugs*, Threepio," Leia interrupted. "He was using the term pejoratively."

"He was?" C-3PO asked. "Might I suggest that this is a particularly poor time to insult insects, Captain Solo. You and Princess Leia seem to be the only mammals in this hangar."

"Like I hadn't noticed," Han grumbled. He unbuckled his crash webbing and initiated the shutdown cycle, but remained in his seat staring out the forward canopy. "Leia, do you notice anything strange about the Killiks loading those transports?"

"Now that you mention it, yes," Leia said. "They really don't look like Lizil."

"That, too," Han said. Unlike Lizil workers, these Killiks were nearly two meters tall, with powerful builds, blotchy gray-green chitin, and short curving mandibles that looked like bent needles. "But *I* was wondering why there aren't any coming *down* the ramps."

Leia studied the ships for a moment, then said, "Good question."

"Actually, the answer is rather clear," C-3PO said. "Those Killiks aren't loading the transports, they're boarding them."

"It certainly appears that way," Leia agreed. "The Chiss may be in for a big surprise."

"A surprise?" C-3PO said, missing the obvious as only he could. "What sort of surprise?"

"You *did* notice all those S and K transports hanging out in the entrance tunnel?" Han asked.

"Of course," C-3PO said. "All one hundred twenty-seven of them."

Han whistled. He had not thought it was so many. "Okay, let's say each one of those tubs can transport three hundred bugs . . . that's close to forty thousand troops, counting these ships."

"A full division," Leia said. "That's going to be a very *nasty* surprise for the Chiss—especially if the Killiks strike someplace they're not expecting."

"Oh, dear," C-3PO said. "In that case, perhaps we

should return to our own territory and send a messenger to warn Commander Fel."

"Not a chance," Han said, rising. "The Chiss are on their own—at least until we get our daughter back."

He led the way back to the aft hold, where Meewalh and Cakhmaim were waiting with the hoods of their Ewok disguises tucked under their arms. The huge Magcannon Max that had once been stowed here was gone, now headed for a pirate base somewhere in the Galactic Alliance. If Lando's engineers could be trusted, the weapon would blow itself apart the first time it was live-fired.

Han instructed the Noghri to put on their Ewok heads. After he and Leia checked their own disguises—Arkanian and Falleen—he turned to the cargo lift controls and was puzzled to find a pair of Fefze staring at him from the external monitors. The black, meter-high beetles were standing beneath the cargo lift, staring up into the vidcam, frantically waving their forward legs for the cargo lift to be lowered.

"What now?" Han demanded. He turned to C-3PO. "Didn't Grees say his Flakax goons would be the ones meeting us?"

"I believe his precise words were 'Tito and Yugi will be there to take care of you,' " C-3PO reported. "And he *was* pointing at the Flakax at the time."

"So what do these two want?" Han asked.

Leia closed her eyes a moment, then said, "Let them in. I think we know them."

"*Know* them? If I'd ever met a puker, I'd remember." Han was referring to the Fefze habit of regurgitating food paste whenever they grew frightened. "You're sure about this? I don't want to spend the rest of the trip in a stinky—"

"Han, their presences are familiar." Leia reached past him and depressed the lift control. "Let them in."

The lift had barely touched down before the Fefze scrambled over the safety rail and began gesturing for it to be raised again. Han glanced at Leia uncertainly, then— when she nodded—brought the two insects up. The pair's antennae had barely risen above floor level when one of them began jabbering in muffled Ewokese.

C-3PO shot something back in the same language, then turned to Han.

"You were quite justified in your reluctance to let them aboard, Captain Solo. I haven't been spoken to quite so rudely since the *last* time we had dealings with that dreadful Ewok."

"Ewok?" Han went over to the lift. "I think I'd rather have the bug."

The Fefze jumped onto the deck of the hold, then reared up on its rear legs and began to flail its forelegs about haphazardly. A moment later, its head popped off and fell to the floor, revealing another head inside—this one black and furry, with large dark eyes and little round ears.

"Tarfang!" Leia exclaimed, coming to Han's side. "What are *you* doing here?"

Tarfang began to chitter rapidly, waving his remaining Fefze legs excitedly.

"Oh, dear," C-3PO said. "He says if he tells you, he will have to kill you."

The Ewok added two more syllables.

"Your choice," C-3PO translated.

"That's okay," Han said. The last time they had seen Tarfang, Admiral Bwua'tu had just offered him and Jae Juun positions as military intelligence affiliates. "We can guess."

The second Fefze joined them and began to flail its arms around, as had Tarfang. Han reached over and twisted the head off, exposing a bug-eyed face with grayish, dewlapped cheeks.

"Juun!" Han slapped the Sullustan on the back of his costume. "I'm glad you're still alive, old buddy—and a little surprised, too!"

"Yes, all of our missions are very dangerous," Juun said, beaming. "Admiral Bwua'tu always sends Tarfang and me when the mission is likely to be fatal."

"You certainly appear to be beating the odds," Leia said. "How can we help?"

Tarfang pattered something impatient.

"He says they're here to help *us*," C-3PO translated.

"The Squibs have put a death mark on your heads," Juun explained. "Over a thousand credits—*each*."

"What?" Han scowled. "That doesn't make any sense."

Tarfang twattled a sharp reply.

"That's hardly fair," C-3PO replied. "It's been nearly two decades since Captain Solo had a death mark on him. He has every right to be frightened."

"I'm not scared," Han said. "I just don't believe it. We have a deal with the Squibs."

"And *they* have a deal with Tito and Yugi," Juun said. "Tito said we could eat your brains if we helped."

"Did they say *why* the Squibs want us killed?" Leia asked.

Juun shook his head. "Only that it wouldn't be much of a job, because you'd never see it coming."

The Sullustan pulled his Fefze head back on, then turned toward Tarfang, who had noticed the two Noghri in their Ewok disguises and gone over to glare at them.

"Tarfang, let's go," Juun said. "The Flakax are already on their way."

Instead of retrieving the head of his own disguise, Tarfang let out an angry yap and shoved Meewalh. She reacted instantly, dropping the Ewok to the deck with a foot sweep and landing atop him in a full straddle-lock that left him completely immobilized.

"Tarfang!" Juun snapped. "What are you doing? We have to leave before the stingers arrive."

Tarfang burbled an angry reply, purposely spraying saliva into the face of Meewalh's costume.

"I don't care if it *is* an insult," Juun replied. "We don't have time for this. If we blow our cover, Admiral Pellaeon will never know where this division is going."

Han's brow shot up. "*Pellaeon* asked for this mission?"

"Uh, er, I'm really not at liberty to—"

"Yeah, sure," Han said. "What I don't get is why the GA's Supreme Commander would be that interested in a bug division headed for Chiss space."

"I do," Leia said. "If Pellaeon can tell the Chiss where these Killiks are headed, he just might convince them that the Galactic Alliance isn't siding with the Colony. It's a long shot, but it's probably the galaxy's best chance to avoid a three-way war."

Tarfang let out a long, fading gibber, and Cakhmaim moved over to threaten him with a stun stick—not that it was necessary, with Meewalh still straddling him.

"It doesn't look like you'll be killing anyone to me," C-3PO said to the Ewok. "Princess Leia's bodyguards appear to have you very well under control."

"Relax," Han said. "Your secret is safe with us—and you've got to get out of here before the trouble starts."

He motioned for the Noghri to release Tarfang. Meewalh growled low in her throat but quietly slipped off the Ewok.

Tarfang's eyes darted from one Noghri to the other, and it seemed to Han that he was trying to estimate his chances of launching a successful attack while still lying on the floor.

"Your devotion to operational security is admirable," Leia said, using the Force to set the Ewok back on his feet.

"But Captain Juun is right. We don't pose a threat to your mission, and you *do* need to be going."

Han picked up the head of Tarfang's Fefze disguise and plopped in place before the Ewok could utter more threats, then shoved him onto the cargo lift with Juun.

"The next time we see Gilad, we'll be sure to tell him how brave you two are," Han said. "And thanks for the warning—we owe you."

Cakhmaim activated the lift, and the two spies dropped slowly out of sight.

Han went to Leia's side. "Now, *that* was a surprise."

"What? That they lasted this long?" Leia asked. "Or that they'd risk their lives to help us?"

Han shook his head. "That they're crazy enough to come back to this place in bug costumes."

"You're right." Leia reached up adjusted Han's wig. "That *is* crazy."

Han frowned. "It's different for us," he said. "We're good at this stuff."

"Sure we are," Leia said. "That's why the Squibs are trying to kill us."

"Yeah, I don't get that," Han said. "We had a deal."

"Maybe they don't like us having something on them," Leia suggested.

Han shook his head. "That doesn't make sense. The Squibs know we can't tell Lizil anything without exposing ourselves. Trying to take us out just adds to the chances we'll be caught, and they know we'd try to settle the score by telling Raynar who helped me and Luke on Woteba."

"Maybe they think they can kill us before we talk," Leia said.

"They're arrogant, not stupid," Han countered. "Even taking us by surprise, there's a big chance we'll survive. Any way you look at it, attacking us *here* is a risk."

"Then it doesn't make sense," Leia said. "They should

be trying to cover for us, not kill us—at least while we're still in the nest."

"Right." Han rubbed the synthetic skin of his disguise, then said, "So they're trying to hide something—something big enough to risk angering Raynar."

"Something to do with the black membrosia?" Leia asked.

Han thought for a moment, then shrugged. "I can only think of one way to find out."

"Ask the Flakax?" Leia asked.

"May I point out that Flakax males are noted for being unhelpful and rude?" C-3PO asked. "I really don't think they're going to tell you much. Perhaps it would be better to leave before they arrive."

"Too late." Leia closed her eyes for a moment. "They're here—and they feel very dangerous."

Han went to the control panel and checked the external monitors. The two Flakax had arrived with four Verpine assistants. They were each bearing a crate labeled GREEN THAKITILLO or BROT-RIB or some other delicacy that the Squibs had pressured the Solos into carrying as part of the agreement to help them reach Jaina and Zekk in the war zone.

"Six of 'em," he reported. "All carrying crates."

"Their weapons are probably in the crates," Leia said. "I'll take care of those first."

"Right," Han said, motioning Cakhmaim and Meewalh to follow him. "We'll get the drop on them from behind."

C-3PO started to clunk away in the opposite direction. "I'm sure you don't want me in the way. I'll wait on the flight deck until you sound the all-clear."

"Good idea," Leia agreed. "Keep a watch on the external monitors."

"And if it looks like any Killiks are coming this way, get out there and stall," Han said. "We can't have the bugs stumbling on this fight any more than the Squibs can. It could blow our chances of joining the convoy."

"Stall?" C-3PO stopped at the threshold and let his head slump forward. "Why am I always assigned the dangerous tasks?"

Han drew his blaster pistol—a 434 "DeathHammer," which Lando had given him to replace the trusty DL-44 that Raynar Thul had taken on Woteba—then he and the Noghri each slipped into one of the cramped crawlways hidden behind the service hatches in the back of the hold.

Han sat in the dark, waiting and thinking about how Leia's devotion to her Jedi training had changed things between them. There had been a time—not that long ago—when he would never have agreed to let her stand bait. But now, even the Noghri recognized that her Force abilities were adequate protection. She radiated a calm confidence that seemed as unshakable as the Core, as though her Jedi studies had restored the faith she had lost in the future after Anakin died.

Han was glad for the change. Leia had always been his beacon star—the bright, guiding flame that had kept him on course through so many decades of struggle and despair. It was good to have her brightening the way again.

The soft whir of the cargo lift sounded from the other side of the service hatch and sent a chill racing down Han's spine. He had not been thinking about his experience with the Kamarians when he squeezed into the crawlway to set up an ambush, but the darkness and the cramped confines and the likelihood of a bug fight set his pulse to pounding in his ears. It had been over forty years, but he could still feel those Kamarian pincers closing around his ankles, hear his nails scraping against the durasteel as he tried to keep them from dragging him out of his hiding place . . .

Han grabbed his earlobe and twisted, *hard,* trying to break out of his thought pattern with pain. His hands were already shaking, and if he let the memory progress into a full-fledged flashback, he would end up lying there in a ball while Leia and the Noghri dealt with the Flakax.

The lift clunked into place, and Leia's muffled voice sounded through the service hatch. "Are these the crates the Squibs, er, the *Directors* wanted us to take to Tenupe?"

"Right." The Flakax ended his answer with a throat-click. "Where do you—queen's eggs!"

Han pushed open the service hatch and saw the heads of all six insects turned toward the far corner of the hold, where the crate Leia had just Force-ripped from the pincers of the first Flakax was crashing into the wall. It broke open, spilling a rifle version of the Verpine shatter gun and a variety of thermal grenades.

"Why, that doesn't look like green thakitillo," Leia said.

She pointed at the box in the second Flakax's arms. That crate, too, went flying, and the insects finally recovered from their shock. The four Verpine ripped the tops off their crates. Before they could pull their weapons from the boxes, Cakhmaim and Meewalh opened up with their stun blasters and dropped all four from behind.

Han leveled his DeathHammer at the Flakax. "Take it easy, fellas," he said. "No one has to get—"

The pair launched themselves at Leia, clacking their mandibles in fury and spewing a brown fume from their abdomens. Han fired twice, but their chitin was so thick and hard that even the DeathHammer's powerful bolts did little more than blast fist-sized craters into it.

Leia vanished beneath the two creatures, and Han stopped firing. The chances of hitting Leia were just too great, especially when all he could see through the growing haze of brown fume was thrashing arms and swinging insect heads. He called for Cakhmaim and Meewalh and raced forward. As he gulped down his first breath of bug vapor, his nose, throat, and lungs erupted into caustic pain.

Within two steps, his eyes were so filled with tears he could no longer see. A step after that, he grew weak and dizzy and collapsed to his hands and knees, coughing, retching, and just generally feeling like a thermal grenade had detonated inside his chest. He crawled the last three meters to the fight and reached up to press the muzzle of his blaster to the back of a greenish thorax.

With its large compound eyes and a fully circular field of vision, the Flakax had already seen Han coming. It caught him in the head with a lightning-quick elbow strike. The DeathHammer bolt went wide, ricocheting off the deck before it burned a hole through the wall.

Then a muffled *snap-hiss* sounded from beneath the insect, and Han was nearly blinded when the tip of Leia's lightsaber shot up through the Flakax, just a few centimeters from his nose. He barely managed to roll out of the way as the blade swept toward his face, opening the thorax from midline to flank and spilling bug blood all over Lando's deck.

"Hey, watch—" Han had to stop and cough, then finished, "—that thing!"

Han staggered to his feet and pointed his blaster in the general direction of the tear-blurred melee in front of him, trying to separate his wife's shape from that of the Flakax attacking her.

Then Cakhmaim and Meewalh came leaping in, hacking and gasping as they slammed into the writhing pile. An instant later the two Noghri went flying in the other direction, riding the surviving Flakax as Leia used the Force to send it tumbling across the hold.

"Han!" Leia's voice sounded as raw and burning as Han's felt. "Are you—"

"Fine." He reached down and pulled her to her feet. "Why didn't you do that in the first place?"

"Hard to concentrate with those . . . mouthparts snapping in your face." She deactivated her lightsaber and led Han after the Noghri and the Flakax. "Why didn't *you* blast them?"

"I *did*," Han said. "Someone ought to make armor out of those bugs."

"Han!" Leia coughed. "They're sentient beings!"

"Fair is fair," Han countered. "If they get to wear it, so should we."

They stepped out of stink cloud to hear Cakhmaim and Meewalh snarling as they continued to wrestle with the second Flakax. Han wiped the tears from his eyes and found the bug lying facedown on the deck with the two Noghri sitting astride it, still in their Ewok disguises. Cakhmaim had the insect's arms pinned together behind its back at the elbow, while Meewalh was holding its ankles, pulling its legs back against the hip joints every time it tried to open the gas duct in its abdomen.

Leaving Leia to deal with the fray, Han secured the unconscious Verpine and stowed the impressive array of weaponry the insects had brought aboard. By the time he had finished, Leia and the Noghri had the Flakax kneeling with its arms bound behind its back and its abdominal gas duct plugged with a piece of cloth.

Leia waved the tip of her lightsaber in front of the insect's head, causing the facets of its compound eyes to quiver and rustle as they followed the glow.

"Which one are you?" she asked. "Tito or Yugi?"

"Tito!" The Flakax sounded insulted. "I'm the handsome one. Everyone knows."

"Yeah, those eyes of yours are really something," Han said. "Now, why don't you explain why you were going to kill us?"

Tito spread his mandibles in the buggish equivalent of a shrug. "Thought it would be fun."

"Obviously," Leia said. "We're talking about the *other* reasons."

"We know the Squibs put you up to this," Han pressed.

Tito cocked his head to the side, turning one bulbous eye toward Han. "You know that, you know why."

"Stop playing dumb," Han said. "You understand what we're asking. The Squibs want us dead for a reason. What are they trying to hide?"

The Flakax's mandibles spread wide, and a yellow mass of regurgitated *something* shot out and covered Han's chest. "Kill me now. Better than what the Directors will do, if I break my quiet swear."

"Quiet swear?" Han repeated. "You mean like a vow of silence?"

Tito tried to raise his abdomen, straining to clear the plugged gas duct. Cakhmaim drove the point of his elbow down on the nerve bundle where the thorax connected, and the abdomen dropped to the deck again.

Leia turned to Han. "I thought those crime vows were supposed to be reciprocal?"

"They are," Han said, seeing where Leia was headed. "But you know the Squibs."

Tito's head swung from Han to Leia and back again, and finally he could no longer resist asking, "The Directors?"

Han and Leia exchanged looks, then Han asked, "Should we tell him?"

Leia shook her head. "It would just be cruel, since we're going to have to kill him anyway."

"What would be cruel?" Tito asked.

Meewalh pressed her blaster to his head, but Tito seemed a lot more concerned about what they were keeping from him than the likelihood of being killed.

"Tell!"

Han frowned. "You're sure you want to know? No one likes to die knowing they've been set up."

Tito began to work his mandibles. *"How?"*

"You don't want to know," Leia said. She turned to Meewalh. "Go—"

"Wait!" Tito said. "You tell me, I tell you."

Meewalh asked if she should fire.

"Not yet." Leia frowned down at the prisoner. "You're sure you want to know? It'll just make you angry."

"*Really* angry," Han said. "You just can't trust Squibs."

"Flakax *never* get angry," Tito said. "Never get *anything*. Have no useless feelings like humans."

"Okay," Han said. "I'll give you a hint. Aren't you curious about how we knew you were coming?"

Tito turned one eye toward Leia. "Squibs not tell you. They want you dead."

"That's right." Leia made a small motion with her hand, then added, "And we're not the only ones."

Tito spread his antennae. "They want *us* dead, too?"

"That's the way we hear it," Han said. "Before the Verpines, the Squibs asked a couple of Fefze to help you, right?"

"How you know?"

"Because they're the ones who sold us the warning about you," Leia said. "And we're not the only ones they were asked to kill."

Tito clattered his mandibles. "Fefze kill Flakax? That is funny." He turned to Meewalh. "I much amused. You pull trigger now."

"It's not *that* funny." Leia made another motion with her hand. "Remember, you were going to be fighting *us*."

"I don't suppose you noticed the thermal detonator in the brot-rib crate?" Han asked. He had not found any thermal detonator when he stowed the weapons that had spilled from the crate, but that hardly mattered. Han could always produce one from their own stores and claim the Squibs had slipped it into the box when Tito was looking the other way. "Even a Fefze could set a detonator and take off while you were busy fighting *us*."

"Though, of course, I think the Verpine were a much better choice," Leia said, casting an eye at the unconscious insects. "They're so much more technological."

Tito considered this for a moment, then let out a long throat rattle. "The Directors broke their own swear!"

"That's the way it looks, isn't it?" Han replied.

Leia nodded. "And now that we've kept our part of the bargain—"

"The Directors want you dead because Lizil isn't sending you to Tenupe, like they promise," Tito said. "Lizil told them, 'Two-legs are more use in Alliance. Send them with convoy.' "

Han's jaw fell. "Wait a minute! You're saying this convoy is headed for *Alliance* territory?"

Tito clacked his mandibles shut, then looked from Han to Leia. "Maybe."

Leia's brow rose, now with shreds of Falleen disguise hanging from it after the fierce fight. "No wonder they want us dead!"

"Yeah," Han said. If this convoy was headed for Alliance space, there could only be one purpose for all the war cargo they had seen being loaded. "The Colony is supporting a coup—maybe a whole string of them!"

"I think so." Leia's gaze grew troubled, and she slowly turned to Han. "Somebody has to warn Luke."

Han nodded. "I know. Maybe we can find—"

He caught himself and stopped short of saying *Juun and Tarfang*, then took Leia by the elbow and led her away from their prisoner.

Leia did not even wait until they reached the front of the hold. "Han, we have to do this ourselves."

"We're busy," Han said.

"Think about all the Alliance insects we've seen here," Leia pressed. "Verpine, Flakax, Fefze, Vratix, Huk."

"I *have* been thinking about them," Han said. "I've been thinking about them a *lot*."

"If those governments fall, the Defense Force will be so busy in Alliance territory that it won't be able to keep the pressure on in Utegetu—much less carry the war to the rest of the Colony." Leia stopped and turned him to face her. "You know we can't trust this to Juun and Tarfang, Han."

"Of course we can!" Han said. "You heard Juun. Bwua'tu believes in those two."

"But do *we*?" Leia asked. "Even assuming they would be willing to disregard their orders on our say-so, are you ready to place the Alliance in their hands?"

"It'd serve the Alliance right," Han grumbled. "The rehab conglomerates are claim-jumping everything anyway."

"At least the rehab conglomerates aren't spreading the war," Leia said. "And that's what will happen if we let the Colony overthrow the Alliance's insect governments."

Han let his chin drop to his chest, wondering why it always came down to him and Leia, why they always had to be the ones in the right place at the wrong time.

"Well, I guess there was never any doubt," Han said.

Leia frowned. "Doubt?"

"About going back," Han said. "You *still* have to do the right thing. You just can't help yourself."

Leia thought about this a moment, then nodded. "I guess that's true. I just couldn't live with myself if we let the Colony topple those governments."

"Well, don't be too hard on yourself," he said. "With a Squib death mark on our heads and the Killiks determined to send us back to the Alliance, we didn't have much chance of reaching Tenupe anyway."

"Not this time," Leia agreed. "But we'll be back."

"Yeah, there's always next time." Han allowed himself a moment to curse the universe, then nodded toward Tito and the Verpine. "What about them?"

"We can't take them back as prisoners," she said. "Especially not Tito. He's not all that psychopathic for a homeless Flakax, but that will change now that his buddy is dead. We just can't take the chance."

"Then I guess there's only one thing to do," Han said, starting back toward the insect.

Leia caught him by the arm. "Han, you're not going to—"

"Yeah, I am." Han disengaged his arm. "I'm going to send him back to the Squibs."

NINE

With an artificial waterfall purling in the corner and a school of goldies swimming laps in the catch pond, the conversation area of Luke's outer office was designed to encourage a peaceful, relaxed exchange. The lighting was soft and warm, the floor was sunken to separate it from the rest of the office, and the padded benches were arranged at an oblique angle so that any negative energy arising from a discussion would not fly directly at the conversers.

All of this was, unfortunately, wasted on the current situation. Jacen had chosen to remain standing, feet spread and arms crossed in front of him, facing off against Luke and Mara both. Sensing that Jacen knew exactly why he had been summoned, Luke wasted no time coming to the point.

"Jacen, your fellow Jedi Knights had some very disturbing things to say about the raid on the Chiss supply depot."

Jacen nodded, his expression unreadable. "I imagine."

"They claim that it was very clear the Chiss weren't preparing for a surprise attack," Luke pressed. "They believe you started the war unnecessarily."

"They're wrong."

When Jacen did not elaborate, Mara asked, "Okay— what do you know that *they* don't?"

"Just what I saw in my vision," Jacen said. "I couldn't let

the Chiss attack on their own terms. I had to force their hand."

Luke could not sense a lie in his nephew's words—in fact, he could not sense anything at all because Jacen had closed himself off from the Force. He was trying to hide something.

"Jacen, I've never liked being lied to," Luke said, acting on instinct. "And I absolutely refuse to tolerate it now. Tell me the truth or leave the order."

Jacen recoiled visibly, then seemed to realize he had betrayed himself and began to study Luke in slack-jawed surprise.

"Don't think about it," Mara ordered. "Just do it."

Jacen's shoulders slumped, and his gaze shifted to the pool at the base of the waterfall. "It doesn't change what had to be done, but I did have to alter one detail of my vision to persuade Jaina and the others to help me."

Luke had a sinking feeling inside, more disappointment than anger. "*Which* detail?"

Jacen hesitated, then said, "In my vision, I didn't see who attacked first. I just saw the war spreading, until it had consumed the entire galaxy."

"So you thought you would just go ahead and get things started?" Mara asked, incredulous. "What were you *thinking*?"

"That the war *was* already started!" Jacen retorted. "The Colony had been attacking us—the Jedi and the Alliance—for months. All I did was wake everyone up to the fact."

Given what he and Han had discovered on their trip to Woteba, Luke could hardly argue the point. In addition to the fleet of nest ships the Colony had been constructing inside the Utegetu Nebula, it was now clear that the Killiks had caused many of the problems plaguing the Galactic Alliance, by harboring pirates, providing a market for the

Tibanna tappers, and aiding the smugglers of black membrosia.

But that was hardly an excuse for provoking the Chiss into an attack.

"Jacen, what you did was wrong," Luke said. "And I suspect you know it, or you wouldn't have needed to trick your sister and the others into helping you."

"What else was I *supposed* to do?" Jacen demanded, turning on Luke with heat in his eyes. "You were trapped on Woteba, Mom and Mara were stuck in the Murgo Choke, and Masters Durron and Horn had the entire Jedi order locked in a contest of wills."

The reply hurt because it was so true—and because the breakdown had been Luke's failure.

"I understand, but that's never going to happen again." Luke locked eyes with his nephew and put some durasteel in his voice. "And neither will something like the trick you pulled on your sister and the others. Is that clear?"

Jacen let out a breath of exasperation, but nodded. "The next time, I'll come to you."

"And if Luke's not available?" Mara asked.

"I'm sure he'll have designated someone to oversee the order in his absence." Jacen gave Luke a wry smile. "I'm not the only one who learns from his mistakes."

"Let's hope not." Luke reached out and was unhappy to find his nephew still closed off from the Force. "Now, what else are you hiding?"

Jacen was not surprised this time. He merely nodded, then said, "It has nothing to do with the Jedi—and I wouldn't be hiding it if it wasn't very important."

"Does it explain why you want to kill Raynar so badly?" Luke pressed.

Jacen smirked. "That's no secret," he said. "I want to kill Raynar because it's the only way to stop the war. Lowie and Tesar *don't* want to because he was our friend at the academy."

"You don't think they're being influenced by Raynar?" Mara asked.

Jacen considered this for a moment, then shrugged. "If Raynar had known what we were considering, sure. But they're not complete Joiners, so it's hard to believe they would've been in close enough contact for him to know that the Masters were discussing his death."

Luke nodded. Raynar had already proven—when he originally summoned Jaina and the others to the Colony's aid—that he could use the Force to exert his will over non-Joiners. But Cilghal's experiments had established that he was not able to read minds—even Joiner minds—over long distances any better than Jedi could communicate through the Force. It was all feelings and notions; at the most, Raynar would have felt a vague sense of danger and unease.

"Good," Luke said, relieved Jacen had not seized such an obvious opportunity to cast doubts on the judgment of his rivals. At least he was still trying to be fair and balanced in his actions. "That's the way I understood the situation, too."

"Of course," Jacen added, "now that Tesar and Lowie have told Madame Thul about the debate, we can assume Raynar has been informed via more conventional means."

Luke frowned. "How do you know about *that*?"

"Tesar and Lowie?" Jacen's gaze flicked away, and he could not quite hide his frustration with himself. "I didn't realize it was supposed to be a secret."

"*We* haven't told anyone about it," Luke said. "And since I sent the three of them to Dagobah to consider whether they truly want—"

"You sent Tahiri, too?" Jacen gasped. "But she didn't tell Madame Thul *anything*!"

It was Mara's turn to frown. "And how would you know *that*?"

Jacen hesitated a fraction of a second, then seemed to realize he had made a mistake and said, "Tahiri and I still talk."

"About what Lowie and Tesar are doing?" Mara demanded. "Is she *spying* for you?"

"We *talk*," Jacen insisted. "Sometimes their names come up."

"I can't believe this!" Luke rolled his head back and shook it in despair. Had matters really gotten so out of hand that the order's Jedi were *spying* on one another? "Maybe I should send *you* to Dagobah to join them."

"*I* didn't betray the Masters' confidence," Jacen replied evenly. "But if that's your decision, of course I'll go."

"I'll think about it," Luke said darkly. "In the meantime, no more spying. If we can't trust each other, we don't have a chance of pulling together."

"Actually, spying *builds* trust." Jacen was quoting a maxim that Luke had often heard Leia use as the New Republic's Chief of State. He must have sensed Luke's displeasure, because he quickly added, "But it looks like I won't be talking to Tahiri anytime soon, anyway."

"Thank you," Luke said.

"You're welcome," Jacen said. He glanced toward the exit. "If that's all, I really should be—"

"Nice try," Mara said, blocking Jacen's exit. "I still want to know what you're hiding."

Jacen did not even pause before he shook his head. "I'm sorry. I can't tell you."

"Does it involve what you did to Ben?" Mara's voice grew as sharp as a vibroblade, for she had been even more alarmed than Luke when he reported what Lowie and Tesar had told him. "Blocking his memories?"

Jacen did not seem as surprised as he should have. "Not at all," he said. "I did that to protect him."

"From what?" Mara demanded.

"We were sleeping near an Ewok village when a Gorax attacked," he explained. "Before we could get there, it had wiped out half the village and was heading home."

Luke felt Mara's ire fading. Gorax were primate behemoths, standing as tall as the trees on the forest moon, and they were well known for their brutal natures. "I see. You were afraid the memory would traumatize him."

"No, actually not," Jacen said. "Ben knows better than most kids his age that the galaxy is filled with monsters, so I'm sure he could have handled what he saw with a little adult guidance."

"You're more confident of that than I am," Luke said. "Did he feel their deaths in the Force?"

Jacen nodded. "And he sensed what the Gorax's captives were feeling, too."

Mara's hand went to her mouth.

Luke asked, "So that's why you blocked—"

"No," Jacen said. "I blocked Ben's memory to keep him from recalling what *I* did."

"What *you* did?" Luke asked.

"Ben started to scream that I had to save the Ewoks, and that drew the Gorax's attention," Jacen explained. "But I couldn't take him into the fight with me, and I could sense another Gorax in the forest behind me—"

"So you couldn't leave him alone," Mara finished.

Jacen nodded. "I used the Force to hide us."

When Jacen remained silent, Luke prompted, "And?"

"And Ben was very sensitive that night," Jacen continued. "He felt what happened to the prisoners in the cave."

"*That's* what you didn't want him to remember," Mara said.

"By morning, he was already beginning to withdraw

from the Force again," Jacen said. "He's still young; I think he blames it for the bad things he feels in it."

"I think he does," Luke said. He and Mara had postulated a similar theory themselves, shortly after the war, when it began to grow clear that Ben was withdrawing from the Force. "And how, exactly, did you block this memory?"

"It's a form of Force illusion," Jacen explained. "The Adepts call it a memory rub."

Luke frowned. "That sounds pretty invasive for the Fallanassi," he said. "And I don't recall any White Current techniques that can permanently affect another person's mind."

Jacen smiled and spread his hands in a gesture of helplessness. "Well, Akanah *did* say I was only the second-worst student she ever had."

"It's good to know I'm still number one with her," Luke said, not laughing at the joke. He paused a moment, then continued, "I see why you blocked the memory. I'll probably even be grateful, when I've had time to think about it."

"I'm grateful now," Mara said. Luke could feel that she had already forgiven Jacen completely. "I hope you can teach me that technique."

"I'm not nearly the guide Akanah is," Jacen replied. "But I can certainly try."

"First, I want to know why you didn't just tell Mara and me what happened," Luke said. "I understand you wanted to protect Ben, but that doesn't make sense."

"That's right, Jacen," Mara said, forcing herself to be stern again. "There's no excuse for keeping secrets from *us*."

"I'm sorry," Jacen said, shame crawling up his face. "I should have told you, but it was reckless of me to put him in that position."

"And so you decided to hide what happened from us?" Luke demanded.

"I don't know why, but I sense that he needs *me* to guide him into the Force," Jacen said. "And I thought if you knew what had happened, you wouldn't trust me with him."

"Jacen!" Mara's voice was incredulous, but her relief flooded the Force. "How could you think that?"

Jacen looked a little confused. "I'm not sure. I just thought—"

"You thought wrong!" Mara said. "You've been wonderful for Ben, and there's no one else I'd rather trust with him. But no more secrets." She glanced over at Luke. "Okay?"

"We'll see." He was a little less inclined than his wife to forgive all. There was no doubt about the effect Jacen had on Ben, but Luke remained uneasy about the way his nephew continued to shut his emotions off from the Force. "You're *still* hiding something from us. And I want to know what it is."

"I know you do," Jacen said. "But telling you any more would betray a confidence, and I won't do that."

"Jacen, if you're going to continue being a Jedi, you have to put the order first," Luke said. "We can no longer have divided loyalties."

"I understand that, and I'll leave the order if—"

"Nobody wants *that*," Mara interrupted. Luke shot a blast of irritation her way through their Force-bond, but she ignored it and continued, "We just need to know that this secret won't interfere with your duties as a Jedi."

"It won't," Jacen said, relief showing on his face. "In fact, I can promise that it makes me even *more* determined to be a good Jedi—and to keep our order strong."

Jacen revealed just enough of his presence to confirm he was telling the truth—that whatever the nature of this

secret, he saw the Jedi order as the best means of protecting it.

"I guess we'll have to trust you on that." Luke's tone was
measured. "Don't let us down."

Luke was about to dismiss his nephew when a guilty
heaviness began to weigh on the Force from the direction
of his inner office. He went to the door and found Ghent
lying under the work station in the corner, affixing something to the underside of the writing table. Mara slipped
through the door past Luke.

"Ghent!"

The slicer sat up, banging his head, and the guilt in the
Force changed to fear. His gaze shot across the room
toward R2-D2, then he pulled a tiny electronic device off
the underside of the table and swallowed it.

"Have you been planting listening devices in Luke's office?" Mara demanded.

The tattoos on Ghent's face darkened with embarrassment. "S-s-sorry."

She used the Force to pull the slicer out from under the
table, then began to go through his pockets, pulling out a
truly impressive assortment of eavesdropping bugs.

"Did Chief Omas put you up to this?" Mara asked.

Ghent nodded. "He said it was for the good of the Alliance." He plucked one of the bugs out of Mara's hand
and began to fidget nervously with the tiny wire antenna.
"And he said that I couldn't help you with Artoo any more
unless I did it."

"I see," Luke said, joining them.

He looked around for a moment, eyeing an out-of-place
datapad on the surface of his work station, a recording rod
that had mysteriously turned itself on, a holocube of Ben
and Mara that was facing the wrong way on the shelf.

"Were you finished?"

Ghent looked confused. "N-n-not really."

"Well, then." Luke waved Mara and Jacen toward the door. "I guess we had better leave you to your work."

"You're going to let him *finish*?" Jacen asked.

"Of course." Luke nudged his nephew toward the outer office. "Didn't you just tell me that spying builds trust?"

TEN

Three jumps after departing Lizil, Han was running a systems check while Leia plotted the course to the Rago Run, the long hyperspace lane that would take them back into Galactic Alliance territory. So far, the *Swiff* had performed flawlessly, even reminding them to eat when the ship's droid brain noticed that none of the processing units in the galley had been activated in twenty hours.

"I don't like it," Han said, studying the nacelle-temperature history. "No machine is this reliable."

"To the contrary, Captain Solo," C-3PO said. "When properly maintained, operated in the appropriate environment, and not pushed beyond performance parameters, machines are *very* reliable. Malfunctions most often result from a biological unit's inattentiveness. I can tell you that has been true in my own experience."

"Watch it, Threepio," Leia advised. "It's not smart to insult the hand that oils you."

"Oh," C-3PO said. "I certainly didn't mean to imply that you or Captain Solo have *ever* been neglectful. I have had other owners, you know."

"Other owners? Now *there's* a thought." Han looked over to the copilot's station, where Leia was seated in one of the cockpit's self-adjusting, supercomfortable Support-Gel flight chairs. "How are those jump coordinates coming along?"

"Almost done," she said. "The navicomputer's a little slow, at least compared with the *Falcon*'s."

Han felt a small burst of pride. "That surprises you? The *Falcon* has top-notch—"

He was interrupted by the sharp pinging of an alarm.

"I knew it!" Han said, looking for a flashing indicator on the hyperdrive section of the expansive control board. "That warp stabilizer was running a couple of degrees hot at the end of our last jump."

"Actually, Captain Solo, the *Swiff*'s systems status remains at optimum," C-3PO reported. "Aboard a *Dray*-class transport, that chime indicates a proximity alert."

Han shifted his gaze to the sensor area of the console and found the flashing beacon.

"*That* can't be good." He reset the alarm, then activated the intercom. "Be ready back there."

The Noghri replied that they were *always* ready, and a bank of status beacons turned amber, indicating that the *Swiff*'s weapons systems were coming online.

Han brought up his tactical display and saw that a space–time hole had opened behind them. An instant later, the distortion closed and a bogey symbol appeared in its place.

"I *knew* getting out of there was too easy," Han said. After putting Tito and the Verpine off the ship, they had simply lifted the *Swiff*'s boarding ramp and pushed through the air lock membrane before the confused Killiks had a chance to stop them. "Someone must've slapped a homing beacon on our hull."

"Maybe," Leia said. After departing Lizil, they had done a security sweep of the interior of the vessel as a standard precaution, but there had been no time to do an external search without actually landing somewhere. "It's not going to do them much good, though. We'll be ready to jump in thirty seconds."

"As long as they don't start shooting in twenty." Han went to work on the sensors, trying to determine what kind of vessel was following them. "When it comes to a fight, this thing is no *Falcon*."

Before Han could get a sensor readout, the vessel's transponder code appeared, identifying it as a Mon Calamari *Sailfish*-class transport named *Real Deal*. A moment later, a chirpy Squib voice began to hail them over the open comm channel.

"Solo, you there?"

The *Deal* fired its ion engines and began to approach.

Han glanced over at Leia, who appeared just as surprised as he did, then activated his comm. "We're here."

"What are you doing?" asked a second Squib, probably Grees. "You're going the wrong way."

"We were starting to feel unwelcome," Han said. "And that's close enough, you three. The Noghri are still a little sore about those hit-bugs you sent."

"Hey, we *knew* they didn't stand a chance against you," Sligh said. "But we had to try."

"That was good, the way you turned Tito on us." Grees sounded more angry than admiring. "He got Krafte and Seneki before we could stop him."

"But no hard feelings, okay?" Emala asked. The *Deal* finally decelerated, but continued to drift toward the *Swiff*, slowly closing the distance. "We're the ones who started it, so fair is fair."

"Sure," Leia said. "But why do I doubt you followed us out here to mend partition barriers?"

"*That's* what we like about you guys," Sligh said. "Nothing gets past you."

"We could use someone like you in this thing of ours," Emala added.

The Squibs paused expectantly.

"You're trying to *hire* us?" Leia scoffed.

"*Recruit,*" Sligh corrected. "*Hire* is such an ugly word."

"War is very good for business," Emala added. "And this one is just going to keep getting bigger and better. Trust me when I say that we can have a very profitable relationship."

"Not a chance," Han said. He checked the weapons systems and found all of the status beacons green. If the Squibs continued to close, they were going to be in for a big surprise. *Real Deal* might be better armed than the *Swiff,* but the *Swiff* had Noghri gunners—and Han Solo in the pilot's seat. "But thanks for the offer."

"Let me put it to you plainly, Solo." Grees's voice was low and menacing. "This isn't an offer you want to refuse."

"I just *hate* it when someone tells me what I want." Han looked over and, seeing that the calculations for the next jump were complete, signaled Leia to transfer the coordinates to the guidance system. "So why don't you—"

"You're really not getting this, are you?" Grees interrupted. "Jaina is still in Colony space. We can help you get to her—or we can get to her ourselves."

Leia's finger hovered over the transfer key. "Are you threatening our daughter?"

"Not at all," Emala said. "We're giving you a chance to protect her."

Han's rage boiled over. "You try *anything,* and not only will I stop you, I'll personally drag you out of your fur and feed you to a Togorian."

"Now who's making threats?" Grees asked. "You think you're too good for us, so what choice do we have?"

"It's your own fault," Sligh said. "*We're* not responsible for what happens."

"That's it!" Han grabbed the yoke and throttles, preparing to bring the *Swiff* around to attack. "There's not going to be enough left of you—"

Leia reached over and pulled his hands off the yoke. "Han, no."

Han frowned. "No?"

"Think about it." Leia deactivated the comm microphone. "Why did they *really* come after us? Why did they put a death mark on us?"

Han thought about it. "Right. They still haven't come clean with the Killiks about Juun and Tarfang—"

"No." Leia shook her head. "The Squibs vouched for us to Lizil. If we tell the Alliance what the Colony is planning, it's on *their* heads."

Han let out a long breath. "So they're trying to distract us."

"Exactly," Leia said. "They don't need to hire us or kill us. If they can just delay us for a while, maybe even get lucky and actually put us out of commission—"

"We're going to keep going, aren't we?" Han interrupted.

Leia nodded. "We have to."

She transferred the jump coordinates to the guidance system, and Han's heart suddenly felt as heavy as a black hole. Even if the Squibs talked their way out of being held responsible for "Lord Rysto's" betrayal, they were sure to lose a fortune when the coups failed—and Squibs *hated* losing money. They would do their best to make good on their threat.

The *Deal* began to accelerate, then the lock-alarms began to chirp, announcing that the *Swiff* was being scanned by targeting sensors. Sligh's voice came over the comm channel.

"I can't believe you're making us do this, Solo. Don't you love your daughter?"

Han tried to ignore the Squib, but the question was too painful. *Of course* he loved his daughter. He would move stars to protect both of his children, to keep from losing them as he and Leia had lost Anakin. But that was growing more difficult every day. First Jaina had become a Jedi, then a Rogue Squadron pilot, and now she and Zekk were Joiners, fighting on the wrong side of a war that might never end. When you had a daughter as headstrong as Jaina, there was only so much a father could do—even when that father was Han Solo.

"They're not bluffing, Leia," Han said, leaving his comm microphone off. "You know they'll do it."

"They'll try," Leia said. "Jaina can take care of herself."

"Yeah, I know." Han pushed the throttles forward and began to accelerate away from the *Deal*. He knew Leia was right, that any assassin the Squibs sent after Jaina would be sorely outmatched—but that did not make it any easier to place the Alliance's welfare ahead of her safety. "I guess it runs in her blood."

"What runs in her blood?" Leia asked.

"Being a Jedi," Han answered. The attack alarms began to screech as the *Deal* opened fire. "Whatever Luke does with the order, it's pretty clear you'll be staying in it. Duty always comes first with you."

Leia looked hurt, but reluctantly nodded. "I'm not the only one, Han."

"I know, Princess." The *Swiff* shuddered as the *Deal's* first salvo hit the rear shields. Han activated the hyperdrives, and the stars stretched into an opalescent blur. "And Luke won't even give *me* a lightsaber."

ELEVEN

The convoy was only minutes from the Verpine capital, arcing over the distant yellow dot that was the Roche system's sun, on final approach to the glow-speckled lump of asteroid Nickel One. With their underpowered ion drives and puffed-wafer silhouettes, the Slayn & Korpil Gatherers looked more like a long line of returning foragers than a deadly assault force. Mara could sense only a dozen presences aboard each ship, but some of those presences were a little too diffuse to be Verpine, and there was an electric hum in the Force that reminded her of one of those hot jungle nights when all creation seemed ready to erupt into war. There was definitely *something* wrong with that convoy.

She slid her StealthX into attack position behind the last vessel in line, then waited patiently as Luke and Jacen worked their way forward, using the Force to redirect the attention of the belly gunners as they passed beneath the ungainly Gatherers. Despite the diffuse presences they sensed aboard the transports, Luke was pouring caution into the battle-meld, urging Mara and Jacen to show restraint.

The holo the Solos had sent warning of a massive insect coup had been so flickering and distorted that even R2-D2 could not confirm that the voiceprint was Leia's. Luke and several other Masters had immediately suspected that the message was a forgery, designed to trick the Jedi into attacking legitimate convoys. Luke had decided to dispatch a team to each insect culture belonging to the Alliance, but with strict orders not to engage in battle unless it grew clear that the Killiks were indeed staging a coup.

That was why Mara was so confused when a flash of white brilliance erupted at the front of the convoy. It looked like a shadow bomb detonation, but there had been no warning from either Luke or Jacen, nothing on the tactical display to suggest that a coup was actually under way.

The convoy began to cluster—standard procedure when the leader wanted overlapping defenses—then continued toward the asteroid.

"Nine," Mara asked her astromech droid, "is there any sign of a battle down there?"

The droid reported that a very large baradium explosion had just destroyed a light transport on final approach to Nickel One.

"I *saw* the shadow bomb," Mara said. "I mean, is there anything on the surface . . ."

The meld suddenly stiffened with shock, then abruptly collapsed as Luke withdrew. Mara could feel his anger through their Force-bond, a searing pressure that meant he had already answered the question she had been about to ask her astromech. There was no hint of a battle on the surface of the asteroid.

Jacen had attacked without provocation.

Mara looked down to find a long list scrolling up her display: SHIELD PROJECTORS, AIR LOCK ENTRANCES, BLASTER CANNON EMPLACEMENTS, DEFENSIVE BUNKERS, TRANSPARI-STEEL VIEWING PANELS, GUIDANCE LAMPS . . . everything her astromech could identify on the surface of the asteroid.

"That's enough, Nine," Mara said. "I think I have my answer."

She reached out to Jacen and found him filled with impatience, determined to stop the Gatherers before they reached Nickel One.

Mara urged him to withdraw.

Another shadow bomb detonated at the head of the convoy, spraying specks of flotsam and torn hull in every direction.

Mara grew so angry that she had to break off contact. Anger was too dangerous to share during a battle. It corrupted the discipline of everyone it touched, tainted their judgment and made the killing personal.

A Verpine belly gunner caught a glimpse of Mara's StealthX and began to stitch the surrounding darkness with cannon bolts. She rolled away without firing and sensed Jacen trying to establish the meld again, reaching out to her and Luke in confusion and frustration. One of the StealthXs' drawbacks—and the reason only Jedi could fly them—was that the rigid comm silence protocols prevented actual conversation. Instead, pilots had to communicate using the combat-meld, which relied on emotions, impressions, and the occasional mental image.

The convoy had pulled into a tight, three-dimensional diamond formation and was continuing to approach Nickel One, its gunners firing indiscriminately toward the surface. Whether the gunners were trying to suppress the asteroid's defenses or were simply reacting to Jacen's attack was impossible to say. Like Luke, Mara kept her own weapons silent.

A moment later, she felt Luke opening himself to the battle-meld again, and Jacen's relief flooded the Force. He renewed his call to the attack, sharing his alarm and fear through the meld. Luke responded with disapproval and condemnation, urging Jacen to withdraw.

A sudden spark of understanding flashed through the meld, followed by a sense of hurt and indignity. Mara guessed that Jacen had finally realized that his wingmates doubted his judgment, that they did not believe an attack was appropriate simply because he initiated one.

The thought had barely flashed through Mara's head before the gaping rectangle of a hangar entrance appeared in her mind's eye. The turbolaser batteries in its four corners all sat quiet, their turrets ripped open by internal blasts. A single Gatherer sat on the asteroid surface next to the hangar, with a line of pressure-suited Killiks streaming out of its air lock.

"Nine!" Mara was practically shouting. "Didn't you tell me there were no signs of battle on the asteroid?"

The droid replied that there *were* no signs of a battle.

"Then what about those turbolaser batteries?" Mara demanded. "And the Killiks?"

Nine reported that the turbolaser batteries were nonfunctional. And the Killiks appeared to be debarking, not attacking.

"Never mind." Mara felt at once relieved and ashamed—relieved that Jacen had attacked for good reason, ashamed that she and Luke had allowed their reservations—which now seemed unjustified—to compromise the team's effectiveness. "Select targets by expediency, Nine."

The droid illuminated a transponder symbol near the back of the convoy, and Mara swung in behind the Gatherer it represented. She launched her first shadow bomb and immediately peeled off, accelerating toward the next target. An instant later, space brightened behind her, and her tactical display filled with static. She launched her second shadow bomb without even bothering to glance back and check the damage caused by the first. The light transport had not been built that could withstand a direct hit by a Jedi shadow bomb.

More shadow bombs detonated near the middle of the convoy as Luke joined the battle. The StealthXs swirled around the Gatherers, attacking from all directions. Unable to catch more than a glimpse of the darting Jedi ships, the convoy's gunners set up rolling walls of laserfire. The Jedi, in turn, let the Force guide their moves, slipping around and under these barrages until they had obliterated another half a dozen vessels.

Finally, the convoy pilots seemed to recognize they were fish in a barrel. They dispersed, each Gatherer continuing toward a different corner of an imaginary square. As they fled, their gunners continued to blindly spray bolts into space, and now many of Nickel One's surface batteries joined in, trying to provide safe lanes of approach for their surviving "friends." That was the beauty of a coup: confusion worked in favor of the attacker.

Mara took out two more Gatherers and felt Luke destroy another one, then realized that she had lost track of Jacen. She could still feel him in the meld, but his presence had become cautious and furtive. She reached out to him, curious and concerned. His response seemed at once cocky and defiant, as though he was daring her to doubt him again.

"Whatever you're doing, hotshot, just don't screw up," Mara muttered aloud. She was counting on Jacen to keep nurturing Ben's interest in the Force, but that was not going to happen if her nephew continued to behave like a rogue Jedi. "Too much depends on you."

Jacen seemed puzzled by the sentiment, then a sea of turbolaser fire flowered between Mara and her next target, and her astromech began screeching for her to evade. She juked but continued toward her mark, then took a glancing strike on her flank and lost all her shields at once.

"Shhhhubba!" she hissed, still unwavering from her course.

Nine began to bleep and whistle frantically, filling the display with all manner of dire warnings about what would become of them if she failed to withdraw from combat at once. Mara ignored him and launched her last shadow bomb.

The attack caught the Gatherer just above its wing and punched through the shields in a blinding eruption of white. The StealthX's blast-tinting darkened, and she felt a terrible ripping in the Force as the vacuum tore the crew from its ruptured ship.

The StealthX shuddered as something large thumped into its canopy. Mara cringed and held her breath, half expecting to hear the curt *whoosh* of a catastrophic vacuum breach. But when the blast-tinting returned to normal a moment later, the only thing wrong with the canopy was that the exterior was so smeared with bug guts, that she could not find the nose of her own starfighter.

Mara immediately felt Luke reaching out to her in concern. She assured him she was fine, then switched to instrument flying and was relieved to discover she was telling the truth.

"Nine, can you do anything to clear the canopy?"

The droid promised that he would activate the defogger.

"Don't you dare!" Mara ordered. "That stuff is disgusting enough without having it run all over!"

Mara checked the tactical display and saw that only three Gatherers remained, two on Luke's side of the asteroid and one on hers. She swung her StealthX after the nearest target, trusting the Force to guide her safely around the faint streaks of color that were flashing past her blurry canopy. Her astromech droid posted a polite but urgent message on the display, reminding her that they had lost their shields.

"Relax, Nine," Mara said. "I never take more than one hit per sortie."

The droid chirped doubtfully, then asked if she usually flew blind.

"I'm not blind," Mara reminded him. "I have the For—"

Nine interrupted her with a shrill whistle, reporting that they were receiving a desperate message from the Nickel One hive mother.

"Then put it on the comm speaker," Mara ordered.

Nine replied that the message was not coming in over standard comm channels. Instead, it was being transmitted via radio frequencies that the Verpine used to communicate organically.

"Fine. What's she saying?"

A message appeared on Mara's display. HELP! THE HEART-CHAMBER IS UNDER ATTACK BY OLD ONES AND VER-PINE MEMBROSIA-TRAITORS!

"Old Ones?" Mara asked.

Nine believed the hive mother was referring to Killiks.

"Tell her to lock herself in," Mara said. "We'll be there as soon as we can."

Almost instantly, a question appeared on her display. WHO?

"Just tell her we're Jedi," Mara replied. "The ones who have been attacking the convoy."

The droid tweeted an acknowledgment, and the hive mother's reply appeared on the display half a second later. THE HIVE ASKS THAT THE UNSEEN JEDI HURRY. THE MEMBROSIA-TRAITORS HAVE ALREADY INVITED THE OLD ONES INTO THE HEART-CHAMBER, AND THE MALES-WHO-DIE-FOR-THE-HIVE-MOTHER ARE ALREADY IN BATTLE.

Nine added a message of his own, noting that the ground emplacements were now targeting the Gatherers and suggesting that the Jedi would only get in the way if they continued to attack the same targets.

Mara checked her tactical display; the Verpine weapons emplacements *did* finally seem to be attacking the convoy—what was left of it, anyway.

"This had better be legitimate, Nine," she said. The R9 series was notorious for self-enhancing their preservation routines. "If you're altering data just to get me to turn back, I'll schedule you for an op-system reinstallation faster than you can count to a million and ten."

The droid reassured her that he was only reporting the truth, and as evidence, he pointed out that the salvos had stopped exploding around their vessel. Realizing that Nine was probably right—at least, she could no longer see any streaks of color flashing through the thick gunk on her canopy—Mara decided to believe him. She reached out to Luke, calling him to her side.

"Okay, Nine," she said. "Tell the hive mother we're coming in."

The hive mother's reply appeared on the display almost instantly. YES, YOU ARE VERY FAST. WE CAN SEE YOU NOW, CUTTING THE OLD ONES DOWN WITH YOUR CRYSTAL-FOCUSED BLADE.

"She can see us?" The reason occurred to Mara as soon as she had voiced the question. "Jacen!"

The happy swell of pride that suddenly filled her Force-bond with Luke told Mara that her husband had reached the same conclusion. While the two of them had been fretting over Jacen's trustworthiness and nearly blowing the mission, Jacen had been doing what needed to be done—and preventing the coup. He was already in the heart-chamber.

Jacen was, indeed, a *very* good Jedi.

"Ask the hive mother if it looks like we need any—"

Mara was interrupted by the chime of an arrival alarm, and the transponder codes of a Galactic Alliance task force began to appear on her tactical display. Nine ran a message across the screen, informing Mara that he was not altering *this* data, either.

A moment later, a familiar age-cracked voice came over the speaker in Mara's cockpit. "This is Supreme Commander Gilad Pellaeon aboard the Galactic Alliance Star Destroyer *Megador,* advising Nickel One that we are here on a peaceful mission. Please acknowledge."

Mara's droid reported that the hive mother was acknowledging, though it might take the *Megador* a moment to realize this, since she was still using Verpine radio waves.

"This is Supreme Commander Pellaeon aboard the *Megador,*" Pellaeon continued. "I repeat, we are here to aid you. We have reason to believe that a hostile force may attempt to overthrow your government."

It was Jacen's voice that answered, sounding over his personal comlink. "Consider your suspicions confirmed, Admiral Pellaeon," he said. "But there is no reason for alarm. The Jedi have matters well in hand."

"The Jedi?" Pellaeon asked. He sounded relieved, perturbed, and not at all surprised. "I should have known."

Mara felt Luke's curiosity pour into the meld, and Jacen asked, "Why's that?"

"Because I've been getting reports that there were Jedi waiting almost everywhere that the Killiks have attacked so far."

This time, Luke did not even have to pour his curiosity into the meld. Jacen simply asked, "Almost?"

"I'm afraid so, Jedi Solo," Pellaeon said. "I *am* speaking to Jedi Jacen Solo, am I not?"

"And the Masters Skywalker," Jacen replied. "We're here together."

"Yes, that's what Master Horn reported," Pellaeon said. "Regretfully, our garrison intercepted his team before they could prevent the Killiks from landing on Thyferra."

The meld filled with alarm, though Mara could not say whether it was hers or Luke's or Jacen's, and Jacen asked, "You don't mean to say—"

"I'm afraid I do," Pellaeon replied. "The Killiks have taken control of our bacta supply."

TWELVE

A thousand fingers of silver fire stabbed down from orbit, slicing through the emerald rain clouds. The downpour turned as bright as the Core, and the ground shook so hard that the view in the periscope jumped like a bad holo signal. Still, the image remained clear enough to tell that the last wave of drop ships—at least those few Jaina could actually see through the deluge—had landed almost unchallenged. Their passengers were already debarking in armored hover vehicles, streaming forward to join the hundreds of thousands of troops already massing behind the defensive shield at the drop-sector perimeter.

But the Chiss success was not the cause of the icy knot between Jaina's shoulder blades, nor the reason her stomach refused to settle. UnuThul had always known the Colony would not be able to stop the enemy landing. After all, Tenupe was the linchpin of the Killik front, the gateway to the Sparkle Run and the Colony's heart, and the Chiss had committed two-thirds of their offensive forces to its capture. So there was nothing unexpected about the success of the landing, nor even all that alarming. Jaina was reacting to something else, something the Great Swarm had not yet discovered.

Jaina pulled away from the periscope and blinked for a moment as her eyes readjusted to the dim shine ball light inside the rustling tunnel. The air was hot and humid and filled with the bitter smell of battle pheromones, and the Force was charged with the same pre-combat anxiety common to soldiers of every species. The passage was literally packed with Killiks: millions of thumb-sized Jooj, an endless line of massive Rekkers, a scattering of knee-high Wuluws. There were also a few dozen volunteers from other insect species—mostly mantis-like Snutib hunters, shriveled-looking Geonosian warriors, and a handful of Kamarians who kept asking about her father.

Jaina even saw a pair of greasy black-furred Squibs, armed with repeating blasters and thermal detonators, who seemed unable to take their big eyes off her. She smiled and reached out to them in the Force, trying to offer reassurance and calm their fears. She was not very successful; they merely curled their lips and continued to watch her.

Jaina eyed them suspiciously. It was hard to imagine why a couple of young mercenary Squibs would join this fight—unless they were desperate *and* stupid. On the other hand, it was hard to imagine them posing much of a threat, either. More likely, it was something else prickling her danger sense—something to do with the Chiss.

Jaina would have liked to know whether Zekk sensed anything unusual, but he was posted on a mountain more than a hundred kilometers away, too far away for her to share what was in his mind. With their own nest—the Taat—still trapped inside the Utegetu Nebula, their mindlink only functioned when they were within a few dozen meters of each other.

Jaina reached out to Zekk in the Force, communicating in the clumsy way Jedi usually did. When she felt nothing unusual, she withdrew from his presence and turned to a knee-high Killik standing beside her.

"Wuluw, inform UnuThul that we, er, *I* am having danger ripples." As she spoke, Jaina was absentmindedly running her wrists along its antennae. "Ask him if Unu is *sure* the scouts have found all of the Chiss reserves."

Wuluw acknowledged the order with a curt *"Urbu."* With yellow, oversized eyes and chitin so thin that it could be cracked by a stiff wind, the Killiks of the Wuluw nest hardly made ideal soldiers. But Wuluws mind-shared over a much greater distance than most Killiks—nearly half a kilometer, compared with a typical range of a few dozen meters—and so they were posted throughout the Great Swarm to serve as a communications net.

A moment later, Wuluw reported that UnuThul did not sense any danger in the Force. He wanted to know if she and Zekk were trying another trick like she had at Qoribu—

"No," Jaina interrupted. "We want to destroy the landing force, too. Maybe a big defeat will make the Chiss rethink the wisdom of pressing this war."

Wuluw relayed an assurance from UnuThul that they would soon teach the Chiss to respect the Colony. Then a murky Force pressure rose inside Jaina's chest, urging her and the rest of the Great Swarm to action. The tunnel filled with a loud clatter, and Wuluw rumbled a more specific order from UnuThul, telling Jaina to prepare her horde for the assault.

Jaina looked down a side tunnel to a large underground chamber, one of hundreds that the Killiks had been excavating since the drop ships landed. A steady shower of moist jungle soil was pouring down from the ceiling, partially obscuring the pale white chitin of the four Mollom burrowers already digging their way toward the surface.

"Tell UnuThul we'll be attacking the command craft any moment," Jaina said. She opened herself to the battle-meld—primarily with Zekk, but she knew UnuThul would also be monitoring it—then motioned to her insect troops and started down the side corridor. "We'll hit—"

"Ur ruub," the lead Rekker rumbled. *"Uuu b ruu."*

"Right," Jaina said. "We just need to be sure the volunteers—"

"Fassssst and 'arrrrrd," a Snutib whistled.

"UnuThul told us," a Geonosian added.

"Good," Jaina said, wondering why UnuThul had bothered to name her and Zekk subcommanders if he wanted to run the entire battle himself. "Ask if you have any questions."

She stopped just inside the entrance and waited in silence for the Mollom to break through to the surface. Thankfully, the jungle soil was too moist to raise dust as it fell, but as the burrowers neared the surface, the dirt changed to mud, and the chamber floor quickly grew slick. Finally, the Mollom boomed a warning down the shaft, and a loud sucking noise sounded from the surface.

An instant later the heat-blackened nose of a drop ship crashed down into the chamber, its shield generators overloading and exploding as they struggled to push back the cramped shaft the Mollom had dug beneath it. Rain began to pour down the hole, and the craft's forward beam cannons continued to fire, filling the room with heat and steam and color, and blasting bantha-sized craters into the walls and floor.

Jaina made a scooping motion with her hand, using the Force to hurl a huge mass of soil at the cannons, driving the mud down the emitter nozzle and packing it tight around the galven coils. The weapons exploded an instant later, blowing off the turret and leaving a five-meter breach in the top hull.

The Killiks rattled forward in a boiling wave, the tiny Jooj swarming along the walls and ceiling, the mighty Rekkers springing directly onto the drop ship. The Rekkers boomed their thoraxes in glee and dived through the breach left by the destroyed turret. A few seconds after the first insects had entered, the drop ship's hull began to reverberate with muffled sizzles and dull pings.

Jaina clicked her throat in approval, then reached out in the Force to see if she could sense Jagged Fel's presence aboard the vessel. They were enemies now, but she did not want him to die. As a skilled tactician and a high-ranking Chiss officer, he would be a great asset to the Colony—assuming he could be captured and brought into a nest.

And if Jag became a Joiner, she mused, the Dawn Rumble would be so much more—

"R u u buruub!" Wuluw burst out. The little Killik started to turn and flee back down the tunnel. *"Bur!"*

"No!" Jaina caught the insect by an arm. "This way."

If the Chiss were arming the drop ship's self-destruct mechanism, the last place they wanted to be when the shock waves hit was underground. Dragging Wuluw along, Jaina Force-leapt onto the drop ship's hull, then sprang again, leaping half a dozen meters to the surface.

She found herself standing in the heart of the Chiss landing zone, a clearing of mud and ash surrounded by a circle of blast-toppled mogo trees. A hundred meters away, the landing zone abruptly gave way to a skeleton jungle, a leafless tangle of trunks and limbs stripped bare by Chiss defoliating sprays. In the distance, barely visible through the pouring rain and the naked timber, she could see the up-ended tail of another drop ship, rising out of a hole similar to the one from which she had emerged.

A flurry of shrill sizzles erupted as a Chiss squad opened up with their charric rifles. Wuluw tried to dive back underground, but Jaina jerked her in the opposite direction.

"I told you, this way!" Jaina started across the clearing, dodging and weaving and dragging Wuluw along. "It's safer!"

"Bur ub bbu!"

"*Of course* they're shooting at us." Jaina reached the edge of the clearing and dived for cover. "They're the enemy!"

They landed between a pair of fallen mogo trees, and the sizzles became crackles as the charrics began to chew through the speeder-sized trunk.

"*R-ruu u-u b-b-burr,*" Wuluw stammered.

"Don't worry." Jaina unslung her repeating blaster. "We're Jedi, aren't we?"

Wuluw thrummed her thorax doubtfully.

Jaina popped up and began to pour bolts back across the clearing. The nearest drop ship—the one she had bounded up—had not yet self-destructed, and the Jooj were swarming up the hull and pouring out across the landing zone. The Rekkers were coming, too, springing out of the pit by the dozens, booming their thoraxes in glee and spraying shatter gun pellets in every direction.

But the Chiss were recovering from their shock and making their presence known. Nearly half the leaping Rekkers tumbled back into the hole, their thoraxes trailing arcs of gore or their heads vanishing in the flash of a maser beam. And many of those who *did* reach the jungle floor landed in pieces or limp, oozing heaps.

Jaina did her best to cover them, but the Chiss troops were camouflaged in color-shifting, fractal-pattern armor that made them nearly impossible to see. She reached out in the Force and felt perhaps a hundred enemy soldiers scattered throughout the area, all confused, frightened, and—typically for Chiss—still resolute. She began to rely on the Force rather than her eyes to find targets and saw a bolt strike what appeared to be a mogo limb—until it dropped its charric rifle and whirled away clutching a wounded shoulder.

Then a powerful jolt shook the ground. The nearest drop ship's tail erupted into a ball of shrapnel and orange flame, and the Force shuddered with the anguish of a mass death.

Jaina dropped back behind the tree and turned to pull Wuluw down beside her. She found only a shard of white-hot durasteel, lodged in a blood-sprayed mogo trunk behind where the Killik had been standing.

Jaina had seen—had *caused*—so much carnage in combat that she had believed herself numb to the storm of emotions it spawned. But the loss of the frightened little Wuluw brought it all back—all the fear and the anger and the guilt, the despair and the loneliness and the soul-scorching rage that had been lurking just beneath the surface since the deaths of Anakin and Chewbacca and so many others.

Jaina leapt up again, eager to blast a hundred Chiss, to make the invaders pay for the deaths of Wuluw and so many others, but apart from her own fading battle cry, the area had fallen suddenly quiet. All that remained of the drop ship was the black smoke streaming out of the pit and a few shards of white-hot metal embedded in fallen mogos. Chiss and Rekkers alike remained tucked down among the tree trunks around her, momentarily too stunned to continue killing, and even the surviving Jooj seemed disoriented, swirling across the ground in rambling swarms of brownish green.

In the distance, Jaina could make out more columns of smoke rising toward the emerald sky. Every few moments, a fresh thud sounded somewhere in the rain, marking the destruction of another drop ship. Each detonation brought the death of thousands of insects, but an entire drop fleet of detonations would not change the battle's outcome. What the Chiss failed to understand—what they would refuse to understand until it was too late—was that they could not win a war of attrition against the Colony.

A Killik could lay a thousand eggs a month, and within a year, those eggs would be battle-ready nymphs. In two years, the survivors would lay eggs of their own. Kill one Killik, and ten thousand would take its place. Kill ten thousand, and a million would take *theirs*. If the Chiss wanted to survive this war, they had only one choice: withdraw to their own borders and sue for peace. It was that simple.

After a moment, the Jooj started to find their way into the fallen trees the enemy was using for cover. Chiss soldiers began to leap out of hiding, screaming and ripping their armor off, slapping and even shooting at the thumbnail-sized insects that had slipped past their defenses. Jaina understood their panic. The Jooj were not attacking so much as feeding, injecting their prey with a flesh-dissolving enzyme and sucking the liquefied flesh back into their mouths. Supposedly, victims felt as if they were being burned alive.

The surviving Rekkers began to take advantage of the enemy's panic, pounding them with shatter gun pellets the moment they showed themselves. Other Chiss returned fire, and soon the battle was in full swing again. Jaina stretched into the Force and poured blasterfire at soldiers she could sense but did not see. The sharp *phoot*s of insecticide grenades began to detonate all around her, and she felt Killiks dying slow, anguished deaths as their respiratory spiracles swelled shut.

Finally, Killik reinforcements began to pour out of the smoking pit again, the Rekkers springing into view with their weapons blazing, the Jooj scuttling over edges and spreading outward in all directions. The Chiss, disciplined even when it was clear they had no chance of survival, responded with a desperate assault, hurling vape charges and insecticide grenades into the hole in a futile effort to turn back the Killik tide.

Jaina felt an enemy presence behind her and turned to find a trio of Chiss soldiers leaping over a mogo trunk. Their charric rifles were already swinging in her direction. She swept her hand across her body, using the Force to redirect their aim. Maser beams sprayed harmlessly past, filling the air with smoke, splinters, and heat.

The leader was on Jaina instantly, his red eyes shining with hatred behind his helmet as he clubbed at her head with his rifle butt. She ducked, using the Force to pull him over her back and send him crashing into the trunk behind her.

The other two Chiss arrived a step later, one bringing an armored knee up at her face. Jaina blocked with her blaster, at the same time squeezing the trigger and pumping fire into the stomach armor of her other attacker. The bolt ricocheted away and sent the soldier stumbling back, but not before he slammed the barrel of his own weapon down on the back of her head.

Jaina found herself kneeling on the ground, her vision narrowing, her hands empty, and the deafening crack of the blow still echoing inside her skull. She tried to stand and felt the strength drain from her body.

No!

Zekk touched her through their battle-meld, pouring strength into her through the Force, urging her to stay conscious.

Jaina fell flat to the ground—then unhooked her lightsaber and activated the blade as she rolled away, slicing both soldiers at the knees. They screamed and crashed down behind her. She felt her blade move and recoil as a maser beam crackled into it. Her vision cleared, and she found herself facing the first Chiss who had attacked her.

She deflected the next shot back into his helmet visor, sending him tumbling backward over a mogo trunk. His body lay still and silent, the small plume of smoke that rose from it stinking of charred flesh.

Jaina spun on a knee and found the other two Chiss lying on their bellies in front of her, groaning in pain as they struggled to prop themselves on their elbows and open fire. She used the Force to rip their weapons from their hands, then stood and raised her lightsaber to finish them off.

Only the revulsion that Zekk poured into the meld stayed

Jaina's blade. She was still so filled with battle lust that she had not even realized she was about to kill the two Chiss in cold blood. It was happening again. She was surrendering to the rage that had consumed her after Anakin died—giving herself to war, with no thought to anything but vengeance and victory.

Shuddering in disgust, Jaina deactivated her lightsaber and knelt next to the two soldiers. Her blade had cauterized their wounds, so they were not losing much blood. But they were both shivering and much too quiet. She rolled them onto their backs, then removed the first soldier's helmet. His blue skin was covered with perspiration, and his red eyes were distant and unfocused.

Jaina shook him by the chin, trying to bring him back to alertness. "Where's your medkit?"

The Chiss clamped a hand weakly over her arm. "Why?"

"You're going into shock," she explained. "You need a stim-shot, or you'll die."

"You?" the second soldier gasped inside his helmet. "Trying . . . to save us?"

"Isn't that what we just said?" Jaina demanded.

"No!"

The first soldier pushed her away, surprising her with his strength.

"Don't be afraid." Jaina poured soothing emotions into the Force, trying to calm and comfort the pair. "The Colony will take care of you. We'll even give—"

The second soldier snapped a vape charge off his utility belt and pulled the activation pin. "We know what you'll . . . do."

"Hey!" Jaina did not dare use the Force to yank the canister from his hand—the charge would detonate the instant he released the trigger. "You're not getting this. The Colony is *good* to prisoners. You'll hardly know—"

"That your bugs are eating our insides?" The Chiss nodded to his companion, then said, "We'll be waiting on the other side, Jedi—"

Jaina sprang into a backward Force flip and tumbled away in a high arc, thumbing her lightsaber active again and batting aside a flurry of maser beams as she came down in the murky ribbon of a jungle stream.

The vape charge detonated as she splashed into the water, a dazzling flash of white that tore the air itself, stealing the breath from her lungs and leaving her half blind, shaking, and confused. She was not all that surprised the two soldiers had refused to surrender—but the reasons they had given distressed her. Could they really believe the Colony fed its prisoners to its larvae?

Jaina had no time to debate the question, for another cold shiver of danger sense was racing up her back. She brought her lightsaber up and spun around to block . . . and found the two Squib volunteers peering down the streambank at her, their dark heads and power blasters poking out from beneath the trunk of a fallen mogo.

"Take it easy, lady," the one on the left said. His muzzle was a little longer and sharper than that of his companion, who had a crooked streak of white fur tracing an old scar down one cheek. "We just came to see if you were still alive."

"Apparently so," Jaina said. She lowered her lightsaber, but did not deactivate the blade. "Be careful. I sensed something dangerous up there."

"You don't say?" Longnose exchanged glances with Scarcheek, then said, "Then I guess it's a good thing we came along."

"Yeah," Scarcheek agreed. "You're real lucky to have us looking out for you."

THIRTEEN

Deep beneath the new Defense Force command compound on Coruscant—already known among military personnel as "the Dark Star"—there lay a dozen planning facilities so secret that Luke had never officially been informed of their existence. At the moment, he was in PaAR Five—*PaAR* being the acronym for "Planning and Analysis Room." That Cal Omas had actually summoned him—and Mara and Jacen—into one of the secret rooms, he took as a good sign. Perhaps the Chief of State was ready to put the trouble between the Jedi and the government behind them.

Their escort led them along a dimly lit walkway past a projection pit displaying a three-meter hologram of the planet Thyferra. Around the edges of the pit were arrayed several banks of work stations where dozens of communications officers, intelligence analysts, and system operators labored to keep the information displayed on the hologram up to the minute. From what Luke could see, the situation wasn't good. The green swaths of continental rain forest were speckled with colored lettering that showed the dispositions of various villages, forces, and facilities. The planet's largest city, Zalxuc, and most of its villages had already turned red, indicating they were known to be under enemy control.

At the end of the walkway, the Skywalkers and Jacen were admitted onto a secure command platform where

Chief Omas stood poring over holofeeds with Admiral Pellaeon. Han and Leia were already there as well, studying a second bank of holodisplays along with a Vratix—one of the mantiform insects who inhabited Thyferra. When the guards announced their arrival, Omas pretended to be engrossed in a holofeed of the Thyferran rain forest, leaving a surprised Pellaeon to wave them toward the holobank.

"Masters Skywalker, Jedi Solo, please join us." Despite his aged face and bushy white mustache, Pellaeon—an ex-Imperial admiral—continued to look the part of the shrewd command officer he was. He gestured toward the insect at his side. "Do you know Senator Zalk't from Thyferra?"

"Only by reputation." Luke inclined his head to the Vratix. "I'm sorry the Jedi weren't able to prevent the coup on Thyferra, Senator Zalk't."

Zalk't scuttled over and greeted Luke by rubbing a massive forearm across his shoulder. "The fault was not *yours*, Master Skywalker." His speech was filled with whistles and clicks. "Thyferra thanks the Jedi for their efforts on our behalf."

"As does the entire Galactic Alliance," Pellaeon added. "Had the Jedi not responded so quickly, we would have lost far more than the Thyferra system." He cast a meaningful glance in Omas's direction. "Isn't that correct, Chief Omas?"

Omas finally tore his attention away from the holo and met Luke's gaze. He looked even more careworn than usual, with ashen skin and bags beneath his eyes as deep as those of a Yuuzhan Vong.

"Yes, it was a relief to find the Jedi serving the Galactic Alliance for a change," Omas said.

"The Jedi have always served the Galactic Alliance, Chief Omas." As Luke spoke, he was pouring goodwill into the Force. He could sense the anger that Omas's comment had raised in Han and Leia and even in Jacen, and he could not allow this meeting to degenerate into a shouting match. "But the issues have not always been clear, and sometimes we have taken the long view without talking to you. I apologize for our mistakes."

Omas's jaw dropped, as did those of Han, Leia, and Jacen. Only Pellaeon and Mara did not seem surprised—Pellaeon because the Galactic Alliance and the Jedi order clearly needed each other to deal with the Killiks, and Mara because she was the one who had suggested to Luke that it was the duty of the Jedi order to support the Galactic Alliance. Imperfect as it was, the Galactic Alliance remained the galaxy's best hope for achieving a lasting peace.

Omas finally recovered from his shock. "Thank you, Master Skywalker." There was more suspicion in his words than relief, and he quickly turned back to the bank of holofeeds. "I trust the Jedi won't find the issues too confusing today."

Almost all of the holofeeds showed a small squad of Killik commandos leading a few Vratix "tarheads"—insects addicted to black membrosia—into a village of graceful, multibalconied towers. The tarheads would enter one or two of the towers, then return with a few Vratix and present them to the Killiks, who did not even bother lining the prisoners up before spraying them with shatter gun pellets. Sometime during the process, the holo would usually show a Killik approaching the holocam, and the signal would go to static.

"The traitorsss are bringing out the village anirs," Zalk't explained in his whistling Basic. "But the coup actually began in Zalxuc. Before we realized what was happening, tarhead traitors had slain our high canirs and their assistants, and the Killiksss were hunting down every noninsect in the city."

"Cutting off the head so they can control the body," Leia said. "Standard coup strategy."

"Yeah, but this one has a twist," Han added. "Black

membrosia will be running in the streets. Half the population will be addicts—and the bugs will be their suppliers."

"It gets worse," Leia pointed out. "If the Killiks hold Thyferra long enough, the Vratix will become Joiners."

Luke nodded. "*If* the Killiks hold it long enough." He turned to Jacen. "How long would it take for the Vratix to start becoming Joiners?"

"It doesn't matter," Jacen said, shaking his head. "The Killiks are trying—"

"That's *not* what I asked," Luke snapped. He could feel in the Force that Omas remained too suspicious of the Jedi to take advice from Jacen. "Just answer my question."

Jacen scowled at the rebuke. "Cilghal would have a better idea than I do," he said. "Normally, an outsider has to spend several months in a nest to become a full Joiner, but it might go faster for insect species."

"In the meantime, our bacta supply is cut off," Omas said. "And if we launch a counteroffensive, the damage could be even worse."

"The fighting will be widespread, and the xoorzi crop will suffer," Zalk't said.

"Xoorzi crop?" Han asked. "I thought bacta was made out of a couple of kinds of bacteria."

"It is," Zalk't replied. "Xoorzi fungus is the growth medium for the alazhi bacteria. It occurs only in the wild, in the deepest shade of the forest floor. The slightest disturbance will cause it to release its spores and shrivel."

"As you can see, a conventional battle would be devastating," Pellaeon said. "We were hoping the Jedi would be able to handle the situation a bit more delicately." He turned to Omas, his expression carrying an unspoken demand. "Weren't we?"

Omas swallowed hard, then said, "Yes. The Galactic Alliance would be very grateful for the Jedi's help."

Luke kept a sober expression, but inwardly he was smiling. The Jedi's quick response to the coup attempts had regained some measure of respect from Chief Omas, and now he was asking for the Jedi's help—albeit reluctantly.

"Of course." Luke felt a bolt of alarm shoot through the Force as Han, Jacen, and even Leia grew worried that he was allowing political concerns to undermine his judgment. "The Jedi would be delighted to help."

"If you and Admiral Pellaeon think that's best," Mara added, obviously sensing the same objections from their companions.

Omas frowned at her. "We do."

"Then that's what we'll do." Luke noticed Pellaeon's brown eyes studying Mara with their usual shrewdness. He nudged the admiral through the Force, feeding Pellaeon's doubt and urging him to question the situation. Outwardly, he simply bowed to Chief Omas. "If you'll excuse me, then, I'll start recalling our Jedi Knights—"

"Not yet," Pellaeon said. His gaze flickered briefly between Luke and Mara, and Luke knew the admiral had figured out that he was being played. That did not prevent him from asking the right question. "You don't think sending the Jedi to Thyferra is a good idea, do you, Master Skywalker?"

Luke kept his gaze fixed on Omas. "The Jedi are willing to go wherever Chief Omas feels we are needed."

"Blast it, Luke!" Pellaeon barked. "That's not what I asked. If you know something we don't—"

"It's not anything we *know*," Leia interrupted. "It's just experience."

"*What* experience?" Omas looked suspicious, but he was clearly unwilling to deny his Supreme Commander the leeway to pursue his own line of inquiry. "With the Killiks?"

"Precisely," Leia said. "I'm sure it hasn't appeared this way from your position as the Chief of State, but the Jedi are convinced that much of the Colony's aggression since Qoribu has actually been directed at the Jedi order."

"That wouldn't surprise me in the least," Omas said icily. "As I'm sure you recall, I didn't want the Jedi involved with the Colony in the first place."

"I don't see how that has any bearing on the current situation," Pellaeon said sharply. "And you feel these coups are directed at the Jedi *how*?"

"Not *at* us," Luke said. "They're diversions, to keep us on the defensive instead of destroying the Colony's strength at a crucial time."

"The Killiks are launching something major," Leia said. When Omas's brow rose, she raised a hand to forestall his question. "I can feel it through Jaina—there's a big battle going on, one she seems confident of winning."

This was news to Luke, who had not been able to get a clear Force reading on his niece since she became a Joiner, but Pellaeon nodded in agreement.

"Bwua'tu feels they're preparing another breakout attempt in the Utegetu," the admiral said. "And they certainly wouldn't want the Jedi interfering in *that*—not after the role you played in spoiling their first attempt."

Omas looked at Pellaeon with a dropped jaw. "You believe them?"

"I do. The Colony can't fight the Alliance and the Chiss at the same time. I never believed the coups were meant to be anything more than a diversion—and I'm certainly willing to consider the possibility that it wasn't the *military* they were trying to distract." Pellaeon turned to Luke. "Can the Jedi really destroy the Colony's strength?"

Luke nodded, using the Force to project more confidence than he felt. "We can."

"You'll forgive me if I want to know how," Omas said.

"Simple." It was Jacen who said this. "We take out Raynar Thul."

Pellaeon and Omas exchanged uneasy glances, then Omas asked, "By 'take out,' you mean—"

"We mean do whatever is necessary to remove him from power," Luke said. He was still not ready to commit to killing one of his own Jedi Knights—at least not publicly. "But to destroy the Colony, we can't stop there. I'll have to find and kill Lomi Plo."

Pellaeon's eyes narrowed. "And you can do that? I thought she was invisible."

"She won't be invisible this time," Luke said. "And we have a backup plan."

"We do?" Han asked, raising his brow.

Luke nodded. "Something Cilghal developed while you and Leia were scouting Lizil."

Luke avoided any reference to the mission being unauthorized. Despite Leia's misgivings about him assuming sole leadership of the Jedi, she was obviously still dedicated to the Alliance and the order—she had proved *that* when she and Han returned to sound the warning about the coups instead of continuing after Jaina and Zekk.

When Luke did not elaborate, Pellaeon grew impatient. "Master Skywalker, you obviously have a plan to end this entire crisis. Would you please stop wasting the Chief's time and tell us?"

Luke smiled. "Of course."

He laid out the basics of the plan that he and Mara had been developing for some time, outlining what he would need from the Defense Forces, how the Alliance's Jedi would be used, and what they would need from Chief Omas. By the time he finished, there had been a clear shift in the mood on the command platform.

"Just so I'm sure I understand," Omas said. "This will destroy the Colony, but not the Killiks?"

"That's right," Luke said. "And even if the Colony does somehow form again, it won't be able to expand."

Omas nodded, then caught Luke's eye and held it. "And you really said 'the Alliance's Jedi'?"

Luke laughed, trying to keep hidden the sense of loss he felt inside. "I did," he said. "The Jedi serve the Force—but we can't serve it in a vacuum. We need the Galactic Alliance as much as it needs us."

"Well, then!" Omas's face brightened, and he turned to Pellaeon. "What do you think of our Jedi's plan?"

Pellaeon grew thoughtful, absentmindedly twisting the ends of his mustache, then frowned in approval. "It's sneaky," he said. "I like it."

FOURTEEN

A terrible ripping noise growled down out of the clouds, and Jaina looked up to see another flight of Chiss missiles arcing through the downpour. It had been days—more than a week—since the Great Swarm had boiled out of the ground beneath the enemy's drop ships, and the missiles had not stopped. They came day and night, painting streaks of white fire across the sky and trailing green plumes of insecticide, grating nerves raw with their endless growling.

Jaina made a sweeping motion with her hand, using the Force to hurl three missiles back toward their launchers. The other two dropped into the defoliated jungle behind her and detonated in a blinding pulse, hurling trunks in every direction and flashing killer radiation through the naked trees for a hundred meters.

Killiks died by the hundreds in an instant, and they would die by the thousands as the plumes of poisonous vapor settled to the jungle floor and began to take their toll. It did not matter. UnuThul was urging the Great Swarm onward, filling every thorax with the same irresistible compulsion to *attack, attack, attack* that Jaina felt hammering inside her own chest. The Killiks had to overrun the Chiss lines; they had to do it now.

There was just one problem.

Already, the jungle floor lay buried so deeply beneath

dead Killiks and pieces of dead Killiks that Jaina could barely walk. In places, she was literally wading through pools of insect gore or scrambling over mounds of broken chitin, and the enemy lines remained as unattainable as ever. For every hundred meters the Great Swarm advanced, the Chiss pulled back a hundred and one. Eventually, of course, they would run out of room to retreat—but Jaina was beginning to worry that the Colony would run out of Killiks first.

Jaina slipped behind the trunk of a giant mogo and dropped to her knees, keeping one eye on the flickering battle ahead as she uncapped her canteen. The problem was not that the Killiks were failing to kill the enemy. Jaina could see half a dozen panicked Chiss ripping at their armor to get at the Jooj underneath, and every few moments, a Rekker would spring over a breastwork and send a Chiss soldier bouncing off the trees—often in pieces.

The problem was that—with UnuThul's Will compelling them to attack almost mindlessly—the Killiks were a lot less efficient than the Chiss. They were running headlong into walls of charric fire, while the enemy remained concealed and protected behind their temporary fortifications, exposing themselves to attack only when there were so many Killik bodies piled in front of them that they had to withdraw to a clear position.

Jaina turned, looking for her newest communications assistant—she lost at least one Wuluw a day—and found only the two black-furred Squibs who had assigned themselves to watch her back.

"Wuluw?" she called.

A soft clatter sounded from the base of the mogo tree, and she looked down to find the little brown Killik crawling out from beneath a root-knee. "What are you doing down there?"

"*Ubb.*"

"Okay." Jaina sighed. "Just don't disappear entirely."

Wuluw withdrew back under the root, leaving visible the tiniest tip of one antenna.

The rain-soaked Squibs snickered openly, mocking Wuluw for being a coward—until a passing charric beam singed a hand-wide band of fur off the side of Longnose's head.

"*Rurub,*" Wuluw thrummed from her muddy hole.

"I know you're not laughing at *me,* bug." Longnose started to raise his repeating blaster. "Because you aren't that brave."

"Knock it off," Jaina said. She used the Force to push both Squibs away, then addressed herself to the mouth of Wuluw's hiding place. "Tell UnuThul this isn't working. We have to slow down and fight from position—"

"*Bb!*" Wuluw relayed.

"We *have* to," Jaina said. "At this rate, the swarm will run out of soldiers!"

"*Bruu ruu urubu,*" Wuluw thrummed, still relaying Unu-Thul's message. "*Ur bu!*"

"Even the Colony's army isn't that big!" Jaina protested. "The Chiss are slaughtering us by the millions."

"*Ur bu!*" Wuluw repeated. "*Urub bub ruuur uur.*"

"What do you mean you're going to be out of touch?" Jaina demanded. "You're the commander, UnuThul! You can't just leave the battle!"

"*Ru'ub bur,*" Wuluw relayed. "*Ur bu!*"

The "trust me" command was accompanied by the dark pressure of UnuThul's Will, urging Jaina to continue the attack, to overrun the Chiss lines. Everything depended on that.

"What choice do we have?" Jaina grumbled. "But before UnuThul goes, there's something he should know about the Chiss."

"*Ub?*"

"They're not surrendering," Jaina reported. "Even when they have no way to keep fighting, they make us kill them."

"*Uuuu,*" Wuluw rumbled. "*Bu?*"

"They seem to think we're laying eggs in them," Jaina reported, "and letting our larvae eat them, like what the . . ."

Jaina could not remember the name of the nest that had been doing those terrible things at Kr.

"Like what happened at Qoribu," she finished.

Wuluw relayed UnuThul's response quickly—too quickly. "*Buub urr bubb.*"

"It's more than a rumor," Jaina objected. "We saw what happened at Kr. So did you, UnuThul."

"*Ubbb ruur?*" Wuluw asked for UnuThul. "*Burrubuur rububu ru.*"

"Maybe," Jaina said. The pressure to attack had turned to a dark weight now, pressing down inside her chest, urging her to reexamine her memories. "It *was* dark in the grub cave. We could have misunderstood what we were seeing."

"*Buuu ururub,*" Wuluw relayed. "*Rbuurb u rubur ruu.*"

"That's probably it," Jaina agreed.

She knew that UnuThul was forcing the conclusion on her, that somewhere down inside she remembered events another way. But Zekk was still hiding in the mountains with the airborne swarm, too far away to share her thoughts and bolster her resolve, and without him, she simply lacked the strength to resist UnuThul's Will.

"It would be just like the Chiss to make that up," Jaina said. "That must be what happened. They must be afraid their soldiers will surrender and join the Colony."

"*Bur.*"

Wuluw went on to reiterate UnuThul's orders, instructing Jaina to continue pressing the attack on all fronts. Of course, it was not actually necessary for her to issue the order herself. The entire swarm simply felt the same pressure in their thoraxes that Jaina did in her chest, and they began to redouble their efforts, the Rekkers springing over the Chiss breastworks in waves, the Jooj swarming through the jungle in a droning brown-green cloud.

Taking care to make certain Wuluw stayed with her—and that she always knew where those Squibs were—Jaina started toward the mountains in the distance, hidden though they were by rain and mist. She could have turned toward any quadrant, since the swarm was attacking the Chiss from all directions inside the perimeters. But the mountains were where Zekk was waiting, and Jaina longed to be as near to him as possible. With Taat still trapped in the Utegetu Nebula, he was her entire nest now—the words that completed her thought, the beat that drove her heart—and if she was going to die today, she wanted to do it near him.

Suddenly, the sizzle of the charric rifles began to fade and the swarm began to advance more rapidly. Jaina finally waded free of the Killik gore and saw nothing ahead but scurrying limbs and fanning wings. There were no Chiss anywhere, no beams of death flickering out to slow the Colony. Jaina could not believe they had actually broken the legendary Chiss discipline, that UnuThul's last exhortation had been all that was needed for the swarm to push through the enemy lines.

Something was wrong.

Jaina stopped and turned to Wuluw. "Halt! Tell them to stop. It's a—"

The crackle of an incoming barrage echoed through the trees, then the jungle erupted into a raging storm of detonating artillery shells and splintering wood. Whole treetops began to crash down from above, crushing thousands of unlucky insects, and wisps of green vapor began to spread through the mogos and sink toward the forest floor.

The Killiks stopped and drummed their chests in alarm,

working their wings and trying to keep the mist from set-
tling on their bodies, but the artillery shells continued to
come. The wisps of vapor turned into a ground haze, then
the haze to a fog. The rain only seemed to make the fog
grow thicker, as though the insecticide was water-activated.
The river of Jooj stopped advancing, the jungle floor grew
crowded with convulsing Rekkers, and Jaina began to gag
on the sickly-sweet smell of the deadly gas.

She used the Force to clear a hole through the green fog.
Before she could pull the electrobinoculars from her utility
belt, the hole grew congested with charging Rekkers. She
started to hop up on a mogo trunk so she could see over
them, then realized how exposed that would leave her and
thought better of it.

"Tell those soldiers to wait!" Jaina said to Wuluw. "I
need to see."

Wuluw had barely acknowledged the order before the
Rekkers dropped to the jungle floor. Jaina set the electrobinoculars to scan and peered down the tunnel she was
keeping open through the green cloud. Even with all the
foliage stripped away by Chiss defoliators, it was nearly
impossible to see very far through the thick timber. But
eventually, she did glimpse a muzzle flash from beside a
fifty-meter mogo. She gave the tree a fierce Force shove and
sent it crashing to the jungle floor.

A flurry of Chiss charric beams reduced the upended
roots to a spray of dirt and smoking splinters, but Jaina
wasted no time searching for the attackers. The fire had
been quick and precise, which meant it had come from dismounted infantry, and that told her much of what she
needed to know.

The rest Jaina discovered when another muzzle flash
filled the viewfinder of her electrobinoculars. She centered
the flash, magnified the image, and found herself looking at
the blocky silhouette of a MetaCannon, one of the Chiss's

largest drop-deployable field pieces. The MetaCannon could fire maser beams, blaster bolts, or even primitive artillery shells with a "quick-and-easy" change of the barrel.

What it could not do, however, was react quickly to changing tactics.

"Everybody into the treetops," Jaina ordered. The Chiss insecticide would not be as effective in the jungle canopy, since it would rapidly be dispersed by the wind or sink to the ground. "Advance rapidly until the enemy starts to fire into the jungle canopy, then drop to the ground and continue. Expect small-arms fire in—" She checked her range-finder. "—approximately one kilometer."

Having already relayed the orders, Wuluw started up the nearest mogo. The Squibs followed close behind. Jaina returned her electrobinoculars and lightsaber to her utility belt, then started after them, giving orders as she climbed.

"Report to all nests that it looks like the Chiss have brought their heavy artillery back to stop us."

Wuluw stopped climbing and spun her head around backward, her mandibles spread in alarm as she looked down her back at Jaina.

"B-b-bu?"

"Really," Jaina said. "Don't worry. We're not going to let anything happen to you."

Wuluw flattened her antennae doubtfully. *"Buur urbu ruub u."*

"I mean it this time." Jaina fluttered her hand, using the Force to whisk away a bank of insecticide drifting their way. "Just keep climbing . . . and do your job! The other nests need that report."

Wuluw expelled air through her respiratory spiracles, then turned her head around and resumed climbing. A moment later, she began to drum her chest, relaying the other nests' pleasure at how well the battle was progressing. Kolosolok would be attacking the perimeter soon.

They finally climbed above the vapor layers into the remains of the jungle canopy. All the foliage was gone, of course, leaving the great mogos scratching at the rain clouds with the crooked fingers of their naked crowns. The artillery barrage had opened surprisingly few holes in the gray expanse, and there were even a few confused birds still circling low over the wet treetops.

To Jaina's relief, thousands of Rekkers had survived the dangerous climb from the jungle floor. They were already advancing through the rain, springing from treetop to treetop with a power and grace that even Wookiees would have envied—had they been able to overlook the Rekkers' six limbs, antennae, and long pendulous abdomens.

The Jooj were advancing somewhat differently, winding across the treetops in huge sinuous blankets, circling gaps in the canopy or creating long boiling bridges out of their own bodies. The Chiss artillery continued to savage the jungle below, occasionally sending the crown of a mogo plummeting into the poisonous tangle while panicked Killiks leapt to safety in adjacent treetops.

But mostly, the Colony's advance was unhindered. Rekkers and Jooj continued to rise into the canopy behind Jaina, and as far as the eye could see ahead, an unstoppable tide of insects was boiling across the jungle top toward the Chiss lines.

Jaina turned to Wuluw. "How good are you at jumping?"

"*Bub bu,*" the insect admitted.

"That's what we thought," Jaina said. She turned her back to the Wuluw. "Hop on."

The Killik leapt up and wrapped all six limbs around Jaina's body.

"What about you two?" Jaina asked the Squibs.

They folded their wet ears flat. "Don't worry about us, doll," Scarcheek said. "We'll be right behind you."

"Sorry—didn't mean to insult you," Jaina said. She nodded them toward the Chiss lines. "Why don't you lead the way?"

They fixed their dark eyes on her for a moment, then slung their repeating blasters across their backs and scampered away on all fours. When they came to the end of the limb, they spread their arms and glided nearly twenty meters into the crown of the next tree.

When they stopped to wait for Jaina, she paused to speak over her shoulder to Wuluw.

"What do the nests know about those two?"

"*Urubu bubu rbu,*" Wuluw answered.

"I know they're Squibs!" Jaina said. "What are they doing *here*?"

"*Bubuu urrb.*"

"*Besides* killing Chiss," Jaina said.

"*Ruubu bu,*" Wuluw answered. "*Ub rur uru.*"

"It's *not* enough," Jaina said, exasperated. "People don't cross most of the galaxy just to fight in someone else's war—especially not Squibs."

"*Urub r buur.*"

"What thing sent them?" Jaina demanded.

"*Urub u ur r Buur.*"

"Just *The Thing*?" Jaina asked. "We've never heard of The Thing."

"*Rburubru uburburu buu,*" Wuluw explained. "*Urb u?*"

"Okay."

Jaina clicked her throat in irritation, but knew there was no sense in interrogating Wuluw any further. Insects had unsophisticated motivations, so if a trusted transacting partner offered to send someone to help fight the Chiss, the Killiks were not likely to ask a lot of questions. She warned Wuluw to hold on tight, then began to Force-leap after the Squibs.

They were perhaps halfway to the MetaCannons when

a descending whine broke over the jungle. Jaina looked toward the sound and saw the dark flecks of an AirStraeker squadron approaching through the rain.

"Son-of-a-Sith-harlot!" Jaina cursed.

Zekk and his swarm had visited a battering on the AirStraekers during the initial landing, so she had not expected the Chiss to risk what remained of the wing in the middle of a downpour.

Jaina pointed at the center of the formation, then reached out in the Force and began to shove one of the AirStraekers toward a wingmate. The second evaded, and the first aircraft began to struggle against her grasp. The rest of the squadron opened fire a second later. A wall of smoke erupted in the jungle canopy and began to roll toward her.

"Tell Zekk to get the Wing Swarm down here, *now*!" Jaina said over her shoulder.

"*Bb.*"

"No?" Jaina screeched. "We've got fireflies!"

Wuluw explained that UnuThul's orders had been clear. The airborne swarm was not to attack until the Chiss began to evacuate.

"The Chiss aren't *going* to evacuate if we don't stop those AirStraekers!" Jaina protested. "They won't have any reason to, because all that's going to be left of the Great Swarm is a jungle full of maser-popped bugs!"

"*Rruub uru bubub,*" Wuluw reported. "*Ubbuburu buub.*"

"I don't care if the Kolosoloks *are* attacking," Jaina said. "That's not going to do us much good up *here*, is it?"

"*Urbuubur, buubu ururbu.*"

"Oh." Jaina was quiet for a moment, still struggling to Force-shove the AirStraeker into a wingmate. "When you look at it that way, maybe we are expendable."

A fireball erupted over the jungle canopy as Jaina finally

succeeded. With any luck, one of the AirStraekers she had downed had been the commander, but she knew better than to think that this would throw the squadron into disarray. The Chiss were far too organized to let a little thing like casualties disrupt their plans.

Wuluw began to tremble on Jaina's back. "*Uuuu buuuu . . .*"

"Ah, don't be that way," Jaina said. The squadron was so close now that she could see the droop-winged silhouettes of individual AirStraekers. "Maybe it's not that bad."

"*Bu ubu ru—*"

"Look, you shouldn't believe everything we say," Jaina said.

"*Urbur?*"

"Really," Jaina replied. She fixed her gaze on the AirStraeker squadron, then reached out to Zekk, concentrating hard and trying to make him feel her alarm through the battle-meld. "Humans *do* exaggerate."

Wuluw stopped shaking and remained curiously quiet for a moment, then reported, "*Burubu rurburu.*"

"He is?" Jaina gasped, feigning surprise. "Well, Zekk's StealthX isn't going to give anything away, is it? The Chiss can't even see that."

"*Ur!*" Wuluw clacked her mandibles in delight, then began to rub her antennae over Jaina's face. "*Burrb u!*"

"All right! That's enough!" Jaina laughed. "If we're going to get out of this, I still need to see."

Wuluw folded her antennae back immediately.

As soon as her view was clear again, Jaina realized that she had lost sight of the Squibs. Probably, they had dropped back into the jungle as soon as the AirStraekers appeared, preferring to take their chances with the MetaCannons. There was no time to worry about it. She could see the AirStraekers sweeping back and forth now, spraying a wall of maser beams ahead of them and setting aflame a kilometer-wide swath of jungle canopy.

Jaina reached out and tried her Force shove again, but the Chiss learned quickly. Her target simply peeled away from the squadron and climbed, fighting against her Force grasp until he entered the clouds and she lost sight of him. Thinking that disruption was as good as destruction, she began to Force-shove the rest of the squadron. They all vanished into the clouds—then dropped back into view a few moments later, in perfect formation and closer than before.

"Hurry, Zekk!" Jaina said under her breath.

"Ubr?"

"I said we need to keep pressing the attack," Jaina replied, not wanting to alarm her Wuluw again. "Let's see if we can find a good observation post."

Jaina Force-leapt into an especially tall mogo, then used the Force to make herself light and ascended high into the smallest twigs until she had clear view all the way to the mountains. Through the tangle of barren tree limbs, several MetaCannons were visible on the jungle floor, about half a kilometer ahead. Jaina retrieved her electrobinoculars and saw that the crews were busy changing the configuration of their weapons, replacing the ballistic barrels with fan-tipped beam emitters more suited to close-in fighting.

"Have the Rekkers jump those MetaCannons now!" Jaina instructed Wuluw. "If they don't get there in the next thirty seconds, those maser fans will tear them apart."

"Ru."

Jaina checked on the progress of the AirStraekers and found them so close now that she could see the underwing emitter fans flashing individual maser beams—and she could hear the wood cracking as mogo trees burst into flame. She tried her Force-shove attack again, and again she succeeded only in sending the entire squadron into the clouds for no more than three seconds.

Jaina reached out to Zekk again, urging him to hurry. In response, the meld filled with reassurance.

Jaina returned the electrobinoculars to her eyes and began to scan the rest of the battlefield. Five kilometers beyond the MetaCannons, the Chiss perimeter shield was glowing through the battle smoke, a golden wall that flickered and flashed as the Colony's hordes attacked with catapults, magcannons, and other primitive field pieces. The Chiss were responding with maser cannons mounted on armored personnel carriers, directing most of their fire at a line of about fifty moss-covered hillocks that seemed to be ambling slowly forward.

Kolosolok was attacking.

Jaina watched in awe. More than fifty meters long and ten meters high, the enormous insects resembled freighter-sized spider-roaches, with broad, slightly humped carapaces that covered their entire backs. Their heads were slightly beetle-like, however, with a thicket of stiff black antennae that looked more like horns.

Though the Kolosoloks appeared sluggish and torpid, they were covering so much ground that the throngs of Killik soldiers following in their wake were having trouble keeping pace. Maser cannons were useless against them. The beams ricocheted harmlessly off their thick head chitin, or blasted craters three meters deep into the green, spongy moss that covered their thoraxes. And when a cannon strike did penetrate their chitin, the brief geyser of brown blood seemed to go unnoticed—at least by the victim.

The crackling of the fires in the jungle canopy became a building roar, and Wuluw began to tremble on Jaina's back again.

"*Rurb u brubr ub.*"

"Can't leave yet." Jaina did not lower her electrobinoculars. "Those MetaCannons should be opening up with their maser fans about—"

A tremendous roar erupted down in the jungle, shaking Jaina's tree so hard that she had to Force-stick herself to the limb on which she was sitting.

"—*now!*" she shouted. "Hold on!"

A flurry of loud, long crashes began to sound from the area near the MetaCannons, and ancient, hundred-meter mogo trees began to drop to the jungle floor, their bases heat-blasted from beneath them.

Jaina continued to study the perimeter shield. That was the key, the place where the battle would be won or lost. The Chiss defenders changed tactics, standing atop their personnel carriers to launch gas grenades and vape charges. The gas grenades seemed to sicken the Kolosoloks, causing them to shudder and stumble when one actually struck them. The vape charges opened gaping holes in their chitin, sometimes resulting in a flood of blood and organs large enough to drop them to their bellies. Even then, the huge warriors continued to crawl forward.

The Chiss weapons were simply too light to stop Kolosolok. More than half of the nest reached the perimeter alive and began to butt into the curtain of energy, snapping at the relay pylons with their mandibles, clawing huge pits into the ground, serving as siege towers for the rivers of Killik soldiers who streamed up their backs.

A cold prickle rose in the middle of Jaina's spine. She lowered the electrobinoculars and spun on her heel, staring down into the jungle toward the spot that seemed to be the source of the feeling. She saw nothing but shadow. She started to stretch out in the Force, but then the whine of an approaching AirStraeker became a scream and the heat of the burning canopy began to warm her face, and she knew Zekk had not made it in time.

Jaina spun back toward the sound and found herself looking through the canopy bubble directly into the red eyes of a Chiss pilot. There was no emotion in the woman's face as she twisted her control stick, swinging the maser fans in Jaina's direction.

Wuluw screeched, and Jaina felt her own hand rising as though to ward off a blow. But instead of turning her palm toward the emitter fans, she flicked her fingers sideways, reaching out with the Force to bat the AirStraeker's control stick out of the pilot's hand.

The Chiss's eyes widened in surprise. She lunged after the rebellious stick, and Jaina did not see what the woman did after that. The AirStraeker simply dipped into the jungle canopy and vanished, and an instant later an orange plume of fire boiled up through the trees. Jaina felt a gush of heat in the soles of her feet, and Wuluw shrieked again and clung to her even more tightly.

The rest of the squadron roared past, spraying crimson curtains of death fifty meters to either side, filling the Force with the anguish of thousands of dying Killiks, instantly turning the air so hot that Jaina's throat stuck closed.

Then the prickle between Jaina's shoulder blades became a cold shiver. She leapt without taking the time to look and found herself dropping through the smoke-filled jungle with no idea what lay below—no idea beyond the danger that she sensed. She was in someone's sights, and she knew it.

A flurry of blaster beams began to stitch the air around her, forcing Jaina into an ungainly Force tumble that sent Wuluw flying. She twisted around, reaching out to draw the Killik back to her . . . and saw Wuluw's thorax shatter as a blaster bolt tore through it.

Jaina felt the Killik's death as though it were her own. A terrible fire blossomed inside her and began to crackle on her fingertips, longing for release, for vengeance. A mogo limb appeared out of the smoke below, and she reached for it in the Force, pulling herself over to it and lighting on it as gently as a feather.

A handful of blaster bolts tore into the tree's trunk, then abruptly stopped when her attackers realized she was protected. Jaina snapped her lightsaber off her belt and Force-leapt to the branch above, then crept close to the trunk and peered around it, toward the source of the blaster bolts. As she had suspected, Longnose and Scarcheek were crouching in a trunk notch in the next tree, their large dark eyes scanning the area where she had disappeared.

Jaina scowled. *Hit-Squibs.*

She began to scan the surrounding branches, planning a route that would take her behind the two assassins, unsure in her anger whether she meant to capture them or simply take her vengeance.

That was when Zekk touched Jaina through the meld, wondering if she was hurt, urging her to focus. Vengeance was not important—it was *never* important. The battle was all that mattered now. She had a responsibility to the Colony.

Jaina glanced skyward. The smoke was so thick that she could barely see the green rain clouds above, but they were still there, still pouring water down onto the burning jungle.

Jaina wondered what had taken Zekk so long to reach her, and the image of attacking clawcraft filled her mind. Of course—the Chiss would never attack without top cover. She returned her lightsaber to her utility belt, then used the Force to snap a small branch about thirty meters behind Longnose and Scarcheek.

The two Squibs leapt out of their hiding place and started down the tree headfirst, moving so fast that Jaina wondered if they were falling. Once the pair had vanished from sight, she whispered after them, using the Force to carry her hard-edged voice.

"We'll finish this later," she said. "If you stay alive that long."

A pair of startled screams echoed up through the smoke.

A moment later, the hum of a StealthX's repulsor drives passed by overhead. She looked up to see a black streak flashing after the AirStraekers, its laser cannons ripping the sky open.

The MetaCannons were continuing to chew through the jungle, but now Jaina could hear other sounds, too—the wail of enemy voices, the pinging of shatter gun pellets on metal armor, the chain-thunder of exploding ammunition. The Rekkers had reached the Chiss lines.

Seeing that the lower levels of the jungle—at least in the direction of the fighting—had erupted into a solid wall of flame and smoke, Jaina returned to the canopy. She could see Zekk's StealthX in the distance as it hunted down the AirStraekers, but not much more.

Jaina retrieved her electrobinoculars, then used the Force to clear a hole through the smoke. The MetaCannons had cut a trench three hundred meters into the jungle. A solid wall of smoke and steam was pouring out of this trench, while thousands of Rekkers and millions of Jooj were swarming into it. Clearly, the situation at the MetaCannons was under control.

The battle at the perimeter was going more poorly. The Chiss had massed opposite the Kolosoloks, flinging vape charges and gas grenades at the great insects and firing their charric rifles from the roofs of their personnel carriers. The Killik tide pressed the attack, pouring shatter gun pellets over the shield or simply leaping into the horde of defenders.

The Chiss were too disciplined to panic and too well trained to break. Support units poured in by the squad, by the platoon, by the company. Bodies, both insect and Chiss, began to lie three and four and then ten deep. Personnel carriers exploded or became so riddled with shatter gun fire that the crews could be seen lying in pieces inside. The Kolosoloks were butting the shield, filling the air with golden sprays of discharge sparks, recoiling stunned and unsteady, then hitting it again and again . . . and still the perimeter held.

Then Jaina saw a Chiss vape charge fly astray when the soldier who had thrown it was hit by a line of shatter gun pellets. Responding more by instinct than by plan, she reached out for the vape charge in the Force. Her control at such a distance was almost nonexistent, so she simply nudged it toward the nearest relay pylon and watched in surprise as the distant speck struck the post—then dropped to the ground and simply lay there.

Jaina cursed under her breath, then lowered her electrobinoculars. "The rodder didn't thumb the—"

A brilliant detonation dot appeared through the smoke, and a sudden jolt of surprise shot through the Force. Jaina raised the electrobinoculars again, then cleared a viewing hole through the smoke and was astonished to see that the relay pylon had disappeared after all. Killiks were pouring through the gap in the perimeter shield, enveloping a company of Chiss defenders and fanning outward in an unstoppable tide.

The Colony had broken the enemy line. Now the Chiss would *have* to evacuate.

FIFTEEN

The vastness of the *Megador*'s Hangar 51 rumbled with activity as a small army of technicians, droids, and support personnel rushed to ready the entire wing of Jedi StealthXs for combat. The StealthXs were temperamental craft with specialized equipment, so even simple tasks like fueling and arming required twice as much work and made three times as much noise as the same work on a standard starfighter. And the systems checks caused a cacophony in their own right, as furious bleeps and tweets flew back and forth between the StealthXs' security-conscious astromechs and the *Megador*'s self-important diagnostic droids.

As a result, Jacen could not overhear what Luke and Mara were saying to Saba and to his parents at the *Falcon*'s boarding ramp. But he doubted it was a problem. They were all holding hands and embracing, and he could feel their concern and warm feelings in the Force.

Probably, Luke had just called Jacen over to say goodbye before his parents departed on their mission against the Chiss. Jacen would have liked to save them the trip—to make them see that the Chiss would keep attacking the Killiks whether Luke's crazy scheme worked or not. But he did not dare.

Lowbacca and Tesar's accusations had left him in a tenuous position with Luke and Mara, and Jacen could not risk aggravating the situation by openly opposing Luke's plan. Everything depended on the Chiss winning this war, and he had to remain in a position to make certain they *did*.

Jacen reached the foot of the *Falcon*'s boarding ramp and stopped, waiting his turn to embrace his parents and wish them a good journey. Despite his father's graying hair and the crow's-feet creeping out from the corners of his mother's eyes, he did not think of them as old. They were just experienced—*vastly* experienced.

They had been going on missions like this together for over thirty years—since long before he and Jaina had been born—and Jacen was just beginning to truly understand the sacrifices they had made, the risks they had taken. How often had they faced dilemmas like the one he faced now, had to choose between a terrible evil and an absolute one? How many secrets like Allana had they kept hidden—how many were they *still* hiding?

The time had come for Jacen and his peers to take up the beacon his parents and their friends had been carrying all these years—not to push aside the previous generation, but to carry the burden themselves and allow the old heroes a well-deserved rest. He knew he and his fellows were ready; a group of Jedi had not been as carefully selected and pre-pared since the days of the Old Republic. But when Jacen looked at his parents and recalled how they had changed the galaxy, he found himself wondering whether he and his generation were *worthy*.

Sometimes, given their secure childhoods and formal training, he even wondered whether the new Jedi were too soft. Compared with the filthy, overcrowded freighter that his father had called home as a boy, or the dusty Tatooine moisture farm that had shaped his uncle Luke's early life, the Jedi academy on Yavin 4 had been luxurious. Even his mother, raised in the Royal Palace of Alderaan, had understood true danger as a child, with the deadly gaze of Palpatine always turned her family's way.

"Jacen?"

Jacen felt his father's eyes on him and realized everyone was looking in his direction.

"You here?" Han asked. "You're not having another of your visions, are you?"

"No, just . . ." He was surprised to find a lump in his throat. ". . . just thinking."

"Well, stop it," Han ordered. "You're scaring me."

Jacen forced a smile. "Sorry. I wouldn't want that." He turned to his mother. "You can't talk him out of this?"

Leia must have sensed something despite his defenses, because she ignored the joke and said, "Is there a reason I should?"

Jacen rolled his eyes, but silently cursed his mother's perceptiveness. "It was a joke, Mom." He spread his arms and wrapped her in a tight hug so she would not be able to examine his face too closely. "I just came to wish you a safe trip."

He released her and turned to embrace his father. "Good . . ." Had Jacen realized he was going to have such a hard time concealing his emotions, he would have found an excuse to be busy doing something else when his parents departed. ". . . bye, Dad."

"Take it easy, kid. We're coming back." Han suddenly stiffened, then pulled back and eyed Jacen nervously. "Aren't we? You haven't seen something—"

"You're coming back, Dad—I'm certain of it," Jacen said. "Just be careful, okay? Raynar isn't going to believe you—and it won't help that you're telling the truth."

"Is *that* what you're worried about?" Han sounded relieved. "Look, kid, we've been over this about a—"

"We'll be fine, Jacen," Leia interrupted, finally warming to him and squeezing his hand. "This is the only way to make the Chiss understand how difficult it would be to win a war against the Killiks."

Saba stepped up behind Leia, looming over her the way Chewbacca used to loom over Han. "Everything will be fine, Jacen. Your mother is a powerful Jedi—az strong in her way as you are in yourz."

Jacen nodded. "I know that." He leaned down and kissed Leia on the cheek. "May the Force be with you, Mom."

"And with you, too, Jacen," Leia said. "*We're* not the ones who'll be attacking Gorog's nest ship."

Han's face suddenly fell. "*That's* not what you're worried about—is it?" he asked. "Did you see—"

"I didn't see *anything,* Dad," Jacen said. "Really." He shooed his father up the ramp. "Go on. I'll meet you when this is over."

Han studied him for a moment, then finally nodded. "I'll hold you to that, kid. Don't let me down."

He took Leia's hand and started up the ramp.

Saba remained behind, one slit-pupiled eye fixed on Jacen, and began to siss in amusement. "You are alwayz full of surprisez, Jacen Solo." She started up the ramp. "Alwayz so full of surprisez."

Jacen had to fight down a moment of panic. He knew that Ben found the Barabel Master frightening, and he was beginning to understand why—she was just so hard to *read.*

Before starting up the ramp after Saba and the others, C-3PO paused in front of Jacen and tapped him lightly on the shoulder. "Pardon me, Master Jacen. But did whatever you saw have anything to do with me?"

Before Jacen could answer, Han's voice sounded from the top of the boarding ramp. "Threepio! If you're still on that ramp in three seconds, you'll be riding to Tenupe cargo-clamped to the hull!"

"Threats are hardly necessary, Captain Solo!" C-3PO clumped up the ramp after Saba and the others, his golden hands paddling the air. "I'm coming, I'm coming!"

Jacen smiled and waved a last farewell to his parents, then retreated to safe distance and watched with Luke and Mara as the boarding ramp retracted and the *Falcon* slipped out of the hangar. The ship hung below the *Megador* for a moment, a mere teardrop of white durasteel framed by the hangar's huge mouth, then spun toward the Star Destroyer's stern and streaked off deeper into the Unknown Regions.

Luke's hand suddenly clasped Jacen by the shoulder, and Jacen barely stopped himself from cringing. He could not afford to show any hint of surprise . . . or guilt.

"I'll bet it seems like they've been doing that your whole life, doesn't it?" Luke asked fondly.

"It does," Jacen said, nodding. "And I couldn't be prouder."

"No?" Mara slipped a hand through his other arm. "Well, neither could they."

"Uh, thanks." Jacen felt the lump forming in his throat again and swallowed it into submission. "Maybe I ought to get back to my fighter. Neufie has been giving those diagnostic droids—"

"In a minute," Luke said. "First, I'd like you to come with us."

"Sure." Jacen's heart began to pound so hard he had to use a Jedi calming exercise to quiet it. "Where?"

"Ghent is ready to show us the rest of Artoo's secret files," Mara said. "But he still hasn't finished duplicating the omnigate, so this may be the only time anyone gets to see the holos of your grandparents. Luke and I thought you'd like to be there."

"You did?" Jacen said, almost allowing his relief to show. "I mean, yes—of course!"

"It's okay—I'm nervous, too." Luke laughed uneasily, then added, "Scared, even."

"Well, *I'm* not."

Mara's tone was a little too light. The Skywalkers joked openly about Alema Rar's insinuation that Mara might have played a role in the death of Padmé Amidala, but Jacen knew how hurt his aunt had been by the whole incident.

The question had to be answered—and it had to be answered before the Jedi attacked the Gorog nest ship. Luke could not face Lomi Plo otherwise. She would find any trace of doubt—especially *that* doubt—and use it to veil herself completely.

That was one of the reasons Jacen believed *he* ought to be the one to confront Lomi Plo. He had no doubts—of any kind. Vergere had scorched them out of him in a crucible of pain.

They found Ghent in a small briefing salon that overlooked Hangar 51, sitting on the floor beside R2-D2, surrounded by the usual litter of tools, circuits, and snack wrappers. The lanky slicer was peering through an access panel with his magnispecs flipped down, manipulating a micrograbber in each hand and muttering to himself in a high-pitched, staccato manner that sounded alarmingly like machine code. Afraid to cause a mishap by startling him, they stopped just inside the door and waited for him to remove his hands from inside the droid's casing.

"What are you standing there for?" Ghent asked without looking away from his work. "You won't see anything from the door."

"Sorry." Luke led the way forward. "Are you ready?"

"Don't I look ready?" Ghent asked. "All I have to do is snap the omnigate back in place."

"Oh," Luke said. "When I saw all the circuits—"

"Standard maintenance," Ghent interrupted. "No wonder this droid acts up. Some of those circuits haven't been cleaned in twenty standard years. They had carbon molecules stacked a hundred moles high."

As they drew closer, Jacen realized the slicer must have been working on R2-D2 for a couple of days straight—at least it smelled that way. In any case, Ghent had clearly not found time for a decent sanisteam lately. They stopped several paces away and watched as he snapped a circuit board back in place.

"All set." He rocked back on his heels, then looked up and said, "I don't think you should do this, you know."

"You told us already," Mara said.

Ghent's brow rose. "I did?"

"Several times," Luke said.

"Oh." Ghent ran a hand over his tattooed head, then said, "It's just that I've almost got the omnigate figured out. Another three weeks—no more than six, really—and I'd have it for sure. Then you could look at these files anytime you liked."

"We don't have six weeks." Luke checked his chrono. "We're due to launch in six *hours*."

Ghent's eyes widened. "That soon? I thought we had three days!"

"It *has* been three days," Mara said patiently.

Ghent looked around him in a daze, then said, "I guess he was in worse shape than I thought."

"Ghent, we really need to see that holo now," Mara pressed gently. "A lot depends on it."

"Yeah, I know," Ghent said. "But I don't think you understand. That's the Intellex Four designer's original back door. If we fry it before we've copied it, we're destroying a whole sub-era of computer history."

"Ghent, it's really important," Luke said.

The slicer sighed, then flipped R2-D2's primary circuit breaker without saying anything more.

The droid came to life with a startled bleep, then swiveled his dome around, carefully studying the stacks of tools and discarded circuit boards around him. After a moment, he began to roll back and forth on his treads, extending various utility arms and whistling in approval.

Then R2-D2's photoreceptor swung past Ghent's face. He gave a startled buzz, then looked at Luke and began to back away.

"Artoo, stop it!" Luke ordered. "Come back here. We need to see what happened to my mother after my father came back from Mustafar."

R2-D2 tweeted an explanation in machine code. Jacen was not really surprised when Ghent translated it.

"He says Anakin Skywalker didn't come back."

"He didn't?" Luke frowned. "What happened?"

R2-D2 remained silent for a moment, then abruptly blurted out an explanation.

"Padmé went to see your father," Ghent reported.

"Then show us *that*," Luke said to R2-D2. "And no tricks. I need to see this."

R2-D2 whistled doubtfully.

"He says—"

"Artoo, just do it," Luke interrupted. "We're going into combat soon, and you need time to calibrate yourself with the StealthX."

The droid trilled an excited question.

"*If* Ghent thinks you're up to it," Luke said. "And *if* you don't keep stalling."

R2-D2 tipped forward and activated his holoprojector. The image of a green starfighter appeared on a landing platform on some distant world that could not be identified from the image. A young man in a dark robe appeared, running into the image from the direction of the starfighter. As he drew closer, it grew apparent that he was Anakin Skywalker. He appeared tired and grimy, as though he had just come from battle. That fit what he had told Padmé in the last holo that Jacen and the Skywalkers had seen together: that he was going to Mustafar to end the war.

"Padmé, I saw your ship," Anakin said.

Padmé appeared, entering the image from the opposite direction, and they embraced.

"Anakin!" Her back was to the holocam, but it was clear that she was trembling.

"It's all right, you're safe now." Anakin looked down into her eyes. "What are you doing out here?"

"I was so worried about you!" Padmé's voice was somewhat muffled, since she was still facing away from the holocam. "Obi-Wan told me terrible things."

Anakin's face clouded with anger. "Obi-Wan was with you?"

"He said you've turned to the dark side," Padmé continued, avoiding a direct answer. "That you killed younglings."

"Obi-Wan is trying to turn you against me," Anakin said darkly.

Padmé shook her head. "He cares about us."

"Us?"

"He knows." Padmé paused a moment, then said, "He wants to help you."

"And you." Anakin's voice was full of jealousy now. "Don't lie to me, Padmé. I have become more powerful than any Jedi dreamed of, and I've done it for you . . . to protect you."

"I don't want your power." Padmé pulled away from him. "I don't want your protection."

Anakin drew her back to him. "Is Obi-Wan going to protect you?" he demanded. "He can't . . . he can't help you. He's not strong enough."

Padmé's head fell, and she was silent for a long time.

Perhaps R2-D2 had attuned his communications routines to Luke's moods over the years, because he seemed to sense the dread in Luke's presence as clearly as Jacen did. The droid took advantage of the long silence to whistle a long, worried-sounding question.

"He's afraid this is going to overload your circuits," Ghent reported. "And I *know* we're stressing his. Do you hear that warble in his interrogative pitch?"

"Keep going." Luke's tone grew a little softer. "It's all right, Artoo. I'm fine."

Jacen nodded his approval. There was an irrational and dangerous edge in Anakin's voice, and Jacen understood why R2-D2 had been so reluctant to show these holos to Luke. But pain was only dangerous when it was feared— that had been one of Vergere's first lessons. Luke *needed* to see the end of the holo. He needed to embrace the pain.

After a moment, Padme raised her head again in the holo.

"Anakin, all I want is your love."

"Love won't save you," Anakin snarled. *"Only my new powers can do that."*

"At what cost?" Padmé demanded. *"You're a good person. Don't do this."*

"I won't lose you the way I lost my mother." Anakin's face belonged to someone else now, someone angry and frightened and selfish.

Padmé did not seem to see the change—or, if she did, she remained determined to bring the other Anakin back again. She reached for him.

"Come away with me," she said. *"Help me raise our child. Leave everything else behind while we still can."*

Anakin shook his head. "Don't you see? We don't have to run away anymore. I have brought peace to the Republic. I am more powerful than the Chancellor. I can overthrow him, and together you and I can rule the galaxy . . . make things the way we want them to be."

"*I don't believe what I'm hearing!*" *Padmé backed away, stumbling as though she had been struck.*

Luke sighed audibly, clearly dismayed at the arrogance that had led his father down the dark path of the oppressor. But Jacen found himself responding to his grandfather far more sympathetically, almost with admiration. Anakin Skywalker had understood his own strength, and—at one time, at least—he had tried to use that strength to bring peace. Vergere would have approved. Power unused was power wasted, and whatever had happened to him later, Anakin Skywalker had at least attempted to use *his* for a good end.

For a moment, R2-D2's hologram began to flitter, and everyone held their breath. Then the droid gave a click and a whir, and the scene continued.

Padmé had stopped retreating from Anakin.

"*Obi-Wan was right,*" *she said.* "*You've changed.*"

"*I don't want to hear any more about Obi-Wan!*" *Anakin started after her.* "*The Jedi turned against me. The Republic turned against me. Don't you turn against me.*"

"*I don't know you anymore,*" *Padmé said.* "*Anakin, you're breaking my heart. I'll never stop loving you, but you're going down a path I can't follow.*"

Anakin's eyes narrowed. "*Because of Obi-Wan?*"

"*Because of what you've done! What you plan to do!*" *Padmé's voice grew commanding.* "*Stop now.*" *She was silent for a moment, then her tone softened.* "*Come back. I love you.*"

Anakin's gaze shifted, and he seemed to be looking over Padmé's shoulder toward the cam. "*Liar!*"

Padmé spun around, and for the first time it grew clear just how advanced her pregnancy was. Her jaw fell in dismay. "*No!*"

"*You're with* him!" *Anakin's gaze had returned to Padmé.* "*You've betrayed me!*"

"No, Anakin." Padmé shook her head and started toward him again. *"I swear . . . I—"*

Anakin extended his arm, his hand shaped into an arc. Padmé cried out, then grabbed her throat and began to make terrible gurgling sounds.

Luke cried out in disbelief, and the Force grew heavy with grief and outrage. Even Jacen—whose time among the Yuuzhan Vong had taught him never to be surprised by the brutality one being could inflict on another—felt his stomach turn at the sight of his grandfather using the Force to choke the woman he supposedly loved.

An ominous but barely audible whine arose somewhere inside R2-D2. The holo began to flicker again, and a familiar voice spoke from outside the holo frame.

"Let her go, Anakin."

Arm still extended—and Padmé still choking—Anakin turned to sneer at the speaker. *"What have you and she been up to?"*

Obi-Wan Kenobi stepped into view, wearing the sand-colored robes of a Jedi. Though his back was to the camera, his shape and bearded profile were clearly recognizable.

"Let . . . her . . . go!"

Anakin whipped his arm to one side, and Padmé flew out of the holo.

Anakin started forward to meet Obi-Wan, saying, *"You turned her—"*

A sharp pop sounded from R2-D2's interior, and the holo dissolved into static.

Ghent flipped his magnispecs down, then peered through R2-D2's access panel and cried out as though a blaster bolt had pierced his heart. He lowered his micrograbbers through the opening and clicked something, then retrieved what appeared to the naked eye to be a smoking dust speck.

"I knew this would happen!" the slicer cried. "It's an omni*ash* now!"

No one answered. Luke was stiff and ashen, fighting back tears. Mara was staring at the spot where Padmé's limp form had vanished from the holo. Jacen was trying to decide where his grandfather had gone wrong, trying to puzzle out what flaw had made him a slave to his temper. Even R2-D2 remained silent, continuing to project a column of holostatic onto the floor.

After a moment, Ghent seemed to realize that the loss of the omnigate was not the most serious one of the day. He laid his hand on Luke's shoulder and gave it a comforting squeeze.

"Well, at least we know it wasn't *Mara* who killed your mother."

"Ghent!" Mara's eyes looked ready to loose a flight of blaster bolts.

"What's wrong?" Ghent seemed genuinely confused. "Isn't that what we were trying to find out?"

"Drop it," Mara ordered.

Tears were escaping down Luke's cheeks now, and Jacen could sense him struggling with the anger he felt toward his father. It left a fiery, bitter taste in the Force, all the more powerful because of the forgiveness that Luke had already granted Anakin Skywalker.

Ghent remained entirely unaware of all this history, of course. "But now we know," he insisted. "It wasn't Mara!"

Jacen sighed. "Ghent, we really *don't* know that," he explained. "We only saw Anakin throw Padmé. We don't know that my grandmother actually died."

R2-D2 trilled a series of sad notes.

"You see?" Ghent asked, as though everyone else could understand what the droid was saying, too. "Do you want to see it?"

"See what?" Mara demanded.

"Her death," Ghent replied. "This is what Artoo has been trying to protect Luke from, but now that the secret is out—"

"No—I've seen everything I need to." Luke rose and wiped his face dry, then added, "We have a battle to prepare for."

Jacen did not like the hollowness in his uncle's voice. Luke was retreating from his pain, avoiding that last file because he knew how devastating it would be to watch his mother die. And pain you feared was pain that could be used to control you. Luke was not ready to face Lomi Plo, would not be ready until he accepted the tragedy that had befallen his parents—until he *embraced* it.

"Are you sure?" Jacen asked. "It couldn't take long, and who knows when Artoo is going to be this cooperative—"

"I'm sure!" Luke snapped. "Don't you have some flight checks you should be doing?"

Mara nodded toward the door, but Jacen remained where he was. "This is more important. We need to talk about it."

Luke sighed, then went over to a briefing chair and sat down. "Okay, Jacen. Let's hear it."

Mara cringed, then closed her eyes and touched Jacen in the Force, urging him not to press the matter.

Jacen took a deep breath, then said, "I'm not sure you're ready to win this fight, Uncle Luke."

"That's not your decision to make, Jacen." Luke's tone was stern. "But go ahead."

Jacen did not hesitate. "You haven't committed yourself yet," he said. "You're afraid to look at the last file—"

"I don't *need* to look at it," Luke said. "I know what happened. I knew the instant that I saw my . . . that we saw *Darth Vader* raise his hand to my mother."

"You're afraid of the pain," Jacen accused.

"Pain isn't always good, Jacen," Mara said. "Sometimes it's just distracting."

"And I *don't* need to be distracted right now." Luke pointedly started to rise. "What I need is to prepare myself for combat . . . and so do you, Jacen."

"It's not only the file," Jacen pressed. He was certain now that *he* should be the one to face Lomi Plo; that he was the only one who had no doubts about what they must do. "You're not going to kill Raynar, either."

"I haven't decided anything yet," Luke said.

"You may think you haven't decided," Jacen said. "But you're not going to—and it's a mistake."

Luke cocked his brow. "I see." He fell silent for a moment, then returned to his chair. "I don't know what you've foreseen, Jacen, but I can promise you this—regardless of Raynar's fate, the Colony will be destroyed. The war in your vision won't come to pass."

"I'm sorry, Uncle Luke, but promises aren't good enough," Jacen said. He would not trust Allana's life to good intentions. "We must be *sure* the Colony dies—and that means we must act."

Mara came and sat beside Luke in front of Jacen, then asked, "So you're going to kill a man—someone who was once your friend—just to be certain?"

"I won't enjoy it," Jacen said. "But it's necessary."

"I know you think so, Jacen," Luke said. "But I'm not convinced. Not yet."

"We can't afford to doubt ourselves," Jacen insisted. "We must decide . . . and act."

Luke sighed in exasperation. "Vergere again." He shook his head. "Look, I know her instruction saved your life—"

"And helped us win the war with the Yuuzhan Vong," Jacen pointed out.

"And helped win the war against the Yuuzhan Vong," Luke admitted patiently. "But I'm not sure we should embrace her ideas as the core of our Jedi philosophy—in fact, I'm sure we *shouldn't*."

"Why not?" Jacen demanded.

"Because we're no longer at war with the Yuuzhan Vong, for one thing," Mara said. She shook her head, then pointed at R2-D2's holoprojector. "Didn't you learn anything from what you just saw?"

Jacen scowled, genuinely puzzled. "I don't know what you mean."

Luke's voice grew sharp. "There's more to being a Jedi than being effective, Jacen." He looked away, then continued in a gentler tone. "Since the war ended, I've been growing more and more troubled by Vergere's teachings, and I think I finally understand why."

Jacen lifted his brow. "Why?"

"Because their ruthlessness reminds me so much of what my father believed." Luke turned and looked into Jacen's eyes. "Of what the Emperor *taught* him to believe."

Jacen was astounded. "You can't be serious!"

"I'm not saying Vergere's teachings are immoral," Luke replied. "In fact, they don't concern themselves with morality at all. They provide no guidance."

"Exactly!" Jacen said. "They're about ridding ourselves of illusions, about seeing that nothing is ever truly dark or light, completely good or evil."

"So a Jedi is free to take any action necessary to achieve his goal?" Luke asked. "His only duty is to be effective?"

"His first duty is to *choose*," Jacen said. "Everything follows from that."

Mara and Luke looked at each other, and something passed between them that Jacen barely perceived.

Finally, Luke said, "But Jacen, that isn't what a Jedi *is*."

Jacen frowned. He could not understand what his uncle was trying to tell him, except that it had to do with principles and responsibilities—with those ancient shackles that

Vergere had taught him to open. Could Luke really be saying that the Jedi should don them again; that they should let the opinions of others dictate their actions?

"Very well," Jacen said cautiously. "What *is* a Jedi?"

Luke smiled. "I suggest you spend some time meditating on that," he said. "In the meantime, just remember that we *aren't* bounty hunters, okay?"

Jacen nodded. "Yes, Master." He understood that he was being told in no uncertain terms not to assassinate Raynar—at least not without Luke's permission. "I understand, but I sense that you still have doubts about the morality of your plan. Perhaps *I* should be the one to confront Lomi Plo."

Luke's face showed his astonishment. "Is *that* what this was about?"

"I might be the better choice," Jacen said. "*I* don't have any doubts about this plan—or anything else, for that matter."

Luke stood, a smile of relief spreading across his face, and clapped Jacen on the shoulder.

"Jacen, you *are* a good Jedi," he said. "Thank you."

"Uh, you're welcome." Now Jacen was really confused. "Does that mean you agree with me?"

"Not at all—you're mistaking fairness for doubt," Luke said. He motioned R2-D2 to follow, then pulled Jacen toward the door. "I *am* going to kill Lomi Plo."

SIXTEEN

The Chiss survivors had withdrawn to a chain of islands in the great river, a defensible position but not an impregnable one. For days, the defoliated jungle had been reverberating with the crashing of the Colony's field artillery. The trebuchets were flinging rough-edged boulders, the catapults hurling waxes filled with hanpat incendiary. Every now and then, the Killiks even sealed a few thousand of their smaller fellows into a flight of wax balls and cast *them* onto one of the islands.

Nothing shook the Chiss. They remained hunkered down behind their breastworks, smothering the flames, tending to the wounded, picking off any Killik foolish enough to show itself outside the soilworks that shielded the field artillery. The Chiss still numbered nearly a hundred thousand, more than enough to prevent an assault across the river's swift current. After so many weeks of constant, raging battle, even the Colony was beginning to run low on soldiers, and Jaina knew that any attempt to seize the islands would end in the destruction of her army.

But a Chiss relief force might be arriving at any time, and UnuThul was growing impatient. He remained out of mind-touch with the ground forces and did not understand what was preventing the final push. His Will had become a constant dark pressure inside Jaina's breast, urging her to press the attack and force the enemy's hand. Soon, she feared, he would grow weary of waiting for her plan to work and simply exert his Will over the Killiks. She needed to find a way to dislodge the Chiss *now*.

Jaina slipped a few meters down the muddy embankment, then spun around so she was facing the trebuchet it protected. Several dozen meter-tall Sotatos Killiks were crewing the piece, working the windlass with such coordination that the firing arm looked as though it were being retracted by a power winch. The weapon was being supplied with boulders by a long line of Mollom, who were quarrying the stones from a rare outcropping of stone, then carrying them two kilometers and loading them directly into the trebuchets. Despite being from two different nests, the two groups were so well coordinated that the trebuchet never sat idle, and no Mollom ever had to stand waiting to load a boulder.

Jaina's fragile Wuluw communications assistant joined her when she reached the bottom of the embankment. *"Rubbur bu uubu,"* she reported. *"Urr buur rrububu."*

"Tell Rekker to *unmass*," Jaina ordered. "Even if they can jump over to the islands, now is no time for a leap-charge. We can't get anyone there to support and exploit."

"Bur u buuur rrub," Wuluw objected.

"I *am* doing something!" Jaina snapped. "These aren't Imperials we're fighting, they're Chiss! They're not going to fall apart just because we throw a few million bugs at them!"

A sudden silence fell over the jungle, and Jaina realized that every Killik in sight had turned to stare at her.

"Blast it!" Jaina shook her head at the temperamental insect ego. "Don't be so touchy—we're fighting a war!"

She went into the jungle behind the trebuchet, then slid down a muddy bank into a shallow stream beside the emplacement. Wuluw followed behind her, landing on all six limbs and never breaking the surface of the water.

"Ruburu ubu?"

Jaina started downstream, circling back around the trebuchet toward the Chiss islands. "Doing something."

An approving drone arose in the jungle, and Wuluw skated along on the surface of the stream beside her.

"Ubu?"

"Don't know yet," Jaina answered. "But it'll be good."

As Jaina waded through the water, she was careful to keep her eyes level with the terrain next to the stream, her gaze always turned in the direction of the islands. The jungle floor was piled high with shriveled foliage and splintered mogo wood. Thousands of dead Killiks—perhaps tens of thousands—lay in the detritus, sometimes in twisted pieces and sometimes with their thin limbs reaching toward the sky, always stinking in the jungle heat, always with their insides spilling out through a huge burn hole in their body chitin.

Finally, only a narrow spit of jungle floor separated Jaina from the great river. The Chiss islands lay on the other side of a fast-moving channel, beneath the still-constant hail of boulders and burnballs from the clacking catapults and booming trebuchets of the Killiks. At this distance, Jaina could barely make out the barricade of felled trees that the enemy had erected at the edge of the river. The island was too flat and smoke-swaddled to see the terrain beyond the breastworks, but Jaina knew the Chiss well enough to be certain that there would be a second and a third line of defense beyond the first—probably even a fourth.

Still being careful not to show her head above the streambank, Jaina brought the electrobinoculars to her eyes and found a mass of red eyes and blue faces peering out from between the mogo logs, scanning her side of the river for any hint of Killik activity. Here and there protruded the long barrel of a sniper rifle, surmounted by the dark rod of a sighting sensor. She continued to study the breastworks, wondering if Jag was out there somewhere, reaching out to see if she could sense his presence. She was not sure why she cared.

Wherever he was, Jagged Fel certainly hated Jaina for taking the Colony's side in this war—and for starting it in the first place. And truthfully, she could hardly blame him. Had he led a team of Chiss commandos against the Galactic Alliance, she would undoubtedly have hated *him*. That's how humans—and Chiss—were. Only Killiks fought without hate.

Jaina continued to study the Chiss defenses. She was not sure what she hoped to find—maybe someplace where the defensive lines did not have a clear view of the river channel, perhaps a cluster of mogo trunks that could be brought down atop the heads of the defenders. Twice, she thought she spotted weaknesses where the Chiss did not have clear fields of fire. They turned out to be traps, one designed to channel the attackers into a large expanse of quicksand, the other protected by the few pieces of field artillery that the Chiss had managed to salvage during their retreat.

Jaina's gaze reached the end of the first island. She turned her attention to the near riverbank, this time looking for a natural place to launch a crossing—then felt somebody looking back at her.

"Cover!" Jaina warned.

She pulled the electrobinoculars away from her face and dropped down behind the streambank—then saw a pair of bright flashes explode into the slope in front of her. The attack was coming from *behind* her.

Jaina dropped underwater. Her ears filled with a fiery gurgling as blaster flashes lit the muddy stream around her, instantly superheating liters of water and sending it skyward in a thin cloud of steam. She pulled herself along the silty creek bed, moving upstream and reaching out in the Force in the direction of the attack.

She felt two presences, both very familiar. *Squibs.*

Blast it! Couldn't those two wait until *after* the war to try killing her?

When Jaina judged she had traveled far enough upstream to be out of the Chiss line of fire, she yanked the lightsaber off her utility belt and rose out of the water. The air around her immediately erupted into a storm of flashing and zinging, but she had already activated her lightsaber and brought it up to block. She batted half a dozen bolts aside, several times narrowly escaping injury when her blade had to be in two places at the same time.

After a couple of moments of frantic parrying, Jaina finally sorted out the source of the attacks and realized the Squibs had her in a crossfire. She began to redirect their bolts toward each other, forcing them to worry about their own cover as well as attacking her, and it was not long before she found the chance to extend a hand and Force-jerk one of her attackers out of his tree.

The Squib's alarmed squeal was followed by a soft thud—then by a shrieking storm of maser beams as the Chiss sharpshooters reacted to the disturbance in the manner of most soldiers under stress: by shooting at it. Fortunately for the Squib, their angle was poor and he was far enough from the river to be well protected by the trees, but the attacks did at least force him to keep his head down.

Jaina used the Force to wrench his blaster away, then flung it into the jungle and turned her attention to the second Squib. She batted five or six blaster bolts straight back into the tree root behind which he was hiding, and when a big chunk of wood flew skyward, he finally stopped firing. Then she Force-jerked him out of his cover and pulled him straight to her—not minding that the Chiss sharpshooters did their best to pick him off as he passed between trees.

As the Squib approached—it was Longnose—he tossed his repeating blaster aside and reached for a thermal detonator hanging from his utility harness. Jaina flicked her fingers, and the silver orb sailed away before he had a chance to arm it.

Longnose's shiny eyes widened in surprise, then grew squinty and hard. "It don't matter what you do to me, girlie. You're—"

"If you had any brains, you'd watch who you called girlie," Jaina said. She dumped the Squib into the muddy water, then held the tip of her lightsaber so close to his nose that it melted his whiskers off. "Don't move—don't even breathe."

Longnose's eyes crossed as he focused on the tip of Jaina's blade, and she slowly let him sink.

"C-c-can I t-t-tread water?"

"If you can do it with your hands over your head," Jaina said.

Longnose's hands went over his head, then he sank so far into the stream that he had to tip his head back to keep his chin above water. Satisfied, Jaina turned her attention back to Scarcheek and was relieved to find him firmly in the grasp of a handful of Mollom, threatening and flailing as he tried to free himself.

Jaina turned to tell Wuluw to have the Squib brought over—and found the little Killik floating a few meters downstream, bobbing lifelessly in a slick of gore and shattered chitin.

Longnose tipped his head. "Sorry."

Jaina eyed the Squib sternly. "Jedi can sense when you're lying, you know."

Longnose's ears went flat. "Hey, it's not our fault!" he protested. "We were aiming for *you*."

Jaina risked sticking her head above the streambank long enough to call the Mollom over with the second Squib. As the Killiks dashed from tree to tree, dodging maser beams, she pushed Longnose up onto the bank. She unbuckled his utility harness and tossed it—and the holdout blaster and vibroknives hidden on the underside—back into the water.

"Hey!" he demanded. "Those are my clothes!"

"It's warm," Jaina retorted. "We're on a jungle planet."

She studied Longnose for a minute, touching him through the Force to make him uneasy, then deactivated her lightsaber and leaned in close.

"Why are you trying to kill me?" she demanded.

"I'm not talking," Longnose retorted.

"Are you sure about that?" Jaina asked. She used the Force to press him into the muddy bank. "Because you and your friend get to live if you answer my questions."

"You're bluffing," Longnose said. "You can't kill us in cold blood. You're a Jedi!"

"You're right—but there's no time to watch you, either." Jaina cast a meaningful glance toward the approaching Killiks. "So your fate will rest in Mollom's hands. What do you want me to tell them?"

Longnose's lip curled into a sneer. "You wouldn't dare. I know about the dark side. If you . . ."

Jaina made a pinching motion with her fingers. Longnose's mouth continued to work, but his voice fell silent.

"If you're not going to say anything useful, there's no use in your talking."

Jaina turned her attention to Scarcheek, whom the Mollom were bringing down into the stream. The Killiks had been none too gentle with their prisoner, tearing off an ear and leaving him half bald. They deposited him in the mud next to Longnose, then took up encircling positions and stood there clacking their huge mandibles.

Jaina snatched Scarcheek's utility belt off him and tossed it into the water with Longnose's. "How about you?" she asked. "Feel like answering a few questions?"

"No."

"Too bad," Jaina said. "Because if you do, you leave here alive. Otherwise, I'll let Mollom deal with you."

Scarcheek glanced at his Killik tormenters and could not suppress a little shudder. Then he shrugged and tried to appear unintimidated. "Depends on the questions, I guess."

"Fair enough," Jaina said. "Why are you trying to kill me?"

"Dumb question," Scarcheek retorted. " 'Cause we took a contract. What do you think?"

Longnose rolled his eyes and began to shake his head.

"Don't listen to your buddy," Jaina said. "He's got a death wish."

Scarcheek nodded. "Goes with the business."

"Who put out the contract?" Jaina asked.

Longnose continued to shake his head, now drawing his finger across his throat.

"Why not?" Scarcheek demanded of her. "Nobody said nothing about keeping quiet. They just want her dead."

"You see?" Jaina gave them both a little Force-nudge, then locked eyes with Scarcheek. "Who wants us dead?"

"The Directors," Scarcheek said. "And it's just you. They said to leave your boyfriend out of it, unless he got in the way."

"Zekk isn't my boyfriend," Jaina said. "And you haven't answered my question—not really. Who are the Directors?"

Longnose rolled his eyes again and tried to speak, but could only choke.

"Ready to say something useful?" Jaina asked. When he nodded, she released his vocal cords. "Let's hear it."

"It'll go bad if you make them send someone else," Longnose said. "You'd be better off just letting us do you now."

"Yeah," Scarcheek agreed. "We'll make it real painless."

"I'll take my chances with the next crew," Jaina said. "I'm sure they wouldn't be any better than you."

Longnose perked his ears in pride. "You're a smart girl, Jedi. We like that in a target."

"Then how about telling me who these Directors are?" Jaina made a pinching motion with her thumb and forefinger. "Or is your partner the only one getting out of this alive?"

"I guess there's no harm—it's not like you're going to live long enough to go after *them*," Longnose said. "The Directors are the head of the family—our great-great-great-grandparents."

"Grees, Sligh, and Emala," Scarcheek finished. "Your parents had some dealings with them on Tatooine."

Jaina nodded. "I've heard about that. Why do they want me dead?"

Longnose shrugged. "Didn't say."

"You owe them money?" Scarcheek asked.

Jaina shook her head.

"Your parents owe them money?" Longnose asked.

"I doubt it," Jaina said.

The two Squibs glanced at each other, then Longnose nodded. "Well, you're costing them money somehow. That's the only reason the Directors *ever* put out a contract."

"Or maybe your parents are," Scarcheek added. "If they ignored a warning."

Longnose nodded enthusiastically. "That's usually what it is when they send us after the kids."

"Dad never heard a warning he took seriously, so that part makes sense." Jaina was more mystified than ever. "But I still don't know how my parents could be mixed up with your, uh, the Directors. What business are they in?"

"What business *aren't* they in?" Longnose snorted.

"But right now it's a lot of war stuff," Scarcheek said. "Double-billing supplies, gouging for fuel deliveries, vouchering meals that were never served—"

"You know: the usual stuff," Longnose continued. "War is always good for a few billion credits in off-the-book profit."

"Okay—now it makes sense," Jaina said.

If she knew her parents—and her uncle Luke and the rest of the Jedi—they would be working to end this war as quickly as possible. And if their efforts had upset these "Directors" enough to put a hit on a Jedi, then whatever they were doing was effective. Maybe her parents actually had a chance of stopping the war.

Jaina shifted her gaze to the hit-Squibs' Mollom guards. "Get these two out of here. Turn them loose."

"*Burrub?*" boomed several of the Mollom together.

"A deal's a deal," Jaina said. She shifted her gaze to the Squibs. "But your contract is finished, you understand? If we see you again—anywhere—you're speeder-kill. Okay?"

The Squibs' muzzles fell open in surprise, and they both nodded enthusiastically.

"Yeah, sure."

"Whatever you say, doll."

"And *don't* call me doll," Jaina hissed. She motioned to the Mollom to take the Squibs away. "Tell Wuluw I need a new—"

"*Bu.*"

Jaina turned around to see a new Wuluw communications assistant standing on the water behind her. She smiled at the little Killik.

"What took you so long?"

Wuluw flattened her antennae in apology. "*Urru bu, urbru, uu bu ru—*"

"It was a *joke,*" Jaina said. "Don't any of your nest's Joiners have a sense of humor?"

"*U,*" Wuluw answered. "*Bu urb r urubu bubu ur burbur?*"

"No, *that* was serious," Jaina said, feeling guilty about

the number of Wuluws she had lost. "I'll—*we'll* try to do a better job of protecting you this time."

Wuluw rattled her mandibles in gratitude, then asked if Jaina had a plan to exterminate the Chiss on the islands yet.

"The plan's coming along," Jaina exaggerated. "We—just need to check out a few last details." She started down the stream, waist-deep in water and crouching to keep her eyes level with the top of the streambank. "Stay low. Those sharpshooters are good."

Wuluw splayed her limbs, lowering herself to within a few centimeters of the water, and followed close behind. The banging of the catapults and trebuchets continued unabated, filling the jungle with the simmering pressure of a star waiting to go nova. When the enemy islands came into view, Jaina stopped and lifted the electrobinoculars to her eyes again.

This time, she was doing more thinking than observing. After hearing about the trouble her parents had been causing the Squibs, she found herself wondering whether she really *did* need to develop a plan. If her parents were close to ending this war, perhaps the best thing to do would be to stall. The lives she saved would number in the millions—and that was Killiks alone.

But if Jaina was wrong about the reason the Squibs had put a hit on her—or if her parents failed to move quickly enough—a relief force would arrive to spoil UnuThul's trap. The Chiss would grow even bolder and attack deeper into Colony territory. Trillions of Killiks and millions of Chiss would die, and the war would continue more ferociously than before.

Fortunately, Jaina had a way to find out. She reached out to her mother in the Force and felt a jolt of happy connection—not as clear as a battle-meld, but stronger and more permanent. She filled her mind with thoughts of

peace, then added curiosity. Her mother seemed at first relieved, then puzzled, then worried.

Clearly, Leia did not understand at all. Jaina tried again,
this time filling her mind with hopefulness. Her mother
seemed more confused than ever, and Jaina gave up in exasperation. Some things never changed.

She felt Leia touching her through the Force, urging patience, and suddenly Jaina had the feeling that she would
be seeing her parents again soon.

That was all she needed to know.

Jaina lowered her electrobinoculars and turned to
Wuluw. "Have the trebuchets start dropping short, into the
water," she ordered. "We're going to fill that channel with
boulders—and we mean that literally."

"Burubr?" Wuluw demanded. *"Ubru urb uburb!"*

"Then we'd better get started, hadn't we?" Jaina said.

Actually, Jaina thought it would take even longer than a
week to fill the channel with stones. But if she could make
it appear to Wuluw and the rest of Great Swarm that she
was preparing a foolproof attack across a broad front, she
hoped UnuThul would sense the swarm's confidence and
be patient.

But the banging of the trebuchets continued to echo
through the jungle. Boulders continued to sail over the
channel onto the Chiss islands, and the pressure inside
Jaina began to grow more powerful. She found herself on
the verge of ordering an all-out assault. Her plan had created more impatience in the Great Swarm than confidence,
and now UnuThul was warning her to get the assault
going—or he would.

Jaina took a moment to perform a deep-breathing exercise, gathering herself to oppose UnuThul's Will.

Her meditations came to an abrupt end as a series of
high-pitched squeals echoed down from the treetops. At
first, she thought it might be a missile or a bomb dropping

from orbit, but then she realized that the squeals were moving *across* the sky, flying from the direction of the Killik trebuchets toward the Chiss islands.

Jaina spun around in time to see a pair of spread-eagled forms spinning through the air toward the Chiss islands.

"What are those?" Jaina demanded.

"Burru."

"I *know* they're Squibs." Jaina watched as the two figures arced down toward the island and landed about thirty meters inside the Chiss breastworks. "Why did they fly across the sky like that?"

"Ruru bu rur," Wuluw reminded her.

"Trebuchets!" Jaina gasped. "I didn't mean get them out of here like *that*. Wait here."

Jaina climbed out of the stream and started up a mogo tree, staying on the back side where she would be protected from Chiss snipers. When she judged she was high enough to see over the breastworks, she used the Force to stick herself in place, then raised her electrobinoculars and cautiously leaned out to peer around the trunk.

To her surprise, Jaina found both Squibs back on their feet, staggering around, wiping their eyes and spitting something dark from their mouths and nostrils. She thought for a moment that both rodents had suffered grievous internal injuries when they landed—until a squad of Chiss came staggering up to take them prisoner. The soldiers were smeared head-to-foot with mud, and every time they took a step, they sank knee-deep into the wet ground.

The island was practically underwater.

A circle of coldness suddenly formed between Jaina's eyes, and she pushed off the mogo, launching herself into a backflip just as a maser beam scorched past the trunk. She sensed more beams flying in her direction and dropped the electrobinoculars, snatching her lightsaber off her belt and activating it in the same swift motion.

Jaina's wrists flicked three times, intercepting and redirecting three maser beams in less than a second before she splashed feet-first into the stream. The sniper attack stopped as abruptly as it had started, and suddenly it sounded as though a tremendous wind were blowing through the jungle, rustling leaves that no longer hung on the trees. Jaina had to listen a moment before she realized that she was hearing the clicking of millions of stick-thin legs.

The Great Swarm was on the march.

"Wait!" Jaina turned to find Wuluw.

The insect was floating down the stream, pressed flat to the water with a huge dent in the chitin where the electrobinoculars had bounced off her delicate thorax.

"No!" Jaina used the Force to draw the wounded insect back to her, then rubbed a forearm along her antennae. "We're sorry!"

Wuluw tried to thrum something and succeeded only in pumping a long gush of insect gore into the water.

"Don't try to talk." Jaina started back upstream. The rustling had become a murmur now, and she could see the first Rekkers springing through the trees toward her. "We'll get you some help, but first you have to stop the Swarm. Attacking now is a terrible mistake!"

Wuluw managed a barely audible mandible tap, and the murmur of the Swarm's advance rose to a drone.

"I have a plan!" Jaina cried. "A good one."

All six of Wuluw's limbs stiffened and began to tremble, and a milky tint appeared deep inside her eyes.

"Hold on, Wuluw—tell the others we're going to dam the river." Jaina began to pour Force energy into the insect, trying to keep her alive long enough to complete the message. "Tell them we're going to flood the Chiss off those islands!"

SEVENTEEN

The pearlescent blur of hyperspace had barely winked back into the star-sparkled velvet of normal space before the *Falcon*'s proximity alarms began to scream. Han hit the reset so he could think, and the alarms screamed again.

"What the blazes?" Han demanded. There was nothing ahead but the swirling disk of a cloud-swaddled planet that he assumed to be Tenupe, and it was still no larger than his fist—far too distant to have triggered the first proximity alarm, much less a repeat. "What's out there?"

"Working on it!" Leia's hands were flying over the control board, adjusting static filters and signal enhancers. "These sensors don't calibrate themselves."

"Okay, take it easy," Han said. "I didn't mean anything."

He hit the reset again, and again the alarms reactivated themselves. The repeats could mean that more hazards were appearing, or that the original hazard was drawing rapidly closer. Seeing nothing between them and the planet, he began to accelerate. Tenupe swelled rapidly to the size of a Bith's head, and the azure blots of hundreds of cloud-free inland seas began to mottle its creamy disk.

"Is it wise to accelerate while we're sensor-blind?" Juun asked from the navigator's station. At Luke's request, Pellaeon had arranged for him and Tarfang to serve as the Solos' guides to Tenupe. "We still don't know where—"

"You see something in front of us?" Han interrupted.

"Only Tenupe."

"Same here." Han reset the alarms, then cursed as they instantly reactivated. "So whatever keeps triggering those alarms is coming at *us*."

"And we are *running*?" Saba was incredulous. "We do not even know from what!"

"Think of it as getting out of the way," Han replied. He activated the intercom so he could speak to the Noghri. "Get into the cannon turrets and let me know if you see anything suspicious."

Tenupe had swollen to the size of a bantha's head now. Hanging to one side of the planet, Han could see a shadow-pocked lump that might be a small red moon. On the opposite side, a cluster of tiny, wedge-shaped specks were circling above the clouds.

"That doesn't look good," Han said. "Leia, how are those sensors—"

Han's question was interrupted when Meewalh and Cakhmaim announced that there were ion trails closing on the *Falcon*'s stern from all directions.

"Chisz?" Saba asked.

Tarfang chuttered something sarcastic.

"Tarfang believes so," C-3PO translated helpfully. "He points out that Killik fighters still use rocket propulsion."

"Of all the luck!" Han complained. "The Chiss are already here—and we enter the system in the middle of a patrol!"

A trio of crimson bolts flashed past barely a dozen meters above the canopy. Then a gruff Chiss voice came over the hailing channel.

"*Millennium Falcon,* this is Zark Two." The woman's Basic was thick-tongued and awkward. "The Chiss Expansionary Defense Fleet demands that you bring to a dead stop your vessel. Stand by for boarding."

Han activated his comm microphone. "Uh, just a second." He glanced over at Leia, then pointed at the control panel and raised his brow. When she gave him a thumbs-up and began to bring the sensors online, he continued, "Sorry. You'll have to say again. Your Basic is a little—"

Another flurry of energy beams flashed past the cockpit, this time so close that they left spots in Han's eyes.

"That is clear enough, *Falcon*?" Zark Two asked. "This is a war zone. If you disobey, we fire for effect."

Han's tactical display came up, and he saw that the *Falcon* had an entire squadron of clawcraft on her tail. The fighters were escorted by two heavy gunboats and an assault shuttle—a standard package for a boarding company.

But it was what Han saw near the planet that really alarmed him. As he had suspected, the wedge-shaped flecks circling above the clouds were a huge Chiss battle fleet, clustered together over one tiny area of the planet.

"Leia, see if you can—"

"Working on it," Leia said.

A moment later, the image from a cloud-penetrating sensor scan appeared on Han's display. Most of the planet's land surface seemed to be covered by lowland jungles or mountain rain forests, but the area directly beneath the Chiss fleet was a brown smudge. A huge river ran through one edge of the smudge, and a tiny area along one bank shined red with thermal energy.

The lock-alarms began to chime incessantly, announcing that the *Falcon* was being targeted by her pursuers.

"*Millennium Falcon*, this is our final warning," Zark Two commed. "Bring your vessel to a dead stop."

Han pushed the throttles to the overload stops and dropped into an evasive corkscrew. Laser bolts instantly began to streak past on all sides, and the cabin lights flickered as the *Falcon*'s shields began to take hits.

"Captain Solo, the squadron leader's accent must be confusing you," C-3PO said. "She ordered us to *stop*."

"I heard." Han's eyes remained fixed on the image of the riverbank. "But that looks like a battle down there. A big one."

"How do you know that?" Juun sounded more amazed than doubtful. "I thought it was a jungle fire!"

"A jungle fire? With a fleet to provide space cover?" Saba reached over from the comm station and slapped the Sullustan's back. "So funny!"

Tarfang rushed to help Juun off the floor, then whirled on Saba and chittered so angrily it made the Barabel's scales ripple.

"Sssorry," she said. "This one did not know he was serious."

A depletion buzzer activated as the Chiss continued to pound the rear shields. Realizing he would never escape a dozen clawcraft with fancy flying alone, Han activated the intercom again.

"Are you two taking a nap back there?" he demanded. "Shoot something!"

The *Falcon* shuddered as the Noghri immediately cut loose with the big quad cannons.

Leia's eyes widened. "Han, I don't know if this is a good idea," she said. "Killing Chiss is only going to aggravate—"

"Look, *I'm* not the one setting the stakes here," Han said. "If I know my daughter, she and Zekk are in the middle of that battle down there, and that means the Chiss are trying to kill *them*. So pardon me if I return the favor."

"Han, I feel the same way," Leia said. "But we have to think of the mission. Luke wanted to do this without killing more—"

A damage warning began to scream, and suddenly the yoke felt like an angry snake, snapping from side to side and forward and back, twisting right, whipping left, then kicking and bouncing like a kid on his first bound-stick. The *Falcon* went into a shuddering vortex, and more alarms screamed as delicate systems began to take secondary damage from the violent shaking.

"Sh-sh-shut down n-n-number four n-nacelle!" Han ordered. At least he thought it was number four—with all the quaking and shaking, it was hard to be sure which status light he was seeing. "And if that doesn't work, try the others!"

Leia's fingers were already stabbing at the control panel, trying to catch the correct glide-switch. In the midst of it all, a synthesized boom reverberated from the control panel speaker, and Han glimpsed a Chiss designator-symbol vanishing from the tactical display. Even with all of the shaking and spiraling, one of the Noghri had hit a claw-craft. Han was not that surprised.

Leia finally managed to shut down the number four nacelle. The *Falcon* stopped shuddering, but her acceleration slowed and the yoke grew stiff and sluggish. Han struggled to bring the ship's wild spiral back under control.

"Han?" Leia's voice was brittle with fear. "You know what I was saying about aggravating the situation?"

"Yeah?"

"Forget it," she said. "They're already mad."

"Yessssz." Saba's hiss had an air of thoughtfulness. "Master Skywalker did not know how far the situation has deteriorated."

"Thanks for your opinions," Han grumbled. "Now could someone get back there and disconnect the number four vector plate? We're handling like a one-winged manta right now!"

"Mantaz can fly with one wing?" Saba gasped.

"No, Master," Leia explained. "That's the point."

"Oh." Saba jumped up and tapped Tarfang on the shoulder, then started toward the back of the flight deck. "Why did you not say it was so bad?"

A jolt ran through the *Falcon* as they took another hit, and Han saw on the tactical display that the clawcraft were beginning to close the distance more rapidly.

"Jae, how long before we're in the clouds?"

"We won't reach them," Juun announced immediately.

"What are you talking about?" Han demanded. "Of course we'll reach them!"

Juun shook his head. "I've done the calculations. By the time we decelerate to enter the atmosphere—"

"Who says we're decelerating?" Han demanded.

Juun's voice grew even more nasal. "We're not going to decelerate?"

"Captain Solo never decelerates in these situations," C-3PO reported. "He seems to enjoy seeing how close we can come to crashing without actually doing so. I can't tell you the number of times that we have been statistically doomed, only to escape at the last possible mo—"

Another boom reverberated from the control panel speaker, announcing the destruction of a second clawcraft.

"You see?" C-3PO continued. "But I *am* pleased to report that our odds of survival have increased by three one-thousandths of a percent."

The boom had barely died away before the hailing channel grew active again.

"Captain Solo, that is *quite* enough!" The voice this time was male . . . and very familiar. "Come to a dead stop at once!"

"Sorry—someone's shooting at us." Han continued to corkscrew toward Tenupe, which was now so large that its cloud-blanketed face filled the entire forward viewport. "Is that you, Jag?"

"It is," Jagged Fel confirmed. "And I will *not* tolerate any more casualties."

"Then I advise you to order Zark Leader to stop pursuit," Leia retorted.

"I *am* Zark Leader," Jagged replied coolly. "And I am not at liberty to end this pursuit. If you do not stop immediately, there is only *one* way this can end."

"You're a *squadron* leader now?" Han asked, ignoring Fel's threats. "What'd you do to get busted down that far?"

"*Nothing.*" The cockpit speaker crackled with Jagged's indignation. "My rank remains intact. Bring the *Falcon* to a—"

"You're the same rank?" Leia broke in. "Are you telling me a *commander* is leading this squadron?"

"Captain, actually," Jagged replied.

"*Captain?*" Han began to feel sick to his stomach. The Chiss Expansionary Defense Fleet used the naval system of ranks, so captain was a command-grade rank—the equivalent of colonel in terms of Galactic Alliance ground forces—and Han could think of only one reason a command officer would fly a patrol mission. "You're here because of us! You *knew* we were coming!"

"I should have thought that was obvious, Captain Solo," Jagged said.

Han did not respond. He was too busy trying to bring the *Falcon* out of her spin . . . and silently promising a painful death to whoever had betrayed them to the Chiss. Only a handful of people outside the Jedi order had known of the Solos' destination, so it would not be difficult to track down the spy and put a blaster bolt through his head.

"But now that you understand," Jagged continued, "perhaps you see how hopeless your situation really is."

"Hopeless?" Han scoffed. "I'm not even worried!"

He shoved throttles one through three past the overload stops. The *Falcon* began to spiral even more wildly, and a slight tremble returned to the yoke.

"Han," Leia said.

"Yeah?"

"*I'm* a little bit worried."

"Rel-l-lax." The yoke was vibrating so hard in Han's hands that it made his teeth chatter. "Those are rain clouds down there."

"So?"

"So when we pull up under them," Han explained, "they'll put out the entry burn."

"You're entering a gravity dive?" Juun's voice was filled with awe. "May I have permission to record? We should document how you pull out—especially given the damage to our controls."

"*If* we pull out," Leia groaned. She *hated* gravity dives. "But go ahead. What can it hurt?"

"We'll pull out," Han said, "assuming Saba and Tarfang get that vector plate disconnected. And we'll need to know if there are any mountains in that mess. Better run a terrain scan."

"I'll *try*," Leia said. "It's difficult to get a reading while we're spiraling out of control to our deaths like this."

"Who's out of control?"

Leia began to activate the imaging scanners, struggling to keep her hands on the appropriate switches as the *Falcon* bucked and shook. Zark Squadron continued to zing cannon fire at their stern, but the Noghri's accuracy seemed to have a chilling effect on the Chiss. Despite the renowned speed of their clawcraft, Fel's pilots were closing the distance much slower than Han had expected—and not nearly fast enough to keep them from reaching the planet, as Juun had calculated.

"Wait a minute!" Han said. They were so close to Tenupe now that all they could see ahead was pale mass of green clouds, marked here and there by a blue blob of cloudless sea, spinning past the forward viewport ever more quickly. "Something's not right."

"You can say that again." Leia sent the terrain scan to his display. "Look at this."

The map showed a rugged jungle planet of high mountains and vast drainage basins, with no large oceans, but rivers wide enough to see from orbit. It also showed a dozen cruisers converging on the *Falcon*'s point of entry, their course and original locations clearly outlined by the huge vapor trails they were leaving in their wakes.

"Get a tactical readout on those—"

The data appeared on Han's tactical display. As he had expected, they were drop cruisers—terrible in space combat, but ideal for supporting planetside operations. And the energy blooms on their hulls suggested they all had fully charged tractor beams.

"This is a setup!" Han pulled the three functional throttles back to three-quarter power—not suddenly, but enough to buy a little reaction time. "Jag is trying to drive us into a trap!"

"*Trying,* Han?" Leia asked.

"*Trying,*" Han growled. "Nobody traps Han Solo."

Han waited until the Tenupe's little red moon showed through the top of the canopy, then jerked back on the yoke. A series of muffled crashes rumbled up the access corridor—the inertial compensators could not quite neutralize the high g forces—but the planet's cloud-swaddled face vanished from the forward viewport.

Jagged Fel's voice came over the cockpit speaker immediately. "I *told* my superiors that trap wouldn't fool you. But if you check your tactical monitor, you'll discover your situation has only grown more hopeless."

Han checked his display and had to agree. A pair of Chiss Star Destroyers had appeared on Tenupe's horizon, eliminating all hope of escaping around the curve of the planet. Zark Squadron was cutting the corner behind the *Falcon,* approaching at an angle and continuing to fire.

"Don't force me to destroy you and the Princess, Captain Solo," Jagged said. "Things didn't work out between Jaina and me, but I still remember you all fondly."

"Do what you have to, kid." Han pushed the three functioning throttles back past their overload stops. "I always liked Kyp Durron better anyway."

Leia slapped the comm microphones off. "Han! Are you crazy?" she demanded. *"Kyp?"*

"Relax." Han gave her a crooked smile. "I'm just trying to make him mad. I know Kyp's way too old for her."

Leia closed her eyes and shook her head. "Do you really think *now* is a good time to make Jag angry? He has an entire *fleet* at his disposal."

"Nothing to worry about," Han said. "He's bluffing."

"Han, Jagged was raised by *Chiss*. They don't know how to bluff."

"Must be why they're so bad at it." Han winked at her. "Send Meewalh and Cakhmaim to help Saba and Tarfang with that vector plate. I don't think we're going to need them in the turrets much longer, but it would be nice to have control of this tub again."

Leia activated the intercom and relayed the order. The laser cannons had barely stopped firing before Jagged's voice came over the comm again.

"You have stopped firing on us—thank you." He sounded genuinely relieved. "But I cannot stop firing on *you* until the *Falcon* comes to a dead stop."

"Jagged, we all know that if you were serious about this, we'd already be space dust," Leia replied. "What I can't figure out is *why* you're going to so much trouble to save us."

"Your confusion surprises me, Princess," Jagged said. "I should think the reason would be obvious to someone of your diplomatic and military background. You and Captain Solo will be valuable prisoners—and so will Master Sebatyne and Bwua'tu's master spies, the Ewok and the Sullustan."

"You're very well informed, Jag," Leia said. "But not well enough. If you knew our mission, you'd know we're trying to *end* the war. You would be helping—"

"I know you and Captain Solo came here to find Jaina and her, ah, *companion*," Jag retorted. "I also know you want to help them smuggle a Killik commando squad into one of our command and control centers. I know your brother believes—wrongly—that this maneuver will prove to us how difficult it would be to win a war against the Killiks. He also believes it will make it easier for him to persuade the ruling houses to accept the peace that he intends to impose on the Colony. Is there anything *else* about your mission that I should know?"

"No, that about covers it," Han said, speaking through gritted teeth. He had assumed that some spy eavesdropping in a hangar or briefing room had betrayed them. But clearly, it been someone a lot closer to the Jedi order than that—someone close enough to know Luke's entire plan. "You think it'll work?"

"No," Jagged said icily. "I'd have to kill you first."

"Yeah, that's what I figured," Han said.

Zark Squadron continued to pour fire after the *Falcon.* Another damage alarm started to scream—prompting Juun to take C-3PO and rush aft—but the clawcraft began to drift back on the tactical display. The Star Destroyers began to lay barrages of fire ahead of the *Falcon,* trying to channel her into tractor beam range, or force her to stop and wait for boarding.

Still fighting a sluggish yoke and an out-of-control spiral, Han dropped them back toward Tenupe and continued toward the planet at an oblique angle.

"Uh, Han?" Leia sounded worried. "What are we doing?"

"This d-d-doesn't make any ssssense," Han said. The yoke had started to shake again, and he was fighting to keep it from swinging around at random. "They know our plan. They ought to be coming after us hard."

"Han, this *is* hard." Leia's gaze was fixed firmly forward, where a green sliver of planetary horizon was slowly rolling around the edge of the viewport as the *Falcon* spiraled toward Tenupe. "There's a whole task force after us."

"That's what I mean," Han said. "You saw that battle down there! Do you think the theater commander really wants Jag wasting his time chasing *us* right now? They should just blast us back to atoms and be done with it."

"They won't *need* to," Leia said. "Han, we're heading for—"

"Whoever double-crossed us made them promise to take us *alive*," Han continued. The boiling red curtain of a Star Destroyer barrage blossomed ahead, jolting the *Falcon* and spreading spots before his eyes. "Leia, it had to be someone close to us."

"Okay, Han!" Leia pointed forward, where the hazy blur of Tenupe's atmosphere was whirling around the center of the viewport. "But what are you *doing*?"

"Just what it looks like—a planet-skip." Han activated the intercom. "Hold on back there!"

An instant later, tongues of red flame began to flicker over the viewport as they entered the thin gas of Tenupe's upper atmosphere. The *Falcon* bucked so hard that Han slammed against his crash harness, and the clamor of flying gear echoed up the access corridor. Han fought against the sluggish controls, struggling to keep the ship's spiral from growing any tighter and faster . . . and *that* was when the yoke went loose.

Before Han realized it, he had pulled it completely back

against his thigh, and the *Falcon* was flipping out of its spiral in a weld-popping wingover. He quickly moved it back to center . . . and the wingover gradually slowed.

The *Falcon* stopped about three-quarters of the way through her roll and hung there, then languidly began to drift back toward upright—now headed straight for a rolling barrage of megamaser blossoms. Han pushed the yoke all the way forward, trying to dive under the fiery wall of death, and could only grit his teeth as the *Falcon* dropped her nose a mere five degrees.

Leia leaned over and grabbed Han's hand. "Han, I love—"

The barrage vanished as suddenly as it had appeared, leaving nothing ahead of the *Falcon* but the blotchy red surface of Tenupe's moon.

"Yeah, me, too." Han pulled the throttles back to the overload stops, gripping the handles tightly to keep his hands from shaking. "See what I mean? They killed that barrage to keep from vaping us."

"Yes. Okay. I believe you." Leia's voice was still shaky. "They promised *someone* not to kill us."

"Yeah." Han's tone was bitter. "I wonder who *that* could have been?"

"You're thinking Omas?"

"That's the only thing that makes sense," Han said. "Cal Omas would sacrifice us in a minute if he thought it would convince the Chiss that the Alliance isn't at war with the Ascendancy."

Leia shook her head. "Why would he bother making them promise to keep us alive?"

"Because he needs the Jedi, too," Han said. The moon ahead had swelled into a lumpy, fist-sized ovoid laced with a spidery web of dark rifts. "And if his double cross ever comes out, Omas would never be able to make peace with Luke if we were dead."

Leia frowned. "Maybe . . ."

"Look, it's either him or Pellaeon or someone in the Jedi," Han said. "And Pellaeon never double-crossed anyone, even when he was an Imperial."

"I guess, when you put it like that."

Leia still sounded doubtful, but their discussion was interrupted by Jagged Fel's astonished voice.

"I'm finally starting to understand Jaina," he said. "Insanity runs in her family. Only a madman would attempt a planet-skip in a damaged ship."

"Han's not crazy," Leia said. "Just good."

"I'm sure you believe that, Princess Leia," Jagged said. "But I'm warning—no, I'm *advising*—you not to attempt taking refuge in that moon cluster."

"Moon cluster?" Han peered more closely at the red lump ahead and saw that the rifts might, indeed, be interstitial spaces. He deactivated his comm microphone, then asked, "What the blazes *is* that?"

"I'll find out," Leia said, reaching for the terrain mappers. "In the meantime, stall."

"Stall *Jag*?" Han turned his microphone back on, then commed, "Thanks for the advice, Jag, but we were planning on going around anyway."

"Really?" Jagged sounded smug. "Then the *Falcon* must be even faster than Jaina always claimed."

Han glanced down at his tactical display and saw that the Zark Squadron had taken advantage of his planet-skip to put on their own burst of acceleration. They had stopped firing—a sign that they now felt certain of a successful capture—and were arrayed in a semisphere around the *Falcon*. The squadron's escort was not far behind, and the Star Destroyers had already closed to within tractor beam range of the moon cluster's near side.

Han cursed under his breath, but said, "Just watch, kid. You'll be surprised."

"I have no doubt," Jagged said. "But please believe me about the moon cluster. It's gravitationally unstable. Every one of our scoutships has been smashed flat. You'll be much safer surrendering to us, and I give you my word that we won't torture or humiliate you during your interrogations."

"Thanks, that's real good of you," Han said. "Let me think it over for a second."

Han closed the comm channel, then experimented with the yoke, pushing it around and feeling almost no reaction from the *Falcon*.

"How bad is it?" Leia asked. She was still staring at the terrain mapper, frowning and adjusting the controls.

"Bad," Han said. "How about those moons?"

"Even worse than he said." Leia looked out at the moons, which were close enough now for her to see that they were all shifting around, bumping against each other. "It looks like something shattered the old moon into fifty or sixty pieces. It must still be in there, because I'm detecting . . ."

Leia let her sentence trail off, then gasped and stared out the viewport.

"Yeah?" Han asked.

Leia raised her hand to quiet him, then closed her eyes in concentration.

Han frowned and leaned over to look at the terrain scanners. He saw only the shattered moon she had described, with a density reading near the center that suggested a metallic core—probably whatever had shattered it in the first place. He tried to be patient, waiting for Leia to do whatever Jedi thing she was preparing, but they were running out of time. The two Star Destroyers had activated their tractor beams and were already reaching out toward the moon cluster, trying to block any chance the *Falcon* had of slipping into one of the crevices.

Han activated the intercom. "Somebody back there get

to the repulsor beam now! We've got some rocks to move
out of—"

"Han, no!" Leia opened her eyes and turned to him,
shaking her head. "We have to surrender!"

Han frowned. "Look, I know the yoke's a little sloppy—"

"It's not that." Leia reached over and pulled the throttles
all the way back. "It's Raynar and the Killiks—those moons
are teeming with insects!"

EIGHTEEN

The Jedi StealthXs appeared—as always—as though by magic, an entire wing of dark X's hanging against the crimson veil of the Utegetu Nebula. They floated there for just an instant, then drifted over to the black ribbon of a stellar dust cloud and vanished, darkness merging into darkness. It all happened so quickly that any picket ship pilots who happened to be looking in that direction would blink, question what they had seen, and check their instruments. And their instruments would assure them that their eyes had been mistaken.

The StealthXs continued their approach in full confidence that they remained undetected, and soon the bright disk of the yellow planet Sarm began to swell in the forward panels of their cockpit canopies. The Jedi pilots kept a careful watch for sentries—both on their sensor screens and by reaching out in the Force—and easily avoided a single inattentive blastboat operated by pirates. The StealthXs reached Sarm unobserved . . . and unsettled. The Jedi knew better than to underestimate a foe—especially during a war. The Killiks would not leave themselves exposed like this without good reason.

As the wing drew nearer the yellow planet, a network of ancient, world-spanning irrigation canals grew visible on the surface—all that remained of the beings who had inhabited Sarm before being blasted from the galactic memory by the Utegetu Nova. The Jedi had time to ponder those channels as they closed on their destination, reflecting on the destiny of civilizations in a violent universe, glimpsing the anonymous end to which every culture ultimately came. What did battles matter when a galactic burp could erase whole civilizations? Could any amount of killing ever change the fundamental brutal transience of existence?

Perhaps the Killiks knew the answers. After all, they lived in harmony with the Song of the Universe, killing and being killed as the melody demanded, abounding and vanishing, fighting and dancing as the mood moved them. They did not concern themselves with right or wrong, feelings of love and hate. They served the nest. What benefited the nest, they desired. What hurt the nest, they exterminated.

Not so with the Jedi. They struggled with their fates, worried over whether something was moral or immoral, peered into the future and tried to bend it to their desires. And then, when their grasps slipped and the future snapped back in their faces with all the force of an impacting meteor, they were always so surprised, always so shaken, as though their wills should have been strong enough to steer the course of the galaxy.

And so the Jedi continued toward Sarm in their StealthXs, silent and grim of purpose, readying themselves to kill and be killed, to sing in their own way the Song of the Universe. Their targets came into view just as Admiral Bwua'tu's intelligence officer had promised, eleven pale spheres in orbit around the planet, each the size of a *Super*-class Star Destroyer, all but one enveloped by the diffuse Force presence of a Killik nest.

The StealthXs swung wide around the planet, positioning themselves to descend on the nest ship with no Force presence. It was in the lowest orbit, where it would be screened from attack by the rest of the fleet. That was the Dark Nest's vessel, the one where Lomi Plo would be hiding, and Luke's plan was simple. The Jedi would sneak into position around the vessel and wait for Admiral Pellaeon to arrive with the *Megador* and the rest of the Alliance strike fleet. When he did, they would destroy any craft attempting to leave the Gorog nest, and then they would go inside and flush Lomi Plo from her den.

But Sarm was too quiet. There should have been smugglers and membrosia runners flitting in and out of the nest ship hangars, and an entire flotilla of pirate vessels hanging in orbit. There should have been maintenance barges hovering over the nest ships, repairing the damage the Jedi had inflicted at the Murgo Choke. Instead, the fleet looked almost abandoned. Save for the presences they felt in the Force, the Jedi would have believed it was.

Then blue halos of ion efflux appeared around the sterns of the nest ships, and the vessels began to accelerate. Now the Jedi understood the reason Sarm was so quiet. The Killiks had already repaired their battered fleet. They were breaking orbit and deploying to challenge the Alliance blockade.

Luke dropped into a power dive, swinging wide around two nest ships to avoid the sharp eyes of the Killik sentries. Mara and Jacen and the other Jedi followed close behind, grasping the change of plan through their combat-meld. Kenth Hamner took his squadron and circled back behind the first two nest ships, decelerating so their attack would hit at the same time as Luke's. Kyle Katarn's squadron peeled off and started for the far side of the planet. Tresina Lobi and her squadron broke in the opposite direction, heading for the front of the Killik fleet.

The remainder of the wing continued toward the original target: the Dark Nest of Lomi Plo. As they descended, Luke allowed his alarm to fill his thoughts and reached out to Cilghal in the Force, trying to impress on her the urgency of the situation. She was still aboard the *Megador* with Tekli and the collection crews, and Pellaeon would listen if she told him the attack fleet had to jump *now*. She seemed at first surprised by Luke's contact, then worried, but quickly focused on what he was trying to tell her and returned his touch with reassurance.

The Gorog nest ship grew steadily larger in Luke's forward viewport as he drew nearer, and soon its pale ovoid began to obscure Sarm's yellow surface. The planet took on the appearance of a huge, golden halo behind the immense vessel. Luke pointed the nose of his StealthX straight at the ship's heart, using its own shadow to shield his squadron from Sarm's planet-glow.

The strategy did not prove very effective. Insect eyes were especially adept at detecting movement, and barely a moment passed before R2-D2 scrolled a warning across Luke's display.

TARGET ENERGIZING WEAPON BATTERIES.

"Thanks, Artoo," Luke said. The three squadrons broke in different directions, then broke again and split into shield trios. "Good to have you riding the socket again, old friend."

IT'S ABOUT TIME, R2-D2 replied. YOUR SURVIVAL HAS BEEN IMPROBABLE WITHOUT ME!

"There *have* been a few close calls," Luke admitted.

The nest ship was close enough now that Sarm had completely disappeared behind its pale orb. Luke could see a double row of turbolaser barrels protruding up from among the knobby heat sinks that covered its hull. The smaller weapons that would be attacking the StealthXs remained concealed in a grid of dark shadows.

Luke began evasive flying, leading his shieldmates on a random, wild descent toward the target. Mara and Jacen followed as though their controls were linked to his, entering each roll almost before he did, coming out behind him so quickly their transponder codes looked like a single entry on his tactical screen.

A burst of elation filled the battle-meld as Kenth Hamner's squadron attacked. The tactical display showed repeated detonations in the sterns of three nest ships, and a string of white flashes erupted in a high orbit behind Luke's squadron. But none of the vessels seemed to be slowing down.

"Artoo, are they deploying—"

A sharp whistle filled the cockpit as R2-D2 warned that the Gorog had opened fire. Luke was already dodging, his hands and feet reacting even before he saw the laser bolts flashing up from the shadows. He rolled away from the burst and took a flak-shell in the forward shields. Mara reached out to him in concern, ready to move into the lead.

No need. R2-D2 already had the shields back at 90 percent. Luke followed the line of laser bolts visually down to their source, then reached out with the Force and shoved the cannon barrels aside. The deadly stream of color changed direction and began to pour harmlessly into space.

Mara made Luke's day by seeming impressed—at least that was what it felt like through their Force-bond. Then Jacen redirected a stream of mag-pellets and somehow located the flak-guns and pushed those aside, too. Mara seemed almost awed.

Luke sighed, then checked his tactical display. He saw no indication that the nest ships were doing anything except continuing to accelerate.

"Artoo, any sign of dartships?"

R2-D2 trilled a sharp response.

"Take it easy," Luke said. R2-D2's testiness made him wonder whether the droid truly was ready to return to combat service. "I just wanted to be sure."

R2-D2 beeped a promise to make certain Luke knew the instant a dartship appeared, then scrolled an additional message across the display: YOU HAVE NO REASON TO DOUBT ME. I WAS ONLY FOLLOWING MY OWNER-PRESERVATION ROUTINES.

"I know that, Artoo," Luke said. "But you can't protect people from the truth."

WHY NOT? THERE ARE NO TRUTH EXCEPTIONS IN MY PARAMETER STATEMENTS.

A turbolaser strike erupted ahead, bucking the StealthX so hard it felt like they had collided with the nest ship—which they soon would, if the squadron did not launch its attack quickly.

"I'll explain later," Luke said. "Right now, arm the penetrator."

R2-D2 beeped an acknowledgment, and Luke sensed the rest of his squadron lining up behind him. Basically a Jedi shadow bomb with a trio of shaped-charge warheads, the penetrator had been specifically designed to unleash a series of powerful, focused detonations toward the interior of a Killik nest ship.

A message appeared on the display announcing that the penetrator was live. Luke dodged past the fiery blossom of a turbolaser strike, then saw a pair of laser cannons flashing up from the dark crevices between a pair of spitcrete heat sinks. He Force-shoved the barrels aside, then released the penetrator and simultaneously used the Force to send the weapon smashing into the nest ship's hull.

His canopy blast-tinting went black with the first detonation, but the two explosions that followed were so bright that they lit the interior of the cockpit anyway. Luke rolled away, then did a wingover and flew back along the attack line.

With no dartships to worry about, he was free to watch on his tactical display as Mara, Jacen, and the rest of his squadron released their penetrators in one-second intervals. Each bomb disappeared into the crater left by the previous one, driving the hole deeper down through the nest ship's layered decks, wreaking increasing amounts of destruction and exposing more and more of the vessel's interior to the cold vacuum of space.

By the time the last weapon detonated, the Gorog were in such a state of shock that all defensive fire had ceased within a kilometer of the impact area. Luke swung his StealthX around and found a cloud of steam, bodies, and equipment tumbling from the crater, so thick it obscured the ship's hull. He could sense by the exhilaration in the meld that Kyp's attack on the stern of the ship had also gone well, but there was a certain heaviness in Corran's squadron that Luke knew all too well: a Jedi had fallen in the assault on the bow.

R2-D2 whistled an alarm, and Luke looked down to see swarms of Gorog dartships pouring from the vessel's hangar bays.

"Thanks, Artoo," he said. "What's the rest of the battle look like?"

The tactical display switched scales, and Luke saw that the other nest ships were bleeding dartships and dropping into lower orbits to support Gorog. Clearly, the Killiks had aborted their attack on the blockade. It was more important to protect the Dark Nest, and the Dark Nest had been wounded.

Luke reached out to Kenth, Kyle, and Tresina, calling them back to the initial target. When Pellaeon arrived with the main attack fleet, there would be fewer casualties from friendly fire if the Jedi were doing their best to follow the original plan.

Once Luke sensed that his squadron had re-formed behind him, he continued forward, using the Force to clear a path through the cloud of flotsam and bodies still pouring from the Gorog nest's interior. He knew by the growing tension of the meld that Corran and Kyp were also returning to begin the second, more dangerous phase of the assault. And he shared in their hope that the Alliance battle fleet would arrive soon. Once the Jedi began the final destruction of the Dark Nest, they were going to need all the support they could get.

Luke reached the breach in the outer hull and activated the imaging system in his helmet visor. The dark interior of the nest ship was immediately transformed into an eerie hologram of vibrant colors, with white-hot lumps of spitcrete rubble and glowing red pieces of Killiks streaming up a long, seemingly bottomless shaft before they tumbled out into the void.

The StealthXs shut down their ion drives and descended into the hull breach under the power of their maneuvering thrusters alone. As much as Luke would have liked to, there was no time to look for traps or counterattacks as they descended past each deck in the bombed-out shaft. The success of their assault depended on speed and ferocity, and their best hope lay in keeping the enemy off balance.

When the squadron had descended ten decks, the rear trio of StealthXs peeled off and glided toward the edge of the shaft. A few moments later, a series of blue flashes spilled out of the darkness as the three pilots came to an air lock and used their laser cannons to blast it open. Luke glanced over his shoulder and saw more flotsam streaming up the shaft behind him. The nest ship's artificial gravity generator had either been destroyed or shut down to conserve power, because even the heaviest pieces showed no sign of dropping toward the center of the ship.

A second trio of StealthXs peeled off after the squadron had descended twenty decks, and a third after thirty. By then, the combat-meld was charged with excitement as the

Jedi blasted their way deeper into the enormous ship from three sides, cutting down waves of vac-suited Gorog warriors with their laser cannons, blasting open air locks and using the Force to hide shadow bombs at critical locations.

Luke and Mara and Jacen passed the fortieth deck and continued down to the fiftieth, the shaft narrowing to barely more than the spread of a StealthX's wings. The excitement in the meld turned to fear and anger and all the other emotions that boiled to surface in the midst of a pitched battle, then Kenth and Kyle and Tresina Lobi began to radiate alarm, warning Luke and Kyp and Corran that trouble was on its way.

Luke was not worried. Dartships were far less maneuverable than StealthXs and would be next to worthless in the twisting wreckage . . . but that thought came to an abrupt end when R2-D2 trilled an urgent warning.

"*B-wings?*" Luke asked. Armed more heavily than XJ-3s, B-wings were some of the most dangerous and maneuverable starfighters in the galaxy. "Are you sure?"

R2-D2 piped an annoyed affirmative.

Luke tore his gaze away from the dust-filled murk ahead just long enough to check his tactical display. At this point, the image showed only the shaft behind them, a flared column of space packed with descending starfighters.

"*Ours?*"

That question was answered when the blue streak of an approaching proton torpedo appeared on the display. Luke instantly poured on some speed and ducked into the exposed decks, leading Mara and Jacen away from the detonation area. The torpedo streaked past behind them, then reached the bottom of the shaft and exploded.

Luke and his wingmates were partially shielded by several layers of deck, but the blast reached them with enough power to beat down their rear shields and hurl them into the next bulkhead. Their forward shields absorbed most of the impact, but their cockpits broke into a cacophony of damage alarms and depletion warnings.

Luke spun his StealthX around while it was still wobbling. The wings banged into a ceiling on one side and the floor on the other, but at least his targeting systems seemed unaffected. A constant stream of laserfire flashed down the shaft as Kyle Katarn and two members of his squadron attacked the approaching B-wings from behind.

Although the hull breach was considerably larger than it had been just a few minutes ago, with the nest ship's artificial gravity nonfunctional, it was so choked with floating dust and rubble that the storm of cannon bolts was barely visible. Luke glanced over and found Mara and Jacen already using their attitude thrusters to move away from him, spreading out to lay an ambush.

As they waited, Luke silenced his alarms and wondered idly, "Where did *Killiks* get B-wings?"

R2-D2 ventured the obvious opinion. After all, B-wings were manufactured by Slayn & Korpil—one of the best known of the Verpine hive companies.

"All right—forget I asked," Luke said. All the Killiks would have needed to arrange a third-party sale was a single highly placed tarhead. "How are the rear shields? Can you get them back up?"

R2-D2 let out a falling whistle, then a pair of B-wings appeared in the storm of laser bolts pouring down the shaft. breach. With their head-like cockpits mounted atop a cross-shaped wing structure, the craft had a vaguely human profile, like a man standing with his legs crossed and his arms outstretched. The first B-wing was descending in the upright position, slowly spinning around to search the adjacent decks for StealthX infiltrators. The second was flying on its back, firing back up the shaft at Kyle Katarn and the other attacking Jedi. from behind.

The first craft started to spin more rapidly, trying to

bring the torpedo launcher on its tail assembly to bear on Luke's StealthX. He grabbed the vessel in the Force and held it in place, then opened fire with his laser cannons. The startled B-wing pilot applied more power, trying to break free. Luke drew on the Force more heavily to counter the maneuvering thrusters, and all of the energy flowing through his body began to make his skin nettle.

Mara and Jacen began to fire, too. The B-wing's shields emitted an overload flash, then went down in a storm of discharge static. An instant later the starfighter itself simply came apart under the combined fury of the StealthX cannons.

The second B-wing gave up trying to hold Kyle and his companions at bay and dropped its tail to bring its torpedo launcher to bear. Luke started to Force-grab the fighter again, but Jacen had already caught it and was holding it in place while cannon bolts pounded its shields from above.

This B-wing did not even try to break free. The pilot simply launched the proton torpedo in the direction it was pointed. Suddenly the electronics in Luke's cockpit were popping and spewing acrid smoke, and the spitcrete ceiling was crashing down on his StealthX, and Mara was touching him through their Force-bond, surprised and worried but somehow confident they were not going to die—not yet.

Then Luke and his StealthX became just so much flotsam, the laser cannons and broken wings tumbling away into the dust and the rubble, the fusial engines banging against the fuselage, still connected by a few twisted shreds of metal. R2-D2 was screeching warnings over the cockpit speaker, his voice barely audible over the roar of escaping air.

Luke sealed his vac suit and activated his helmet comm unit. "I'm okay, Artoo. Prepare to abandon the craft."

R2-D2 ran a message across the heads-up display inside Luke's visor. THE SELF-DESTRUCT CHARGE IS MISSING—AND THERE *IS* NO CRAFT.

"I know. Just unhook yourself."

Luke could feel that Mara was not injured, either, but Jacen was more difficult to read. He had drawn in on himself and vanished from the Force.

Luke opened a comlink channel. "Jacen?"

"Over here." Mara's concern filled their Force-bond. "His canopy is smashed, but his visor is down and I can tell that his vac suit is pressurized. He may still be alive."

Luke's breath left him in a rush of fear. *Not again.* He could not tell Leia that he had lost another of her sons.

"Get him out!"

"I'm *trying*," Mara commed. "Just calm down."

But Luke could not calm down. He felt as though he had been punched in the stomach by a Wookiee. It was bad enough that he had sent Anakin to his death, but this time Jacen had been with *him.* He looked in the direction from which he sensed Mara's presence.

It took a moment to pick out her blotchy red image through all the rubble displayed by the imaging system inside his visor. But she was already wearing her combat harness, and she had her bulky G-12 power blaster slung over one shoulder. The battered remains of her starfighter were bobbing along in the rubble beneath her, and she was hanging on to the empty droid socket behind the shattered canopy of Jacen's StealthX.

Now that he saw that Mara was already with Jacen, Luke began to calm. What could be done, she was doing—but he did not understand how she had gotten there so fast. Before the explosion, she had been on the other side of him.

"How'd you get over there?"

"Bounced," Mara said. She took the lightsaber off her utility belt. "You coming?"

"Be right there."

Luke popped his canopy, then grabbed his own combat harness and slipped out of his darkened cockpit. He pulled the massive power blaster out of the carrying sleeve behind his seat, connected the powerfeed to the energy pack on his combat harness, and slung the weapon over his shoulder.

A trio of Jedi presences arrived behind him, about fifty meters away. Luke glanced back and saw three empty spaces about the size of StealthXs amid all the dust and spitcrete floating in the penetration crater. Even this close, the imaging system inside his helmet was as blind to the starfighters as any sensor system.

"Master Skywalker?" Kyle asked over the helmet coms.

"Jacen's out—we don't know how bad." Luke used the Force to pull R2-D2 out of the astromech socket and used a utility clip to attach the droid to the back of his combat harness. "We'll need a hand evacuating . . ."

Luke let the sentence trail off when an icy knot of danger sense formed between his shoulder blades. He dropped behind his StealthX and felt the fuselage vibrating beneath a hail of shatter gun pellets. He peered under the belly of wreckage, but his attackers were too well covered for his helmet's imaging system to pick them out from the surrounding rubble.

Luke worked to quiet his mind, to sense only the Force holding him in its liquid grasp, lapping at him from all sides. He began to feel a mass of ripples coming at him from the emptiness ahead, from the shifting voids of beings hiding themselves in the Force. There were hundreds of them, Gorog warriors rushing to the attack, pouring into the battle zone through a choke point hidden somewhere deep in the sea of floating rubble.

And there was more, a stillness so fixed it was frozen, a cold hole that seemed to be drawing the Force into *it*.

"Lomi Plo is here," Luke commed. At the same time, he was reaching into the battle-meld, calling Kyp and Corran and the rest of the Jedi to his side, letting them know it was time to close the trap. "She came after *us*."

Shatter gun pellets began to stream through the fuselage on Luke's side of the cockpit, and he knew that his projection was disintegrating fast. Still peering under the StealthX wreckage, he pulled the heavy power blaster off his back, then used the Force to send a speeder-sized block of spitcrete tumbling toward an even larger one where he had detected the nearest group of Gorog.

The two blocks collided in silence and tumbled away in new directions. The shatter gun fire stopped instantly, and images of warm bug gore and crushed pressure shells began to drift across Luke's imaging system. He spotted a trio of Gorog tumbling through the rubble, all six limbs flailing as they struggled to bring their carapace suits back under control.

Luke swung the barrel of his power blaster around and fired one bolt at each insect, using the Force to steady himself against the blowback caused by the weapon's massive energy discharges. Unlike the lighter blasters that Luke and Mara—and Han and Leia—had been carrying the first time they fought the Gorog, the big G-12s had more than enough power to punch through the thick chitin of a Killik pressure carapace. As each bolt struck, it literally shattered the protective shell—and the bug inside.

When no more shatter gun pellets came his way, Luke turned toward Mara. She was crouching on the other side of Jacen's StealthX, trying to use her lightsaber to cut him out of the cockpit. She was not having much success. A small tangle of Gorog were floating toward her through the rubble, spraying Jacen's crippled starfighter with shatter gun pellets as they bounced from block to block.

Luke extended a hand and sent them all tumbling with a violent Force shove. As they struggled to right themselves, he pulled a thermal detonator off his harness, thumbed the activation switch, and sent it after them.

A sharp crackle came over his comlink as the weapon detonated, and his imaging system went momentarily dark. Luke squeezed the trigger of his power blaster anyway, spraying bolts toward the empty ripples in the Force that he could still feel approaching from deeper in the rubble.

By the time the imaging system cleared again, Mara had cut Jacen's canopy open and was depressing a button on his wrist to activate his suit's automatic stim-system. Luke started toward them, somersaulting through the dust and laying suppression fire into the rubble. He no longer needed to search for ripples in the Force to find Gorog—he could see them coming, a growing tide of egg-shaped carapaces springing from one hunk of spitcrete to another, spraying shatter gun pellets as they approached.

Luke reached Jacen's StealthX just as Mara was pulling his limp form out of the cockpit. "How is he?"

"Still alive," Mara said. A string of shatter gun pellets tore into the fuselage, blowing Jacen's R9 unit apart and filling the air with sparks. "For now!"

R2-D2 flashed a message across Luke's visor suggesting that without evasive action, none of them would be alive in a moment.

"Don't worry." Luke pulled a trio of thermal detonators off his harness and thumbed the activators. "I still have a few tricks left."

He tossed the detonators toward the oncoming wave of Gorog, then used the Force to spread them across the head of the entire swarm. This time, the crackle inside his helmet was ear popping. But Luke was looking in the opposite di-

ection as the detonation occurred, pulling himself over
acen's StealthX, and his imaging system did not darken.

Luke retrieved his nephew's combat harness and power
blaster from the cockpit, then caught up to Mara and took
n arm. As they Force-pulled themselves toward a slowly
umbling chunk of spitcrete, Luke's imaging system showed
StealthX-sized bubble pushing past through the flotsam.
Kyle Katarn touched Luke through the battle-meld, reas-
uring him, letting him know reinforcements were on the
vay.

A moment later, the StealthXs turned the battle zone as
bright as day with their flashing laser cannons.

Luke and Mara slipped behind the spitcrete with Jacen.
Luke used the Force to hold the block steady so they could
iide behind it. Mara opened the status display on the fore-
rm of Jacen's suit and checked his vital signs.

"Everything reads okay," she said. "Maybe it's just a
ompression blackout."

"Or a concussion." Luke could hear the relief in his own
oice. Neither type of injury was likely to be a fatal—as
ong as they could get him to help. "Turn up his comm vol-
ume."

Luke started to grab Jacen by the shoulders, but Mara
pointed him toward the edge of the block. "Stand watch.
'll handle—"

An incoherent groan came over the comm channel, then
acen's face grew suddenly pale inside his helmet visor. His
ryes blinked open, and he nearly sent them all tumbling by
rying to sit up.

"No, Jacen." Mara pushed him against the spitcrete.
"Stay put."

He looked confused for a moment, then turned to Luke.
"She's here, isn't she?"

Luke nodded. "I think so."

"Can you see her?" Jacen demanded.

"I don't know," Luke said. "I haven't—"

A deafening pop came over the comm channel, and an orange flash briefly lit the battle zone. Luke felt the sudden anguish of a young Jedi's fiery death, then saw the wings and cannon mounts of a StealthX spinning past along with the gravel and smoke. He slid over and peered around the edge of their spitcrete hiding place and discovered that he could, indeed, see Lomi Plo. The Dark Queen.

She floated about a dozen meters away, surrounded by Gorog warriors and encased in a somewhat cylindrical Killik pressure carapace. A pair of long, crooked arms were still extended from her stooped shoulders, pointing toward the twisted skeleton of smoking durasteel that had been a StealthX just a moment earlier. A second pair of shorter, more human-looking arms protruded from the middle of her body, while one spindly leg jutted out from the side of her hip, giving her an appearance more insectile than human.

Intending to take her out with a sniper shot, Luke started to reach for his power blaster, but Lomi's danger sense was as acute as Mara's. A lightsaber immediately appeared in her lower set of arms, and she started to turn in a slow circle, scanning the rubble and looking for her would-be ambusher.

Realizing there was only one way to do this, Luke snapped the lightsaber off his own belt. "Mara, keep the bugs off me."

"Luke?" Mara came his side. "What are you—"

"Lomi's over there," Jacen said, joining them. "At least I think it's her."

"*You* can see her, too?" Mara asked.

"Sure," Jacen said. "Either that or I'm still unconscious."

"You're awake," Luke assured him. He shrugged out of

is combat harness and sent it toward Jacen. "Keep an eye
n Artoo—"

"I'm not *that* fuzzy," Jacen said. "I'm coming with you."

There was no time to argue, for Lomi Plo had spotted
uke and was staring right at him. The face inside the cara-
ace was the same one Luke had glimpsed during their
ght a few months earlier: a half-melted, noseless face with
ulbous multifaceted eyes and a pair of stubby mandibles
here there should have been lower jaws. The mandibles
oved behind the faceplate, and the Gorog warriors raised
eir shatter guns and started to turn to fire.

Luke sprang toward Lomi Plo, at the same time grab-
ing her in the Force and pulling her toward him. She
unched herself into a backflip, trying to wrench free, but
uke had her too tightly. It was all she could do to bring
erself back around before he was on her, igniting his blade
nd thrusting at her abdomen.

She brought her purple blade down and blocked—then
uke glimpsed a white flash sweeping toward his helmet
nd had to throw himself sideways. Her second lightsaber
wept past his shoulder, barely missing. Luke used the
orce to accelerate his spin, whipping his feet up over his
ead. He landed a Force-enhanced kick to her faceplate,
he tip of his blade tracing a smoky curve up the side of her
arapace.

Lomi Plo whipped both lightsabers around in a counter-
trike, the short purple one driving for Luke's abdomen,
he long white one sweeping toward his knees. He switched
o a one-handed grip, meeting the white blade with his own
nd blocking the other attack by spinning inside and strik-
ng across her elbow, forcing her to lock her arms with
oth blades extended. She countered by bringing her knee
p into his helmet, sending him flipping away, and then
hey fell into a vicious contest of strike and counterstrike,
either one probing for weaknesses or trying to set up a

fatal trick later, both of them fighting just to survive tw
more seconds, all their attention focused on blocking th
next blow, pouring all their strength and speed and skil
into landing their next attack just a little quicker, hittin;
their foe's blocks just a little harder.

Luke was vaguely aware of the larger battle ragin;
around him. He could feel Mara and Jacen protecting hi
flanks, keeping Lomi Plo's bodyguards at bay with blast
ers and detonators and the Force. He could sense mor
StealthXs gliding into the battle zone, lighting it up witl
their laser cannons and penetrating deeper into the rubble
preventing more Gorog from reaching their queen. He coul
hear Kyle Katarn issuing commands over the suit comms
ordering Jedi Knights to leave their StealthXs and form ;
protective ring around their Grand Master.

Then Mara set off the first dazer. A shrill whine filled th
comm channels, and the battle zone shimmered with ;
rainbow iridescence. The air inside Luke's helmet suddenl
smelled like fresh-cut pallies—a side effect, he knew, of th
aura-deadening pulse Cilghal had developed to disrupt th
collective mind of the Killiks.

Deprived of the thoughts and feelings of their nest
fellows, the Gorog warriors froze or launched suicidal at
tacks or simply collapsed in trembling heaps. And Lomi Plo
hesitated, her white lightsaber hanging above her shoulder;
for a heartbeat too long, her lower blade caught out of po
sition defending a flank attack that was not coming.

Luke launched a furious assault, slipping under he
upper lightsaber and catching her lower guard on the back
swing, then driving forward and slashing at her mid
section. She pivoted, dropping one side back, and Luke
switched to a lunge, driving the tip of his blade deep in th
belly of her carapace.

For a breath, the queen did not seem to realize she hac
been hit. Seeing Luke stretched forward and off balance

she snapped her mandibles in delight and brought her short blade around to attack his arm while her long blade descended on him from above.

Luke thumbed off his lightsaber and rolled away sideways, watching in alarm as her long blade slashed past his head just a centimeter from his visor. He rolled once more and saw vapor billowing from the abdomen of Lomi Plo's pressure carapace, then brought his feet up over his head . . . and found himself hanging upside down, caught in a net of golden Force energy.

Luke knew what was coming next: the Myrkr strike team had described how Lomi Plo had used a similar net to dice a Yuuzhan Vong captor into bits. Luke began to push out with the Force, stopping the net from constricting any further and slicing through this vac suit. But he was not strong enough to break the attack outright. Cilghal's Dazer had cut Lomi Plo off from the collective mind of the Gorog, but not from the Force. She could still draw on her nest to enhance her Force potential, and as strong as Luke was, he was not strong enough to overpower an entire nest of Killiks. He would simply have to hold on—and hope she ran out of air before he ran out of strength.

A black, tarry substance began to boil from the puncture in Lomi Plo's pressure carapace, and the vapor plume disappeared. The queen had plugged the hole. She turned and started to float toward Luke, the mandibles on the other side of her faceplate spread so wide he could see the smiling row of human teeth they concealed.

There was no question of reaching out to Mara or Jacen for help. They were busy fending off Gorog warriors, somersaulting and spinning and Force-deflecting shattergun pellets. Instead, Luke risked a split in his concentration and used the Force to send a Wookiee-sized lump of spitcrete hurling toward Lomi Plo's head.

The attack never reached her, of course. She sensed it

coming and raised her hand, deflecting it straight into Mara.

The impact sent Mara spinning, and a Gorog shatter gun pellet slammed into the small of her back. A puff of vapor shot from the hole, then quickly vanished as the vac suit sealed itself.

Luke still felt Mara's jolt of surprise, and to some extent even the numb, deep ache of the wound itself. A fierce rage boiled up inside him, and perhaps that was what gave him the strength to break Lomi Plo's Force-net . . . or perhaps she had just been distracted by the boulder Luke had hurled at her.

It did not matter. Luke pushed, and the net dissolved. He flew at Lomi Plo, determined to finish this *now,* but terrified that he would not be fast enough . . . that he was not good enough to kill the Unseen Queen in time to save Mara.

Lomi Plo turned to meet him, and suddenly she seemed the size of a rancor, with bristling bug arms three meters long and reflexes so quick that her whirling lightsabers were nothing but a blur. Luke drew up short, trying to shake his head clear, trying to calm himself so he could determine the truth of what he was seeing.

But it was no use. Luke was too frightened for Mara. He could feel her starting to slip, feel her fighting to control the pain . . . and the Gorog were still attacking. Luke hurled himself at Lomi Plo again. It did not matter that he would never get past her guard, or that he did not understand what he was seeing. He just had to kill her.

But Lomi Plo had grown weary of fighting Luke. She spun away, her long upper arms lashing out toward Mara. Luke locked his blade on and drew his hand back to throw—then found that his arm would not come forward. Nothing would move at all; his mouth would not even open to voice the scream that rose inside him as Lomi Plo's white lightsaber came arcing down toward the crown of Mara's helmet.

Then Jacen was there, slipping in front of Mara, his lightsaber flashing up to block. He caught the blow above his head and whipped his blade over Lomi Plo's and sent her white lightsaber spinning away into the rubble.

But Lomi Plo had two lightsabers, and she brought the second one up under Jacen's guard, pushing it into the abdomen of his vac suit. The purple tip came out through his back, and still Luke could not move. If anything, he was more paralyzed than ever; he could not breathe, could not blink . . . it seemed to him that even his heart had stopped beating.

The tip of Mara's power blaster appeared under Jacen's upraised arm, and Luke could feel the anger that was driving Mara, the rage at what had happened to their nephew. A blinding bolt flashed from the barrel, taking Lomi Plo full in the chest and sending her tumbling head over heels, leaving her purple lightsaber hanging in Jacen's body.

And suddenly Luke could move again. He used the Force to pull himself over to Jacen and Mara, then deactivated Lomi Plo's lightsaber and tossed the handle aside. By the time he had finished, Mara was already placing a patch over the holes in Jacen's vac suit.

Kyle Katarn arrived in the same instant, emerging from the flotsam with half a dozen other Jedi. They quickly drove the last of the Gorog warriors away, lacing the darkness with blaster bolts and flinging thermal detonators around like confetti, using the Force to create a protective shell of rubble around the Skywalkers and Jacen.

"Where's Lomi Plo?" he asked. "I can't see her. Is she still here?"

Luke barely heard. He could sense that Mara was in pain but still strong, and she remained lucid enough to have applied a pair of emergency patches to Jacen's vac suit. But

Jacen's presence had grown as elusive as when he had been knocked unconscious, and the pattern of dark spray around the suit patches suggested that he had lost a lot of blood.

"Jacen?"

"Don't . . . worry about . . . me!" Jacen's voice was anguished but calm, and his words carried the sharp edge of command. "You're showing Lomi . . . your weakness!"

"It's okay." Luke peered over his shoulder, but saw no sign of Lomi Plo or her Gorog anywhere. "Mara drove her off."

"I *did*?" Mara asked. Obviously, she had not been able to see Lomi Plo, either. "You're sure?"

Jacen shook his head. "We don't . . . know." He grabbed Luke's sleeve and pulled him closer. "You showed her . . . your fear, and she used it . . . against you."

Mara caught Luke's eye, then nodded past his shoulder. "I'll take care of Jacen," she said. "You take care of Lomi Plo."

Luke took Jacen's power blaster and slowly turned around, quieting his own thoughts and emotions, surrendering himself to the Force so that he could feel its currents and search for the cold stillness that would be Lomi Plo. He felt nothing, not even the telltale ripples of her Gorog warriors.

"I think she's gone," Luke said. "I can't see her anymore."

NINETEEN

Interrogation cells were the same the galaxy over: dark, cramped, and stark, usually too hot or too cold. The interrogator usually had a breathing problem, some wheeze or rasp or even an artificial respirator that suggested he had been cuffed to a chair a time or two himself. This interrogator, a blue-skinned Chiss in the black uniform of a Defense Fleet commander, spoke with a wet snort. It was probably caused by the old wound above his black eye patch, a thumb-sized dent deep enough to have collapsed his sinus cavities.

As the officer approached, Leia's nostrils filled with the harsh stench of charric fumes—probably what passed for deodorant aboard a Chiss Star Destroyer. He stopped a meter and a half from her chair, running his good eye over her as though contemplating what a Jedi woman looked like beneath her robes. Leia pretended not to notice. The "undressing" was an old interrogator's trick, designed to make a prisoner feel more powerless than she really was. Leia had endured such scrutiny more times than she wanted to remember—and that applied especially to the time the interrogator had been Darth Vader.

Finally, the interrogator met her gaze and said, "You're awake. Good."

"I'm glad one of us thinks that's good," Leia said.

"Frankly, I would've preferred to sleep until my head stops hurting."

The interrogator's red eye glimmered as he filed this tidbit away for future use. Again, Leia pretended not to notice. She intended to lay a trail of such tidbits for him . . . a trail that would lead straight to the identity of the person who had betrayed their mission.

"Yes . . . the knockout gas." The interrogator's impediment caused him to pronounce *gas* as *khas*. "After the trouble we had taking Jedi Lowbacca into custody, we felt it necessary to be prudent with you and Master Sebatyne."

"You could have asked politely."

The interrogator offered her a thin smile. "We did. You destroyed two of our clawcraft."

Leia shrugged. "There was a little misunderstanding."

"Is that what you call it?" His voice remained steady, but there was an angry heat to it. "Then perhaps we should make certain there are no *more* misunderstandings."

He stepped back and gestured toward a sizable display screen hanging in the corner. On cue, an image appeared, showing Han cuffed into a chair similar to Leia's. Another Chiss officer, younger than the one in Leia's cell but with a harder blue face, stood next to Han. On a nearby table lay an array of nerve probes, laser scalpels, and electrical clips—a virtual smorgasbord of torture.

Leia gasped, her heart suddenly hammering hard. She turned to her interrogator, struggling to regain her composure. "Captain Fel promised there would be no torture."

"*If* you surrendered." A wet rumble sounded from the back of the interrogator's mouth as he inhaled. "Instead, you continued your attempts to escape until he trapped you against the Shattered Moon."

"A *Chiss* is going to hide behind a technicality?"

Leia knew that the contempt in her voice only confirmed to the interrogator that he had found his leverage, but she could not help herself. After discovering that the moon cluster was filled with Killiks, she had been the one who argued against making a run for the planet. With a faulty control system and Zark Squadron and two Star Destroyers ready to blast the *Falcon* to space dust, it had just seemed wiser to surrender and escape later. Now she wasn't so sure. To be willing to break promises and threaten torture, the Chiss had to be in desperate circumstances—and a desperate foe was the most dangerous kind.

The interrogator remained silent, giving Leia's emotions time to build, trying to move her from fear to anger to hopelessness as quickly as possible.

But Leia had already regained control of her feelings and hid her fear behind a cool voice. "I see I'll have to revise my opinion of the Ascendancy."

The interrogator spread his hands in a gesture of helplessness. "That is entirely up to you . . . as is your husband's fate."

On screen, the young officer picked up a laser scalpel and activated the blade. Han responded with a sneer, but Leia could see the fear beneath his show of disdain. The officer brought the blade close to Han's eye, then made a very precise serpentine cut down Han's cheek—just proving that there were no rules for this interrogation. The letter *S* appeared in faint crimson, and blood began to dribble down Han's face.

Han held his sneer, not even flinching. "I can only get prettier."

Please, Han, don't provoke him, Leia urged silently.

"It's just a scratch," the interrogator said. "As long as you cooperate, it's the worst your husband will suffer. But if you refuse, my protégé will be required to demonstrate his skills."

A surge of hatred rose inside Leia, and she had the sudden urge to show this little man who was really in control here, to reach out with the Force and squeeze his throat shut. Instead, she swallowed her anger and settled for narrowing her eyes.

"This may surprise you, but I'm willing to tell you whatever you wish to know." She turned toward the hidden vidcam she sensed to one side of the display screen. "You're already aware of the *Falcon*'s mission, and the Jedi have nothing else to hide."

The interrogator followed her gaze and smiled. "Impressive. Others might guess that a cam exists, but not its precise position. I'm sure you have many such talents, Jedi Solo." His smile faded abruptly, and he leaned in close, breathing fetid air in her face. "But I must warn you against using those talents to escape. Regardless of whether you succeeded, your husband will be in no condition to join you."

He glanced at display screen again. When Leia looked, the cam panned back. Behind Han stood two Chiss guards, their charric pistols pointed at his head. Leia took this in, her hatred of the interrogator now growing to include his superiors and all the others whom she knew were watching, and she expanded her Force-awareness around her.

As expected, she felt two Chiss guards standing behind her, as well. But she also felt a more familiar pair of presences lurking above and behind the guards, approximately where a ventilation duct might be. Cakhmaim and Meewalh had escaped custody—or, more likely, they had never been captured in the first place.

Leia turned her attention back to the interrogator.

"I don't appreciate your threats," she said. It was a code phrase that would alert the Noghri to the fact that she was about to give an order. "But threats *are* sometimes effective. While Master Sebatyne and I can take care of ourselves, I would be very unhappy if any harm were to come to Han or the other members of our crew."

The interrogator frowned, confused by what seemed only an indirect response to his warning. "If you are asking for a guarantee of their safety—"

"I'm not *asking* anything, Commander . . ." Leia paused, waiting for the interrogator's name to rise higher in his thoughts. ". . . Baltke. I'm *telling* you that whatever happens to Han and the others, I'm going to do the same to you." She turned to the hidden vidcam. "And to *you.*"

The tightening of Baltke's lips was barely perceptible, but Leia knew that his superiors would point it out to him later as the moment he had lost control of the interrogation. For now, however, he seemed to believe he was still in charge. He spent a moment trying to stare Leia down—snorting softly with each breath—and she felt the Noghri withdrawing to carry out her instructions.

Finally, Baltke stepped to Leia's side and extended a hand toward one of the guards behind her. The hand returned holding a hypoinjector.

"Don't be afraid, Princess." Baltke pulled up the sleeve of her robe and reached down to press the hypo to her forearm. "This is only something to help you relax . . . and assure that the answers we receive from you are true."

"Oh, I'm not afraid, Commander."

Leia created a loud Force-thunk in the corner behind her, then used the Force to redirect the hypo into Baltke's thigh and depress the injector. He gave a startled cry and pulled the hypo away so quickly that even Leia barely saw what had happened. Given that the vidcam's view had been partially obscured by the commander's back, she hoped the monitors in the control room had not seen it at all.

"Commander?" asked one of the guards behind her. "Is something wrong?"

"Nothing's wrong," Leia said reassuringly. Normally, she

could influence only weak minds with the Force—but the drug was *designed* to make minds weak. She just hoped that it was fast. "I flinched, and Commander Baltke nearly injected himself instead of me."

Baltke frowned and looked at the hypo in his hand.

"Commander?" the second guard asked.

"She flinched." He passed the hypo back to the guard. "I nearly injected myself."

Leia let out a long breath. "The drug must be working, Commander. I'm feeling more relaxed already."

"Good. Slo am I." Baltke's slur was barely perceptible, but it was there. He stepped back in front of Leia, wobbling slightly. "I think we're ready to begin."

"There's no need to stand, Commander," Leia suggested. "Sit down and make yourself comfortable. You're going to find me very cooperative."

"She's going to cooperate." Baltke looked to one of the guards. "Bring me a chair."

Leia felt a growing wave of concern from the two guards, and she did not hear either of them move to obey.

"Forgive me for inshruding." Leia slurred her words to reinforce the impression that she was not fully under control. "But washn't that an order?"

"That's not for you to say, prisoner," the guard retorted.

"'S not my fault," Leia retorted. "*I'm* not the one who injected me with a truth drug."

"That was indeed an order," Baltke scowled at the guards. "Do I have to vocode it?"

"No, sir."

The door whirred opened, and a moment later a black-uniformed guard placed a chair behind Baltke.

"Thank you."

Baltke sat down and studied Leia, snorting softly, his brow furrowed as though he was having trouble remembering what he wanted to ask her. She was going to have to work fast. It would not be long before his superiors realized something was wrong and relieved him.

"I imagine you want to know what the Jedi's plans are," Leia prompted.

Baltke shook his head. "Already know 'em."

Leia frowned. "You do?"

"Aaaaffirmative." He nodded for emphasis. "We want to know *why.*"

"Why what?"

"Why the Jedi are forcing the Galactic Alliance to side with the Colony against us."

"We're not," Leia said.

Baltke snorted sadly, then twisted around to look up toward the display screen in the corner. He clicked the comm unit on his lapel. "She's lying. Cut something off this time."

The officer in the vidimage smiled. Then he activated his laser scalpel and pressed the tip to the base of Han's ear.

"I'm not lying." Leia put the Force behind her words. "It's the truth."

"The truth?" Baltke seemed confused, and Leia realized that the belief she was fighting was deeply ingrained. "But the Killiks ambushed us with a brand-new *Alliance* Star Destroyer at Snevu!"

"Yes, I know," Leia said. "It was the *Admiral Ackbar.* The Killiks captured her in the Murgo Choke. That was shortly before Admiral Bwua'tu prevented the Colony's battle fleet from leaving the Utegetu Nebula."

"The Killiks? *Capturing* an Alliance Star Destroyer?" Baltke was clearly having trouble believing this, even under the influence of the mind-weakening drug. "That doesn't seem very likely, Princess."

The officer in the display began to cut into the skin around Han's ear, prompting Han to clench his teeth and tense against his restraints. His head—wisely—remained still.

"You stupid rodder!" Leia yelled. It required all her willpower to keep from Force-choking Baltke to death, but she held herself in restraint. The Noghri had not yet reached Han, or what she was seeing would not be happening. "I saw it with my own eyes. I was there!"

"You were there?" Baltke continued to watch the display screen, his face blank and disinterested, as though he saw someone's ear get detached in slow motion every day. "I'm sure that's why the *capture* looked so convincing in news-holo footage."

Leia groaned. "Look, *I'm* never going to convince you that it wasn't staged." She could not take her eyes off Han's anguished face. "So why don't you stop cutting and ask your source?"

"Our source?"

"The person who told you about the *Falcon's* mission!" Leia said. Whoever *that* was, he—or she—was also going to pay for what Han was suffering now—assuming Leia could trick Baltke into revealing the traitor's identity. "You clearly have good reason to trust your source."

"An excellent suggestion." Baltke nodded a little too enthusiastically. "I'll pass it along to Commander Fel."

"Maybe you should stop torturing Han until you can confirm my answer." Leia used the Force again, trying to make Baltke think that was a good idea. "I *am* telling the truth."

Balkte stood and pressed his comlink. "Wait."

Han's torturer glanced over his shoulder, then stopped, the laser scalpel still held to Han's ear.

Leia exhaled in relief. "Thank you," she said. "By the time you get a message to Coruscant, there wouldn't have been enough left of him to—"

"Coruscant?" Baltke asked, looking confused.

"That *is* where your source is, isn't it?" Leia focused all her attention on Baltke, alert to any hint of deception . . . in his face or in the Force. "Or is he with the fleet?"

"You'd have to ask Captain Fel." Baltke's tone was helpful, as though he really believed Jagged might tell them. "He's the only one who knows who the source is."

Baltke cocked his head and frowned, no doubt listening to instructions over a hidden earpiece, and Leia tried not to choke on the growing lump of disappointment in her throat. Even if Baltke was somehow defeating his own truth drug, there was no hint of deception in either his face or the Force. As far as *he* knew, Jagged Fel was the only person who knew the identity of the mission's betrayer.

Baltke's face turned a lighter shade of blue. "You're very clever, Princess—but cleverness carries a price." He depressed his comlink again. "Finish it."

The officer resumed cutting, removing Han's ear, then stepped back with the appendage pinched between his thumb and forefinger. Han's mouth opened in a roar, and he shook his head, spraying a line of blood across the man's blue face. Leia grew so angry and sick inside that she had to fight to keep from retching.

"I hope you remember my warning, Commander!" Leia snarled. "Because I certainly do."

"Of course," Baltke replied pleasantly. "And I hope *you* remember what will happen if you attempt anything so foolish." Again, the display screen showed the two guards pointing their charric pistols at the back of Han's head. "Now perhaps we should discuss your daughter's activities."

"There's no point—you know more than I do," Leia said. She was still in shock from what she had just seen. The Chiss were tough, cunning soldiers, but she had not believed they would actually torture a prisoner—especially not when one of their command officers had promised otherwise. Of course, the fact that Jagged had felt it necessary to *make* such a promise suggested that Leia was being a bit naïve. "But I'm sure you won't believe *that*, either."

Baltke looked confused. "I *want* to believe you, Princess. Just tell us why she is leading the Killik ground swarm."

"How do I know?" Leia snapped. "Because she's a Joiner."

Baltke snorted loudly and cocked his head, and Leia began to regain control of herself, to realize that she was not going to help Han or the Jedi by allowing her fear and frustration to control her. She turned toward the hidden vidcam.

"And even if Jaina wasn't a Joiner," Leia said slowly, "the Jedi can't condone speciecide. We're *all* opposed to what you're doing here. Any help we're giving to the Killiks—*that's* the reason." She glanced toward the display, and when the officer remained standing next to Han's bleeding figure, she added, "All the Jedi are trying to do is end the war."

"By defeating *us*," Baltke retorted.

Leia shook her head. "No—by destroying the Colony and restoring the Killiks to their prior state of disorganized nests."

Balkte scoffed. "Perhaps you and Captain Solo are not getting along these days." He glanced toward Han's bleeding image. "Perhaps that is why you keep lying."

Leia used the Force again. "I . . . am . . . not . . . lying."

"You aren't lying?" Even under the power of a mind influence, Baltke sounded unconvinced. "Then the Jedi are fools. What you suggest can't be done."

"We think it can." Leia turned to the vidcam again. "You asked why the Jedi are opposing you. Let me explain."

The floor and interrogation chair began to shudder with a sudden acceleration tremor. Baltke furrowed his dented brow and remained silent for a moment, listening to his earpiece and snorting softly every time he inhaled. The Force became charged with anticipation . . . and with a strange, stoic fatalism.

Leia waited until Baltke's attention returned, then asked, "Something wrong?"

"Not at all," he said smugly. "Everything is going quite well, as a matter of fact."

Leia sensed no deception in his answer. "Then how come you're so ready to die?"

Baltke's eye widened in surprise, but he said, "Because I am a soldier, Princess Leia." He returned to his seat and gestured for her to continue. "But please don't waste our time with more lies. Our session will soon be cut short."

"Very well," Leia said. The vessel continued to tremble, suggesting they were accelerating into battle. "You already know what the *Falcon*'s mission was."

"Yes. Your assignment was to rendezvous with your daughter and her mindmate." Baltke was speaking a bit rapidly now, the truth drug and the excitement of the coming battle serving to agitate him. "Then you were to enter Chiss space and attempt to infiltrate our command and control centers with teams of Killik commandos."

"Not quite," Leia said. "Actually, the plan was to attack only *one* center, using a variation on the same tactic the Killiks used to capture the *Admiral Ackbar*."

Baltke arched the brow above his red eye, then asked in an interested voice, "*Really?*"

"The idea was to get the *Falcon* captured," Leia explained. "While you were interrogating us, a swarm of Killik commandos—they're about the size of your thumb—would be sneaking out of the *Falcon*'s smuggling compartments to infest your facility and take control at an opportune moment."

As Leia explained this, Baltke frowned and pressed a finger to his earpiece without seeming to realize he was doing it.

"Don't worry—your vessel is safe," Leia said. "That part of our plan relied on winning Jaina's cooperation.

Since we haven't rendezvoused with her, we haven't picked up any Killiks yet."

"You'll understand if we want to check for ourselves."

"Go ahead," Leia said. "If you give me a comlink, I'll instruct See-Threepio to show you how to open the compartments."

Baltke started to reach for his comlink, then seemed to catch himself and smiled.

"Nice try, Princess." He glanced at one of the guards behind her. "Bring a vocoder. We'll have her *record* the message."

The guard acknowledged the order, and the door whirred open behind Leia. A moment later the vessel began to buck and shudder more noticeably.

"We're entering the atmosphere!"

"So it seems," Baltke replied calmly. "We're still confused about this plan of yours. How did you expect capturing one of *our* command and control centers to destroy the Colony?"

"We didn't," Leia said. "That was just to get your attention. Luke is destroying the Colony himself."

"Now I *know* you're a fool," he said. "How could one Jedi do that?"

"By destroying the Dark Nest and its Unseen Queen," Leia said. "That should be completed by now."

"You tried that at Qoribu," Baltke pointed out. "You failed miserably."

"This time, we're better prepared," Leia said. "Our scientists have developed a few weapons to disrupt the Killiks' collective mind—and we have an Alliance attack fleet to support us."

Baltke's voice grew derisive. "And once the Dark Nest is gone, you think the Killiks will become 'good bugs' again?"

"Not at all," Leia said. "That's only the first part of Luke's plan. He should be arriving here very soon to complete the second."

"Which is?"

"Destroying Unu and removing Raynar Thul from his role as the Colony's leader," Leia said. "It may take a little time, but our scientists are certain that once Raynar is no longer able to control the nests by exerting his Will through the Force, the Colony will grow disorganized and enter a self-regulating cycle again. Then it won't be a threat to anyone."

"An interesting theory," Baltke said. They began to buck harder than ever, and the cell began to grow warm—an indication that they were descending so fast that the vessel was having trouble dissipating the heat of atmospheric friction. "What exactly do you mean when you say 'remove' Raynar Thul?"

"Whatever it takes," Leia said. "Luke has never liked the idea of a Jedi leading any government, and this is a good example of why."

"So you're going to assassinate him?" Baltke asked.

"That's one possibility, but I don't know what Luke has decided," Leia said. "I can promise you this, though: Raynar Thul is a Jedi problem, and we'll do whatever it takes to fix it."

Baltke considered all this for a moment, then said, "It does sound plausible." He stood, shaking his head and turning to the display screen. "But I can see we're going to have to cut something else off your husband."

"*What?*"

The display screen showed a Chiss medic bandaging Han's ear—and, by the looks of it, enduring the cussing-out of his life.

"Your story doesn't hold together," Baltke told Leia.

"Attacking *one* of our command centers contributes nothing to this plan."

"That's because the Jedi don't see the Chiss as an enemy," Leia said. "Luke never wanted to cause the Ascendancy harm—only to make a point."

"Is that so?" Baltke asked. "I'm afraid we fail to see it."

The lights flickered as the vessel began to fire its heavy weapons. Leia checked the display screen again, wondering why Han was still there. The Noghri should have had him free by now.

She turned her attention back to Baltke. "The point was to show that the Killiks are capable of infiltrating even your most secure facilities. The Alliance learned that the hard way with the *Ackbar*. The Killiks stole it right out from under the nose of our best fleet admiral."

"Bwua'tu might be *your* best," Baltke said. "But I can assure you that no Chiss admiral would make such a mistake—if, indeed, it *was* a mistake."

"I don't think you're very sure of that," Leia said. In the display screen, the medic stepped away and made some sort of joke that caused Han's tormenter to laugh. "If you were, you wouldn't have been so curious when I described the *Falcon*'s mission."

"Merely being prudent," Baltke countered. "An abundance of caution is never wasted."

"If you really believe in caution, then you'll think about what I'm telling you," Leia said. "Killiks can sneak into anyplace. They're *insects*. All they have to do is lay eggs in a few wounded soldiers and let you take them home aboard a medical frigate, and a whole base will be infiltrated. Or they could stow away in a returning supply freighter and then infest an entire planet. Before you know it, your whole society will be swarming with Killiks—and I don't have to tell you what that means. You'll become an empire of Joiners."

"And the Jedi think we would be better off letting the Colony mass nests on our border until they are ready to attack?"

"We think the Chiss would be better off ending the war our way," Leia said. "You'll never win the war your way. It's not *possible* to wipe out the Killiks. They were building nest cities on Alderaan twenty thousand years before the Chiss empire was born, and they'll be building nest cities on your frontier twenty thousand centuries after it's gone."

A confident smirk flashed across Baltke's face, and Leia felt something disturbing in the Force—something cold and menacing and final. Deciding to give up on the Noghri, Leia reached out to Saba, concentrating on the bloody image of Han in the display screen, allowing her alarm to flood her thoughts.

Saba's emotions were oddly reassuring—at least for a Barabel—and Leia received the distinct impression that Han was safe. Unfortunately, Leia was not assured.

Baltke cocked his head again and briefly turned toward the hidden vidcam, then faced Leia. "I'll pass your warning on to my superiors." He started toward the door. "But now I'm afraid I must be off to my duty station. We'll be expecting casualties soon."

"You're a medic?" Leia could not conceal her surprise.

"A battle surgeon, to be precise." Baltke removed his eye patch, revealing a perfectly sound organ underneath, and started toward the door. "Interrogations are a secondary duty."

"Wait!" Leia commanded.

Baltke stopped—clearly in spite of himself. He glared at her angrily.

"When I told you the Killiks would outlast the Ascendancy, you smirked," Leia said. "Tell me why."

"What are you doing? Using a Jedi mind trick?" Baltke

demanded. "It will be your fault if I have to hurt Captai⟩
Solo again."

Leia glanced at the display screen and saw that the medi⟨
was still standing next to Han, laughing with the torture⟩
Something did not make sense. Saba had clearly meant to
reassure her about Han, and yet Leia could see that he had
not yet been rescued—in fact, that he did not even look
close to being rescued.

The remaining guard started to step forward behind
Leia. She grabbed him in the Force, then hurled him into
the corner with the vidcam. He hit headfirst with a loud
thunk, then dropped to the floor and did not move.

Leia looked back to Baltke and put the power of the
Force into her voice. "*Why* do you think the Killiks can'⟩
win?"

Baltke's face twisted into a mask of resistance, but the
truth drug made it impossible for him to lie.

"Because *we* have developed our own solution to the
Killik problem," he said. "And *our* plan will work."

He tried to go to the door again, but Leia Force-shoved
him up against the wall. "What kind of solution?"

"A p-permanent one." Baltke cast a longing look toward
the display screen, then said, "It's not too late to save you⟩
husband. Just release me."

"Han's going to be just fine." Leia used the Force to
begin working the locks of the cuffs holding her in the
chair. "You, on the other hand, are in trouble—or have you
forgotten what I said about anything that happened to
Han?"

"I remember."

"Good." The first cuff came loose. "You might want to
be a little more informative about this 'permanent solution.' "

Baltke shook his head, but he could not resist the power
of his own drug. "P-p-parasites."

"Parasites?" Leia asked. The second cuff came undone. "You're going to infect them with parasites?"

Baltke nodded. "Any minute now," he said. "After the Killiks spring their trap."

"Trap?"

"You know," he said. "Isn't that why you turned back from the Shattered Moon?"

Leia's jaw fell. "You know about the Killiks hiding here?"

"We suspected." Baltke seemed almost proud. "We're counting on them to ambush us."

"I don't understand." Leia stretched her hand toward the unconscious guard and summoned his charric pistol to hand. "Counting on their ambush for *what*?"

A low boom rolled out of the air vent behind Leia, and the whole room rocked.

"To deliver a resounding defeat to us," Baltke said.

Leia understood the rest of the Chiss plan. "And tomorrow, all of the nests will have a huge victory dance."

"That's right," Baltke said. "The Killiks aren't the only ones who can play the infestation game."

"How long?" Leia asked. When Baltke did not answer, she asked again, this time using the Force. "*How long?*"

"We'll have to keep fighting for a while," Baltke answered. "The parasite won't be fatal for a year."

"And by then, it will have spread throughout the whole Colony."

Baltke smiled. "You see? We *can* win the war our way."

"Are you mad?" Leia cried. "That's speciecide!"

She used the Force to open her ankle restraints—then heard the cell door whirring open behind her. Thinking the other guard had returned with the vocoder Baltke had requested—or the officers watching from the control room had sent reinforcements—she threw herself out of the chair and rolled across the floor, then spun around, brought her captured charric pistol around . . . and found herself pointing it at the handsome face of her favorite scoundrel.

"*Han?*"

"Whoa—take it easy, Princess!" Han raised his hands. "I know I'm late, we had to take care of the control room first."

"I don't care!" Leia cried, recovering from her shock. She threw herself into Han's arms, barely noticing as Cakhmaim and Meewalh slipped past to take control of Baltke and the unconscious guard. Then she reached up and touched his ears. "They're both there!"

"Honey, are you okay?" Han moved her back from him and studied her with a concerned look—until he noticed the display screen in the corner, which continued to show the medic and the torturer standing beside Han's bloody head. "Hey! That poor rodder looks like *me!*"

TWENTY

A familiar voice echoing down a long tunnel . . . a hammer pounding inside her head, a centrifuge spinning her through the darkness . . . aching cold below the knees, aching cold from the shoulders up.

Nothing between. Just numb.

Then the voice again, calling Mara back, commanding her attention.

Luke giving orders . . . too fast. Not quite near enough to follow.

Slow down, Skywalker!

Luke continued. "Nothinghaschanged. We're burru-burrub," he was saying, "uruburruplan. Cilghalwillbe in urburbubu collection teams, thenserveas Kyle's scientific adviser urburub dispersal operations inside the Colony proper."

Mara opened her eyes and found herself staring up at a blinding white blur. Everything smelled of stericlean, and there were machines hissing and whirring all around. She tried to sit up and found herself held tight by a strap across her chest.

"Just how volatile *is* this nanotech?" a deep Duros voice asked from somewhere to her right. "Is it going to turn our StealthXs into dirt right under us?"

"Only if you let it escape the stasis jars," Cilghal replied. Her voice and the Duros' sounded somewhat muffled.

"Even then, you would have plenty of time to go EV before the damage grew critical."

The brightness overhead came into focus, and Mara recognized it as the softly lit whiteness of an infirmary ship ceiling. It took her a moment to understand why she was here, then she turned her head and saw the tangle of IV lines hooked into her arm and she remembered: the shatter gun pellet that ripped through her vac suit and abdomen. It had destroyed one of her kidneys, and no healing trance could repair *that*.

The huge head of her Bith physician, Ogo Buugi, appeared above her. "Good, you're awake. How are you feeling?"

"Hararrg oooo aiiig meeeffffing?" Mara croaked. It was supposed to have been *How do you think I'm feeling?* but her throat was as dry as a Tatooine swamp and her tongue was too heavy to lift. "Ooggaf."

Buugi nodded approvingly, his smile half hidden by the epidermal folds hanging from his cheeks. "Good. That's what I was hoping."

Mara considered using the Force to slam him against the ceiling.

"The operation went very well—no complications at all," Buugi continued. "We already have a new kidney growing in the cloning tank. We'll insert it in a couple of weeks, and in a month you'll be ready to start your rehabilitation."

"A *month*?" Mara cried. "Are you a doctor or a—"

"Better let me take over, Doctor Buugi." Jacen appeared at Mara's bedside, seated in a hoverchair with a drainage bag hanging from his side. "Aunt Mara can be a little testy right after she wakes up."

Buugi smiled more noticeably and nodded. "So I see." He placed a delicate, long-fingered hand on Mara's forearm, then said, "You need to be patient with this. Even a Jedi can't grow a new kidney overnight."

"Thanks for the advice, Doctor," Mara answered, softening her tone. "And thanks for patching me up." Mara waited for Buugi to leave, then turned to Jacen. "Shouldn't you be in a bacta tank?"

"With the Killiks still holding Thyferra, the fleet is running short on bacta," Jacen explained, moving his chair closer to her bedside. "I'm out of action for a couple of weeks anyway, so I thought I'd save it for someone who doesn't have a healing trance."

Mara nodded her approval. "Good idea—very thoughtful." She pointed at the drainage bag hanging from his side. "How is it?"

"Inconvenient," Jacen said. "I've got holes in three different organs, and I can't move well enough to fight until I fix them."

"I know the feeling," Mara said. She reached for his arm and winced at the dull ache that the effort sent shooting through her lower back. "Thanks, Jacen. She would have gotten me."

"She nearly *did,*" Jacen said. "If you hadn't been so fast with that blaster, neither one of us would be here."

"All the same." Mara squeezed his arm, then asked, "Do we know what happened to her?"

Jacen's expression turned sober. "Pellaeon's intelligence staff has been reviewing the battle vids. A skiff left Gorog just before we blew it. Nobody challenged it—nobody even seemed to see it, including the combat controllers."

Mara had a sinking feeling. "Lomi Plo."

"That's what Uncle Luke thinks."

Mara used the Force to operate the bed controls and raise her upper body. The shift of position sent another dull ache through her lower back, but she pushed the pain aside and looked out the door into the infirmary lobby, where Luke was meeting with Cilghal and the other Masters.

"And he's sticking to his plan?"

Jacen nodded.

"Who's taking our places?"

"No one," Jacen said, a slight frown betraying his disapproval. "Cilghal offered to lead a team herself so that Kyp, er, *Master* Durron could back Luke up, but Uncle Luke wouldn't hear of it. According to the intelligence maps that Juun and Tarfang left, the collection teams only need to harvest nanotech from fifteen different environments inside the nebula, but they're going to have to seed more than a thousand worlds in the Colony. Tresina Lobi is out of action with some crash burns, and Uncle Luke didn't want to take another Master off the dispersal teams. He thinks it's the nanotech environmental systems that will keep the Killiks in check—in the long run, anyway."

Mara's heart sank. "So he's going after Raynar alone?"

"Admiral Pellaeon is taking the fleet to Tenupe," Jacen said. "Wraith and Rogue squadrons will be assigned specifically to support him, and he'll have a company of Lando's bugcruncher droids—but we both know they won't be able to do much once the Force duel starts."

"And Lomi Plo isn't going to give up, either," Mara said.

"Not likely," Jacen said. "Unless that blaster shot you got off kills her first."

Mara gave him a sour look. "What do *you* think the chance of that is?"

"About the same as you do," Jacen confessed. "He'll have to take both of them out. Lomi Plo and Raynar."

Mara's stomach began to ache with fear. "Jacen, we can't let him do that alone."

"I don't think we have a choice in the matter," Jacen said. "Have you tried to stand up yet?"

Out in the lobby, Luke dismissed the Masters and turned

to enter Mara's room, the faithful R2-D2 trailing close behind.

They had barely crossed the threshold before Mara demanded, "Are you *crazy*?"

Luke stopped and cast a sheepish look back toward the departing Masters before he returned her gaze. "You heard."

"You'd better not have been thinking you'd keep *that* from me, farmboy."

"Of course not." Luke came to her bedside and took her hand, then gave Jacen a stern look. "But I *had* hoped to tell you myself."

"Luke, the Colony isn't going to win this war overnight," Mara said. "Wait until Jacen and I can back you up. Raynar is inexperienced, but he's powerful."

Jacen nodded his agreement. "And Lomi Plo will be—"

"I can't," Luke said, cutting them off. He clasped a hand on Jacen's shoulder. "I've been feeling something urgent from Leia. This war is coming to a head *now*."

"Do you know *how*?" Jacen asked.

Luke shook his head. "All I can tell is that things didn't go well at Tenupe. The *Falcon* never connected with Jaina. I think maybe the Chiss were already there attacking."

Mara's heart skipped a beat, but the corners of Jacen's mouth rose in a near smile.

"Then we shouldn't interfere," Jacen said. "If Mom and Dad can recover Jaina and Zekk, staying out of the Chiss's way might be the best thing for the galaxy."

Luke frowned. "Jacen, you're as bad as your father," he said. "You think the answer to every insect problem is to start stomping."

"Not every insect problem," Jacen said. "Just this one. I thought I'd made that clear."

"You have," Luke said. "You also made it clear that you'd follow the order's leadership in this matter."

"It was only a suggestion," Jacen retorted. "Can't a Jedi Knight express himself around here anymore?"

Luke's expression softened. "Of course," he said. "But half a dozen times should be sufficient. I'm very aware of your opinion about the Killiks, and believe it or not, I *have* given it consideration."

"Okay. Sorry to bring it up again." Jacen looked more disappointed than apologetic—which suggested to Mara that he was sincere about following the order's leadership, even if he disagreed with it. "But I still think you should wait until Aunt Mara and I can back you up. You won't solve anything if Raynar kills you."

"Or if Lomi Plo does," Mara added. She had been growing more impressed with Jacen every day since Luke took sole leadership of the order, and she was even beginning to wonder if he might make a suitable second in command someday soon. "I don't think you can take them both, Luke."

"Then I'll have to take them one at a time," Luke said. "Because if I wait for you two to recover, Lomi Plo will have time to recover, too—and so will Gorog. Lomi is never going to be weaker than she is right now."

Luke's tone was as firm as Mara had ever heard it, and she could feel through their Force-bond that he would not be moved from his plan.

But Jacen, bless him, was determined to try. "And you're *still* not ready to face her."

Luke's eyes flashed with resentment—or it might have been self-doubt. "*I* will be the judge of that, Jacen."

"Of course." Jacen spread his hands in a gesture of surrender, and Mara thought she saw something bright, like moonlight dancing on a river, flicker in the depths of his brown eyes. "You *are* the Grand Master."

"Thank you, Jacen," Luke said. He turned to Mara, and

she felt the faintest tingle of Force energy washing over her body. "And now, if you'll excuse me, I'd like a . . ."

Luke's jaw dropped, then he frowned in confusion. "Padmé?"

"Padmé?" Mara repeated. "Luke, what are you talking—"

"Mara?" Luke sounded disappointed. He shook his head as though to clear it. "I don't understand."

"Neither do I," Mara said.

"Mara?" Now Luke's voice was frightened. "What's wrong?"

"Good question," Mara said.

She turned to Jacen, but he only held a finger to his lips and moved his hoverchair closer to Luke. R2-D2 emitted a confused whistle and raised a hydraulic extension with a medical sensor at the end.

"*Mara!*" Luke turned and hit the emergency summons button next to Mara's bed, but Jacen made a motion with his hands and the button did not depress. Luke did not seem to realize this. He turned back to Mara and placed his fingers to her throat, checking her pulse. "I can't feel a pulse. Artoo, call an EmDee droid. Tell her to hurry!"

R2-D2 spun toward the data jack to obey, but Jacen used the Force to disable the power to the droid's treads.

Mara caught Jacen's gaze. "All right, Jacen. This has gone far enough."

Not yet. The message reverberated without words inside Mara's head. *He must learn.*

Mara felt another wave of Force energy pass over her, and Luke cried out in horror and looked toward R2-D2.

"*Artoo,* what's taking you so long?"

R2-D2 issued a frustrated whistle and spun an accusing photoreceptor toward Jacen. Luke could take it no longer. He raised a hand and began to fill it with life-giving Force energy.

"Jacen, we can't wait. We have to revive her ourselves." He pointed at the emergency respirator hanging on the wall. "Get the respirator."

Luke leaned over Mara and started to place his hand on her chest—until Jacen raised an arm and pushed him away.

"*Jacen!*" Luke screamed. "What's wrong with you?"

"Nothing," Jacen said calmly. "And there's nothing wrong with Aunt Mara."

Luke's gaze swung back to Mara, and she could not decide whether he looked more stunned or relieved. "You're . . . you're alive again!"

"I was never dead," Mara said. "I think Jacen is trying to make a point."

Luke turned back to Jacen, still too confused to be angry. "I don't understand, Jacen. What's she—"

"You're not ready to face Lomi Plo again," Jacen interrupted. "And you just proved it."

Luke's confusion started to fade, and his anger quickly began to build. "*You* did that to me?"

Jacen shook his head. "You did it to yourself," he said. "Your fear betrays you."

Mara suddenly understood what Jacen had done—or rather, what he had *not* done. "Luke, I think you'd better listen to him." She reached out to her husband through their Force-bond, adding a private plea that she knew he would not refuse. "For me."

Luke snorted, but turned to Jacen. "Okay, I'm listening," he said. "And it had better be good. Saving Mara's life does not give you the right to manipulate me."

"I didn't do that," Jacen said. "All I did was bring your fear to the surface. You created the illusion yourself."

"Remember what happened in the nest ship?" Mara asked. "After I got hit, you couldn't move. Luke, you froze."

"And then I couldn't see Lomi Plo anymore," Luke said, growing calmer. He turned to Jacen. "*You* did the same thing to me?"

"I doubt it." Jacen grew uncomfortable, and his gaze slid away. "That was just a mirror illusion I learned from the Fallanassi."

"But it does prove you're still vulnerable to Lomi Plo," Mara said.

"You don't fear for yourself," Jacen said. "You fear for others—and now Lomi Plo knows that. She'll use it against you."

Luke nodded, and a glimmer of recognition came to his eyes. "Fears aren't so different from doubts. I have to face mine—"

"No," Jacen said. "You have to *eliminate* them."

"Eliminate them?" Mara asked. "That's a lot to ask—especially before we reach Tenupe."

"But I *can* do it," Luke said. "I have to."

"How?" Mara demanded. "You can't give up caring about your family."

"He doesn't have to," Jacen replied. "He just has to surrender."

"Surrender?" Mara asked.

"Vergere taught me to embrace my pain by surrendering to it." Jacen turned to Luke. "I made that pain a part of me—something I would never fight or deny. You have to do the same thing with your fear, Uncle Luke. Then it will have no power over you."

"That may be easier said than done," Luke said.

"Not at all—I know just where to start." Jacen used the Force to lift R2-D2 over to them. "The first thing your fear showed you was your mother's face. And before the battle, you refused to see what happened after your father Force-hurled her."

"So I need to see that now?"

"Only if you want to kill Lomi Plo," Jacen said.

Mara wanted to discourage Luke, to spare him the pain of seeing his mother die by his father's hand. But he was determined to kill Lomi Plo and end this war on Jedi terms, and she knew that Jacen was right, that Luke could not succeed until he embraced his fears as Jacen had learned to embrace his pain.

"Jacen's right. If you're going after Lomi Plo, you need to do this." Mara reached for his hand. "You can't change what is in that holo. You can only accept it."

"That's a lot different from accepting you being hurt—or dying," Luke pointed out. "I couldn't do anything to stop what happened to my mother, but when you were hurt, I was there."

"And you still couldn't stop what happened to *me*," Mara countered. "You were pretty busy with Lomi Plo, as I recall."

"I was barely holding my own," Luke acknowledged.

"Some things you can't control," Jacen said. "If you fear them, then those things control *you*."

Luke shook his head. "I'm not sure we have time for this," he said. "And what if you're wrong? What if Lomi Plo's wounds are enough to distract her?"

"I'm not wrong," Jacen countered. "Look, you may think you push your fears aside when you go to battle—that you bury them. But you'll never bury them deep enough to hide them from Lomi Plo, no matter what her condition is. So you'll have to deal with this problem *now*. Because as you've pointed out, Lomi Plo is healing as we speak."

Luke let out a long breath. "Okay." He turned to R2-D2. "Show me the holo where my mother dies."

R2-D2 issued a questioning trill.

"We're going into battle either way," Luke said. "If you

don't want to end up navigating slave ships for Lomi Plo, you'd better start where we left off last time."

R2-D2 gave a plunging whistle, then rocked forward and activated his holoprojector. The image of Padmé, Anakin, and Obi-Wan Kenobi appeared on the floor, Padmé choking, Anakin extending an arm toward her, and Obi-Wan approaching Anakin.

"Let . . . her . . . go!" Obi-Wan was ordering.

Anakin whipped his arm to one side. Padmé flew out of the holo, and Anakin started forward to meet Obi-Wan.

"You turned her against me!" Anakin accused.

Obi-Wan shook his head. "You did that yourself."

The pair left the holo as R2-D2 retreated and turned away from them. For a moment, their voices could be heard arguing in the background, slowly fading as Obi-Wan accused Anakin of falling prey to his anger and his lust for power. Then their voices faded entirely as Padmé's crumpled form returned to the holo, lying on a metal deck.

A lump of sorrow formed in Mara's stomach, and she felt Luke shaking with grief. R2-D2 extended a grasping appendage and started trying to drag Padmé's unconscious form to safety.

From somewhere out of the holo, C-3PO's voice called, *"What are you doing? You're going to hurt her. Wait!"*

The distant sounds of a lightsaber fight arose somewhere outside the holo, then C-3PO appeared and carefully took Padmé in his arms. He started toward the slick-looking skiff they had seen in the last holo, with R2-D2 following close behind, beeping.

"I am being careful!" C-3PO said. "I have a good hold on her, but I'm worried about my back. I hope it's able to hold up under this weight."

C-3PO entered the skiff and laid Padmé on a bed in a stateroom. The holo blurred as R2-D2 advanced it quickly through several minutes of watching her lie there; then Obi-Wan arrived to check on her and brush her hair back.

The holo flickered off for an instant, then restarted in the observation room of an operating theater. Obi-Wan was there with C-3PO, Yoda, and a tall, swarthy human. Mara recognized the man as Bail Organa—someone she would later spy upon when she became the Emperor's Hand. A medical droid entered the observation room and began to speak to Obi-Wan and the others.

"*Medically, she is completely healthy.*" *The droid's voice was tinny, but surprisingly sympathetic for a machine.* "*For reasons we can't explain, we are losing her.*"

"*She's dying?*" *Obi-Wan sounded as though he did not believe the droid.*

"*We don't know why,*" *the droid replied.* "*She has lost the will to live. We need to operate quickly if we are to save the babies.*"

"*Babies?*" *This from Bail Organa.*

"*She's carrying twins,*" *the droid said.*

"*Save them, we must,*" *Yoda added.* "*They are our last hope.*"

The medical droid returned to the operating room, and one of R2-D2's beeps sounded in the holo.

"*It's some kind of reproductive process, I think,*" *C-3PO said softly.*

After a few minutes, Padmé whispered something to the medical droid, and Obi-Wan was summoned into the operating theater. He went to her side, and his voice came out of R2-D2's holospeaker sounding even more tinny and distant than usual.

"*Don't give up, Padmé,*" *he said.*

She looked up at him, seeming very weak. "*Is it a girl?*"

"*We don't know yet.*" *Obi-Wan looked toward the droid operating on her midsection.* "*In a minute . . . in a minute.*"

Padmé winced with pain, then the medical droid lifted a iny bundle into view.

"It's a boy," he announced.

Padmé's voice was so weak that it was barely audible. "Luke . . ." She smiled faintly, struggling to extend a and to touch the baby on the forehead, then repeated, ". . . Luke."

The medical droid produced another bundle. "And a girl," he announced.

"Leia," Padmé said.

Obi-Wan leaned closer to her. "You have twins, Padmé. They need you . . . hang on!"

Padmé shook her head. "I . . . can't."

She winced again and took Obi-Wan's hand. There seemed to be a necklace dangling from her fingers as she did this, but the holo was not clear enough to see what kind.

"Save your energy," Obi-Wan urged.

Padmé's gaze grew distant. "Obi-Wan . . . there . . . is good in him. I know there is . . . still."

She let out a sudden gasp, then her hand dropped out of Obi-Wan's, leaving the necklace dangling from his fingers. He gathered it into his palm, then turned his hand and began to study the jewelry with a shocked expression.

The holo ended, and R2-D2 tweedled a question.

When Luke did not answer, Jacen said, "Thank you, Artoo. That's all we needed to see."

R2-D2 tipped himself upright again, then swiveled his photoreceptor toward Luke and issued an apologetic whistle.

"There's nothing to apologize for, Artoo," Mara said. Although Luke looked outwardly composed, she could feel how hard he was struggling to contain his grief, to keep his anguish from erupting in an explosion of fury and pain. "It had to be done."

Jacen took Luke's elbow, then squeezed until Luke's blank gaze finally turned toward him. "Master, can you change what you saw in the holo?"

Luke shook his head. "Of course not."

"That's right. You can only accept it," Jacen said. "Some misfortunes you can prevent, and you will. But others . . . sometimes all you can do is embrace the pain."

Luke laid a hand across his nephew's. "I understand. Thank you."

"Good," Jacen said. "Now use what you are feeling. Your anger and your grief can make you more powerful. Use them when you meet Raynar and Lomi Plo, and you *will* defeat them."

A sudden wave of disgust rolled through the Force-bond between Mara and Luke, and Luke frowned and pulled his arm away from Jacen.

"No, Jacen," he said. "That's Vergere's way of using the Force. It won't work for me."

Jacen's face grew worried. "But you're one against two, and they'll have the Force potential of the entire Colony to draw on. You'll need all the power you can get!"

"No," Luke said. "I'll need *strength*—and that comes from my way of using the Force."

Jacen cast a worried glance toward Mara, and she began to grow fearful as well.

"Luke, I understand your hesitation," Mara said. "But I'd feel better if you took another Master or two—"

"I've made my decision." Luke smiled and squeezed her arm gently. "Don't fear. *Accept*."

TWENTY-ONE

It had grown clear that—for once—Han and Leia Solo would not arrive at the crucial moment. A ceaseless storm of megamaser fire had turned Tenupe's green sky into a flashing sheet of crimson and the endless downpour into a hot, foul-smelling drizzle. A dozen different kinds of rescue shuttles were hovering over the flooded river, trying to pluck the half-drowned Chiss survivors off their submerged islands. Clouds of fist-sized Qeeq and meter-long Aebea were droning out of the jungle to attack, clogging intake turbines with their puréed bodies and massing on hulls until their weight alone dropped the vessel like a stone into the river.

The crucial moment was past. Maybe Jaina had misinterpreted the situation when she reached out to her mother in the Force, or maybe something had delayed the *Falcon*. It hardly mattered. The battle could no longer be stopped. Zekk was descending out of the jungle's defoliated canopy with her StealthX slaved to his, and all that remained now was to spring UnuThul's trap and watch the Chiss die.

As the StealthXs drew near, Jaina and Zekk's mind-link was restored. It was not as all-embracing as it had been when they were with the Taat—living with other nests had weakened it—but the connection remained strong enough for Jaina to know the sense of urgency that filled every fiber of Zekk's body, and to understand the reason for it. UnuThul was coming with the Moon Fleet.

The struts had barely touched the jungle floor before Jaina's astromech was opening the canopy and tweedling a welcome.

"Nice to see you, too, Sneaky," Jaina said. "All systems go?"

The droid gave an affirmative whistle, and Jaina felt a wave of concern from Zekk. She looked battered and exhausted and bloody. Maybe she was not ready to start flying missions.

"You think the Chiss will wait while we take a nap?" Jaina retorted. Without waiting for a reply, she turned to her Wuluw communications assistant and reached down to rub a forearm along an antenna. "Sorry for getting you killed so many times, Wuluw."

"*Burru,*" Wuluw thrummed. "*U bru.*"

"You be careful, too," Jaina said. "Someday, the Song will have a verse about your bravery at the Battle of Tenupe."

"*Rrrr.*" Wuluw's mandibles clattered in embarrassment, then she waved all four arms in modesty. "*Uburr.*"

Jaina and Zekk laughed, then Jaina stepped over to her StealthX, retrieved her flight suit from the cockpit and gladly changed out of her mud-caked combat utilities.

She was just climbing into the pilot's seat when her mother suddenly touched her through the Force. Leia seemed terribly alarmed and was clearly trying to warn Jaina and Zekk about something, but the feeling was too vague to tell more.

Then Jaina and Zekk felt Saba reaching out to them as well, opening herself to a battle-meld. They did the same, and the situation immediately grew clearer. Saba and Leia were here, somewhere near Tenupe, and they needed Jaina and Zekk in the air. Something terrible was coming, something that had to be stopped.

Jaina hastily buckled her crash webbing, then glanced out at Wuluw, and she and Zekk wondered if this was something they should warn the Killiks about.

Yes! The impression came from both Saba and Leia, so strong that Jaina and Zekk heard it inside their minds as an actual word. *Must!*

Wuluw started to turn around and leave, but Jaina caught her in the Force and floated her back to the StealthX.

"Urubu rububu!" the Killik drummed as Jaina suspended her next to the starfighter. *"Brurb!"*

"Don't worry, you're not coming with us," Jaina said. "And even if you were, I really doubt you'd burst. StealthXs have inertial compensators."

"Urb?"

"You need to warn the swarm," Jaina said. "Something bad is coming."

"Rr?"

"We don't know. My . . ."

Jaina stopped, unsure whether she should reveal the source of her foreboding. She had heard how her parents had interfered with the Utegetu evacuation, and she knew the Colony would disapprove of any effort to end the war, so she and Zekk both thought it was probably best not to mention Leia and Saba.

"We're getting a strong feeling from the Force." Jaina returned Wuluw to the ground. "Warn the swarm—and alert UnuThul!"

Jaina lowered the StealthX canopy and energized the repulsor drives, then followed Zekk up into the top of the jungle, where the defoliated mogos were now shattered and burning. Chiss megamaser strikes were lancing down through the clouds like a Bespinese lightning squall, igniting kilometer-long columns of flash fire and turning the lower sky into a region of flame-storm and hot, buffeting winds.

The two Jedi ascended toward the cloud ceiling half blinded by alternating instants of crimson brilliance and stormy dimness, trusting their stick hands to the Force, weaving and rolling their way through a forest of crackling energy. They were dimly aware of a quiet area by the river, where an erratic stream of Chiss shuttles was diving into the mass of Killiks swirling above the islands. But they did not even consider entering the enemy's rescue corridor. As nerve racking as it was to ascend through a barrage, it was far better than the alternative: being spotted by a rescue pilot and having a squadron of clawcraft jump them.

The cloud cover made the ascent especially challenging. The megamaser beams did not seem to descend so much as manifest from the mist. Jaina and Zekk constantly found themselves reacting rather than anticipating, rolling away from a fading column of flame only to find a new one erupting ahead. To make matters worse, their tactical displays revealed two squadrons of clawcraft circling through the clouds around them—enough to make even Jedi grind their teeth and curse under their breaths.

Zekk wanted it known that he was only responsible for the teeth grinding. Until he had become Jaina's mind-mate, he had never even *heard* most of the curse words that were now ricocheting around inside his head.

As they broke out of the clouds into the emerald vastness of Tenupe's upper atmosphere, both exhaled in relief. A blinding torrent of energy was still crackling down around them, but now that they were above the rain and the clouds, the situation looked a little more like the battles they had grown accustomed to in space—with an emphasis on *little*. The megamaser beams were fanning down from about fifty points overhead. The vessels that fired them

vere still so distant that they were barely flecks against the
ky, but they *were* descending fast, following each other
lown in a large open spiral and trailing long plumes of
;ray entry smoke that gave away their positions.

Jaina wrinkled her brow. A military fleet dropping out of
orbit with batteries blazing might be terrible, but it was
aardly something that Leia and Saba would expect Jaina
and Zekk to stop with a pair of StealthXs. The warning
aad to point to something else—something the two Jedi
Knights had not yet seen.

"Sneaky, give me a full tac on that fleet," Jaina ordered.
"I'm looking for something that doesn't fit the attack pro-
ile."

Sneaky tweedled an acknowledgment, then scrolled a
message across the display: A SPACE FLEET PERFORMING
CLOSE GROUND SUPPORT DOES NOT FIT ANY ATTACK PRO-
FILE IN MY RECORDS.

"Your records don't include the Battle of Bogo Rai,"
Jaina said.

AND YOURS DO?

"ReyaTaat's do," Jaina said. ReyaTaat had once been a
Chiss intelligence officer named Daer'ey'ath. "It's a famous
Chiss battle. The Colony learned about it when Taat found
Daer'ey'ath spying on us and received her into the nest."

OH.

The fleet deployment appeared on Jaina's tactical display. The enemy's ground-support task force consisted of
thirty Star Destroyers and their escorts, a truly awesome
flotilla capable of incinerating the jungle from canopy to
roots for kilometers around. But the Chiss were being
oddly careless, leaving only a handful of Star Destroyers
and their escorts in orbit to provide top cover. When Unu-
Thul arrived with the Moon Swarm, he was going to do
more than bloody the enemy fleet and drive it off—he was
going to smash it against Tenupe.

The Chiss have made their last mistake, Zekk said through their mind-link. *After UnuThul destroys their fleet, they will not be* able *to press the war.*

The Chiss will be weakened, Jaina agreed. Somewhere deep in her mind, she knew that the total destruction of the fleet was a two-edged sword, that weakening the Chiss too much would only embolden the Colony and prolong the war—but it did not seem that way to UnuThul. She could sense his excitement through the Force. It was a dark momentum inside her, growing more powerful each moment and carrying her inexorably into bloody total war. *The tide will change, and the Colony will crush them like bugs.*

Zekk chuckled at the insult, and the sensation of his amusement made Jaina feel a little sad. There had been a time when the chuckle would have erupted from her lips, too, and neither of them would have known—or cared—who laughed first.

Then Jaina sensed something else from Zekk—a sudden surge of alarm—and they quickly dropped back into the clouds where they would be difficult to see. Four squadrons of clawcraft had started to descend ahead of the main task force, escorting a pair of Chiss defoliators and swinging wide to avoid the megamaser barrage.

Jaina and Zekk reached out to the defoliators in the Force and suddenly felt sick and cold. *Those* ships were what Leia and Saba had wanted them to intercept. There was something terrible aboard those two defoliators, something so sinister and deadly that it had overwhelmed their danger sense from nearly a hundred kilometers away.

Navigating by instruments, they swung onto an interception vector, and shortly afterward they escaped the barrage area. UnuThul soon felt the threat, too. A dark pressure arose inside their chests, pushing them after the two defoliators, compelling them to attack *now.* It was all they could do to resist his Will, to remain in the clouds until they were actually in a position to succeed.

Finally, when the two defoliators had moved so close that the main fleet would not risk firing into the fight, Jaina and Zekk raced forward. They remained in the clouds until they were directly beneath their targets, then pulled back their sticks and climbed straight up. Jaina armed a pair of proton torpedoes—the Colony could no longer acquire the baradium needed to make shadow bombs—then designated the defoliator on the right.

"We'll take that one, Sneaky. Let me know when we have a target-lock."

The droid chirped an acknowledgment, and for a moment it looked like their StealthXs might reach attack range unseen.

Then clawcraft from the two trailing squadrons began to drop down to meet them. They seemed to be moving in slow motion, since the atmosphere even this high was thick enough to slow down a starfighter and tear it apart if it maneuvered too sharply. But the distances were also smaller—dozens of kilometers instead of hundreds—and within a few heartbeats, the dark specks of the first Chiss fighters came into view and began to rain cannon bolts down on the StealthXs.

Sneaky reported that they had a target-lock. Jaina confirmed that it was the correct vessel, then sensed Zekk doing the same. They launched their torpedoes together and watched the white dots of the propulsion tails vanish into the green sky.

A second later the first laser bolt slammed into Jaina's forward shields, spilling orange flame in front of her canopy and reverberating inside the cockpit as shield hits never did in space. Zekk slipped in close and slightly ahead of her, buying time for her shields to recover by placing himself between her and their attackers. They continued to climb like that, barely five meters apart, juking and jinking as one, pouring fire back up at the clawcraft.

Then Sneaky chirped in surprise, and Jaina checked her tactical display to find both sets of proton torpedoes detonating twenty kilometers from the defoliators—well short of where any countermeasures should have taken effect.

"What the Hutt happened?"

The tactical display replayed the last several seconds, and Jaina saw four clawcraft come streaking in to intercept the proton torpedoes head-on. One of the pilots was lucky enough to blast his target out of the air with cannon fire, but the other three missed and stopped the torpedoes by crashing into them.

That's spaced—even for Chiss! Zekk said through their shared mind.

Maybe the defoliators don't have countermeasures, Jaina suggested.

Or maybe the Chiss just want to be really *sure those ships deliver their payloads,* Zekk said.

Zekk took a hit in his shields, then Jaina slipped into the forward position. The enemy squadrons were coming head-on, a mad tactic as dangerous for them as it was for their targets. They were coming in waves of four, the leaders already so close that they were the size of fists. Jaina and Zekk picked the second one from the left and fired together, pounding through its shields by landing five cannon strikes simultaneously.

Before the fireball died away, Jaina and Zekk switched targets. The first wave was so close now that they could see the laser bolts streaming from the tips of the forward-pointing "claws" that gave the starfighters their nicknames. The Jedi fired again, aiming where the Force told them the craft was going rather than where it was. The pilot accommodated them by jinking into their line of fire, and the starfighter vanished in a flash of yellow flame.

Jaina and Zekk were just turning their attention to their next victim when the crash of a triple cannon strike shook Jaina's cockpit. Her instrument panel lit up with depletion lights and damage warnings, but she could not hear the alarms—or Sneaky's tweedling—over the roar of the explosion.

Zekk slipped into the lead position, and they began to pour cannon bolts at the next clawcraft. The two survivors from the first wave had swollen in apparent diameter to the size of a Bith's head, but they were barrel-rolling and bobbing and weaving so hard now that, at such short range, the StealthXs could not aim their laser cannons quickly enough to hit the targets.

Sneaky scrolled a message across Jaina's display. IT IS IMPERATIVE THAT WE TURN BACK IMMEDIATELY. WE HAVE LOST OUR FORWARD SHIELD CAPACITOR!

"So?" Jaina asked. "We still have shields for now, right?"

UNTIL WE SUFFER THE NEXT HIT, Sneaky replied. AND IF WE ARE FORCED TO EJECT, I DON'T HAVE A PARACHUTE!

"Relax," Jaina said. "I have the Force."

The Chiss finally rolled the wrong way. A trio of hits punched through his shields and took off an attack claw, sending him into an uncontrolled spin. He vanished into the roiling gray-green clouds below, and then the last clawcraft was on them, not evading, just coming straight at the StealthXs with all four cannons blazing.

Zekk's shields overloaded and flashed out in a second. Before Jaina could move into lead position, his StealthX took a hit in the nose and another in an upper wing, and still the clawcraft kept coming.

Then Jaina realized the pilot had no intention of veering away. With her and Zekk flying in overlap formation, the explosion from a midair collision would be enough to take them both out.

The thought had barely entered Jaina's mind before Zekk was breaking left. Jaina broke in the opposite direction, trying to force a hesitation by making the enemy choose between targets.

The Chiss was too good to hesitate. He smoothly switched targets and took aim at the side of Jaina's StealthX, pounding through her shields and blowing head-sized holes into her fuselage. Unable to shoot back, she used the Force to tip his clawcraft downward, redirecting his fire and forcing him into a dive that carried him beneath her starfighter instead of crashing into it.

As the starfighter streaked past, the Force fairly crackled with the pilot's frustration—with his very *human*-feeling frustration. Jaina reached out to him and felt an all-too-familiar presence. "Blast," she muttered. *Jagged Fel.*

Knowing better than to let a clawcraft pilot—particularly *this* clawcraft pilot—get behind her, Jaina pivoted the StealthX over its wing and started after him.

"Sneaky, open a hailing channel to our target."

The droid squeaked a long objection, which Jaina could barely hear over all the damage alarms—and which she could not read because her display was out.

"Comm protocols don't apply right now," Jaina said, taking a guess at what her astromech was upset about. "The enemy already knows where we are. They can *see* us."

Sneaky whistled in refusal.

"If I have to do it myself, I'm ejecting you," Jaina said.

The channel was open by the time she fell in behind the clawcraft.

"Jag, what are you doing here?" she demanded.

"Trying to shoot you down," Jag said. "But I forget—that's supposed to be a military secret. Now I guess I have to kill you."

Jaina probably should not have been surprised by the

bitterness in Jag's voice, but she was, and he nearly broke free by rolling to the left. Fortunately, Zekk was there pouring laser bolts into the clawcraft's exhaust tail, and Jag had to slip back into Jaina's sights when overload static began to snake across his shields. He tried to escape again by breaking hard to the right, but this time Jaina was ready and forced him back by sending a stream of cannon bolts past his flank.

"Jag, you shouldn't take this so personally," Jaina said. She noticed that he was gradually turning, trying to draw them away from the defoliators. "You and I were over a long time before Zekk and I met Taat."

"You think I *care* whose antennae you rub?" Jagged retorted. "You betrayed your honor."

"Our honor?" Jaina was confused. "We haven't made you any—"

"I guaranteed Lowbacca's parole at Qoribu," Jagged reminded her. "And you returned my courtesy with betrayal. at Supply Depot Thrago and the Battle of Snevu. My family's reputation has suffered."

As had its finances, if Jaina recalled the terms of the guarantee correctly. Aristocra Formbi had said the Fels would have to repay any damages Lowbacca caused if he violated the parole—and before returning to the Alliance, he had taken part in the destruction of not only several million liters of space fuel, but also dozens of clawcraft and a couple of capital ships.

"Jag, I'm sorry," Jaina said. The second wave of clawcraft reached visual range and—ignoring the possibility of hitting Jagged by accident—opened fire on the StealthXs. "In the urgency of the situation, the parole just didn't occur to us."

"Don't apologize. The fault is all mine." Jagged continued his turn and started to climb, trying to set up Jaina and

Zekk for his wingmates. "I should never have made the mistake of thinking Jedi had honor."

The rebuke hurt more than it should have, perhaps because Jaina and Zekk knew it was justified—and because Jaina knew that it reflected Jagged's current disdain for her. But this was war, and they could not allow personal feelings to interfere with stopping those defoliators—not when whatever the vessels were carrying felt so malevolent and deadly.

"Jagged, we—I—want you to know that I still love you. And I always will." Jaina activated her attack sensors and locked Jagged's clawcraft as the primary target. "But if you can eject, you should do it now."

Jaina and Zekk opened fire.

But Jagged had already gone into the Clawcraft Spin, whirling his starfighter around its ball-shaped cockpit and spraying laser bolts in every direction as he fell away in an erratic spiral impossible to target. It was a popular tactic in space combat, but in an atmosphere it was so dangerous and difficult that most pilots would have preferred to take their chances with no shields and one engine. Yet Jagged Fel somehow managed to keep the air resistance from tearing his craft apart, and by the time he vanished into the clouds, he was already emerging from the spin and starting to pull up.

Maybe we shouldn't warn him next time, Zekk suggested.

You're just saying that because you're jealous, Jaina joked.

Yeah, but not over you, Zekk replied. *No one can fly like that without the Force!*

A cannon bolt flashed past Jaina's cockpit—so close that it raised a heat blister in the canopy—and she and Zekk turned and dived. With their forward shields down and the Chiss behaving more like Killik suicide fliers than clawcraft pilots, their only chance of stopping the defoliators lay in catching the two vessels in the clouds, where their StealthXs could remain hidden until they attacked. The clawcraft pursued, but both Jaina and Zekk still had their rear shields and were able to endure the short pounding they received before reaching cover.

They had barely entered the clouds before the dark pressure began to build inside their chests again. UnuThul did not want them to wait. He wanted them to attack *now*. Jaina and Zekk reached out to him in the Force, trying to make him see that they could not possibly succeed, that their StealthXs were barely holding together and their only hope of success lay in concealment.

UnuThul did not understand—or care. The dark pressure grew unrelenting, until they thought their hearts would collapse. Still, they remained in the clouds, calling on each other for the strength to resist UnuThul, Jaina using the Force to steady Zekk's hand when his StealthX began to drift upward, Zekk reaching out to push her stick forward when she began to pull it back. Because Jaina's displays were not working and Zekk's sensor pod had been blasted away, they had to navigate by feeling alone, always keeping the noses of their battered starfighters pointed toward the menace they sensed in the Force.

And even as Jaina and Zekk closed on their targets again, they sensed Leia and Saba struggling with their own troubles far above. Sometimes, her mother felt tense and worried, and other times she and Saba were clearly in combat, filling the battle-meld with fury and fear and determination. Jaina and Zekk ached to help, but they were too well disciplined to ignore the defoliators—even without the influence of UnuThul.

A shock wave of astonishment rolled through the battle-meld, and suddenly Leia and Saba seemed confused, hopeful, and terrified all at once. The dark pressure inside Jaina and Zekk grew more powerful than ever, and they found themselves poking their canopies out of the clouds in spite of themselves.

The defoliators were only a few kilometers above, so close now that Jaina and Zekk could clearly see their hawkish silhouettes—and the drop-shaped outlines of two enormous bombs hanging beneath each wing.

Each of the vessels was tightly ringed by a defensive cordon of clawcraft, with another six starfighters arrayed farther out in intercept position. There would be another dozen Chiss ambushers even farther out, circling low over the clouds, ready to pounce the instant the StealthXs showed themselves.

Far above the defoliators, a distant web of light was flashing back and forth between the descending Chiss fleet and the lower reaches of space. With both of their tactical displays nonfunctional, it was impossible for Jaina and Zekk to tell exactly what was happening . . . but they could guess. UnuThul had arrived with the Moon Swarm and launched his attack prematurely, probably hoping to divert the Chiss's attention and make it easier for them to bring down the defoliators—and judging by the feelings in the battle-meld, Leia and Saba and the rest of the *Falcon*'s crew had gotten caught in the middle of it.

The tactic changed nothing as far as Jaina and Zekk were concerned. Their best chance of success, as small as it was, still lay in the . . .

A new presence joined the meld—the dark, oddly familiar presence of a Twi'lek Joiner. *Alema Rar.*

A wave of revulsion rose inside Jaina and Zekk—and inside Leia and Saba, as well. Alema was the holochild for all that worried Master Skywalker about the Jedi's new view of the Force. She was living proof that there *was* a dark side, for she had ventured into that darkness and lost her way so completely that even Luke had given up hoping of redeeming her. She had become a twisted and angry thing that cast off vows like boyfriends, that turned her back on faithful comrades and betrayed sacred trusts and viciously attacked those who had shown her nothing but kindness.

And none of that mattered, because there she was in a StealthX, hiding in the clouds a few kilometers behind Jaina and Zekk. The Chiss had no idea she was there, and Jaina and Zekk understood now why the dark pressure inside them had grown so strong, why UnuThul was so eager for them to sacrifice themselves in a futile gesture.

They were nothing more than a diversion. Alema—Night Herald of the Dark Nest—was the true firepower. To UnuThul, this was the surest way to stop the evil hanging beneath the defoliators' wings.

Leia and Saba reached out in the Force, urging Jaina and Zekk to resist UnuThul's Will, to stick to their own plan and attack in the clouds.

Jaina and Zekk pushed their throttles forward, then pulled their sticks back and began to climb in a wild corkscrew that made their astromechs shriek structure-stress warnings. With no forward shields left to share, it made no sense to fly in close formation. Instead, they climbed in parallel spirals, angling across the bows of the defoliators to cut off their descent.

The Chiss moved quickly to stop them, the defensive rings shifting to remain between the two StealthXs and their targets, the interceptors diving to confront them with laser cannons flashing. Jaina and Zekk returned fire effectively but without enthusiasm, destroying a clawcraft apiece and knowing that those pilots were being sacrificed to a diversion—just as they were themselves.

"Sneaky, can you get a torpedo lock on either of the defoliators?" The bombs—four on each vessel—were identical to the prototype that Jag had destroyed in the dunes above the Iesei nest.

The droid replied with an affirmative tweet, but added a

long descending whistle that suggested he questioned the wisdom of this attack.

"Don't argue!" Jaina armed all of her proton torpedoes, and sensed Zekk doing the same. "Just let me know when you're ready."

The droid emitted a brief whistle.

Jaina fired her next two proton torpedoes and watched in horrified fascination as a pair of clawcraft dropped down in front of the shrinking efflux dots. A moment later, she was momentarily blinded when a pair of dazzling flashes lit the sky between her and the defoliators.

Guessing that she must be in range by now, Jaina began to pour laser cannon fire into the defoliator Sneaky had targeted. The defensive ring tightened even more, bunching up to absorb the attacks on their own shields and leaving the stern of the vessel badly exposed to a proton torpedo.

Still, Alema did not attack. Was she waiting for the Chiss ambushers to show themselves . . . or for Jaina and Zekk to be blasted out of the sky? The spite Leia and Saba were pouring into the meld made clear what *they* thought.

Two proton torpedoes streaked from Zekk's StealthX toward the second defoliator. A Chiss clawcraft dropped down and obliterated the first torpedo with a volley of cannon bolts. The pilots trying to intercept the second torpedo were blinded by the explosion, and it slipped past the defensive screen to detonate against the defoliator's belly shields. Almost immediately, Jagged Fel and a dozen other ambushers emerged from the clouds to begin hammering Jaina and Zekk's rear shields.

Trapped in a devastating crossfire and badly outnumbered, the only sensible thing for Jaina and Zekk to do was to roll out. Sneaky began to whistle and toot, no doubt extolling the wisdom of presenting their shielded tails to the enemy and fleeing while they still could.

Instead, Jaina launched her last set of proton torpedoes

and accelerated toward her target, pouring a constant stream of cannon bolts ahead of her and doing her best to make it appear that she intended to ram the defoliator. Zekk mirrored her every move, heading toward the second defoliator. Four clawcraft defenders quickly moved to block their torpedoes. The interceptors raced forward on a collision course with Jaina and Zekk, while Jag and his ambushers poured fire into the StealthX tails with no concern for hitting their own starfighters.

Then Jaina and Zekk sensed Alema streaking up out of the clouds, coming up behind the defoliators where there were no longer any clawcraft to challenge her. Jaina's rear shields went down, then one of her fusial engines flamed out, and Sneaky began to trill warnings that she could not understand. She continued to pour fire at the belly of her defoliator, ignoring the pending collision with the clawcraft interceptors and using the Force to dodge what she could of the mad storm of bolts.

One of Zekk's wings came off. His StealthX entered a spin and tried to nose over into a dive, but Jaina felt him using the Force to pull it back into a climb. He continued toward his target, his spiral more erratic than ever and firing with only two laser cannons, but holding the Chiss rapt.

You have nothing to be jealous of, Jaina said through their mind-link. *Even if Jag had the Force, he couldn't do that!*

Who's using the Force? Zekk replied. *This is fear!*

Alema finally launched her first set of proton torpedoes, targeting the nearest defoliator. She was so close that the vessel had no chance to deploy countermeasures. The first torpedo overloaded the vessel's shields and blasted its tail into shards. The second vaporized the entire ship, bombs included, leaving nothing behind but a white flash.

The Force roiled with shock and confusion, but the Chiss

reacted with remarkable swiftness, instantly abandoning Jaina's StealthX to rush back toward Alema.

They were too late; Alema had already sent another set of torpedoes toward the remaining defoliator. One exploded just as the defensive ring arrived at the vessel's stern, and Jaina and Zekk felt a dozen lives wink out in an instant. The other torpedo smashed into a sacrificial clawcraft, but it was so close to the defoliator that both vessels took the hit. The defoliator's fuselage and one wing vanished in another white flash.

But one of the wings survived.

It went fluttering planetward, its silver skin flashing brightly in the blue sun, the two bombs still intact and the clouds below coming up fast.

TWENTY-TWO

High above Tenupe, *Fell Defender* was still shuddering from the Killiks' opening salvo when a grim calm came to the battle-meld, and Leia understood what Jaina and Zekk were about to do.

"We can't waste any more time being sneaky," she whispered. Alema Rar had just joined the meld. Leia could sense the Twi'lek in the atmosphere below, hovering behind Jaina and Zekk, calculating and resolute and slightly amused by the idea of using them for bait. "We need to board the *Falcon* now."

Tarfang chortled something that sounded a little like "impossible." He was the only one in the group who could stand upright in the oily-smelling conveyance tunnel, and he took advantage of the fact by bracing his hands on his hips and vehemently shaking his head as he chittered.

"Tarfang is right." Juun pointed into the bustling hangar, toward an out-of-the-way corner where about fifty Chiss troopers in black deflection armor stood in a tight cordon around the *Falcon*. "They know we're coming. That security platoon is clearly waiting for us."

"Ssso?" Saba rasped. "Maybe they will give us a good fight—for a change."

"Yeah, maybe *too* good," Han said. He was looking out across the gleaming vastness of the Star Destroyer's hangar, studying what had to be an entire maintenance brigade rushing to launch the *Defender*'s starfighter wing. "We can probably take the security platoon, but those maintenance guys are all carrying—"

"Han, Alema Rar has joined the battle-meld," Leia said. "I think Jaina and Zekk are going to serve as her decoys, to pull the escorts off—"

"What are we waiting for?" Han raised the T-21 repeating blaster that Cakhmaim and Meewalh had liberated from the detention center's contraband vault—along with the rest of the group's weapons—then started to duck-walk out of the conveyance tunnel. "Let's go get my ship back."

Saba used the Force to stop Han in his tracks. "A plan would be good."

"You want a plan?" He pointed at Saba and Leia. "Okay, you two make a distraction. Cakhmaim, you and Meewalh sneak aboard and take out the squad I'm sure they've got waiting to ambush us. Tarfang, you and I blast anyone who even looks our way." He glanced back to Saba. "How's that for a plan?"

"Good," Saba said.

"It's vague and incomplete!" Juun objected.

"So?" Han demanded.

"So what am *I* supposed to do?" Juun demanded.

"Keep up," Han replied. " 'Cause the *Falcon*'s not waiting around for anyone."

"Of course not," Juun replied. "In *Spy Primer*, Kyle Katarn makes it clear that every member of an espionage team . . ."

Leia stopped listening as Cakhmaim and Meewalh crept out of the conveyance tunnel. They slipped behind an empty missile rack waiting to be sent back up the tunnel for reloading, then began to work their way along the wall toward the *Falcon*. They were so adept at camouflaging themselves that even Leia lost sight of them within five steps.

Saba pointed at one of the overhead storage gantries where clawcraft were moored before they were prepped for flight. One of the starfighters began to sway in its suspension rack, then suddenly came loose and fell to the floor with a deafening crash.

All eyes in the hangar turned toward the sound, and Leia led Han and the others out of the conveyance tunnel at a sprint, dashing between empty armament racks, crouching behind parked utility carts, hiding behind portable diagnostic units. Saba's distraction proved so dramatic that work came to a standstill as astonished technicians, pilots, and even the security platoon guarding the *Falcon* watched the emergency response team rush to investigate.

By the time the officers recovered from their own shock and began to fill the echoing hangar with shouted commands to return to work, Leia and her companions were kneeling behind a self-portable laser-cannon charging tank. The *Falcon* was only about twenty meters away, the security cordon about half that distance. She could feel the Noghri hiding somewhere in the shadows on the other side of the ship, waiting for their opportunity to slip aboard.

Leia signaled the others to be ready, then used the Force to create a loud creak in the storage gantries directly above the security platoon. The troops immediately looked up, already suspicious enough to raise their charric rifles.

Leia Force-grabbed a clawcraft hanging over their heads and began to swing it back and forth. The troops immediately began to back away from the *Falcon*—until their female officer started barking commands at them. In the next moment the officer was sliding across the deck with her arms flailing, still screeching orders in a panicked voice and gesturing at the gantries.

The soldiers stared after her in confusion, or looked up into the gantries and scowled. None of them noticed the slender, chest-high forms of two Noghri appearing out of the shadows behind them, then slipping up the *Falcon*'s boarding ramp.

Saba thumped her tail on the deck and began to siss uncontrollably.

"Quiet, Master!" Leia whispered. "You'll give us away!"

"Sssorry!" Saba replied. "She is juzt so funny, telling her soldierz to stay while she goes."

"Yeah, she's a laugh a millisecond," Han grumbled. He turned to Leia. "How about getting the rest of 'em to move so we can get out of here?"

Leia gave the swinging clawcraft a violent twist, and it came free of its mountings. The security platoon shouted the alarm and dived for cover, many of them zinging blind reaction shots into the gantries as they moved. An instant later the starfighter crashed down in their midst, scattering cannon arms and pieces of armor plating in every direction.

Leia and Saba were already leading the rush toward the *Falcon*, lightsabers in hand but not ignited. For a moment, the security troops continued to focus their attention overhead, thinking their attackers must be up in the gantries. Then one of them noticed Leia and the others racing toward the ship and shouted the alarm.

Leia and Saba Force-jerked half a dozen charric rifles out of troopers' hands and sent the weapons skittering across the floor. Han and Tarfang began to lay suppression fire, but that did not prevent the security platoon from launching a counterattack.

Leia and Saba activated their lightsabers and began to weave an impenetrable shield of light, synchronizing their movements through the battle-meld so that one blade was always in position to block without interfering with the other. Unlike blaster bolts—which carried little kinetic energy—each maser beam struck so hard that the blow nearly knocked the lightsaber from Leia's hand. Sometimes she called on the Force to reinforce her grasp and batted the beam back at her attacker, and other times she redirected the energy, using it to move her blade into its next position.

But no attacks penetrated their shield, and soon Leia and the others were all backing up the boarding ramp into the *Falcon*. Han raised the ramp, then winced at the sound of the maser bolts pinging into the ship's hull.

"Now that's just uncalled for," he said.

A pair of metallic feet came clanking down the corridor behind them, then C-3PO said, "Thank goodness you're here! They've been tearing the ship apart!"

"Who?" Leia asked.

"Lieutenant Vero'tog'leo and his subordinates," C-3PO replied. "They reactivated me and kept demanding that I tell them where the smuggling compartments were. When I explained that I wasn't authorized to reveal that information, they threatened to pour acid into my lubricators!"

"Where are they now?" Leia asked.

"Waiting with Cakhmaim and Meewalh in the aft hold, I believe."

Leia turned to Han. "Saba and I can handle that. You take Jae and get us out of here."

Han nodded and turned to go—then suddenly stopped. "Where *is* Jae?"

Leia looked around the boarding area and did not see the Sullustan anywhere. "Tell me we didn't leave him outside!"

Tarfang jabbered something angry.

"It's not her fault," Han said. "I warned him to keep up."

Tarfang chittered something else and pointed forward, and suddenly Juun's voice came over the intercom.

"Initiating emergency cold-start procedures," he said. "Secure all hatches."

They all let out long sighs of relief, then Han motioned to Tarfang. "Come on. We'd better get up there, or he'll still be doing circuit tests when the Chiss bring up their laser cannons."

Han and the Ewok started up the corridor at a run, and Leia and Saba went aft. As C-3PO had said, Lieutenant Vero'tog'leo had torn the *Falcon* apart, emptying stowage cabinets, disassembling the medical bay, even opening the service panels in the ceiling. By the time they reached the hold, Leia was mad enough to stow the lieutenant and his squad on the wrong side of a soon-to-be open air lock.

But when she saw how battered and bloody the Chiss already were, she decided that Cakhmaim and Meewalh had punished them enough. Leia herded the limping and slumping squad onto the cargo lift and simply off-loaded them.

The lift was still retracting when the *Falcon* rose from the deck and swung toward the hangar mouth. Chiss being Chiss, Leia was fairly certain that Vero'tog'leo had hidden a tracking device, a bomb, or both somewhere aboard. She sent Cakhmaim and Meewalh to do a security sweep, then she and Saba hurried to the turrets to engage the quad cannons.

Leia had barely buckled into her firing seat before Han had the *Falcon* shooting toward the hangar mouth. A handful of security troops pelted the hull with maser beams, but there was no question of anyone trying to stop them by sealing the barrier field. With the Killiks attacking, the Chiss had more important things to worry about than escaping prisoners. The *Defender* was gushing clawcraft as fast as she could, and the deck master was not going to interrupt the launch for anything.

Before venturing out into the tempest of energy erupting

just beyond the *Defender*'s shields, the starfighters were using the shelter of her expansive belly to form up by squadrons. Han simply dropped the *Falcon*'s nose and dived, leaving Leia—whose turret happened to be facing aft—staring up into the flashing madness of the battle above. The sky was at once black with smoke and descending dartships and dappled with the blue brilliance of blossoming turbolaser strikes, and already the flaming hulks of two Chiss Star Destroyers were plummeting groundward in an uncontrolled gyre.

The *Falcon* suddenly veered out from under the battle, and Han announced, "Got 'em."

Leia checked her targeting display and saw that the *Falcon* was about five kilometers above a pair of Chiss defoliators and closing rapidly. The defoliator escorts were badly out of position, bunched up in front of the two craft as they fired at unseen targets that Leia assumed to be Jaina and Zekk. She could feel them through the battle-meld, grim and determined, driven by Raynar's Will and still focused on destroying the defoliators. She could also feel Alema—close by and just as determined.

Leia spun her turret around and touched Jaina and Zekk in the Force, urging them not to sacrifice themselves. Help was on the way. All they had to do was drop back into the clouds and wait.

But Alema Rar had never been patient. She continued to pour impatience into the meld, demanding that Jaina and Zekk keep attacking. Raynar's Will continued to weigh on the two Jedi Knights, and they began to exchange cannon bolts with the escorts.

Then the blinding dots of two torpedo detonations flared about three kilometers ahead the *Falcon,* and when the static cleared from Leia's targeting display, the trailing defoliator was gone.

"Han, get us there now!" Leia ordered over the inter-com.

"Sure." The *Falcon* accelerated, and long tongues of flame began to lick past the turret canopy. "What's a little entry burn?"

By the time the second set of torpedoes detonated, they were close enough to see the thick cloud of clawcraft swarming around Jaina and Zekk's StealthXs—and to see how clumsily both craft were handling as they dived for the clouds. Even if Leia had not been able to feel it through the Force, she would have known just by looking that her daughter and Zekk were in desperate straits.

And there was no sign of Alema going to help them. The Twi'lek had vanished from the battle-meld as soon as she destroyed the second defoliator, and now she was doing nothing to help her decoys.

"Anybody see what happened to Alema?" Leia asked. "I'd like to send a few cannon bolts her way."

The *Falcon* shuddered as Saba opened up with the belly cannons. "Sssorry! This one misssed," she hissed. "She was on my side, diving for the cloudz."

"It looks like she's going after something," Han said. "And so are the Chiss."

Leia checked her targeting display and saw that eight clawcraft had entered a power dive, chasing something big and slow with an erratic flight pattern. "What is it?"

"A wing!" Juun was silent for a moment, then added, "With two huge bombs attached to it!"

Leia had a sinking feeling. "How close are they to the battle zone?"

"It doesn't matter," Han said. "This time, my daughter comes first. What do I care if her creepy friends get wiped—"

"Han!" Leia swung her turret around and began to pour laser bolts toward the clawcraft harassing Jaina and

Zekk. "You do know StealthXs can eavesdrop on intercom transmissions at this range?"

"They can?"

"The StealthX'z primary mission is spying," Saba reminded him. She opened fire, too, and some of the clawcraft began to disperse and come after the *Falcon*. "But maybe they're not listening."

"Who cares?" Han asked. "Jaina knows I'm just worried about her."

"She also knowz that *you* know she can take care of herself," Saba said. "And that you would never let the Chisz rupture one of those parasite bombz. Even a few eggz might be enough to kill her friendz' species."

Han sighed. "You're saying we have to recover that wing, aren't you?"

"I'm afraid so," Leia said. The cold ache of disappointment in her stomach was only partially relieved by the feelings of encouragement and approval coming from Jaina and Zekk through the meld. "But nothing says you can't edge a little closer on the way past. Saba and I would enjoy some target practice."

The *Falcon* rolled into a dive so steep that it sent all the unstowed equipment and supplies flying around the interior of the cabin and holds. Leia ignored the crashing and banging and continued to fire. She also ignored the clawcraft now pouring cannon bolts after the *Falcon*. Instead, she used the Force to target the craft that continued to harass her daughter and Zekk, far below.

Even at that distance, even in an atmosphere, the *Falcon*'s powerful quad cannons were more than a match for the light shielding of a clawcraft. She sent one tumbling toward the clouds. Another burst into a ball of flame as it seemed to simply fly into a stream of Saba's bolts, then Leia hit a third starfighter with a series of glancing shots that forced it into an uncontrolled spin.

And finally, the two StealthXs had a clear lane down into the clouds. Jaina and Zekk dived into it, smoking and fluttering, with a dozen clawcraft hanging on their tails, but still in one piece. The meld grew warm with their gratitude; then the turret lights dimmed as the nearest clawcraft began to take a toll on the *Falcon*'s shields.

Han rolled again, causing even more crashing in the cabin, and the entry burn grew so intense that Leia could no longer see through the flames. She swung her cannons toward the clawcraft, then forgot about the targeting display and allowed the Force to guide her hand as she squeezed the triggers. The synthetic rumble of the fire-control computer announced one hit, then two, then one more, and suddenly she sensed no more targets.

Leia checked the display and found the thermal blossoms of a dozen dissipating explosions. Incredibly, for every starfighter she had destroyed, Saba had taken out two.

"Rodder!" Leia gasped. "Maybe I'll be able to do that when *I'm* a Master."

"Maybe?" Saba began to siss uncontrollably for some reason no one but a Barabel would ever understand. "Leia, now is no time for your jokez! This one must focuz."

The entry burn paled as the *Falcon* entered the clouds, then faded away altogether as they emerged into a downpour so fierce that Leia could barely see the freight-handling mandibles at the front of the ship. The targeting display showed the eight clawcraft that had followed the defoliator wing down. They were firing at the wing—which was catching updrafts and flittering back and forth so wildly that even Saba would have had trouble hitting it. They were also shooting at an empty area behind the wing, which Leia assumed to be Alema's StealthX. She felt no shame in wishing them good luck with the latter target.

C-3PO's voice came over the intercom. "How helpful!"

he announced. "The Chiss appear to be shooting at their own bombs. Perhaps we should withdraw."

"They're not just shooting at them, chipbrain," Han said. "They're trying to detonate them."

"How odd," C-3PO replied. "Won't they detonate on impact anyway?"

"Only if they're armed," Leia interjected. "And obviously they're not. The pilots weren't on-mark yet when their defoliator was hit."

The fire-control computer began to designate targets in order of threat level, and Leia and Saba opened up with their quad cannons again. A trio of clawcraft erupted in flames before three of the others finally stopped attacking Alema and the wing and rolled out to come after the *Falcon*.

Saba switched to the *Falcon*'s attackers, leaving Leia to stop the other two from rupturing the parasite bombs. Her targets were clever, positioning themselves between the *Falcon* and the tumbling wing, so that she could not fire on them without running the risk of hitting the bombs. She looked out into the blinding rain and found one of the starfighters in the Force, then focused only on that and released all conscious control of her hand.

Leia felt the turret shudder as her quad cannons fired, then the fire-control computer announced the target's destruction with a synthetic rumble. She reached out to the other clawcraft in the Force—and was astonished to feel the familiar presence of Jagged Fel in the pilot's seat.

"Han," Leia said over the intercom. "That last clawcraft, it's Jag!"

"What? How do you . . ." Han caught himself. "Right—forget I asked."

Leia could tell by Han's tone that he was no more eager to kill Jagged Fel than she was, but they did not seem to have a lot of options. Saba was still exchanging cannon bolts with the clawcraft she had not yet killed, and they all knew that it would not be long before the squadron that had chased Jaina and Zekk into the clouds gave up their search and rushed over to help with the wing.

"I guess the shoe is on the other foot," Han said. "What are you going to do? We've got to shoot him down."

"I know," Leia said. "But give me a hailing channel."

"Go ahead, Princess," Juun said.

"Jagged Fel, I'm sure you know who this is."

"Princess Leia?" Jagged did not seem surprised. "I *told* them it's impossible to hold Jedi prisoners."

"Well, they know now." Leia placed her finger on the triggers. "If you can eject, I suggest you do it fast."

Jagged sighed. "I've been hearing that from a lot of Solo women lately."

Leia barely heard him. She was already deep in the Force, focusing all her attention on his starfighter.

She felt her finger twitch, and said, "Good-bye, Jag."

The turret began to shudder and did not stop. Leia felt her hand moving, following Jagged's evasion attempts, but he might as well have been trying to dodge light. She followed his juking and jinking through the Force for a moment, then began to anticipate him, and an instant later she heard the synthetic rumble of the fire-control computer.

But Leia did not feel the shock of his death.

She dropped her gaze to the targeting display and saw the fading blossom of his clawcraft explosion, but the image was not fine enough to determine whether some of the debris she saw fluttering away was an EV unit.

"Han, did he—"

"I don't know," Han cut in. "I might have seen an ejection flare before you fired, but we've got other problems right now."

A green blur, as vast as a planet, appeared out of the rain ahead, and then the *Falcon* pulled up, hard. Leia spun her turret around and glimpsed what was clearly a jungle canopy dropping away behind the ship's stern.

"Han, are you telling me—"

"Afraid so," Han said. "The bombs are down there somewhere."

TWENTY-THREE

Luke found Gilad Pellaeon alone in the *Megador*'s observation deck, his liver-spotted hands clasped behind his back and his gray-haired head tipped back slightly as he gazed out the center of the dome. His attention seemed to be fixed on the cloud-pearled planet ahead, where the red-flashing shadow of the Killik ambush swarm was spreading steadily outward. The insects were striving to keep the Chiss fleet trapped between them and Tenupe's surface, and by the looks of things, they were succeeding. If the Grand Admiral noticed his own huge armada sparkling out of hyperspace all around the edges of the observation dome, he showed no sign.

"I've never seen anything like this, Luke." Pellaeon spoke without taking his eyes off the planet. "The Colony must have a million dartships attacking down there. I can't imagine the logistics."

"*You* don't have a collective mind," Luke said, stepping to the admiral's side. "The Killiks are an extraordinary species. At times, I'm tempted to believe that they *were* the ones who built Centerpoint Station and the Maw."

Pellaeon studied him out of the corner of one eye. "And you don't think that now?"

Luke shook his head. "The nests have a habit of confusing their Joiners' memories with their own." He was surprised that Pellaeon seemed to take the Killiks' claim seriously. "And the technology does seem well beyond them."

"You think so?" Pellaeon returned his gaze to the dome, then pointed a wrinkled finger at the Killik fleet. "I wonder how long it would have taken the *Galactic Alliance* to build that navy."

"Good point." Luke studied Pellaeon carefully, trying to figure out what the cunning admiral was driving at. "But the Killiks don't even have a true science. How could they have the knowledge to build something like the Maw or Centerpoint?"

Pellaeon turned to face Luke. "A lot can happen in twenty-five thousand years, Master Skywalker. Sciences can be lost, knowledge can be forgotten, cultural imperatives can change. That *doesn't* mean we should underestimate our opponent."

"Of course not," Luke said, taken aback by the sharpness of Pellaeon's rebuke. "Forgive me, Admiral—I wasn't thinking on the same level you were."

Pellaeon's face softened. "No apology necessary, Master Skywalker. You had no way to know we were discussing our current attack strategies." He returned his attention to the Killik fleet, then added in a wry tone, "Since the Rebellion, I've become a bit fanatic about keeping an open mind toward my enemy's capabilities."

Luke laughed, then said, "I should have been more alert, especially since I *did* track you down to talk about our strategy."

Pellaeon nodded without looking away from the dome. "Go ahead."

"Thank you," Luke said. A burst of iridescent light flashed across the dome as the *Mon Mothma* and the *Elegos A'Kla* emerged from hyperspace and moved to either side of the *Megador*. "Our vessels appear to be deploying for an enveloping attack on the Colony fleet."

"We are." A hint of a smile appeared beneath Pellaeon's bushy mustache. "It's going to be a thing of beauty, Luke. The Killiks have absolutely no room to maneuver. We're going to smash them against the Chiss like, well . . . like bugs."

"Forgive me for spoiling your fun," Luke said. "But that's exactly what we *shouldn't* be doing."

"*What?*" Pellaeon tore his gaze away from the dome. "The Killiks might as well be dead already. They can't possibly escape us."

"Probably not," Luke agreed. "But we're not here to destroy an enemy fleet. We're here to stop this war."

"In my experience, they're one and the same," Pellaeon snapped.

"Yes, but your experience doesn't include Killiks." Luke's reply was blunt; he had to persuade the admiral to switch tactics *now*. Once the fleet started to deploy its fighter wings, changing battle objectives would become impossible. Not even Pellaeon was a good enough commander to recall several thousand starfighters, change formations, and continue the attack with any expectation of success. "Admiral, we have to concentrate our resources on retaking the *Admiral Ackbar* and neutralizing Raynar Thul."

Pellaeon arched his gray brows. "You know for a fact that Raynar is aboard the *Ackbar*?"

Luke nodded. "I'm certain. I feel it in the Force."

"Then you don't need an entire fleet to trap him," Pellaeon countered. "Admiral Bwua'tu's task force should be more than sufficient to support you."

"You're missing the point, Admiral," Luke said. "Destroying the Colony's fleet will delay the war, but it won't end it. The Killiks will only rebuild and be back with an even larger force next year."

"Then at least we will have bought ourselves some

time." Pellaeon shook his head. "I'm not going to commit *everything* to neutralizing one man, Luke. If you fail—or if you're wrong, and removing Raynar *doesn't* cripple the Colony—we will have squandered the opportunity for a great victory."

"That's sound military doctrine, of course," Luke said. The *Mothma* and the *A'Kla* were now moving into shielding positions just ahead of the *Megador*. "But if you follow your plan, Raynar and Lomi Plo will defeat us—because we'll have lost sight of our true goals."

Pellaeon's eyes remained hard—perhaps even angry—but he did not interrupt.

"Let's assume I do neutralize Raynar and Lomi Plo without the fleet's full support," Luke continued, "and that you destroy the entire Killik fleet. Your strategy will only prolong the war."

"You're making no sense, Luke," Pellaeon retorted. "Without Raynar and Lomi Plo, the Killiks won't be *able* to rebuild their fleet. You've said yourself that neutralizing those two will destroy the Colony's ability to coordinate its nests. Are you telling me it won't?"

"I said removing Raynar would *eventually* destroy the Colony," Luke corrected. "And you're forgetting the Chiss. If you wipe out the Killik fleet here on Tenupe, what do you think the Chiss are going to do next?"

"Thank us," Pellaeon said. "Perhaps they'll finally believe that we're not siding with the Killiks."

"They'll know *that* if we focus on recapturing the *Ackbar* and neutralize Raynar and Lomi Plo," Luke said. "What they *won't* do is use that fleet down there to continue pressing the war against the Colony."

Pellaeon's eyes flashed in alarm; then he scowled and studied Luke as though they were meeting for the first time. Outside, the edges of the observation deck were laced with ion trails; the rest of the fleet was moving into attack formation.

Finally, Pellaeon spoke in a disbelieving voice. "Master Skywalker, I do believe you're suggesting that we leave the Chiss fleet to its own resources."

Luke nodded. "It would be for the best," he said. "They were obviously willing to sacrifice much of it anyway."

"*Before* their parasite weapon was compromised," Pellaeon pointed out. The *Megador* had barely emerged from hyperspace before the *Falcon* had commed an update of the situation on Tenupe. "I suspect they're no longer eager to lull the Killiks into a false sense of security. This battle is going to be bloody."

"No doubt. But it might be wise to let the Chiss have a good taste of what the Killiks can do. Otherwise, the Ascendancy will continue pressing the war—they'll find another way to deploy their parasite weapon." Luke paused, then continued, "As excited as you are about this battle, I know you don't want speciecide on your conscience."

Pellaeon's eyes flashed, and Luke thought maybe he had gone too far.

Then the admiral sighed. "It isn't the killing, you know," he said. "It's the beauty of battles that I love—the choreography and the challenge of executing everything just right—and the challenge of matching your wits against a capable opponent."

Pellaeon's expression began to change from indignant to reluctant. "I guess I carry a little more Thrawn with me than I'd like to believe." He sighed again, then looked out toward Tenupe, now just as heavily blanketed with dartships as it was with green clouds. "The Chiss will lose a lot of ships, you know—and this is a dangerous part of the galaxy, even without the Colony."

"I know." Luke did not like the idea of abandoning so many Chiss to their fates, but the alternative would have

meant *killing* even more Killiks. "The Ascendancy may
have to rely more heavily on its friends for a while—and
that will be good for the Alliance."

"Yes, I suppose it will be—provided they still consider us
friends." Pellaeon stood staring out the dome for another
moment, then sighed regretfully and turned toward the lift.
"Come along, Master Skywalker. Before you join the boarding parties, I'll need a few minutes of your time in TacCon."

TWENTY-FOUR

The strength of the living Force in the jungle overwhelmed Leia's physical senses. Her ears hummed with its energy, her skin prickled beneath its warm pressure, even her vision had begun to cast the rain in a soft green glow. She found herself perceiving with her spirit rather than with her body, becoming a part of the jungle rather than a visitor to it.

Saba was reacting a little differently. She was creeping along the vine-swaddled mogo branches with all the stealth of a hungry rapard, barely stirring the thick foliage except when she suddenly fell on some hissing rodent or popped out of hiding to snatch a passing buzzbird.

Leia might have been bothered by the trail of death that her Master's predatory instinct was laying behind them had she not felt like half the jungle was trying to eat *her.* Through the Force, she could sense everything from tiny bloodbats to packs of Ewok-sized spiders—all of them on the hunt, stalking her through the canopy, watching and waiting for an opportunity to attack.

The prevalence of predators made Leia worry about Jaina and Zekk, who had gone down in their crippled StealthXs. She could feel them somewhere out there in this same ravening jungle, badly battered, but still alive, together, and apparently holed up in a safe place. They actually seemed more worried about Leia than she was about em, and they were pouring reassurance into the Force, ncouraging Leia and Saba to deal with the parasite bombs rst and them second.

That was easier said than done, of course. Han was oing his best to draw the enemy out of the area by flying op cover over a different part of the jungle, but it would ot be long before the Chiss realized it was a ruse. Their ensor sweeps would eventually confirm that there was no netal—and therefore no bomb—in the area Han was pro-ecting.

The soft beeps coming from Leia's scanner finally fused nto a single long whine. She checked the display and saw nat the metal signature she had been following for the last alf hour was in the center of the small screen, indicat-ng she was now on top of the source. She stopped and rouched down on the mossy mogo branch, her lightsaber n hand in case one of the predators stalking her decided to ry its luck.

"Master Sebatyne," she called. "Perhaps you could tear ourself away from your fun?"

Saba popped out of a nearby bough, her mouth ringed y half a dozen bloody feathers.

"Do not be disapproving, Jedi Solo," she said. "This one an eat and search at the zame time. Who found Alema .ar'z StealthX?"

"You did, Master," Leia said.

Saba had found the starfighter hidden high in a mogo ree, camouflaged as a giant curtain of beard-moss and sus-ended nose-down with its rear landing struts carefully ung over a thick branch. They assumed that the Twi'lek vas doing the same thing they were—trying to destroy the arasite bombs before the Chiss arrived to recover them— ut it was not a task that either Master or student wished o entrust to someone else, especially not a Dark Nest oiner.

"Have you checked your scanner recently?" Leia asked.

"Of course." Saba sneaked a look toward her utilit belt, and her dorsal crest rose in surprise. She grinne sheepishly, then said, "This one was merely giving her stu dent a chance to find the bombs first."

Allowing Leia no chance to challenge the statemen Saba leaned out of her hiding place and peered down int the jungle—then sissed in frustration. Leia clipped th scanner to her utility belt, then grabbed hold of an offshoo and leaned away from her own branch until she could se what Saba had found.

The defoliator's wing lay about twenty meters belov bent backward over a mogo branch. Both weapon mount ings were empty, and the bombs were nowhere in sight.

"Bloah!" Leia yelled.

Her outburst sent a troop of long-armed monkey-lizard swinging away through the trees, screeching and hissing i alarm. Saba watched them go with a hungry leer, her lon tongue flickering between her pebbly lips.

"*Focus,* Master," Leia urged. She pulled her scanner of her utility belt, then programmed it to ignore the wing an turned in a slow circle. She was about halfway aroun when the scanner began to beep again, and a contact-bli appeared at the top of the screen.

"Found something!" Leia reported.

"This one, too," Saba answered.

Leia glanced over her shoulder and saw Saba staring i the opposite direction.

"Of course—it would have been too much to ask tha they fall *together,*" Leia complained. "We'll have to spli up."

"It'z okay, Jedi Solo," Saba said. "This one is no afraid."

Sissing with laughter, Saba turned and Force-jumpe down to an adjacent branch. Leia watched the Barabe

vanish into the foliage, worried that perhaps she was ab-
sorbing more than Jedi wisdom from her Master. She actually understood the joke.

Leia took a bearing to her own contact, then selected a
safe-looking branch to serve as her intermediate landing
point and Force-leapt into the rain. She would much rather
have used a repulsor pack, but Saba disdained technological "crutches" when the Force would do instead.

On the way down, a cold shiver of danger sense raced
along Leia's spine, and she felt something hungry descending on her from above. The hiss of air rushing over wing
scales began to rise behind her, and she rolled into a
Force flip and ignited her lightsaber, bringing the blade up
through the body of something huge, green, and musty
smelling.

The snake-bird fell away in two pieces. Then Leia sensed
her target branch coming up behind her—fast. She reached
out to it in the Force and drew herself over to it, landing
backward in the wet moss and nearly slipping off the
branch.

Leia's danger sense continued to ripple.

She could hear a large river purling through the jungle
somewhere far below, but she had no sense of where this
new predator was hiding. She turned in a slow circle. When
she saw nothing but clouds of emerald foliage, she reached
out in the Force, but she felt only the same hunters as before. This danger was something different—something that
could hide itself in the Force.

Leia stilled herself and began to search for an empty
place in the gauzy fog of the living Force on Tenupe. It did
not take long to find. There was an odd calm where her
branch connected to the mogo's trunk, hidden behind a green
curtain of strangle-vines. Still holding her lightsaber in one
hand, she drew her blaster and began to fire into the vines.

The *snap-hiss* of an igniting lightsaber sounded from inside the mass of vines, then a blade so blue it was almost black sliced through the foliage and began to bat Leia's bolts aside. The tangle of vines quickly fell away, revealing a blue-skinned Twi'lek female with an amputated head-tail and one withered arm hanging useless beneath a sagging shoulder. She wore a StealthX flight suit two sizes too small for her slender figure, her front zipper open down to the navel.

Leia stopped firing and touched Saba through their battle-meld, trying to let her knew she had found something as important as the bombs. "Alema Rar. I should have known you'd crawl out of a hole around here somewhere."

Alema's unblinking eyes widened with anger, but she deactivated her lightsaber and bared her teeth in what looked more like an insect's threat display than a smile.

"Come now, Princess," Alema purred. "We are both here to destroy the bombs. Perhaps we should work together."

The Twi'lek's voice was so beguiling that Leia found herself thinking that Alema was not really such a bad girl; that anyone who had had such a hard life was entitled to make a few mistakes along the way. And besides, the suggestion *was* reasonable. The Dark Nest had even more reason than the Jedi to want those parasite bombs destroyed, and any time she and Alema spent fighting each other was time that would bring the Chiss closer to recovering them.

Then an image of Jaina and Zekk diving for the clouds in their battered StealthXs flashed through Leia's mind, and an icy knot of danger sense formed at the base of her skull. This was how Alema Rar—and probably the whole Dark Nest—worked, by offering the promise of something pleasant or reasonable to secure the target's cooperation. But in the end, it was the target who suffered—who played the decoy, or who had to stay and fight while the Twi'lek and the Dark Nest simply faded into the night.

"Thanks, but I'll pass," Leia said. "I've seen your kind of cooperation. It nearly got my daughter killed."

Alema gave a couple of throat-clicks, then said, "It was necessary for the good of the Colony. Jaina and Zekk understood that."

"They understand that you ran out on them," Leia countered. Now that she was alert to it, she could feel the Twi'lek trying to use the Force against her, to dampen her negative thoughts and bolster the positive ones. Fortunately, there *weren't* many positive ones. "And so do I."

"We had to destroy the bombs." Alema put a little urgency in her voice—and complemented it by pushing harder with the Force. "We still *have* to destroy the bombs."

"Okay," Leia said, deciding to switch tactics. She reached out in the Force, trying to make her own voice sound beguiling and reasonable. "I've never been one to hold a grudge. If you want to work together, Alema, just pass over your lightsaber and other weapons."

"Really?" Alema started to unbuckle her utility belt—then blinked both eyes in astonishment and let out a jagged little throat-rattle. "Nice try, Princess—but we don't think so."

"Good." Leia smiled, looking forward to the surprise she was about to visit upon the Twi'lek. "I was hoping you'd say that."

Leia charged, firing her blaster pistol with one hand and activating her lightsaber with the other. There was no question of giving Alema a chance to escape later by working with her now—even if it meant letting the Chiss recover the bomb. Eliminating the Dark Nest was the core of Luke's plan, and the Twi'lek was a big part of that nest.

Alema rushed to meet the attack, igniting her own lightsaber, wielding it with her one good arm and easily deflecting the stream of bolts. They met at a large burl where a smaller limb converged with its parent, their lightsabers coming together in a sizzle of sparks and color.

Leia jolted Alema with a one-handed power attack that hammered the Twi'lek's block down easily, then whipped her blade around in a buzzing backslash at a pulsing span of blue undefended throat. Alema dropped to her haunches and somehow snap-kicked from that impossible position, and Leia's middle exploded into pain.

The Princess exhaled hard, forcing the pain out, and did not yield a centimeter. She swept her blade down to attack the extended leg, but Alema had already drawn her foot back, and she ended up blocking the Twi'lek's blade as it came sizzling in at her knees.

Leia rolled her wrist and sent Alema's lightsaber flying, then brought her blaster pistol around and allowed herself a small smirk as she opened fire.

It was too soon to gloat.

Alema was already twisting away and launching herself backward in the air, her handed extended to recall her falling lightsaber. A pair of bolts burned past the Twi'lek's legs—so close that her flight suit began to smoke—but she rolled into an evasive Force tumble and landed unscathed on the adjacent branch . . . and slipped. She inhaled sharply and started to fall, then hooked the back of her knee over the branch and caught herself.

Leia fired at the knee, but Alema was already swinging around, facing her, deep blue lightsaber in hand, batting blaster bolts straight back at her. Leia stopped firing. The Twi'lek slipped back into the branch moss in a seated position, then brought her leg up and stretched it along the branch, staring at her boot.

Leia's earlier slash had not missed after all. The front half of Alema's boot was missing—along with half her foot. The Twi'lek turned toward Leia, her unblinking eyes wide in astonishment and anger, and that was when Leia's comlink earpiece crackled to life.

"How's it going down there?" Han asked.

"Busy!" Leia said into her throat mike.

"Any sign of the bombs?" Han pressed.

"Not really."

Leia watched in alarm as Alema rose and peered over the branch behind her—no doubt plotting an escape route.

"Gotta go," Leia said. "I'm sort of in the middle of something."

Determined not to let her prey escape, Leia Force-jumped from her branch toward Alema's.

The Twi'lek's withered arm swung up, reaching toward Leia. The princess tucked into an evasive somersault—then felt herself rolling the wrong way as her feet were Force-jerked in the opposite direction. She called on the Force to stop her rotation, but by then the back of her head was *thonk*ing into the side of the branch.

The moss was not as thick on the sides of the branches. The sound echoed inside her skull so hard that Leia thought she would never hear anything else. Then she felt her feet whipping down from above and sensed the darkness rising up to swallow hers and she knew she had come to one of those terrible instants when everything depended on willpower and the stubborn desire to live.

Fortunately, Saba had prepared her well for such moments. Leia found her arms lashing out behind her, one elbow hooking over the branch to stop her fall. Everything remained dark, but she knew she had to keep fighting, to keep her enemy . . . whoever that was—she was having trouble remembering . . . at bay.

Leia felt the blaster pistol in one hand and her lightsaber in the other . . . another of Saba's lessons ringing inside her head, never, *never* drop your weapon, *die* with your weapon sssstill in your hand . . . and Leia started to fire the blaster, pointing it down the branch where the trouble—who was it again?—seemed to lie.

A familiar voice sounded in her ear. "Hey, that sounds like blasterfire!"

Han.

"Yeah . . . it is." Leia started to recall the situation—a jungle, a Twi'lek, a fight—Alema Rar. "Now be quiet!"

Leia shook her head—*big mistake*—then whipped her leg up over the branch, still firing. The darkness faded from her eyes, but her blaster bolts were snaking toward their target in slow motion, while the target—a shimmering blue mirage that seemed to have three heads and six arms—was limping toward her behind a lightsaber moving so fast that it seemed to be weaving a shield of solid light.

Then one of the six blue arms moved. Leia's blaster flew from her own hand and vanished into the billowing greenness of the out-of-focus jungle.

The fight was not going exactly as planned.

Saba always said that planning would be Leia's downfall; that she planned too much and felt too little. She had also said that a shenbit always saves its deepest bite for last.

Leia pushed off the mossy branch and brought her feet up beneath her. The Princess had never met a shenbit, but Saba usually uttered the saying in sparring practice, right before she drove her student into the deck with a flurry of power strikes. Leia began to advance on her three-headed, six-armed opponent, weaving her blade through the frenzied slash-slice-and-rip of a Barabel rage attack.

To Leia's astonishment, the three-headed enemy suddenly stopped advancing, then began to retreat.

"Wait! This is silly!" Again, that beguiling voice and that furtive Force-touch, trying to dampen the negative thoughts and bolster the positive ones. Alema pointed her lightsaber over the side of the branch. "The bomb is right down there."

Leia stopped advancing—more to give her eyes a chance to bring her enemy into focus than because she was considering the offer—and glanced down. There *did* seem to be a big silver blur lying in a bed of green.

"It would be a shame to let the Chiss recover it," Alema said. "Can't we strike a truce long enough to destroy it—*then* finish killing each other?"

Leia pretended to consider the offer while her vision finished clearing, then—when Alema's extra heads and arms disappeared—she shook her own head.

"Let's do it now."

Leia started forward . . . and instantly regretted her decision when the branch bounced and nearly buckled her knees. She noticed it sagging beneath her weight and realized she was farther out on the end than she had perceived in her foggy-headed state. It was a mistake that would cost her dearly. With such unreliable footing, the Princess would be even worse off than her half-footed foe.

Alema was quick to press her advantage, hobbling forward to attack, launching a flurry of strike and Force-push combinations that drove Leia back even farther toward the tip of the bouncing branch. The Princess parried, but her reactions had been slowed by her head blow, and she had to retreat yet another step. She Force-shoved at Alema's knee, but the nimble Twi'lek—who had spent her youth dancing in the ryll dens of Kala'uun—simply lifted her bad foot and pirouetted forward on the good one, driving Leia back another, even longer step.

The branch sagged so precariously that the Princess had to Force-stick herself in place.

"Hey, those sound like lightsabers!" Han observed over Leia's earpiece.

"They *are*!" Leia growled. "Can you *just* hold on?"

Now the branch was bouncing even when the Princess wasn't moving, and her danger sense was covering her back with goose bumps. Had Alema launched a power attack—even a weak one—Leia's only choice would have been to drop off the branch and hope she could catch another one with the Force on the way down. Instead, the Twi'lek seemed content merely to hold the Princess in place with defensive swordplay.

Then comprehension finally burned its way through the concussion fog inside Leia's head. The danger she was sensing had nothing to do with Alema. A predator had landed behind her . . . something large enough to weigh down a limb the size of her thigh.

Alema smiled. "Dinnertime, Princess."

Leia's blood began to burn with a very Barabel-like rage. She would *not* die at the hands of some Twi'lek dancing girl—or at the claws of some jungle flunky. She went on the attack, forgetting her slow reactions and foggy head and uneven footing, and let the battle take her—let her lightsaber block and slash and stab of its own accord, let her feet dance back and forth over the bouncing limb.

Alema came at her just as strongly, kicking with her half foot, stretching out for long lightsaber lunges, pushing constantly through the Force—steadily driving Leia back toward the hungry presence that she could now sense coming up behind her.

Then a wisp of hot breath brushed the back of Leia's neck, and she knew it was time. The Princess tried a throat slash and swung wide, deliberately leaving herself open for a heart thrust. Never having been one to resist temptation, Alema could not help lunging for the kill.

Leia had already flexed her knees and was springing off the sagging branch, bringing her feet up over her head in an open Force flip. She saw the Twi'lek stretched out below her, not quite off balance—but not far from it—her neck craned back as she watched her target fly overhead.

Leia brought her lightsaber down, striking for the head.

Alema could only whip her lightsaber up in a desperate block. The blades clashed in a growling shower of sparks and light, then the Princess was swinging down behind her, twisting around to plant one foot between the Twi'lek's shoulders and send her stumbling toward the shaggy mass that had been creeping up behind Leia.

There was no time to tell what kind of creature the thing was. All Leia saw was something the size of a bantha taking Alema's sword arm in its jaws. The Twi'lek screamed in pain; then four spiky pedipalps emerged from the side of the creature's mouth and began to feed her in.

Alema's legs were still outside, kicking wildly, when Leia felt the thing's attention fall on her and noticed six beady eyes peering out from beneath the mossy scales that covered its head. Before it could spring, the Princess brought her lightsaber down, cutting the branch away at her feet.

Instead of plummeting toward the jungle floor, the creature swung outward, hanging suspended by a thick, ropy tail that ascended more than ten meters to a branch above. It was even larger than Leia had first imagined, with a long slug-like body that had dozens of tiny feet wriggling on the underside. Alema remained in its mouth, kicking her feet and presumably screaming into its throat. Leia locked her lightsaber blade in the on position, then used the Force to send it spinning through the tail.

The predator—whatever it was—did not open its mouth or roar in pain. It simply plummeted groundward, filling the jungle with a terrific banging and cracking as it crashed through the mogo boughs, then finally splashed into the dark river below.

Leia called her lightsaber back to her hand, and had barely switched it off before Han's voice came over her earpiece again.

"Leia?"

"Don't worry, Han," she said. "I'm still here."

"That's good." Han sounded more impatient than relieved—or even surprised. "But about those bombs . . . you'd better hurry. The Chiss' scanners must have picked something up from that fight you and Saba were having, because you've got a bunch of clawcraft headed your way."

"Great." Leia sighed. "Can't a girl catch her breath?"

Still feeling a little unsteady from her fight—especially the head blow—Leia peered over the side of the branch toward the silver blur she had glimpsed earlier.

The blur was gone, and in place of the bough upon which it had been resting, there was only the jagged stub of a broken limb.

"Bloah!" Leia cursed. She snatched the scanner off her utility belt and found a very weak signal down at ground level, slowly moving away. "It's in the river!"

A loud sissing sounded behind her, and Leia looked back to see Saba standing near the mogo trunk, studying her own scanner and holding a thermal detonator in her hand.

"Nothing *ever* goes according to plan, does it?" the Barabel asked. "This one does not know why you bother with planz at all."

"It's a human thing, I guess," Leia said. "Did you destroy the other bomb?"

"Of course," the Barabel replied. "Not all of us were wasting our time fighting bughuggerz and knocking ourselvez in the head. The parasite bomb is destroyed."

"Then what are you doing just standing there?" Leia demanded.

"This one has been watching." Saba displayed her entire set of fangs. "She is very proud."

"*Proud?*" Leia cried. "I could've been killed!"

"No." Saba shook her head. "This one taught you too well."

Leia felt her jaw drop. "Is that a compliment, Master Sebatyne?"

"Yez." Saba thumped her hand against her chest. "This one did very well, given the material she had to work with."

"Gee, that's swell," Han said in Leia's earpiece. "But if you two can break up the mutual-admiration meeting for just a minute, what about that second bomb?"

"No problem." Leia checked her scanner again. The signal had moved perhaps fifty meters in the last few seconds, but it had grown so weak that she could barely find it anymore. "Blast—now it's sinking."

"Yez, that is what happenz when you drop something heavy in the river," Saba said. She activated her thermal detonator, then tossed it in the direction of the bomb and used the Force to guide it to the fading blip on their scanners. "You will have to be more careful next time, Jedi Solo."

The blip faded from the scanner. The tiny *bloop* of something small entering the water sounded from the same direction; then the sharp *wooosh* of an underwater detonation rose up through the trees.

"Did you get it?" Han asked.

Leia checked her scanner. There was still no blip on the screen. "Let's say we did—because even if we didn't, the Chiss will never find it, either." She motioned Saba to start climbing. "Let's go—it's time to go get my daughter."

TWENTY-FIVE

The interior of *Stomper One* filled with soft whirrings and electronic chirpings as the assault shuttle's passengers began their final systems checks. Each soldier worked his servomotors and confirmed the calibration of his targeting systems with two adjacent units, then executed a quick comm scan to be certain he was receiving on all channels. Because this platoon was assigned directly to the assault commander—Jedi Grand Master Luke Skywalker—they all performed a vocabulator check as well. The phrase "check sound, check Basic" reverberated through the passenger cabin thirty-two times—always in the ultradeep, ultramale version of Lando Calrissian's voice, which remained the standard for the entire line of YVH combat droids.

Sitting behind the controls of the assault shuttle, Luke found the mechanical symphony strangely isolating. As the sole biological unit in the assault brigade, he had already felt a bit out of place, and the stark efficiency of his YVH 5-S Bugcrunchers left him feeling more alone than he cared to admit. The droids would perform as well as—if not better than—living beings, but there was nothing like a little laughter to calm a soldier's nerves before combat.

As soon as the YVHs had finished their vocabulator checks, they began to spray vacuum-resistant lubricant into one another's joints. The whole assault shuttle was quickly filled with an oily-sweet odor that gave Luke watery eyes and a queasy stomach. He had never expected to miss the smell of another soldier's sweat quite so much.

The gravelly voice of the *Megador*'s Tactical Control officer came over the flight-deck speaker. "Task Force Stomper cleared for assault. Be advised: Colony capital ships and dartship swarms attempting to return to support *Ackbar*. Time of breakthrough uncertain."

"Acknowledged."

Luke did not bother to check his tactical display for a tally of the enemy vessels—the number was going to be high, and it did not matter. In fifteen minutes, he would either be aboard the *Ackbar* fighting Raynar, or the eternal war that Jacen had foreseen would be erupting into full blossom.

Luke sealed his vacuum suit, then transmitted the attack order to the other fifty assault shuttles in his all-droid brigade and pushed his own throttles forward.

"Stomper in," he reported to the *Megador*.

"Good hunting, my friend." This voice belonged to Pellaeon. "And may the Force be with you."

Luke thanked the admiral for the good wishes and promised that his faith in the Jedi plan was not misplaced, then turned his attention to the assault.

The *Admiral Ackbar* lay only ten kilometers ahead, her bump-nosed silhouette surrounded by a swirling shell of Killik dartships that were rapidly being vaporized by Alliance turbolaser strikes. Her main engines lit space as she struggled to retreat toward Tenupe, but she was ensnared by the heavy-duty tractor-beams of half a dozen "pirate-nabber" Star Destroyers identical to herself.

Raynar would have been much wiser to send his fighter screen out to counterattack his captors, but he appeared to be holding the dartships back to deal with Task Force

Stomper. That was what Admiral Bwua'tu had predicted he would do, and so far the Bothan seemed correct.

Beyond the *Ackbar,* dozens of what Luke thought of as *Shard*-class capital ships were abandoning the battle on Tenupe to rush to Raynar's aid. Somewhat chunky and conical, they ranged in length from a kilometer and a half to nearly ten, but each had one broad, rounded end and several jagged sides. It almost appeared that the strange flotilla had been constructed by shattering an asteroid or a small moon. Judging by the halo of dispersion flashes and fiery streaks around the vessels, each was also very well shielded and heavily armed.

The Battle of Tenupe itself continued to rage, a flashing red stain that now spread across a quarter of the planet. Most of the Chiss fleet was down in the clouds and hidden from sight, but some of the Colony's larger ships were silhouetted against the flickering brilliance below. The four nest ships that had escaped the Jedi at the Murgo Choke were clustered near the heart of the battle, pouring a terrible rain of fire down upon the planet from one side of their hulls while the other hurled turbolaser potshots at the Alliance.

What impressed Luke most was the Killiks' inventiveness in completing their fleet. Arrayed around the edges of the battle were dozens of ancient megafreighters, their distinctive ring shapes surrounded by dark, swirling clouds that suggested the freighters were serving as staging areas for dartship swarms. Meanwhile hundreds of smaller vessels, visible to the naked eyed as triangular specks, were flitting around the center of the fight in erratic flight patterns, each pouring fire down from a single turbolaser. Chiss megamasers were blasting the gnat-like targets out of orbit whenever their gunnery crews could get a target-lock, but it would clearly take a while to exterminate them completely.

The *Ackbar*'s shields began to flicker with overload discharge, then collapsed in a string of bright, colorful flashes.

Control's voice came over the speaker in Luke's helmet. "Target is shields down. All main batteries switch to formation defense, all squadrons released for strafing runs."

The order had little to do with Task Force Stomper, but Luke was glad Control had included his channel in the transmission array. The sound of a nonelectronic voice reminded him that he was not attacking the *Ackbar* alone, that he and his bugcrunchers were merely the tip of a spear being driven by an entire attack fleet.

The Alliance batteries quickly obeyed Control's order and switched fire to the approaching Shard flotilla. The fighter squadrons left the safe stations where they had been waiting out the turboblaster exchange and streaked in to attack, painting whole swaths of space blue with their engine efflux. The *Ackbar*'s close-range cannons weaved a web of laser bolts in their paths, and the Colony's dartships drew back, creating an even tighter shell around the beleaguered Star Destroyer.

Bad mistake.

Bwua'tu had predicted the tactic. The Alliance fighter squadrons blew through the shell behind a flurry of proton torpedoes, then fell on the *Ackbar* like a thousand hawkbats, strafing her weapons turrets and clearing the way for Task Force Stomper.

A squadron and a half of starfighters—the eighteen craft that had been in the maintenance bays when the Killiks captured the *Ackbar*—dropped out of the hangar bay and turned to meet Luke's assault shuttles. Bwua'tu had predicted that, too. Rogue Squadron slashed in from its escort station and eliminated the interceptors in three fiery passes.

By then, Task Force Stomper had closed to within three kilometers of the *Ackbar,* with only the dartships to prevent them from reaching their target. The swarm peeled away from its combat with the starfighter squadrons and came after the assault shuttles.

Exactly as Bwua'tu had expected.

One of the Alliance's pirate-nabber Star Destroyers slid its tractor beam over and simply pulled the dartships away in a tumbling mass. Nothing remained between Task Force Stomper and its target but a thousand meters of laser-laced space. Every second or so, a blossom of color would flare somewhere in the task force as an *Ackbar* cannon bolt dissipated against a shuttle's shields or a stray dartship was destroyed by a YVH gunner. But for the most part, the starfighter squadrons and the pirate-nabber tractor beam did a remarkable job of deflecting the Killik attacks.

Luke activated his task force command channel. "We're on our own now. Fan out and get in fast."

Instead of acknowledgments, he was greeted by a static-filled pause precisely 1.2 seconds long—the standard delay a YVH droid allowed for a biological unit to finish an incomplete thought.

Then an ultradeep Lando Calrissian voice said, "Sir, 'fan out and get in fast' is not a clear order."

"Sorry." Luke sighed, wishing there had been room to add basic soft-logic interpretation to the YVH processing unit. "Disperse to assigned zones and penetrate target hull."

"Stomper Two acknowledging," the platoon's droid leader responded.

"Stomper Three acknowledging."

A long series of deep-voiced acknowledgments began to sound inside Luke's helmet—forty-nine other platoons in all. He passed the time by reminding himself that the bug-cruncher brigade would prove well worth the irritation once Task Force Stomper entered the *Ackbar*. They were better armored and far more deadly than living commandos, and they would be immune to the Force-based influence attacks of Raynar Thul and Lomi Plo.

The assault shuttles were just beginning to fan out when one of them suddenly flew apart. There was no flash or fireball. The passenger cabin simply came apart at the seams, spilling its cargo of bugcrunchers out into the void.

As Luke was checking his tactical display to find the shuttle's number, another one came apart.

He frowned and opened a channel to the pilots. "Stomper Twelve, what happened to your shuttle?"

The reply came in the electronic tones of a voice synthesizer, since Stomper Twelve's pilot was currently floating through a vacuum and unable to produce any sounds with his own vocabulator. "It disintegrated."

"I can *see* that!" Luke said. "What caused . . ."

Luke let the question trail off when he suddenly felt the Force drawing in around him, as though gathering itself for a powerful, violent release. He had just enough time to create a bubble of counterpressure around himself before every damage alarm on his control panel came to life. The cockpit simply came apart around him, and he found himself tumbling through space in the midst of a flotsam cloud.

Raynar Thul.

An electronic voice sounded inside Luke's helmet. "Sir, if you were asking a question—"

"Disregard," Luke ordered.

Another assault shuttle came apart, spilling another platoon of thirty-two bugcrunchers into space. *This* was not an attack Bwua'tu had expected—but that hardly mattered, because the Bothan *always* planned for what he could not foresee. He had been the one who had insisted that the Alliance specify space-assault YVHs as the platform when it purchased its new Bugcruncher Brigade.

Luke opened a brigadewide channel. "All dismounted

Stomper units continue toward original target zones under individual propulsion."

Again came the long string of acknowledgments. Luke used the Force to hitch a ride on a passing droid as his own platoon fired their thrusters and weaved through a blinding tangle of laser bolts, zipping starfighters, and rocket exhaust toward their target zone. They lost two units to lucky cannon strikes and three more to ramming dartships, but the Alliance starfighters were doing a good job of suppressing the enemy defenses, and Stomper One reached the *Ackbar*'s bridge in good order and with more than enough strength to perform their mission.

By then, much of the rest of the brigade had also reached the Star Destroyer and were dutifully reporting their successes as they breached the hull. The entire vessel had been declared a free-fire zone, so Luke really did not need to know more. He released the platoons to their own initiative and told them to report when they had taken their objectives.

Luke reached out in the Force and found Raynar reaching back, descending rapidly from the command deck atop the bridge structure. Raynar's presence was as murky and heavy as always, and as soon as Luke felt it, it began to press down inside, urging him to turn back.

Luke did not resist. He was *going* to leave, he *wanted* to leave . . . with Raynar. Luke began to exert his own will, pulling Raynar toward him, using Raynar's own power against him by binding their presences together with memories from their past: of how Luke had once helped protect Raynar's family from the Diversity Alliance, and how he had later helped Raynar's father destroy a terrible virus that could have caused a galaxywide plague. They were going to leave *together*. UnuThul wished Luke to go, Luke wished UnuThul to go with him, and so they would go together. *UnuThul* wished it.

The weight inside suddenly diminished as Raynar started to retreat. Luke tried to stop him, to find some part of his former student that he could hold on to. But UnuThul still had the power of the Colony behind him, and he called on that power to break the bonds of remembrance the Jedi Master had so quickly woven. His murky presence wrenched free, and the heaviness vanished from inside Luke's chest.

Stomper One and his assistant had already finished placing the breaching charges. The rest of the platoon was arrayed around Luke on the *Ackbar*'s hull, shielding him with their hulking bodies and firing their forearm-mounted blaster cannons at a flight of incoming dartships. Luke could see tiny divots forming in the droids' laminanium body armor as the enemy's weapons silently made their mark.

"What are you waiting for?" Luke commed Stomper One. "Detonate!"

But when it came to procedure, even war droids could not be hurried. "Stay clear!" Stomper One commed. "Fire in the hole!"

Then he detonated the charge.

Luke's faceplate darkened against the brilliance of the blast, but not so completely that he missed the flash of Stomper One's blaster cannons firing into the breached hull.

Then Stomper One pronounced, "Clear!" and began ordering, "Go . . . go . . . go . . ." at one-second intervals, sending a bugcruncher through the hole with each command.

By the fourth *go*, Luke's faceplate had returned to its normal tint, and he could see a steady stream of captured food containers, membrosia waxes, and chunks of spitcrete gushing out the breach into space.

"Grand Master Commander?" the lead droid asked.

"Thanks."

Luke ducked through the hole into the interior of what had once been the junior officers' mess. The lights remained on, so he could see that the chairs that had once been bolted into place along the tables had been removed by the Killiks. The far half of the room had been converted to a nursery, and the larvae were lying half out of their cells, writhing in pain from the decompression blow. Membrosia waxes and Alliance foodstuffs were still tumbling out of their lockers—or rising out of spitcrete bins—and flying out the breach with the cabin's air.

Raynar's heavy presence returned, this time *summoning* Luke.

The Jedi Master started toward the interior exit, where the first bugcrunchers were already trying to override the decompression safety and open the hatch. He was happy to go to Raynar. Again, Luke exerted his own will through the Force, incorporating UnuThul's wishes, but turning them toward his own ends. He recalled his dinner with Aryn Thul, when she and Tyko had asked Luke to spare her son's life. It was time to stop the killing, to end this war, and the Jedi Master would gladly go to Raynar to accept his surrender. UnuThul wished Luke to come, and Luke wished to end the war, and so Luke would come and accept the Colony's surrender.

Again, Raynar withdrew, this time so violently that Luke had no chance to prevent it. UnuThul was coming—not *to* Luke, but *after* him. The Master would have to fight. He had known it would come to this, but knowing did not make his heart any less heavy.

The interior hatch finally irised open, and the decompression blow brought half a dozen Killiks tumbling out. The bugcrunchers opened fire with their blaster cannons, shattering the tough pressure carapaces before the bugs could react, then pushed through the doorway with weapons still blazing. By the time the fourth droid had gone through, a synthesized voice was already sounding the all-clear inside Luke's helmet.

Luke stepped through the hatchway and found himself in a narrow corridor littered with dead Killiks and pieces of shattered carapace. A closed hatchway sealed either end of the short passage. Two confused boxy little mouse droids were trying to make their way through the debris, determined to complete some errand that no longer mattered. A row of sealed hatches lined the opposite wall, which—if Luke recalled the *Ackbar*'s bridge schematic correctly—concealed storage lockers, officers' lounges, and exercise facilities. Each was a dead end, as well as a potential hiding place for ambushers.

The corridor was hardly the ideal place for a lightsaber duel, but it would have to do. Luke could already sense a furious Raynar Thul at the far end of the passage, using his brute Force-strength to wrest open the safety-sealed hatch.

As soon as the last of his platoon had entered the corridor, Luke pointed to the hatch through which they'd come. "Make that hatch airtight."

"Airtight, sir?" Stomper One asked. "Are you certain? As S-series droids, we enjoy a significant tactical advantage in a nonpressurized environment."

"But *I* don't." Luke plucked at the sleeve of his vac suit. "And I don't want to worry about ripping this. The fight is about to get rough."

"Rough?" Stomper One looked up and down the corridor, appraising their position and apparently reaching the same conclusion that Luke had: the corridor was a bad place for a firefight. "As you wish, sir."

The droids quickly went to work, sealing the hatch to the officers' mess and using their blaster cannons to spot-weld the others closed so the platoon could not be ambushed. When Luke noticed they were leaving the hatch directly behind them open, he pointed to it.

"Fix that hatch, too." He started up the corridor toward the hatch at the far end. "We won't be retreating."

Stomper One's synthesized voice assumed a note of approval. "Very good, sir."

Luke felt the Force stir as Raynar made a final exertion. "They're coming. Prepare for—"

The far hatch suddenly ruptured inward, bringing with it a short-lived decompression squall that rocked Luke back on his heels and hazed the corridor with airborne dust. He glimpsed a tall figure in a black pressure suit.

Then the figure flicked one of his hands, and Luke found himself flying backward, bouncing off YVH droids and tumbling out of control. He reached out in the Force, grabbing at passing hatches, the ceiling, even Raynar himself, but he was whirling too fast to catch hold of anything.

He hit the end of the corridor with a tremendous *clung*, unsure whether he was upside down or sideways, then crashed to the floor struggling to remain conscious.

By the time his eyes came back into focus, the corridor had erupted into a crashing storm of cannon bolts and shatter gun pellets. The lower two-thirds of the corridor was blocked by a wall of laminanium bugcruncher armor, but the upper third of the passage belonged to Raynar's Killiks. Still in their pressure carapaces, they were scurrying through the smoke along the walls and ceiling, pouring shatter gun pellets down on the droids' heads, trying to get past so they could launch an attack from the rear.

Luke rolled to his feet . . . and watched in astonishment as his helmet dropped to the floor in two pieces. He glanced at the wall behind him and saw a fist-deep depression where its impact had dented the durasteel.

"Can't let him do *that* again," Luke groaned. He opened the seals on his vac suit gloves, shook them to the floor, and snatched the lightsaber off his belt. Then he averted his eyes and spoke into his throat mike. "Dazers!"

The corridor erupted in rainbow iridescence; then a piercing squeal came over Luke's earpiece and the smell of ripe hubba gourds filled his nostrils. Stunned by the Dazers' aura-deadening properties, several Killiks dropped off the ceiling into the midst of the bugcrunchers. The rest of the insects were soon spread overhead in yellow smears.

Luke had already rushed forward, only to find himself trapped behind his own bugcrunchers and unable to see the rest of the battle. "Make a hole!" he ordered. "Coming through."

Three bugcrunchers blocking his way obediently stepped aside, and Luke found himself staring up ten meters of corridor packed chest-high with Killik corpses and twisted YVH frames. At the other end, with his black helmet lying in a melted gob before him and the fingers of his vac suit gloves burned off by all the Force energy he had been throwing around, stood Luke's melt-faced opponent. Raynar Thul.

Luke jumped onto the pile of chitin and metal in front of him. Two of Raynar's Unu bodyguards immediately popped up and sent a burst of shatter gun pellets zipping down the corridor toward him.

Luke flicked his hand and Force-batted the projectiles into a wall, then the bugcrunchers at his back sent a stream of cannon fire down the hall. Raynar ignited a gold lightsaber and deflected most of the volley, but a few of the bolts made it through and splattered his bodyguards across the walls.

"It's not too late to surrender." Luke started forward at a walk. "I'm not eager to do this."

Raynar's burn-scarred lips twitched in a faint hint of a smile. "*We* are."

Raynar raised his lightsaber and jumped onto the carnage heap.

Luke ignited his own blade and raced forward, using the

Force to keep himself from stumbling over debris. A loud crunching erupted behind him as his surviving droids raced after him, then half a dozen of Raynar's bodyguards leapt up from the other end of the pile and started forward, firing shatter guns with their lower set of arms and carrying flame tridents with their upper pair.

A flurry of cannon bolts zipped past Luke from behind and took out three insects. Raynar pointed at the attacking droids. A muffled thump erupted inside one of them, and it went down in a sizzling, popping crash of laminanium. Luke killed the last of Raynar's bodyguards by Force-slamming them into the wall so hard their thoraxes burst, then the two Jedi were on one another, their lightsabers flashing toward each other's heads with all the speed and might they could summon.

That was the trouble with powerful men—especially younger ones. Awed by their own strength, they so often believed strength was the answer to every problem. Luke was older and wiser. While Raynar swung, he pivoted.

As Raynar's gold blade sliced the air where Luke's head had been, Luke's boot was kicking him behind the ankles, knocking his legs out from under him and stretching him out flat.

But Raynar was a Jedi, and all Jedi were quick. He caught himself in the Force, levitating himself just long enough to bring his golden blade sweeping in at Luke's shoulder.

Luke had no choice but to block with his blade, and no place to block but the forearm. Raynar's lightsaber went spinning off, still securely in the grasp of his three-fingered hand, and caught one of Luke's bugcrunchers squarely in the back. The weapon sliced through six centimeters of laminanium armor before the severed forearm flew free. The blade deactivated, and the hilt disappeared into the tangle of death and destruction at the droid's feet.

The pain of losing an arm might have forced a common Jedi to stop fighting, but Raynar was no common Jedi. He had the Force potential of the Colony to draw on, and he did that now, swinging his remaining hand up to hurl Luke down the corridor as he had done before.

But this time, Luke was ready. He placed his own hand in front of Raynar's and rooted himself in the heart of the Force, and when he did that, he became the very essence of the immovable object. Nothing could dislodge him—not one of Lando's asteroid tuggers, not the *Megador*'s sixteen ion engines, not the black hole at the center of the galaxy itself.

Luke stood that way, waiting, dimly aware that his surviving bugcrunchers were moving into defensive positions, one at his back and the other just inside the burst hatch. Raynar continued to struggle, trying to hurl Luke down the corridor, trying to move him a single centimeter.

Luke did not budge, and finally Raynar stopped struggling and met his eyes with a stunned and anguished gaze.

The Master sighed and shook his head. "What am I going to do with you, Raynar Thul?" he asked. "You learn nothing from your mistakes."

Luke deactivated his lightsaber and picked Raynar up by the collar and slammed him against the wall. He used the Force to pin him there, waiting for an answer to his question, watching as the expression in his captive's pained eyes turned from astonishment to anger to calculation.

But when Raynar's free hand rose, it was not to summon the Force lightning that Luke had expected. It was to call his lightsaber back, to attempt to continue the battle that he obviously could no longer win.

It was in that moment that Luke finally decided that the life of Raynar Thul would be spared. He intercepted the weapon and used the Force to pin Raynar's remaining arm against the wall along with the rest of his body. Then he opened the hilt of the captured lightsaber and removed the focusing crystal. He held it up in front of Raynar.

"Someday I may return this—but for now, it's staying with me." He zipped the gem into a pocket of his vac suit, then reached out to Raynar in the Force and spoke in a softer voice. "Your days as UnuThul are done, Raynar. It's time to surrender and come home."

The eyes beneath Raynar's lumpy brow flashed with alarm. "The Colony *is* our home."

Luke shook his head. "That can't be anymore, Raynar," he said. "The *Colony* can't be anymore. If you stay with the Killiks, the entire species will die."

Raynar curled his scarred lip. "Lies."

"No." Luke touched Raynar through the Force. "You're still a Jedi. You can sense when a person is telling the truth. You can sense it in me, *now.*"

Hoping to force his Will on his captor, Raynar accepted the contact—as Luke had known he would—then gasped in astonishment as he sensed the truth in what Luke was saying. *"How?"*

"Because as long as you are the Prime Unu, Lomi Plo will be the queen of the Gorog." Luke began to press, as though he were trying to force *his* will on Raynar. "And as long as there is a Gorog, the Colony will be a threat to the Chiss."

Raynar began to pull, learning from Luke's earlier tactics and trying to use Luke's own attack against *him.* "The Chiss are a *threat* to the Colony."

Luke went along with Raynar—in fact, he pushed even harder.

"That's right. The Chiss are a threat to the Colony," Luke said. "They have developed a weapon that can wipe out the entire Colony. They tried to use it here. Jaina and Zekk stopped them . . . but we both know they have more."

Backed by Luke's strength, the truth was too much for

Raynar. His Will broke, and his resolve turned to panic. "We know," he admitted.

Luke continued to push. "And they'll use it—if you stay with the Colony."

Raynar shook his head. "We can't let them."

"Then you have to leave," Luke said. "It's the only way to save the Killiks."

A terrible sadness came to Raynar's melted face. He lowered his burned eyelids and reluctantly began to nod—then suddenly stopped and glanced toward the hatch through which he had burst earlier.

"Not the *only* way." Raynar's voice assumed a dark tone, and Luke knew his true target was finally preparing to show herself. "Maybe there is a weapon to kill the *Chiss*?"

Luke resisted the temptation to look toward the hatch. Lomi Plo would not show herself if she knew she was expected.

"Even if there was such a weapon, it wouldn't be right to use it," Luke said. "The Jedi won't permit speciecide against the Chiss—any more than we would against the Killiks."

"But you could . . . if it was self-defense." Raynar bared his jagged teeth in a try at a grin. "Destroying the Chiss would be self-defense, so you would *have* to permit it."

Raynar began to push back now, filling Luke's chest with the dark weight of UnuThul's Will.

"If it *were* self-defense, we might have to permit it," Luke said, playing along—and again using Raynar's own attack against him. "But even that wouldn't save the Colony. It cannot survive as it is. We know that."

"*How* do we know that?" Raynar demanded angrily. "We know no such thing."

"We *might,*" Luke insisted, exerting his own will through the Force again, reeling Raynar in. "If the Colony grew too large, it would devour its own worlds and destroy *itself*."

"There are always more worlds," Raynar countered.

"Not always," Luke said. "Sometimes all of the other worlds are taken. That *could* have been what happened when the Killiks disappeared from Alderaan." He paused, then used the Force to pull as hard as he could, trying to draw Raynar into his own view of reality. "In fact, I'm *sure* that's what happened on Alderaan. The Killiks devoured their own world and tried to take someone else's. That's the reason the Celestials drove the Killiks into the Unknown Regions."

The fight finally went out of Raynar. "You're *sure*?" He folded his cauterized forearm stump across his stomach and cradled it with his other arm, his lips quivering in pain and tears welling in his eyes. "You know—"

The question was drowned out by the roar of a blaster cannon, and Luke glanced down the corridor to see the bugcruncher stationed there suddenly powering down. The droid fell out of the opening backward and crashed to the deck, then Lomi Plo scuttled through the hatchway on her mismatched set of legs—one human, the other insectile. She turned her bulbous eyes and noseless face down the corridor, then extended her crooked upper arms toward the lightsaber in Luke's hands.

The last remaining bugcruncher opened fire, forcing Lomi Plo to ignite the lightsaber in her lower set of hands. Her blocks and parries came so slowly that she was barely able to deflect the cannon bolts and she was forced to swing her upper arms toward the droid and drain its power. Raynar, thankfully, continued to stand dazed—and seemingly impotent.

Determined to reach Lomi Plo before she drained his lightsaber's power cell, Luke sprang down the corridor and leapt off the carnage heap to attack. Lomi blocked his first pass with her white lightsaber. Then, in place of the purple lightsaber she had left in Jacen at the end of their last meeting, she ignited a familiar-looking green blade—the lightsaber Raynar had confiscated on Woteba. *Luke's* lightsaber.

"Now you're just ticking me off," Luke said.

Lomi clacked her mandibles and hissed, then launched a deadly low–high–low combination with her flashing blades. Luke parried, ducked, and jumped, then brought an elbow up under her mandibles and sent her staggering back, all four arms flailing as she struggled to catch her balance on her mismatched legs.

Luke whipped his blade around, cocking it for a death slash across her middle—then had a prickle of danger sense between his shoulder blades and tried to spin away. He almost made it.

Something heavy and huge slammed into his shoulder—a shatter gun pellet?—and sent him tumbling across the floor past Lomi Plo's feet. He tried a reactionary slash as he rolled by, only to discover that was he was no longer holding his lightsaber, and he could not move his prosthetic hand—nor the rest of his arm.

Lomi Plo's two blades began to chop the floor behind him, so he used the Force to accelerate himself and continued to roll, then came to his feet two meters on the other side of her and called his lightsaber back to his good hand.

The weapon arrived just ahead of Lomi Plo, and suddenly Luke found himself on the defensive, being driven into a corner while Raynar Thul—not so impotent after all—used his other hand to fire more shatter gun pellets.

In lightsaber combat, Luke favored two-handed styles, but he could still fight single-handed—even with his weak hand—just as well as anyone in the academy. What he could not do, however, was fight wounded and weak-handed against twin blades while a second party fired a steady stream of hard-to-deflect shatter gun pellets at him.

In short, Luke was desperate.

So he dropped to his side and caught Lomi Plo's human leg in a scissoring motion between his feet. The knee bent backward and popped with a sickening crunch.

She fell, squealing in pain and clacking her mandibles—and redoubled her attacks, slashing so ferociously with her twin blades that Luke's lone hand barely had the strength to block.

Of course, Control picked that moment for an important announcement from the *Megador.* "Be advised that three Killik swarms are diverting to attack *Healing Star.*"

Lomi Plo's attacks slackened for a moment, and Luke realized that she was gently probing him through the Force, searching for any hint of fear or doubt. He put the *Healing Star*—the fleet's main hospital ship—out of his mind and remained focused on the fight. Lomi Plo had almost certainly used the Dark Nest to divert those swarms, to try to create an opening that would give her power over his mind.

Still dodging shatter gun pellets, rolling back and forth on the floor and parrying madly, Luke glanced up the corridor and used the Force to reach into the carnage heap beneath Raynar's feet. He grabbed the largest, heaviest thing he could find—a disabled bugcruncher droid—and jerked it free.

The pile shifted and Raynar crashed down on his back, but Luke barely noticed. He was pulling the droid down the corridor straight at Lomi Plo.

She deflected it easily, of course—but she had to spin away from Luke and wave a hand, and that gave him the chance he needed to Force-spring up the corridor toward Raynar, who was just returning to his feet.

"As I was *saying,*" Luke said, pointing his lightsaber down at Raynar's chest. "You never learn."

Raynar's eyes flashed with alarm and he rolled away—presenting the side of his head for a perfect knockout blow. Luke brought his lightsaber down, but deactivated the blade and flipped it around at the last second to strike at the base of the ear.

The blow landed with a sharp crack that suggested a breaking skull, but Luke had no time to worry about Raynar. Lomi Plo was dragging herself out the hatchway, trying to escape into the general confusion of the *Ackbar's* recapture. He sprang after her, using the Force to drag her back into the corridor.

Lomi Plo whirled around, her lightsabers rising into a guard position but not attacking. Trapped on the floor with a broken knee, she knew as well as Luke did that she could not defend herself; that he could kill her any time he wished.

So Luke was half expecting it when Control's voice sounded in his earpiece again. "Be advised, Killik swarms are opening fire on *Healing Star.*"

Lomi Plo's mandibles opened wide, and a long, gurgling hiss erupted from her throat. Luke did not need to speak Killik to understand what she was saying—or even to probe her meaning through the Force. *She* could call off the attack on the hospital ship.

All Luke had to do was let her go.

Luke snorted. "That's the trouble with you ruthless types—you're all so predictable."

Lomi Plo grabbed hold of the sides of the hatchway with two of her hands, then pulled herself up on her insect leg and cocked her head so that only one of her bulbous eyes was turned toward Luke.

"Mara and Jacen are in a hospital back on Coruscant," Luke explained. "There's nobody aboard *Healing Star* but a few mouse droids. Admiral Bwua'tu *said* you were going to attack it. And by the way, I have no doubts about Mara. She says hello, in fact."

Lomi Plo's reaction came so suddenly that Luke doubted even *she* was expecting it. She just came flying at him with both blades flashing, striking high and low from opposite sides in a desperate attempt to finish him off.

Luke, of course, had anticipated this, too. Lomi Plo had no power over him. He simply stepped inside her attack and flicked his wrist twice, first sweeping his blade upward, then whipping it around in a backslash, and she landed at his feet in four parts.

Luke stood looking down at the pieces for a moment, half expecting them to turn to smoke and vanish, or to dissolve like a bad HoloNet signal. It was hard to believe that a woman of mere flesh and blood and chitin had caused so much trouble—had brought the galaxy to the edge of eternal war—but of course, beings of flesh and blood were *always* starting wars. That's why the galaxy needed her Jedi.

Luke reached down and retrieved the two lightsabers Lomi Plo had been wielding. He tucked the white one inside his flight utilities and hung the green one in its proper place on his belt, then returned to the side of his former student.

Raynar was still unconscious, but his vital signs were stable, and he did not seem to be in any great danger.

Luke broke out a medkit and started to work. "Let's get you patched up, son," he said. "We're going home."

EPILOGUE

The air had long since grown stale and the caf bitter, but the mood in the *Megador*'s cramped briefing room remained upbeat. Aristocra Formbi was more than two standard hours late for the long-distance conference, but no one was surprised. The Chiss had taken a battering even after the Alliance arrived, and the Jedi had prevented the deployment of their "secret weapon"—the insidious parasite bombs. Without a doubt, the Chiss were going to make their displeasure known, and Leia was just happy they were not doing it with megamasers.

Finally, Admiral Pellaeon's comm officer announced that Aristocra Chaf'orm'bintrano had opened a channel. Formbi's jowly blue face appeared on the giant vid display hanging at one end of the room. He did not bother introducing himself—or apologizing for his tardiness.

"The Ascendancy is ready to hear your peace offer," Formbi said. "But I warn you, we are not interested in any proposal that fails to eliminate the Colony threat."

"We understand that," Leia said evenly. "And we have already done so."

Formbi's eyes grew suspicious. "Really."

"As a matter of fact, yeah," Han said. He pointed a thumb at Luke, whose arm remained in a sling from the injuries he had suffered aboard the *Ackbar*. "Luke *killed*

Lomi Plo, and Raynar's going back to the Galactic Alliance with us."

Formbi's face showed his alarm. "You're taking *Raynar Thul* into Alliance space? I thought you had killed him!"

"We've *neutralized* him," Luke said. "Raynar realizes that his continued presence can only bring more disasters like this one down on the Killiks."

"Besides, we have him buttoned up tight in a special brain hood Cilghal designed," Han said. "If he even *thinks* about a bug, he gets zapped with dazers."

Formbi frowned. "The Ascendancy would feel more comfortable if he were dead."

"He will be, if we find our measures are insufficient to keep him isolated until he recovers," Luke said. "Rest assured, the Colony has been destroyed. The Jedi will do whatever is necessary to ensure that Raynar Thul never troubles you again."

Formbi's brow shot up, but he quickly caught himself and assumed a doubtful scowl. "What of the Twi'lek Jedi?" he demanded. "This Alema Rar? Isn't she a Dark Nest Joiner?"

"She *was*," Leia said. "As of now, she is presumed dead."

Formbi's scowl deepened. "We Chiss prefer certainties to presumptions, Princess."

"As do we all," Leia said. "But I'm afraid that's impossible in this case. We were unable to locate her body, and I'm fairly certain that's because she was eaten."

Formbi was too shocked to feign disbelief. "By what?"

"Some sort of spider sloth," Leia said. "I can't actually name it. All I can tell you is that we were fighting on Tenupe when the creature attacked. I escaped and Alema didn't. The creature disappeared into the jungle with her upper body in its mouth."

"If that is what you Jedi mean by destroying the Colony, then I must inform you that your definitions are not acceptable to the Chiss," Formbi said. "If she survived and returns to the Dark Nest, she could restart the entire Colony."

"No, she couldn't," Luke said. "I assume you've been briefed on the nanotech environmental defense agents of the Utegetu Nebula?"

"Of course," Formbi smirked.

"Then you'll be reassured to know that as of our last report, Jedi teams have seeded more than half of the Colony's planets with the appropriate nanotech agents," Luke said. "Before we're done, that number will be as close to a hundred percent as our knowledge of Colony territory can make it."

"The Killiks won't be *able* to reconstitute the Colony," Leia said. "If they start to overpopulate, their own worlds will bring the nest down to a manageable level."

"You might say it's a failsafe," Han said. "It worked like a charm on Woteba."

"So you say," Formbi replied. "But I doubt your guarantees will be satisfactory to the ruling houses."

"They're going to have to be, Aristocra." Pellaeon spoke in a gruff, sharp voice that carried a subtle but definite threat. "The Galactic Alliance is ready to wash its hands of this matter, and our fleet will be returning to our own territory as soon as possible."

"You'll find no argument from us," Formbi said. "The Ascendancy never wanted you involved in the first place."

Pellaeon's voice grew even more steely. "Perhaps, but we need to deal with current realities. The war is over as of *now*, Aristocra. The Killiks have no reason to restart it, and very soon they'll lack the capacity to do so. Therefore, the *Ascendancy* has no reason to restart it, either."

"We Chiss are accustomed to formulating our own policies," Formbi sneered.

"We know that, Aristocra," Leia said. "But *you* know

that those policies affect your relations with the Alliance— and the Galactic Alliance is not in the habit of tolerating aggressors and warmongers. Quite the opposite, as a matter of fact."

"Take a lesson from the bugs and don't hold a grudge," Han added. "*They* went home a week ago. You do the same, and we'll all be happy."

"The Chiss are not interested in what makes you happy, Captain Solo," Formbi fumed. He paused, swallowing a bit of his anger. "But we *are* beings who value peace above all else—and we are willing to take one more risk to achieve it."

Leia breathed an inward sigh of relief, and Pellaeon smiled beneath his mustache. That was nearly the exact statement that Bwua'tu predicted the Chiss would make— just prior to naming their terms.

"We're very glad to hear that, Aristocra," Leia said.

"Don't be," Formbi growled. "You haven't heard our terms."

"I assume you're prepared to remedy that situation," Pellaeon said, perhaps a bit too smugly.

"Of course," Formbi retorted. "The Chiss will agree to your terms, provided the Alliance will promise to come to our aid in the event of another unprovoked Killik attack."

Pellaeon frowned, pretending to consider a request that everyone in the briefing room already knew he was going to grant.

After a suitable pause, he nodded. "Very well. Done."

Formbi's eyes widened just enough to betray his surprise. "You agree? Just like that?"

"Why shouldn't we?" Pellaeon asked. "*We're* the ones who are promising there will be no Killik attacks."

Formbi frowned. "So you are," he agreed. "But this is a formal treaty. Don't you need authorization from Chief Omas?"

Pellaeon smiled broadly. "My dear Aristocra, I *came* with that authorization," he said. "There is nothing the Galactic Alliance desires more than a close relationship with the Ascendancy. You're welcome to send a team of diplomats back with the fleet when we leave, if you'd like to get started on the formal documents."

Formbi looked vaguely uncomfortable, like a sabacc player who just realized he should have called a bluff. "I'm afraid that will have to wait. We didn't bring any diplomats along on this campaign. We were under the impression we were going to war."

Pellaeon chuckled. "Well, war *can* be unpredictable."

"More so every day, it seems," Formbi said. "You may assure the Killiks—or whomever—that our fleet will be leaving within a day."

"Then you've completed your search-and-rescue operations?" Leia asked. Her heart was in her throat, for she was thinking of a certain young captain whom she had shot down.

"You would be safe in assuming that," Formbi replied with typical Chiss evasiveness about military matters.

"Would you happen to know if Jagged Fel was recovered alive?" Leia asked. "As you know, in the past, he has been a close personal friend of our family's."

"I also know that the *Falcon* was the vessel that shot him down," Formbi replied, a little bitterly.

"So he made it?" Han asked.

"I didn't say that, Captain Solo."

"You are not telling?" Saba burst out, speaking for the first time. "Jaina Solo will be a shenbit for a month!"

"I don't see why. It was my impression that their relationship was over long before her parents shot him down." Formbi grew thoughtful for a moment, then finally said, "Unfortunately, Commander Fel has not been recovered yet. His rescue beacon is transmitting from a rift valley inaccessible to recovery craft. We've sent in a team to search for him on foot."

"Perhaps the Jedi can help," Luke said. "We might be able to sense—"

"Your help would not be welcome," Formbi interrupted. "It has cost us too much already."

"I'm sorry you feel that way," Luke said. "Please let us know if you change your mind."

"We won't," Formbi assured him.

"Be that as it may, Jaina still regards Commander Fel fondly." Leia did not mention Zekk; the Chiss were squeamish enough about Joiners without bringing a mind-mate into the love affair. "Jagged's status was the first thing she asked about after Han and I rescued her. If you *do* happen to recover him alive before you depart, please let him know that she and her wingmate are making an excellent recovery from their wounds. They'll be out of the infirmary tomorrow."

"I really don't see why Captain Fel would be interested. Assuming we *do* recover him." Formbi turned to Pellaeon. "You may assure Chief Omas that a diplomatic team will be arriving shortly to formalize the treaty."

With that, Formbi closed the channel and vanished from the vid display, leaving the mood in the briefing room slightly less jovial than before—despite the fact that they had just negotiated a successful end to the war.

After a moment, Han said, "Nice guy." He shook his head in disgust. "No wonder the Chiss get along so well with their neighbors."

"Out here, I'm afraid getting along with your neighbors means keeping them at arm's length," Pellaeon said.

An uncomfortable silence fell over the cabin—which Saba suddenly broke by snatching the lightsaber off Leia's utility belt . . . breaking the clasp in the process. Well accustomed to her Master's stern training exercises—and odd timing—Leia simply turned and bowed her head for the stern rap that she knew Saba was going to dispense for allowing her lightsaber to be snatched away.

When it did not come, Leia looked up to find the Barabel studying her lightsaber with a disapproving eye. "Master?"

"Jedi Solo, where did you get this lightsaber?" Saba demanded.

"I built it," Leia said. "Over twenty years ago."

Saba curled her lip in disdain. "This one thought so." She jammed the hilt into her belt, then added, "It is a terrible weapon, unworthy of your current skillz. You will carry it no more."

"What?" Leia gasped. "What am I supposed to do for a lightsaber?"

Saba blinked her slit-pupiled eyes in reptilian exasperation.

"Princesz Leia, you are a fine Jedi, the equal of any Jedi Knight in the order." She pointed a claw at the empty place on Leia's belt. "What do you think you should do for a lightsaber?"

Leia finally saw what the Barabel was driving at, then felt herself blushing at how long it had taken her to realize the answer. "Build a new one," she said. "A better one."

Saba closed her eyes. "*Finally.*"

Luke laughed, then said, "Congratulations, Leia. I think that means you should consider yourself a full Jedi Knight."

"No kidding? A full Jedi Knight!" Han wrapped his arm around Leia's shoulders, then added, "But I don't see what the big deal is. I could've told you *that* a long time ago."

Leia slipped her arm around Han's waist, then stretched up to kiss him on the lips. "Thanks, flyboy. There's no one I'd rather hear say that."

Pellaeon cleared his throat and looked at the ceiling, obviously a bit uncomfortable. "That reminds me, Master

Skywalker. I've had a messenger from Chief Omas. He wishes to convene a meeting of the Advisory Council as soon as we return. If I were Bwua'tu, I'd predict that he's eager to formalize the Jedi's new role in the Alliance."

Han groaned, and an empty feeling came to Leia's stomach. They had told Luke that they suspected Omas of betraying their mission. Unfortunately, they had no hard evidence of the Chief's treachery, and Luke did not want to damage the delicate relations between the Jedi and the government by making unprovable accusations. Besides, even if Omas *had* betrayed the Solos, it was not technically a crime, since he had been acting for the benefit of the Galactic Alliance.

Luke merely nodded. "I'll be happy to discuss that with Chief Omas myself," he said. "But I'm afraid the Jedi will be withdrawing from his Advisory Council."

By the look on the other faces in the cabin, Leia supposed that her brother's statement had surprised even Admiral Bwua'tu.

Finally, Pellaeon asked, *"Why?"*

"Because the Jedi should serve, not govern," Luke said. "In the Colony, we've seen again how badly matters turn out when Jedi take the reins of state—even with the purest of motives."

"But Jedi advice is important!" Pellaeon objected. "At times, I think you're the only disinterested representatives *in* the government!"

Luke raised his hand to calm the admiral. "The Galactic Alliance will have Jedi advice," he said. "I'm going to establish a new Jedi Council to help run the order, and I'll relay their advice to Chief Omas."

This declaration was received with the stunned silence that Leia would have believed it deserved—had she seen any better way to hold the Jedi order together.

Finally, Pellaeon said, "A workable organization, as long as you're at the head of it. But what happens if you're unavailable?"

An unfocused appearance came to Luke's gaze, and Leia had the impression that he was looking a long distance into the future.

"Good question," Luke said. "I wish I knew the answer."

Read on for a preview of

REPUBLIC COMMANDO

TRIPLE ZERO

By Karen Traviss

The thrilling sequel to

Star Wars: Republic Commando:
Hard Contact

Available now from Del Rey Books!

Tipoca City, Kamino: Eight Years Before Geonosis.

Kal Skirata had committed the biggest mistake of his life, and he'd made some pretty big ones in his time.

Kamino was damp. And damp didn't help his shattered ankle one little bit. No, it was *more* than damp: it was nothing but storm-whipped sea from pole to pole, and he wished that he'd worked that out before he responded to Jango Fett's offer of a lucrative long-term deployment in a location that his old comrade hadn't exactly specified.

But that was the least of his worries now.

The air smelled more like a hospital than a military base. The place didn't look like barracks, either. Skirata leaned on the polished rail that was all that separated him from a forty-meter fall into a chamber large enough to swallow a battle cruiser and lose it.

Above him, the vaulted illuminated ceiling stretched as far as the abyss did below. The prospect of the fall didn't worry him half as much as not understanding what he was now seeing.

The cavern—surgically clean, polished durasteel and permaglass—was filled with structures that seemed almost like fractals. At first glance they looked like giant toroids stacked on pillars; then, as he stared, the toroids resolved into smaller rings of permaglass containers, with containers within them, and inside those—

No, this *wasn't happening*.

Inside the transparent tubes there was fluid, and within it there was *movement*.

It took him several minutes of staring and refocusing on one of the tubes to realize there was a body in there, and it was alive. In fact, there was a body in *every* tube: row upon row of tiny bodies, *children's* bodies. *Babies*.

"Fierfek," he said aloud.

He thought he'd come to this Force-forsaken hole to train commandos. Now he knew he'd stepped into a nightmare. He heard boots behind him on the walkway of the gantry and turned sharply to see Jango coming slowly toward him, chin lowered as if in reproach.

"If you're thinking of leaving, Kal, you knew the deal," said Jango, and leaned on the rail beside him.

"You said—"

"I said you'd be training special forces troops, and you will be. They just happen to be growing them."

"*What?*"

"Clones."

"How the fierfek did you ever get involved with *that*?"

"A straight five million and a few extras for donating my genes. And don't look shocked. You'd have done the same."

The pieces fell into place for Skirata and he let himself be shocked anyway. War was one thing. Weird science was another issue entirely.

"Well, I'm keeping my end of the deal." Skirata adjusted the fifteen-centimeter, three-sided blade that he always kept sheathed in his jacket sleeve. Two Kaminoan technicians walked serenely across the floor of the facility beneath him. Nobody had searched him and he felt better for having a

ew weapons located for easy use, including the small hold-
ut blaster tucked in the cuff of his boot.

And all those little kids in tanks . . .

The Kaminoans disappeared from sight. "What do those
hings want with an army anyway?"

"*They* don't. And *you* don't need to know all this right
1ow." Jango beckoned him to follow. "Besides, you're al-
eady dead, remember?"

"Feels like it," said Skirata. He was the *Cuy'val Dar*—
iterally, "those who no longer exist," a hundred expert
oldiers with a dozen specialties who'd answered Jango's
ecret summons in exchange for a *lot* of credits . . . as long
is they were prepared to disappear from the galaxy *com-
•letely.*

He trailed Jango down corridors of unbroken white du-
aplast, passing the occasional Kaminoan with its long
ray neck and snake-like head. He'd been here for four
standard days now, staring out the window of his quarters
onto the endless ocean and catching an occasional glimpse
of the aiwhas soaring up out of the waves and flapping into
he air. The thunder was totally silenced by the sound-
proofing, but the lightning had become an annoyingly ir-
egular pulse in the corner of his eye.

Skirata knew from day one that he wouldn't like Ka-
ninoans.

Their cold yellow eyes troubled him, and he didn't care
for their arrogance, either. They stared at his limping gait
and asked if he minded being *defective.*

The window-lined corridor seemed to run the length of
he city. Outside, it was hard to see where the horizon
ended and the rain clouds began.

Jango looked back to see if he was keeping up. "Don't
worry, Kal. I'm told it's clear weather in the summer—for
a few days."

Right. The most dreary planet in the galaxy, and he was

stuck on it. And his ankle was playing up. He really should have invested in getting it fixed surgically. When—if—he got out of here, he'd have the assets to get the best surgeon that credits could buy.

Jango slowed down tactfully. "So, Ilippi threw you out?"

"Yeah." His wife wasn't Mandalorian. He'd hoped she would embrace the culture, but she didn't: she always hated seeing her old man go off to someone else's war. The fights began when he wanted to take their two sons into battle with him. They were eight years old, old enough to start learning their trade; but she refused, and soon Ilippi and the boys and his daughter were no longer waiting when he returned from the latest war. Ilippi divorced him the *Mando* way, same as they'd married, on a brief, solemn, private vow. A contract was a contract, written or not. "Just as well I've got another assignment to occupy me."

"You should have married a *Mando* girl. *Aruetiise* don't understand a mercenary's life." Jango paused as if waiting for argument, but Kal wasn't giving him one. "Don't your *sons* talk to you any longer?"

"Not often." *So I failed as a father. Don't rub it in.* "Obviously they don't share the *Mando* outlook on life any more than their mother does."

"Well, they won't be speaking to you at all now. Not here. Ever."

Nobody seemed to care if he had disappeared anyway. Yes, he *was* as good as dead. Jango said nothing more, and they walked in silence until they reached a large circular lobby with rooms leading off it like the spokes of a wheel.

"Ko Sai said something wasn't quite right with the first test batch of clones," said Jango, ushering Skirata ahead of him into another room. "They've tested them and they don't think these are going to make the grade. I told Orun Wa that we'd give him the benefit of our military experience and take a look."

Skirata was used to evaluating fighting men—and women, come to that. He knew what it took to make a soldier. He was good at it; soldiering was his life, as it was for all *Mando'ade*, all sons and daughters of Mandalore. At least there'd be some familiarity to cling to in this ocean wilderness.

It was just a matter of staying as far from the Kaminoans as he could.

"Gentlemen," said Orun Wa in his soothing monotone. He welcomed them into his office with a graceful tilt of the head, and Skirata noted that he had a prominent bony fin running across the top of his skull front to back. Maybe that meant he was older, or dominant, or something: he didn't look like the other examples of aiwha-bait Skirata had seen so far. "I always believe in being honest about setbacks in a program. We value the Jedi Council as a customer."

"I have *nothing* to do with the Jedi," said Jango. "I'm only a consultant on military matters."

Oh, Skirata thought. *Jedi. Great.*

"I would still be happier if you confirmed that the first batch of units is below the acceptable standard."

"Bring them in, then."

Skirata shoved his hands in his jacket pockets and wondered what he was going to see: poor marksmanship, poor endurance, lack of aggression? Not if these were Jango's clones. He was curious to see how the Kaminoans could have fouled up producing fighting men based on *that* template.

The storm raged against the transparisteel window, rain pounding in surges and then easing again. Orun Wa stood back with a graceful sweep of his arms like a dancer. And the doors opened.

Six identical little boys—four, maybe five years old—walked into the room.

Skirata was not a man who easily fell prey to sentimentality. But this did the job just fine.

They were *children*: not soldiers, not droids, and not units. *Just little kids.* They had curly black hair and were all dressed in identical dark blue tunics and pants. He was expecting grown men. And that would have been bad enough.

He heard Jango inhale sharply.

The boys huddled together, and it ripped at Skirata's heart in a way he wasn't expecting. Two of the kids clutched each other, looking up at him with huge, dark, unblinking eyes: another moved slowly to the front of the tight pack as if barring Orun Wa's path and shielding the others.

Oh, he *was*. He was defending his brothers. Skirata was devastated.

"These units are defective, and I admit that we perhaps made an error in attempting to *enhance* the genetic template," Orun Wa said, utterly unmoved by their vulnerability.

Skirata had worked out fast that Kaminoans despised everything that didn't fit their intolerant, arrogant society's ideal of perfection. So . . . they thought Jango's genome wasn't the perfect model for a soldier without a little adjustment, then. Maybe it was his solitary nature; he'd make a rotten infantry soldier. Jango wasn't a team player.

And maybe they didn't know that it was often imperfection that gave humans an edge.

The kids' gaze darted between Skirata and Jango, and the doorway, and all around the room, as if they were checking for an escape or appealing for help.

"Chief Scientist Ko Sai apologizes, as do I," said Orun Wa. "Six units did not survive incubation, but these developed normally and appeared to meet specifications, so they have undergone some flash-instruction and trials. Unfortunately, psychological testing indicates that they are simply too unreliable and fail to meet the personality profile required."

"Which is?" said Jango.

"That they can carry out orders." Orun Wa blinked rapidly: he seemed embarrassed by error. "I can assure you that we *will* address these problems in the current Alpha production run. These units will be reconditioned, of course. Is there anything you wish to ask?"

"Yeah," said Skirata. "What do you mean by *reconditioned*?"

"In this case, *terminated*."

There was a long silence in the bland, peaceful, white-walled room. Evil was supposed to be black, jet black; and it wasn't supposed to be soft-spoken. Then Skirata registered *terminated* and his instinct reacted before his brain.

His clenched fist was pressed against Orun Wa's chest in a second and the vile unfeeling thing jerked his head backward.

"You touch one of those kids, you gray freak, and I'll skin you alive and feed you to the aiwhas—"

"Steady," Jango said. He grabbed Skirata's arm.

Orun Wa stood blinking at Skirata with those awful reptilian yellow eyes. "This is uncalled for. We care only about our customers' satisfaction."

Skirata could hear his pulse pounding in his head and all *he* could care about was ripping Orun Wa apart. Killing someone in combat was one thing, but there was no honor in destroying unarmed kids. He yanked his arm out of Jango's grip and stepped back in front of the children. They were utterly silent. He dared not look at them. He fixed on Orun Wa.

Jango gripped his shoulder and squeezed hard enough to hurt. *Don't. Leave this to me.* It was his warning gesture. But Skirata was too angry and disgusted to fear Jango's wrath.

"We could do with a few wild cards," Jango said carefully, moving between Skirata and the Kaminoan. "It's good to have some surprises up your sleeve for the enemy. What are these kids really like? And how old are they?"

"Nearly two standard years' growth. Highly intelligent, deviant, disturbed—and uncommandable."

"Could be ideal for intel work." It was pure bluff: Skirata could see the little twitch of muscle in Jango's jaw. He was shocked, too. The bounty hunter couldn't hide *that* from his old associate. "I say we keep 'em."

Two? The boys looked older. Skirata half turned to check on them, and their gazes were locked on him: it was almost an accusation. He glanced away, but took a step backward and put his hand discreetly behind him to place his palm on the head of the boy defending his brothers, just as a helpless gesture of comfort.

But a small hand closed tightly around his fingers instead.

Skirata swallowed hard. *Two years old.*

"I can train them," he said. "What are their names?"

"These units are *numbered*. And I must emphasize that they're unresponsive to command." Orun Wa persisted as if talking to a particularly stupid Weequay. "Our quality control designated them Null class and wishes to start—"

"*Null?* As in no *di'kutla* use?"

Jango took a discreet but audible breath. "Leave this to me, Kal."

"No, they're not *units*." The little hand was grasping his for dear life. He reached back with his other hand and another boy pressed up against his leg, clinging to him. It was pitiful. "And *I can train them*."

"Unwise," said Orun Wa.

The Kaminoan took a gliding step forward. They were such graceful creatures, but they were loathsome at a level that Skirata could simply not comprehend.

And then the little lad grasping his leg suddenly snatched the hold-out blaster from Skirata's boot. Before he could react the kid had tossed it to the one who'd been clinging to his hand in apparent terror.

The boy caught it cleanly and aimed it two-handed at Orun Wa's chest.

"Fierfek," Jango sighed. "Put it down, kid."

But the lad wasn't about to stand down. He stood right in front of Skirata, utterly calm, blaster raised at the perfect angle, fingers placed just so with the left hand steadying the right, totally focused. And *deadly* serious.

Skirata felt his jaw drop a good centimeter. Jango froze, then chuckled.

"I reckon that proves my point," he said, but he still had his eyes fixed on the tiny assassin.

The kid clicked the safety catch. He seemed to be checking it was *off.*

"It's okay, son," Skirata said, as gently as he could. He didn't much care if the boy fried the Kaminoan, but he cared about the consequences for the kid. And he was instantly and totally *proud* of him—of all of them. "You don't need to shoot. I'm not going to let him touch *any* of you. Just give me back the blaster."

The child didn't budge; the blaster didn't waver. He should have been more concerned about cuddly toys than a clean shot at this stage in his young life. Skirata squatted down slowly behind him, trying not to spook him into firing.

But if the boy had his back to him . . . then he *trusted* him, didn't he?

"Come on . . . just put it down, there's a good lad. Now give me the blaster." He kept his voice as soft and level as he could, when he was actually torn between cheering and doing the job himself. "You're safe, I *promise* you."

The boy paused, eyes and aim still both fixed on Orun

Wa. "Yes sir." Then he lowered the weapon to his side. Skirata put his hand on the boy's shoulder and pulled him back carefully.

"Good lad." Skirata took the blaster from his little fingers and scooped him up in his arms. He dropped his voice to a whisper. "Nicely done, too."

The Kaminoan showed no anger whatsoever, simply blinking, yellow, detached disappointment. "If that does not demonstrate their instability, then—"

"They're coming with me."

"This is not your decision."

"No, it's mine," Jango interrupted. "And they've got the right stuff. Kal, get them out of here and I'll settle this with Orun Wa."

Skirata limped towards the door, still making sure he was between the Kaminoan and the kids. He was halfway down the corridor with his bizarre escort of tiny deviants before the boy he was carrying wriggled uncomfortably in his arms.

"I can walk, sir," he said.

He was perfectly articulate, fluent—a little soldier way beyond his years.

"Okay, son."

Skirata lowered him to the floor and the kids fell in behind him, oddly quiet and disciplined. They didn't strike him as dangerous or deviant, unless you counted stealing a weapon, pulling a feint, and almost shooting a Kaminoan as deviant. Skirata didn't.

The kids were just trying to survive, like any soldier had a duty to do.

YOU'VE WITNESSED THE CREATION OF DARTH VADER, BUT THE STORY HAS JUST BEGUN

STAR WARS®: DARK LORD
THE RISE OF DARTH VADER

By JAMES LUCENO

The thrilling sequel to the blockbuster movie, *Star Wars*: Episode III *Revenge of the Sith*

Revenge of the Sith ends with the destruction of the Jedi and the collapse of the old order. The Republic has become an Empire, ruled by a brilliant Emperor and his terrifying enforcer, Darth Vader. In a galaxy reeling from civil war and the destruction of all they once believed in, a few Jedi survive—and some are determined to make a stand. One of Darth Vader's first assignments will be to crush any resistance to the Empire, and it is this mission that will lead him to discover his true strength, as he settles into his new role as the Emperor's iron fist.